THE
DEVIL'S
HALF
MILE

Paddy Hirsch

CORVUS

First published in the United States of America in 2018 by Forge,
Tom Doherty Associates, an imprint of Macmillan Publishing Group,
LLC, New York.
First published in hardback in Great Britain in 2018 by Corvus,
an imprint of Atlantic Books Ltd.

This edition published in 2019.

1 2 3 4 5 6 7 8 9

A CIP catalogue record for this book is available from the British Library.

Hardback ISBN: 978 1 78649 350 7
Trade Paperback ISBN: 978 1 78649 351 4
Paperback ISBN: 978 1 78649 352 1
E-book ISBN: 978 1 78649 353 8

Printed and bound by CPI Group (UK) Ltd, Croydon, CR0 4YY

Corvus
An imprint of Atlantic Books Ltd
Ormond House
26–27 Boswell Street
London
WC1N 3JZ

www.corvus-books.co.uk

To Eileen, for helping me give myself permission

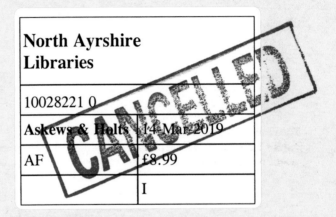

New York, 1799

ONE

Monday

Justy Flanagan leaned on the gunwale of the *Netherleigh* and watched two big men square up to each other on the wharf below. They were like a pair of cart horses, one black, the other white, their fellows in a half circle behind them, grim looks on their faces.

"How goes the negotiations?" Lars Hokkanssen leaned on the rail. He was a giant of a man, with a shaved head and a ragged red beard. Justy was six feet tall, which meant he saw over the heads of most men, but the *Netherleigh*'s first mate was nearly a foot taller, and wider. His build and his name came from his Norwegian father. His red hair, his Galway accent and his politics were all courtesy of his mother.

"Negotiations?" Justy asked.

Lars gave him an amused look. "How long is it you've been away?"

"Four years."

"A lot's changed in that time. This isn't the town you grew up in, I'll tell you that. There's a lot more free Negroes here, for one thing, and they all want to graft. They're forming gangs and taking work, either by force or by selling their labor cheap. The Irish aren't happy about it. There's been a few small riots. Men killed, even." He nodded at the two men, who were now circling each other, ready to come to blows. "This here's the way they usually decide who gets to unload a ship."

A shout went up from the other side of the wharf. The two fighters dropped their fists, and the crowd broke up as men rushed to the water's edge.

One man called for a gaff. Then the crowd went quiet, and Justy knew it was a body. They pulled it up onto the huge granite blocks, and when they all stood still for a moment, their heads down and their caps off, he knew it was a woman.

Four men picked her up. Justy saw the head roll backwards as though it had detached from the body. One of the Negro longshoremen vomited, and there was a ripple through the small crowd as the men in front stepped back.

Two men carried the body to a cart beside the *Netherleigh*'s gangway. They heaved the corpse up and pulled a tarpaulin over it, but as they walked away the wind gusted and pulled the canvas loose, showing the dead woman's legs, her dark skin turned gray by the seawater.

The Negro workers were arguing, and one of them, a short, wiry man in a peaked cap, climbed onto a crate and started haranguing his fellows. Justy couldn't hear the words, but the white longshoremen began edging closer to one another, the gang closing in tight and facing outwards, like a squad of soldiers caught in an open field.

Stung by the words of the small man in the peaked cap, the black workers turned and started shouting at their rivals. The white workers shouted back, stoking themselves and their mates towards the point where they would hurl themselves across the narrowing gap between the two gangs.

"I'm glad I'm up here and not down there," Lars muttered.

Business on the wharf had stopped. People knew the difference between a labor dispute and a fight. Shoppers were hurrying up the streets, away from the docks. Stall owners were hastily packing boxes and stowing their goods away. And the open space of the emptying wharf was filling with a trickle of men, both black and white, coming to join their fellows on the dock.

A long whistle blast made Justy look up towards the Broad Way. Another whistle, and then a half-dozen watchmen, dressed in their long dark coats and leather firemen's hats, were pushing through the crowd of shoppers. The watchmen forced their way onto the dock and ran down between the two groups of men. They made a wall, some facing the Irish stevedores, the others facing their black rivals. The watchmen stood firm, slapping their long billy clubs into their palms, their eyes steady as the workers screamed abuse and spat.

A man in a red coat was pushing his way through the gang of white workers. The men parted way, until he was face-to-face with a white-haired man with a ruddy face and a knit cap perched on the back of his head. They spoke for a moment, and then the white-haired man nodded and shouted something to his fellows.

For a moment, nothing happened, and then the Irish gang began to move slowly away from the water. It was clear some men weren't happy about leaving, but the white-haired man shouted again, and the protestors fell into line, unwilling to be left alone on the dock without their fellows. The black workers fell silent and watched as the Irish withdrew, followed by the watchmen.

When they reached the street, the white-haired man spoke a few words to his men. He took off his cap, and those who were wearing hats followed his lead. He turned towards the docks and nodded at the small, dark, wiry man who was still standing on the crate. And then he turned away and led his men into the town.

The wiry man stepped off the crate. The black crew went to work.

Lars exhaled loudly. He winked at Justy. "So, welcome back to New York, *a chara*. You glad to be home?"

Justy shrugged, and Lars laughed. "Glad to be three thousand miles away from the bloody English, though, eh?"

"There are plenty of English here."

"Aye, but they don't have bayonets fixed and artillery support."

Justy said nothing.

"Jesus, look at the face on you!" Lars said. "You look like you're about to stab someone. And speaking of which . . ."

He dug in his pocket and held out a small bundle of filthy linen. Justy unwrapped it carefully. It was a folding knife, a six-inch length of steel tucked into a handle made of a single piece of carved teak. Justy smiled at the weight and the feel of it, the warm, smooth wood and the cool, polished metal bands under his thumb. "You oiled it."

"Only a couple of times. I was worried about rust." Lars grinned. "Plus a good piece of steel needs to see the light of day every now and again."

"So long as you didn't shave with it. That beard of yours would blunt an executioner's axe." Justy tucked the knife into his boot. "And the other thing?"

Lars fumbled in the band of his breeches with both hands and pulled out a thick canvas belt. It was gray with dirt and sweat. He handed it over. "I stashed it in the galley, behind the hardtack. No one wants to steal that stuff, let alone eat it, so I figured it'd be safe there."

Justy quickly strapped the money belt around his waist. "I hope you took a few coins for yourself."

"The pleasure of being of service is payment enough."

"Jesus, you took that much?" Justy smiled at his friend. "Don't spend it all in the one tavern, will you?"

The big sailor frowned. "That's a terrible thing to say."

"The truth cuts like a sharp blade, *a mhac*," Justy said.

Shaking hands with Lars Hokkanssen was like getting to grips with a bear. They stood for a moment, hands clasped, not saying any of the things they were thinking.

Justy was the first to let go. "Thanks for finding a place for me."

"A small thing, after what you did."

"You don't owe me."

"You'll let me be the judge of that."

Justy nodded farewell to his friend and went to the top of the *Netherleigh*'s gangway. He pushed his face into the gust of wind that carried the smell of the city down the hill to the docks. Woodsmoke from a thousand hearth fires, urine from the tanners' shops, horse shit from the streets, sewage from the septic tanks, fresh blood from the abattoirs, rotting meat and produce from the tips. Bad breath, sour beer, raw spirits, stale sweat. It was like a pungent cloud rolling down the Broad Way to the water, a slap in the face of every newcomer who arrived in the city.

Justy smiled. It was the smell of home.

And then he remembered why he had made the long trip back from Ireland. He thought about what he had to do and his mouth set into a thin line.

The cart that held the woman's body was at the bottom of the gangplank. Her head was wedged against a pile of sacks, so that her chin was touching her right shoulder, but as Justy came down the gangplank he could still see the ragged purple wound in her neck. Close up, her skin looked darker, and there was a cut on her right cheek. She looked as though she was barely thirteen years old.

A man wearing the gorget of an accountant of the harbor-master's office pushed past to look at the corpse. The man was bald, with skin the milky color of a dead fish. He sniggered and wiped his nose. "I'd say she was a pretty one, for a Negro bobtail."

"She wasn't a whore."

"She was surely," the man said. "Look at the mark on her face."

"That cut's fresh. Someone did that to make fools like you think she was a whore. Or they did it for spite."

The accountant leaned over to peer at her face. "Maybe," he said. He reached for the tarpaulin. "I wonder if he cut her up some more."

"Leave her."

The man shrank back. "I was only going to cover her up."

"She doesn't need help from the likes of you. Get away from here."

The man ducked his head and slunk away.

Justy took one more look at the dead girl. A young man was leaning against a stack of crates, watching him. He was dressed in a black coat and breeches, with cheap peg-soled shoes and a white shirt that was grubby at the collar. He looked like any apprentice, but his dark green caubeen hat was unusual. The caubeen was a kind of oversized beret, popular with the old-timers who came over on the boats from Ireland but rarely worn by anyone so young.

The man grinned. His teeth were white in his tanned face, and Justy felt a prickle of recognition.

"He was only wondering what the rest of us are wanting to know," the young man said.

"What's that?"

"Why, whether it's the same man going about killing Negro girls. That's the third in less than a week."

Justy looked back at the body. He felt the skin prickle at the back of his neck.

"Were they all killed the same way?"

"What do you mean?"

"I mean did they all have their throats cut like this? And were they marked like that? The cut on the cheek?"

The man looked at Justy thoughtfully. "New in town, are you?"

"I've been away."

"I'd say you have, indeed." The grin flashed.

Justy looked down at his stained breeches and threadbare coat. He had worn the same clothes for nearly a month. His spares had been chewed to ribbons by rats on the voyage, and he had thrown them over the side. At least his boots looked like the sort of thing a gentleman might wear.

The man held up his hands. "No offense." He tapped two fingers to the brim of his hat.

"I'll see you," he said, and slipped into the crowd of tradesmen and shoppers. Justy stood for a moment, watching him go, struck by the feeling that he knew the man from somewhere.

He shook his head. He had traveled for months, and now that he had arrived, back in New York, he wasn't about to dawdle. There was work to do, and still a full half day to do it in. He would not waste the time searching his memory for half-forgotten faces.

He set off up the hill.

The sun was high in the sky, and the streets were crowded with gigs and horses. Coachmen and riders cursed and shouted as they tried to navigate around one another. The air was heavy with the smell of horse manure, and the cobbled streets were slippery with it, despite the piles of straw thrown onto the ground.

The sidewalks were equally busy. Shoppers and passersby competed for space with a crush of handsellers and their carts: chive fencers selling cutlery, swell fencers touting the sharpness of their sewing needles, flying stationers flogging their penny ballads and histories, crack fencers offering bags of nuts, and everywhere the cakey pannam fencers, whose trolleys were piled with pies, sweet bowlas tarts and savory chonkeys, the minced-meat pasties that no true New Yorker could resist.

Justy was at the top of the hill, crossing Wall Street across from Trinity Church, when he saw the young man in the green hat again. He was striding across the Broad Way, dodging carriages and carts, but as he stepped up onto the sidewalk he stumbled, staggering into a man dressed in ivory breeches, an immaculately cut sky-blue coat and an old-fashioned powdered wig that slipped over his forehead.

"God damn it, you fool!" the bewigged man shouted, groping at the horsehair.

"Sorry, sir!" The young man bowed. "I slipped in some horse shit. There's just too many carriages on the road. My apologies."

The gentleman brushed him aside. "Out of my way!"

Clutching his wig to his head, he puffed past Justy, clearing a way through the crowd with his cane. Justy turned to watch him go, and when he looked back up the hill the young man had disappeared again.

TWO

Justy had felt the eyes on him as soon as he stepped off the ship. Not that he was surprised. Any new arrival in New York was fair game, even one dressed in rags and carrying no baggage.

There were three of them, all dressed in loose homespun breeches, wooden shoes and threadbare coats. Street bludgers, thieves who weren't small enough to burgle, or deft enough to pick pockets, and who relied on violence and intimidation instead. He felt the crew hemming him in after he passed Wall Street, a touch of a shoulder in the crowd edging him gently to his right. One man in front, another behind.

The man ahead of him stopped suddenly on the other side of an alley. Justy was supposed to stumble into him, so that the man on his flank could crowd him down the alley. Instead, he deliberately stepped to his right and took four quick steps down the dank, stinking lane. The bludger on his left had committed to a shoulder charge, but there was no one there to receive it, and he came staggering down the alleyway, slipping in the mud and falling flat on his face in front of Justy.

His mates crowded in behind the man, who tried to struggle to his feet.

"Stay down," Justy ordered.

One of the men sneered at him. He had lost his front teeth, and a stream of snot ran down from his nose and over his upper lip.

"There's three of us, so," he said, his accent a mangle of West Coast Irish and New York waterfront. "And there's just the one of you. So let's have what you've got hidden in your breeks there and we'll let you go without a hammering."

The man on the ground began pushing himself up.

"I told you, stay down," Justy said.

"Or what?"

Justy had left New York to study law at the new Royal College of St. Patrick in Maynooth, just west of Dublin. But he had done much more in his four years away than page through books and take exams. The Monsignor of St. Patrick's believed that travel was an enriching experience and had included a number of cathedral tours in the first year of the syllabus. Justy had attended every trip, more as a way to see other cities, rather than the churches themselves. On a visit to the cathedral of Saint Marie in Sheffield, Justy had grown bored by a lecture on stained glass and slipped out into the streets of the town. Sheffield was famous for its cutlers, and Justy went from shop to shop, comparing blades, learning about steel and shanks and hafts and curvature, so that by the time he crept back into the chapel for evening prayers he knew more about cutlery than he thought possible.

He also had possession of the unusual knife that he had left with Lars for safekeeping during the voyage.

Folding blades were common on the streets of every modern city, but what made this one different was the spring in the blade, and the release catch in the side under Justy's thumb.

Which he now pressed.

With a tiny click, six inches of polished steel appeared magically in the air. It was dim in the alley, but the light caught the blade well enough. The eyes of the man on the ground flickered, the whites showing in the gloom, and he let himself slide back into the mud.

Justy felt his heart thump a little harder at the feeling of power over another man. "I'm not some culchie just in from the old country. I'm a New Yorker, same as you. And I don't appreciate being welcomed home in this unfriendly way by you filthy scamps."

The two men still standing were looking at him, wide-eyed. The leader ducked his head. "Sorry, mister. We thought yiz might be good for a lift, ye know?"

"No. I don't know. Now pick up your boy and fuck off."

The men looked at each other again and then lifted the third man to his feet. Without looking back, they hurried up the alley to the Broad Way.

Justy leaned on the wall of the alley. He felt sweat on his forehead and his pulse hard in his temples. And something else. Shame. The look in the man's face, the fear in his eyes, had made Justy feel things he hadn't felt in a while. And hoped he'd never feel again.

He folded his knife and tucked it back into his boot.

"Welcome home, *a mhac,*" he muttered to himself, and followed the men back up to the street.

THREE

The New Gaol was located in the middle of the Common, a large expanse of open land sandwiched between the Broad Way, which ran along the spine of Manhattan Island, and Chatham Row, which curved east, towards the Bowery. The jail was a solid, square three-story building, with a small dome on its roof. Its walls had been recently whitewashed, making a stark contrast with the black iron of the bars on the windows and the railings that separated the jail from the sidewalk.

A small gate in the railings opened on to a narrow path that led to the door of the jail. Two benches placed on either side of the path faced each other, and Justy sat down to gather himself.

He thought about the long road that had brought him back to New York. Four years, and scores of letters written, hundreds of miles traveled and dozens of people seen. Few of the letters were answered, and only a handful of the interviews revealed anything useful, but in the end a man in London named William Constable had given him two names. Isaac Whippo. And William Duer.

The last was a name Justy already knew. Everyone in New York had heard of Duer, a businessman and a politician, part of the Continental Congress and a friend and onetime ally of both George Washington and Alexander Hamilton. But as wealthy and well-connected as Duer was, he was also a reckless speculator who lost everything in the Panic of 1792—a panic many said he started—and was sent to debtors' prison.

He had been there ever since.

Justy looked up at the white walls and the barred windows. They all had curtains. This was hardly a prison. Not like Kilmainham Jail, in Dublin. So perhaps the rumors were true. The word was Duer's friends may not have helped him with his debt, but they paid handsomely to be sure he was comfortable. They said he had a suite of well-furnished rooms, a personal library, his own wine cellar, even his own privy.

Justy tried to remember what Duer looked like. His father had introduced him once, when Justy was twelve. It was the autumn of 1790, two years before the Panic. They were in one of the coffee houses that stock traders used to do business, buying and selling commodities, company shares and paper debts. He recalled a tall man, with a narrow face and a quick, dry handshake. Duer's small, cold eyes had flicked up and down, summing him up and then looking away. It had made him think of a snake.

His father had not felt the same way. He had been quick to laugh at Duer's witticisms, eager to please. He had gazed at Duer like a priest enraptured by an image of the Christ child. Justy had seen a flash of contempt in Duer's eyes. He recalled feeling the same in himself.

"This man will make us wealthy," his father had whispered, after Duer had gone. "You'll see."

But instead, Duer had killed him.

———•———

The bench was hard, and the late summer sun was hot on his neck, but Justy didn't move. He had been in such a hurry to get here, but suddenly all of his questions seemed foolish. What if Duer denied everything? What if he said nothing? Justy imagined the tall, thin man waving him off with a languid flick of his bony wrist. It was a long way to come for such a short conversation.

He heard the Trinity Church bell strike three, and suddenly he had an image of his father, hanging in the stairwell of the house on Dutch Street. The grotesquely tilted head, the rictus grin, the bruises and scratches on his neck, the half-opened eyelids showing a spray of red dots on the whites of his eyes. Justy felt the anger build in his chest, making his teeth clench, his muscles taut, his face pale.

He stood up and walked to the door.

<hr>

It opened on to a long hallway, lit by a simple chandelier and a window set high in the wall above the door. There was a strong smell of wood polish. Behind a heavy wooden desk sat a heavy-set man dressed entirely in black. His bald head was flat on one side, like a bruised piece of fruit. There was a large, purple brand mark on his right cheek. His eyes were like two blue lights in his battered face. They flicked up and down, taking in Justy's long hair and ragged clothes.

"What d'ye want?"

"I'm here to see one of your prisoners."

The jailer said nothing. Justy tried to see what he saw. A young man in his early twenties, unkempt fair hair, scruffy, stinking. But he was tall, with good bearing, and even though the coat and the breeches were patched and dirty, they were obviously tailored. Justy's boots were the clincher. They were the color of summer honey, made of soft leather, a little scuffed here and there, but gleaming with a luster that spoke of a valet's care. Justy was glad he had gone barefoot during the voyage. He had oiled the boots and wrapped them in linen and hidden them in a barrel to keep them from the rats. His bare feet had been blistered and scraped and shredded by splinters, but it had been worth it.

Without taking his eyes off Justy's face, the jailer opened a ledger, turned it around and pushed it across the polished surface of the desk.

"Sign in."

Justy plucked the quill pen from the inkpot, tapped it and wrote: Monday, 15 July 1799; Justice Flanagan; William Duer; 1pm.

The jailer took a long time reading the entry. Without saying a word, he tucked the ledger under his arm, turned and walked up a short flight of stairs at the end of the hall. He disappeared through a door.

Justy sat on a plain, upright chair and let the silence fill his ears. He closed his eyes. For nearly two years while he was in Ireland, Justy had served with the Defenders, one of the many Catholic rebel groups that joined forces in the ill-fated Rebellion against the British. They had trained him, how to use a pistol and a knife, how to move silently and how to watch and wait. How to measure time by counting breaths. Ten breaths, in and out, made a minute. The discipline had the added advantage of calming him, so that after a hundred breaths his pulse was level, his head was cool and the anger in him had congealed to a cold resolve. He had counted 421 when he heard the sound of two sets of footsteps beyond the door. He stood up.

The jailer came down the stairs, the same blank expression on his face. He put the ledger on the table and stood to one side as an enormously fat man, dressed all in black, made his way slowly down, holding tight to the banisters and wheezing every step of the way. He stood opposite Justy, sweat breaking out from under his wig. He pulled a handkerchief from his sleeve and mopped his face.

His eyes glistened, like two currants peeping out of a scone. "You are here to see William Duer?" He used the lazy, affected English drawl that had fallen out of favor during the Revolution but that had become popular again in certain circles in New York.

Justy looked him in the eye. "I am."

"Who are you?"

"My name is Justice Flanagan."

"So you have written. But who are you?"

"I'm an attorney."

The fat man looked surprised.

"You don't look like one."

"I've just arrived in New York. It was a hard passage. I came straight here."

"To see Mr. Duer."

"That's right."

The fat man smirked. "Well, Mr. Duer has no further need of legal representation."

"I'm not here to represent him. I'm here to talk with him."

"I'm afraid that's not possible."

The fat man glanced at the jailer, who behaved as though he were made of stone.

Justy felt the pilot light catch inside him. "You are the Marshal?"

The fat man drew himself up. "I certainly am."

"And what is your name?"

"What business is that of yours?"

"I am an attorney-at-law, Marshal, come to see Mr. William Duer in the services of my client. As such, I would appreciate it if you paid me the courtesy of furnishing me with your name, so that I can note it in my files. Unless, of course, you would prefer that I pursue my inquiries at Federal Hall."

The fat man looked startled. "That won't be necessary, of course," he said, quickly. "I am Henry Desjardins."

Justy nodded. "Thank you. And forgive my tone. I've come a long way. It's an important matter. I'd appreciate it if you could ask Mr. Duer if I might speak with him immediately."

The fat man cleared his throat. "You misunderstand me, sir. It is not a matter of Mr. Duer not wishing to speak with you. It is a matter of his not being able to speak with you."

"Not able?"

"No, sir."

"Mr. Duer is ill?"

"No, sir." The fat man frowned and mopped his face. "Mr. Duer is dead."

FOUR

Justy sat on the bench outside the New Gaol. He stared into the distance, away from the city, towards the Collect Pond and the bare hump of Bayard's Mount beyond.

He went over the words again and again. *Mr. Duer is dead.* Desjardins had told him Duer had died at the beginning of May, while Justy had been in Liverpool, seeking passage to New York. And Duer hadn't even died in jail. That gross slug of a Marshal had allowed him to go home for his last days, to live with his wife.

Justy's mouth tasted foul. A film of bile coated his tongue. He spat into the grass and rubbed his face with the heel of his hand. He had come all this way for nothing. The man who had all the answers about his father's murder was dead.

The sound of singing made him turn in his seat. A half-dozen men and women had assembled in the northwest corner of the Common and were grouped around a man who was standing on what looked like a fruit crate. The singers were all solidly middle-class, the women wearing bonnets and long dresses of subdued colors, the men dressed in black. The song was "Soldiers of Christ," which made them Methodists, and Justy watched over the stretch of grassy Common as the hymn drew to a close and the man on the platform began to address them.

The man brandished a pamphlet in the air as he spoke. His voice did not carry well, but Justy heard enough to tell he was pressing his audience to boycott enterprises that used slaves. The gathering began to attract attention, and soon there was a small crowd standing in the corner of the Common. Most were middle-class people, like the chorus, but soon a number of laborers joined them, marked by their battered straw hats, their long trousers and shapeless linen coats that hung like sacking on their backs.

"Tarrywags!" one of the laborers shouted, his voice coarse with rum and tobacco and what sounded to Justy like the north end of Dublin city. "You'd set them fuckers free to take our jobs? Keep 'em in chains, I say. Or send 'em home."

"Or drown 'em!" one of his companions shouted.

The speaker said something Justy couldn't hear, but the first laborer went red in the face. "Just because I'm a Catholic don't make me unchristian, you Quaker madge. Set the bastards free, then. Unleash the black tide, and see what that does to this city. We'll either drown in it, or we'll burn."

He stopped. Everyone in the crowd turned to look at something in the street. It was a moment before Justy saw a team of slaves, all dressed in identical homespun shirts and long trousers, hauling an enormous cart, loaded with stone blocks, along the top of the Common. The six men doing the heavy work were barefoot, drenched with sweat, leaning hard into the wide leather straps slung over their shoulders. The seventh man walked behind them, carrying a coiled bullwhip. He wore cheap, heavy boots, a black coat and a battered white wig that denoted his status of overseer.

The team trudged, heads down, heavy-footed, past the small, silent crowd. The overseer kept his eyes front.

"Goddamned snowball!" one of the laborers shouted. No one laughed or spoke. The overseer walked on, and in his wake the crowd began to disperse.

The stone on the cart looked like the granite Justy had seen ten years ago, stacked up on Wall Street, the last time his father had taken him down to his place of business. Francis Flanagan had been a stock trader, a jobber who bought and sold the pieces of paper that represented debts, shares in banks and ships' cargoes. Like all traders, he did his business in one of the riotous coffee houses where the other jobbers gathered to exchange information and gossip and to buy and sell. His favorite was the Merchant's Coffee House at the corner of Water and Wall Streets.

But before going inside the Merchant's that day, Justy's father had pointed to the building being demolished on the other side of the road and the new stone that had been piled up, ready to form a foundation for the building that was to take its place. The Tontine Coffee House. A new kind of gathering place, his father had said, a membership club, for traders and brokers only, unlike the free-for-all coffee houses like the Merchant's, the Exchange and the notorious King's Arms. Justy recalled his father's excitement, and his anticipation that he would be one of the first members of the Tontine. But he hadn't lived to see the cornerstone laid.

Justy hadn't set foot on Wall Street since that day, but he knew the Tontine had been built. He wondered what it looked like. The Merchant's had been a crammed, riotous, run-down place, albeit one with plenty of history. No doubt the Tontine was much more genteel—the word was that it had cost $43,000 to build. A fortune.

"A penny for 'em."

The young man in the green caubeen hat was leaning on the small iron gate.

Justy took a long look at the floppy beret-like hat, feeling the same prickle of recognition he'd felt before.

"It's the fashion now, to wear a tile like that, is it?"

The young man gave him a careful look. "Not really."

"There's a woman I know wears one just like yours."

The man flashed his grin, white against the tanned skin. "Is that right? Maybe I know her."

"You're more likely to know her niece. She's about your age."

"Oh aye? What's her name then?"

"Kerry O'Toole."

The young man blew out his cheeks. "O'Toole? That's a name to be sharp about, around this way."

"It's good to know some things haven't changed."

The young man swung the gate open. "Mind if I rest a bit?"

"Be my guest."

He sprawled on the bench opposite Justy. "So are you after finding this Kerry lass? You're sweet on her, are you?"

Justy laughed. "Sweet on her? No. She was barely fourteen when I last saw her. She'll be all grown-up now. A different person altogether. I doubt I'd even recognize her."

"What about you? Do you think she'd twig you?"

"I don't look so different."

"A lot can happen in four years to change a man."

He had the sensation of something falling into place in the back of his mind. The last time he had seen Kerry O'Toole, she was still a girl, wearing a long blue dress. He remembered her coil of back hair, pinned up behind her head, her wide smile, blinding white against her caramel skin, and her startling sea-green eyes. And now, four years later, he saw the same smile, the same eyes, the color of the sea on a bright day. But now she was wearing a man's clothes and shoes, and it was a farmer's hat holding up her hair.

"Who said I've been away four years?" he asked, trying to stop himself from smiling.

"Did you not just say so?" she asked, trying to look casual.

"I did not, indeed." Justy folded his arms. "Let me see that hat."

"I will not, so."

"You'll take that thing off now and hand it to me." Justy

29

thickened his accent. "Or I'll knock it off with my fist, and your head with it."

She rolled her eyes, and that did it. It was the same thing she'd done when he'd tried to teach her how to read, so many years ago.

She reached behind her head, pulled out a long hairpin and took off the hat.

Her hair uncoiled itself slowly, like something stirring after a long sleep. She shook her head slightly, and her hair slid down over her shoulders, all the way to her waist.

Justy felt as though the world had stopped. There was nothing but the girl in front of him and the pulse in his throat, the sound of his heartbeat in his ears.

He had known Kerry O'Toole from the day she was born. Her father was from the same village as the two Flanagan brothers. O'Toole had hired himself out to them as a porter in return for passage to America. Justy's father had hired him on for the voyage, but it was Justy's uncle Ignatius, the Bull, who had seen O'Toole's long-term potential. When Francis Flanagan took the high road to Wall Street, the Bull stayed on the waterfront, with O'Toole beside him as his bodyguard and his enforcer.

The free blacks and the Irish may have fought each other ceaselessly when it came to finding paid work, but they mixed freely in the cheap, dank taverns and rickety dance halls that had sprung up on the waterfront. Relations between Irishmen and the free Negro girls of the town were common. Some even had black mistresses. But the unwritten rule of the Irish community in New York was that no one ever married outside his race. O'Toole didn't give a damn for the rules. He fell in love with a black woman and married her. She gave birth to Kerry but died on the same day, and the story was that O'Toole had picked up the little brown baby, taken her down to St. Peter's, made a bed for her out of the green silk altar cloth and left her screaming on the steps of the sacristy.

Then he went to get drunk.

The priest had called the Flanagan brothers, and while Francis looked after the child the Bull went in search of the father. It took him nearly two days to find O'Toole, who had vowed to drink himself to death. But the Bull laid him out with a single punch and had his lads carry him up to the Collect Pond. It was February, and the water was frozen solid. The men had to cut a hole, and then they tossed O'Toole in. The shock of it brought him round and they pulled him out again, but only after he swore to take care of his responsibilities.

He had taken the pledge and stopped drinking, but he became a sour, morose man, given to sitting in the dark in the front room of his narrow house on the rare occasions he was home and not out breaking heads for the Bull. Kerry was raised by her aunt Grainne, she of the green hat, and because Justy lived only a few doors down, he had come around every day, to play with Kerry and read her stories.

He remembered how she used to be: lanky and scrawny, as though she never got enough to eat. Now she was even taller, almost as tall as him. Not scrawny anymore, but wiry instead, filled out and muscled, with long legs, slim hands and broad shoulders. She looked like she would be quick on her feet, quicker than he was, maybe. Her flat chest and narrow hips meant the clothes she had chosen fit her well, and she passed easily for a man, with her long hair piled under the spacious caubeen.

He tried to think of something to say. A gaggle of children hurried past. One of them grabbed another's hat, and they screeched with laughter as they tossed it about.

Finally: "It looks like you haven't had a haircut since I last saw you."

31

She pulled a face. "Is that so? Well, you look like you haven't had a shave."

He smiled, rubbing his stubbled chin. He wondered how bad he smelled.

He nodded at the caubeen on her lap. "So what does your auntie Grainne think about you wandering about the place in men's clothes, wearing her hat?"

"She doesn't think. She's dead."

He bowed his head. "I'm sorry. I didn't know."

She shrugged. "I would have written you. Except I still don't have my letters."

"I thought O'Toole agreed to let you go to school."

She laughed drily. "Oh sure, his mouth opened and he said the words all right. But when it came to putting his hand in his pocket . . ."

"I'm sorry."

"You'd best cheese saying that."

"All right." He paused a beat. "I'm sorry."

They grinned at each other.

"You'd better put that tile back on, if you're not to be caught," he said.

She wrapped the long rope of her hair around her fist and tucked it quickly under the caubeen. The long hairpin flashed as she put her hands behind her head and pinned the hat into place.

"You really had me fooled there. You have your act down exact," Justy said.

"Well, I've been called a long-meg mopsie so many times, I may as well make use of what God gave me."

"I saw you fish that mackerel out of that fat fella's pocket earlier."

She gave him a cool look. "Are you going to tell me off?"

"Not at all. I thought you did a fine job."

He meant it. She was an excellent thief. She was daring, aggressive, and as quick as a cat. He looked at her hands. She had long, slim fingers, perfect for dipping into a man's coat pocket.

Kerry looked amused. "So it's all right with you? Me being a street knuckler? Dressing up in men's clothes?"

Justy felt suddenly embarrassed. He avoided her eyes.

"I didn't have much of a choice," she snapped.

"How's that?"

"Look at me. Half Negro, half gangster's daughter. No one's going to marry this, black or white. So it's either get on my knees and scrub floors or get on my back and put Madge Laycock to work."

He felt himself flush. "Jesus, Kerry!"

"What?" Her face was tight. "You think I'm joking? My own cousin offered to get me started on the game. He said my light skin would make up for the fact I've got neither heavers nor crackers and a body like a boy."

"What did you say to him?"

Kerry smirked. "Not much. I did give the madge a good kick in the tarrywags, though. He didn't mention it again after that."

Justy didn't know what to say. She seemed cool and collected, an entirely different person from the one he'd known before. He wondered whether she really had kicked her cousin in the balls. He looked at the tilt of her chin and the tight line of her mouth and decided she had.

She kicked her heels out and stretched, arms up, arching her shoulders over the back of the bench.

"So now you're back, where are you staying? With the Bull?"

Justy shook his head. "I'll go to see him, but I'll not stay. I'll find a room in a boardinghouse somewhere."

She nodded. "Aye, I'd be a bit skittery, staying with him just now."

"Why's that?"

"You saw that carry-on down at the dock today, didn't you? It's not a safe time to be out and about on the waterfront. Or in Canvas Town. Or anywhere else there's gangs. You'll see."

"So where's safe?"

She smirked. "There's a lady I know in the New Town who rents rooms. Her name's Mrs. Montgomery. She made the mistake of marrying an Englishman who got milled in the war. But she's pals with O'Toole, and he gave her some money to buy a place and start over. She's a lively old girl. You'll like her."

They walked slowly along the side of the Park and up to Chambers Street. It was getting dark, and the lamplighters' carts were squeaking their way up the main thoroughfares. Candles illuminated a thousand windows around them, silk and muslin curtains filtering the light into a patchwork of colors.

Justy glanced at her. She looked strong and confident, her head up, her shoulders thrown back, cock of the walk in her boys' clothes. He was suddenly uncomfortably aware of the patched, grubby rags he was wearing.

They crossed the Broad Way. Down the hill, closer to the town, the main streets had been fitted with new lanterns that hung from iron posts every twenty yards or so. But here the streets were dark, the town houses only recently built.

"This is the New Town," Kerry said. "They're building all the way to Greenwich Village, can you believe it?"

Justy peered north, into the darkness. "They'll have to. The way things're going in Ireland, I can imagine people coming over by the shipload."

"To this hole of a city?"

"Better here than there, let me tell you. You wouldn't believe the way we're treated in Ireland. I'd say slaves in America are better off."

"Fuck off." Her lip curled.

34

"It's true. The English treat the Irish like animals. Worse. Certainly they treat their horses better. I've seen folk living in caves there, like wild beasts. The English take everything. Land, livestock, food, even children, to work their fields and serve them at table. And they pay nothing in return."

"It's not the same as being a slave." Her mouth was a tight line.

He felt a surge of anger. "No, it's not. In a way, it's worse. At least an owner looks after his slaves. The bastard English just strip the land bare and leave the people to starve."

She stopped. She was almost as tall as him, and they stood, eye to eye.

"You should try being a slave sometime yourself, Justice Flanagan." Her voice was quiet, but her eyes burned. "Then maybe you'd know the kind of shite you're talking."

"Kerry?"

But she was already walking away. He hurried to catch her.

"I'm sorry, Kerry. That was a benish thing to say."

She ignored him. Her face was tight, her chin thrust upwards. He could feel the anger coming off her, like heat from a fire.

He matched her stride, kept his mouth shut. It was a few moments before she spoke. "So what were you doing at the jail?"

"Do you remember my father?"

"Sure. He used to take us to Drammen's shop on Saturdays. He always bought me butterscotch."

Justy smiled. "I forgot that."

An old woman came slowly up the hill towards them, bent double under the weight of an enormous linen bag, stuffed with laundry. Her ankles were as thin as rails, and her white hair floated over her dark brown skin like a puff of smoke. She glanced up and smiled gratefully as Justy and Kerry separated to let her pass.

"Do you remember how my father died?" Justy asked.

Kerry looked away. "He hanged himself."

He kept his eyes on her until she looked back. He had the sudden feeling that he needed her to understand what he was doing there. "What if I told you he didn't? Hang himself, I mean."

"But you're the one who found him."

"I know. And he had his neck in a noose, right enough. But what if that wasn't how he died?"

"I don't know what you mean."

He stopped under a streetlight. Clouds had rolled in with the dusk, so that the sky looked like a low roof over the town.

"Do you know what I was studying, while I was away?" he asked.

"You told me you went for the law."

"I did. But I studied a lot more than the law. I was in France for a while, my second year. They have something there called a police force. It's like the Marshals and the bailiffs and the Watch all rolled into one, but better."

"Well, they couldn't be worse."

He smiled. "Their constables go after lawbreakers, especially murderers and thieves, and try to bring them to trial. I spent a summer with them in Paris, to see how they investigate crimes and suspicious deaths. It was fascinating. They have a whole library there, full of pictures and sketches, showing how people die."

She shivered. "They sound like a bunch of ghouls, so."

"Not at all. They use it to decide whether a death is suspicious or not. Someone only has to describe a body for an investigator to get a good idea of how someone died. You can tell if it's a natural death or an accident or a murder. And if it is a murder, you're already halfway to catching the killer."

He leaned close. "I'll never forget finding him, Kerry. I

36

remember it, like it was this morning." He tapped his temple. "There's a picture in here, as fresh and exact as though someone painted it the moment I walked into the house and saw him there. But there was something wrong with that picture, I always knew it. I never really believed he was the kind to kill himself, but it was more than that. Something just wasn't right."

Kerry shrugged. "It's hard to accept, someone topping themselves."

"I know. You always hear people saying he or she never seemed the type. But the more I thought about it, the more certain I was that something didn't fit. So I copied out that picture in my head, every detail of it. And then I went to the archive and went through every report I could find that mentioned hanging and suicide. I read every word and examined every sketch, and I compared them to mine. I went out with the police, too. I saw dead bodies. Murdered people, hanged people . . ."

He stopped. She had a wary look in her eye. He knew that if he wasn't careful she'd think he was mad. But it was too late to worry about that. "He didn't do it, Kerry. I know I sound like one of those people, but I'm certain now. He didn't kill himself."

She said nothing.

"Did you hear me?"

She frowned. "I hear you, right enough. Do you hear yourself?"

He took a deep breath. The night was cool, but he still felt warm. He pushed his hair back from his forehead, felt the sweat, slick under his palm.

"I know it sounds like I'm cracked, but I'm telling you, if he'd died in Paris and not here, it would never have been ruled a suicide. They'd have called it what it was."

"Which is what?" Her face was grim.

"Murder."

She stopped, looking down the hill at the lights of the town. Her jaw was set tight. Justy saw a small pulse in her cheek.

"Jesus!" He jumped as a carriage hammered past them out of the dark, sweat on the horse's flanks, the coachman slashing down with his whip. "What's the hurry this time of night?" Justy shouted.

She grinned at him. "You've been away too long, *a chara*."

He shook his head. His heart was pounding. "I'd forgotten the way people drive in this bloody place."

She chuckled and walked on across a side street, taking long strides to avoid the horse manure clumped on the cobbles. They stepped to the side as three young lads ran past, barefoot and dressed in ragged breeches and coats several sizes too big for them, hooting and laughing at some prank they had pulled.

She gave him a long look. "You're sure about this?"

"I know what I saw. And I know my father wasn't the kind to kill himself. You remember what he was like."

"I remember he loved you. You were always together. I remember wishing O'Toole was the same."

They walked on in silence. The surface of the street was uneven here, the cobbles newly laid, the mortar that held them in place not fully bedded down yet. Justy trod lightly, careful not to trip. "You were too young to remember my mother," he said.

Kerry nodded. "O'Toole talked about her once. He said she was a grand lass."

Justy felt a sudden wetness in his eyes, a tingling in his nose. He was glad it was so dark. "The day we buried her, my father sat me down. It was just before we went down to the church. We were in the house on our own, I remember. He held my hand and told me he would never, ever leave." He could hear the tremor in his voice. "He kept his word. He was always there. He did everything for me, but I was an ungrateful mouth, you know? I wanted to be down on the waterfront, living that life. I wanted excitement, not books, but he wasn't having it. He locked me in and made me study. All the time. I cursed him for it. I hated him. When he died, part of me was glad. Can you believe that?"

He stopped. Kerry stepped close and wrapped her arms around him. He hugged her, his face buried in the pillow of her hat, his tears soaking into the coarse green fabric. His chest ached, as though his ribs were broken. "I never got to thank him. I never got to tell him how much I loved him. I owe him so much. But he's gone."

She squeezed, and he felt her heartbeat against his chest. He closed his eyes and waited for the tears and the trembling to stop, and then he let go.

He wiped his face. "Sorry for snotting all over your tile."

She smiled. "It's seen worse, I'm sure."

They started walking again, slowly now, like two people stretching out the time.

She took a deep breath. "All right then. Say he was murdered. So who killed him?"

He felt a rush of something, relief tinged with excitement. And gratitude. "I don't know. But I'm ready to find out. And to do something about it."

"And that's why you went to the jail?"

"The man I came to see knew what happened; I'm sure of it. But now he's dead, too."

"Who was he?"

"William Duer. Have you heard of him?"

"Sure. A Wall Street cove, right?"

"Aye."

She made a face. "Making him a bigger thief than me. What did he have to do with it?"

"He was a swindler, and Francis was one of his marks. The old man worshiped Duer. He was forever trying to find a way to do business with him. Bank shares, government bonds, whatever.

Duer always turned him down. But one day he brought him in on a scheme. Francis was over the moon. I remember him coming home that day; he skipped through the house."

He thought about his father dancing about the place, powder from his wig dusting the shoulders of his black coat. "The next thing I know, the Panic happened. Duer ran out of money and everyone who had invested with him lost all their capital."

"Including your da."

"That's what everyone told me. That he put every penny he had into the venture, and then went to the bank and borrowed a whole lot more. And he wasn't the only one. Duer had plenty of other dupes. Some of them killed themselves, too."

He felt Kerry looking at him. He kept his eyes front. It had been months since he had drunk anything stronger than weak ale, but he suddenly craved something strong and harsh. Anything to dull the raw edge of his feelings.

"Did you know all of this before you went away?" she asked.

"Only some of it. I found out a lot from a fella named Constable. I met him in London. He knew my father quite well. And I wrote a lot of letters. It's taken me nigh on a year to piece it all together. But I needed to speak to Duer for the whole picture."

She glanced at him. "And what will you do now? Go back to Ireland?"

"Jesus, no." He avoided her eyes. "I'm here now. And there's still some people I can talk to about my father. Do you know a man called Jarlath Cantillon?"

"Carrots Cantillon, the lawyer? Sure, everyone knows him."

"He's an old friend of my father's. I'm hoping he'll help me."

They walked in silence down a shallow hill, towards what looked like the aftermath of a battle. Smoke from hundreds of fires hung over a forest of grimy tents and wooden shacks, and the night air hummed with the sound of thousands of people, crammed into the few acres of land between the New Town and the river.

Canvas Town. A tent city, populated by free Negroes, runaway slaves, deserters, criminals and the desperate poor. It was slowly being pushed north by developers who were throwing up cramped tenements and narrow town houses, like the one Kerry stopped beside; a three-story house on the corner of a mud lane, still wreathed in scaffolding.

She jerked her head. "This is it."

"Mrs. Montgomery's?"

"Aye. Just tell her you know me."

A light burned behind the ground floor window. The moon had broken through the clouds and the light glistened on the rutted surface of the street.

"Are you not going to introduce me?"

She made a face. "Dressed like this? I don't think so."

They stood looking at each other. He could feel the heat in his cheeks, his heart alive in his chest.

She broke the silence. "I've been thinking about what you said. About your father. Why did you start so late?"

"What do you mean?"

"You've been away four years. You said you've spent the last year trying to find out what happened to your da, but why didn't you start two years ago, after you got the idea something wasn't right when you were in France? What happened to the year in between?"

There was a gust of wind and he caught a scent of pine, carried from the forests and farmland north of the city. He had a flash of memory, razor sharp, of walking through a forest in the dead of night, the silence loud in his ears, his knife in his hand and the iron taste of fear on his tongue.

Kerry frowned. "Justy? Are you all right?"

Her words seemed muffled. He had the sensation of looking at her through a thick pane of glass. He was sweating. He opened his mouth to speak, but it was as though he didn't know how. He was afraid words would be strangled and distorted by the time and space between them. He felt close to her and far away from her at the same time.

"What happened, Justy?" Her voice was soft. "You can tell me."

He shook his head. He felt as though he had taken a long step backwards and was looking at her from a distance. He wanted to reach out and take her by the hand, but he had the mad idea that it would be like trying to pull a piece of white-hot metal out of a fire.

She gave him a long look, dark green eyes like the middle of the ocean. Bottomless.

"Right you are, then," she said. "Maybe I'll see you around."

FIVE

The room at Mrs. Montgomery's was plain but comfortable. Justy paid her a week in advance, refused a bowl of what smelled like corn chowder and went straight back out into the night.

As he walked down the hill towards Dover Street, he thought about Kerry and tried to make sense of his feelings. She was a wee slip of a girl when he left. Now, four years later, nothing was the same. She was harder, that was for sure. Not surprising. Being called ugly and ungainly was hard for any young girl. She would have built some strong defenses for herself. But there was more to her anger than that.

Perhaps it was him. He had felt sick about leaving her, in that cold house, with her vacant father. He had always felt protective of her because they had both grown up without a mother. His own had died in a yellow fever outbreak when he was seven. Then his father. Justy knew what it was like to have everyone leave you. And yet he had left her. He had felt bad about it then. Now he was back, seeing that look in her eye, he felt worse.

Dover Street was a dark, muddy lane that branched off Pearl Street and dropped in a steep, straight line to the river. Like all the lanes in the poorer areas of the city, it was only cobbled for the first few feet away from the junction with the main road. After that, the surface became packed mud, sand and gravel.

Most of the other side streets in the city were pitted with sink-holes that would fill with rainwater in winter and sewage in the summer, but Dover Street was as smooth as a slipway. Its holes were always filled with loose stones, broken from rocks by men who had offended the Bull in some small way. He gave them a choice: break rocks or lose an eye.

Justy started down the lane. None of the buildings were more than three stories high, but the narrowness of the lane made them loom above him, blocking out the night sky. Lights from a tavern flickered at the bottom of the hill. The rest of the street was pitch-black. Justy's feet crunched on the gravel.

A shadow detached itself from the darkness. The man was as tall as Justy, but heavier. His cap was pulled low over his eyes. Justy didn't recognize him. "I've come to see the Bull."

"The Bull don't waste his time with beggar scum." The voice was deep, the Galway accent dragging like slurry.

"I'm his nephew."

The man said nothing but turned and led Justy to a black-stained slab of heavy wooden planks. The man banged on the door, and a small hatch snapped open at eye level.

"He's here," the man said, and the door was unlatched and swung open. Another big man stood in the doorway. He could have been the first man's brother. He wore a stained shirt and mud-colored breeches that had split in the crotch and were stitched together with a dirty piece of string. His nose looked as though someone had smeared it across the right side of his face, and his mouth hung open as he breathed. He scratched his belly.

"What time do you call this?" The same Galway slur.

"Do I look like I'm wearing a watch?"

The man's eyes narrowed. "Maybe not. But I see that chive in your boot." He held out his hand. "Give it over."

Justy cocked his head and stared into the man's eyes. "You want it, you'll have to take it yourself."

The guard's eyes flicked to the side. "The Bull says no blades in his house."

"Then what does he cut his meat with?"

The guard said nothing, but the look in his eyes and the twitch in his cheek said he was close to breaking both of Justy's arms.

"I'm his nephew, for Christ's sake," Justy snapped. "He'll not thank you for keeping me standing shivering in the street while you bleat about cutlery."

The guard chewed the inside of his mouth for a second, then stood back.

The doorway was narrow. Justy squeezed past the man into a long, white-painted hallway.

"On the right there!" the man called out. Justy ignored him and kept walking. He knew where the Bull would be.

———⋄———

Ignatius Flanagan was a big man, almost as tall as Justy, but half as wide again. He wore plain clothes, but of good materials, tailored to make his bulk less obvious. In his youth he had been a wall of muscle, but while age and comfortable living had turned much of the hardness to fat, it had not softened his brain or dulled his edge. He was now the most powerful landowner in the lanes that led down from Pearl Street to the East River. He might no longer have the strength or the stamina to hack his way through a room of opponents with a cleaver in one hand and a club in the other, but he had plenty of men who would, and he would not turn a hair before calling down all kinds of bloody mayhem on anyone who got in his way.

He sat in a heavy wooden chair by the fire, watching Justy, his face blank. "There's no tea. You're too late for that."

Justy said nothing. His uncle had taken him in, had fed and clothed him and sent him to school. He had done everything a man should do for his dead brother's orphaned son. Every time Justy had thought of his uncle over the last four years, he had felt anger at his obligation, hatred for being treated like a piece of valuable furniture, and contempt for a man who, he told himself, was nothing but a gutter criminal. But now, standing in the glow of his kitchen, with the warm smell of baked bread lingering in the air, Justy felt the surprise of something heavy, deep inside in his chest.

"I'm fine," he said.

"Come on in and sit, then."

Justy pushed himself off the wall and went to the chair at the end of the table.

He watched the fire. Someone had mixed a piece of green wood with the logs. It steamed as the flames licked around it.

"So, did you get your bachelor's?" The Bull's voice was flat.

"I did."

"Well, that's something."

They watched each other. The Bull's eyes were small and hard and dark, a pair of pistol balls, drilling into him. "You look different," he said.

"Do I?"

"You were a bright-eyed colt bowler when you left. Now you seem like you might be someone to be reckoned with."

Justy said nothing.

His uncle shrugged. "Truth is, I'm surprised you came back here at all. I thought you'd be off in Dublin or London by now."

Justy felt as though the words were stuck in his throat. He wanted to tell his uncle that he had come back to New York because he was sure his father had been murdered. Because he wanted to find out why and by whom. But something stopped him.

"The place has changed a bit while I've been away. Street lanterns."

"Aye. We have them all over the town now. Not just where the quality live. Makes life tricky for the toolers and coat-buzzers."

"I saw a fight down on the docks today. Irish on one side. Negroes on the other. The Watch had to come down and break it up."

The Bull grunted. "Bloody darkies. You heard about the abolition bill the state government passed in July? It's made those black bastards damn bold, I'll tell you. They're bidding low for every job on the waterfront. Picking our pockets. If someone doesn't get them back in line soon, the city'll be aflame."

He took a poker and stabbed savagely at the green log in the fire. "So. What will you do, now you're back?"

"What do you know about Jarlath Cantillon?"

"Carrots? I know he's as Irish as a plate of poundies, but he does his damndest to make everyone think otherwise. That orange head of hair of his gives the game away, mind."

"I'm thinking about going to ask him for a clerkship."

"You know he works on Wall Street."

"What of it?"

The Bull smiled. It was like a crack opening in a slab of granite. "Well, well. So you're bound for the Devil's half mile, are you? And there was Francis hoping you'd make an honest living."

"I don't know what you mean by that."

"I mean there's more prigs and screwsmen working on Wall Street than there is on all of New York's waterfront. They may wear prettier duds and prefer a pen to a blade, but they'll pick a man's pocket just as clean. Still, if you're going to start a life of crime, you may as well begin at the top."

Justy felt the heat leap into his face. "You have me wrong, sir."

"You sound like your father."

"Aye, well, he made the hard choice, to make his living square. I'll do the same."

Men had been whipped until their spines showed for saying far less. But the Bull seemed to understand his nephew wanted to provoke him. The thin smile stayed on his face. "You think lawyers make an honest living? They're the biggest thieves of the lot."

A hissing sound came from the grate. The flames had charred the bark of the green log and were now working on the young, uncured wood.

Justy waited for a moment before looking his uncle in the eye. "I know there are plenty of dishonest lawyers. But I won't be one of them."

The Bull said nothing.

Justy stood. "I came here to thank you, Uncle. I owe my education and my position to you. I'm grateful, and I'll pay you back one day, when I can."

The Bull gave him a blank look. "What were you doing at the jail today?"

Of course. The Bull's people wouldn't have just passed the word when they saw him at the docks. They would have followed him. He recalled the three young lads who had run past him and Kerry in the street. And the other group of children, tossing a hat about. Children like that were his uncle's eyes and ears, all over the city. His water rats, the Bull called them.

"I went to see William Duer."

"A wasted trip, then. What did you want with a dead man?"

Justy thought about lying. But the Bull could smell a lie from a hundred yards.

"He was in business with my father."

"Him and a dozen others. So what?"

"I wanted to know what kind of business."

The Bull spread his arms wide. "Who knows? Bonds? Shares? Land? Some stupid scheme that amounted to nothing. Why do you care?"

Justy closed his eyes and saw his father hanging, his head twisted to the side, the marks on his neck. "I think it was something else."

"Like what?"

"I don't know. But whatever it was, I think it got him murdered."

His uncle was very still. "Murdered. Did I hear you right?"

"You did." Justy realized his hands were trembling.

"That's not a word to throw about lightly."

"Do I look like I'm making a skit? I'm the one who found him!"

"And I'm the one who cut him down! Do you remember that?" The Bull slammed his open hand down on the tabletop.

The room was silent. They stared at each other. The Bull's eyes shifted. "You were barely fourteen."

"Don't treat me like a chip." Justy fought to keep his voice steady. "I know what I saw. I saw him when he was hanging, I saw you cut him down, and I saw him when you laid him out. And I know now, he didn't kill himself."

The Bull's face hardened. His eyes were cold. "You've no idea what you're talking about."

"I know exactly what I'm talking about. I have a picture in my head of him, just as he was when you cut him down, before the dustmen took him away. I've spent the last four years comparing it with real corpses. Some hanged, and some throttled. With rope, with hands, and with wire. I've come to learn what a self-murder by hanging looks like, and I can tell you for certain, my father wasn't one."

"That's slicing the gammon pretty thick."

"Is it? Let's talk about the rope, then."

"Don't test me, boy." The words were a low growl. Justy ignored them.

"We had a length of rope in the scullery. It was six feet long, left over from the move to the big house. I remember Father telling the cook to hang it behind the door. It would have been perfect. But the rope that hanged him was a piece of ship's hawser. Inch-thick hemp, with a stitched loop. And it was tarred. I remember how black it was against his neck. And filthy. Where did that rope come from? Father never went near the docks."

The Bull said nothing. His hand tightened into a fist.

"And what about the knot?" Justy went on, ignoring the acid in his guts. "Father didn't know one end of a rope from the other. But the knot on the banister was a perfect bowline."

He drew a breath. "And then there were the marks on his neck. There was no diagonal rope mark, which there always is on a hanged body. There was just tar, smeared all over his throat. The tar wasn't ground into his skin, which it would have been if he'd thrashed back and forth. And there was that thin line lower down, below his windpipe. I asked about it, but that drunk of a surgeon said it must have been made by the rope when he first put it over his head, before he jumped. I can't believe I accepted it then, but I was a child. No one was listening to me. But I've seen marks like that since, many times. Garrote marks."

Justy was standing now, his head pounding, the blood thumping in his temples. He pointed at his uncle. "You know I'm right. I can see it in your eyes."

The Bull ran a hand over his face. Suddenly he looked old. "I had to take an axe to that rope. There was bits of tar flying everywhere. It felt like it took me forever." His voice was soft.

Justy sat down. "There was no way he could have tied it. Even if he knew the knot. You'd need hands like iron for a job like that."

"Aye. And Francie's hands never saw a day's hard labor, right enough." The Bull looked away, something in his eyes.

"So you did suspect something."

The Bull said nothing.

"Uncle?"

He shook his head. "Even if you're right, and I'm not saying you are, it was near eight years ago. What are you going to do about it now?"

Justy reddened. "Find out who did it, and why."

"Look at you, breathing smoke and spitting fire." The Bull's smile reaching his eyes.

"Don't mock me."

"I wouldn't dream of it."

There was a loud crack from the fireplace, and a large ember flew across the floor. Justy ground it out under his heel. "I want to know who else was in the partnership that Duer had with my father. I don't suppose you'd know anything about it."

The Bull gave him a blank look. "We had an agreement, your father and I. He didn't bother himself with my affairs. And I didn't bother myself with his." He thought for a moment. "Who did you speak to, up at the jail?"

"A Marshal, name of Desjardins."

"That fat madge. Was Callum Drummond there? He's chief of the guard."

"There was an older man at the desk. Bald. With a brand on his cheek. You know him?"

"Aye. He's an old soldier. A broken pisspot like most of them. But he's been a jailer there for years. He was there when Duer was locked up."

"Do you think he might know something?"

The Bull shrugged. "Maybe. No harm in asking."

"Let me do it. I want the truth, not some story he'll make up to stop you cutting off his tallies."

The fire cracked again, and Justy felt a wave of tiredness wash over him. "I should go."

The Bull heaved himself to his feet. "You're welcome here, Justice. My lads told me you've taken a place in the New Town, but your old room's still made up for you, if you want it."

Justy stood up slowly. "Thanks, but no. I'll take a few things now. I'll send for the rest when I'm settled."

"As you like."

He stuck out his hand, and, without thinking, Justy took it. His uncle pulled him close.

"You'll be back, and not just for your tackle." The Bull's eyes were narrow and his face was set hard. Justy could smell the meat on his breath. "You're young and you think you're invincible, but one day you'll need something from me, from my world. And then we'll find out who you really are."

SIX

Tuesday

When Justy awoke, it was still dark outside. He washed quickly in the basin in the corner of his room, strapped on his money belt and dressed in the clothes he had brought from his uncle's house. He appraised himself in the mirror as he tied his white cravat. The cream-colored hunting breeches that had been too tight for him when he left now fit perfectly. His black waistcoat was snug—he had let out the belt at the back as far as it would go. But he had only one coat that could fit across his shoulders, a dark green formal affair with a black velvet collar. It was a little tight, but tight clothes were the fashion in Europe, so it would do.

He went by the market and paid a cent to a butcher's boy to rub tallow into his boots. A barber had set up beside the butcher's shop. His gray linen shirt was rolled up to his sleeves, showing the tattoos on his forearms, a web of dark lines against his tobacco-colored skin. He already had a line of customers and he pointed Justy to a stool. There was a pamphlet on it, an anti-slavery tract calling for more boycotts and advertising a Manumission conference that coming Saturday.

After the barber had finished running the razor over his face, Justy gave him another coin for a haircut. He knew it was important to give a good impression, if he was to be offered a clerkship by his father's old friend. He could get away with a too-tight coat, but fashionably long hair would not do for a lawyer in conservative New York.

Jarlath Cantillon had been friends with Francis Flanagan for as long as Justy could remember. He had spoken at Francis' funeral and had asked Justy to call on him before he sailed to Ireland to start his studies in the law at St. Patrick's College. The lawyer had told him that if he ever decided to return to New York he should be sure to call on him again.

Justy was sure Cantillon wasn't expecting to see him so soon.

Or quite so early. Justy didn't know whether Cantillon worked from home or in an office somewhere. But he reasoned that the lawyer was unlikely to leave his house before half past eight, given the farthest commercial district in New York was no more than a thirty-minute walk away.

William Street was a quiet street, lined by three-story redbrick town houses, built in the same uniform style that Justy had seen in London. Cantillon's door was shiny with thick black paint and adorned with the number 9 and a knocker made of brass.

The sound of the knocker echoed inside the house. There was a thump, and Justy stepped back to look up at the window. A curtain twitched. He glimpsed a frizz of orange hair, a chalk-white face and a pair of panicked eyes that flicked up and down the street.

A moment later he heard the sound of footsteps through the door. "Who is it?" a voice snapped.

"Mr. Cantillon?"

"Identify yourself!"

"My name is Justice Flanagan, Mr. Cantillon. Forgive me for calling on you so early. You said if I was ever back in New York, I should come and see you."

There was a long pause, and then the sound of bolts being drawn. The door opened a crack.

The past four years hadn't changed Jarlath Cantillon much. The lawyer was a little older, a little rounder, but he still had the shock of red hair that earned him the nickname Carrots. He was wearing a scarlet silk dressing gown, wrapped tight around his round body. He looked Justy up and down with narrow eyes.

"Come in, then." He opened the door just wide enough to let Justy inside, then slammed it shut and threw the bolts back into place.

"This way." He led Justy into a parlor. The room was cold and smelled of old ash, like the inside of a funerary urn. But it was clean, the grate swept and the surfaces free of dust. The room was dominated by a suite of four overstuffed armchairs, upholstered in a gaudy tapestry. A large painting of a woman hung above the fireplace.

Cantillon waved Justy to a chair, then disappeared. He returned a few moments later with a pewter jug of water. He filled two glasses, then sat down, glancing out of the window and tightening his dressing gown around him.

Justy wondered what the lawyer was scared of. New York had its problems: foul water, bouts of yellow fever, a growing and increasingly restless population of free Negroes and European immigrants, and the occasional fire, but otherwise it was a fairly safe place. Unless things had changed in the four years since he'd been away.

Cantillon tried in vain to soothe his shock of red hair. "Forgive my appearance. I was working late last night."

"I'm sorry for coming so early without warning, Mr. Cantillon. I can come back later, if you'd prefer."

"No, no. You're here now." The lawyer settled in his chair and tried a smile. "So, Justice Flanagan. Returned from the old country. Tell me what you've been about."

Justy told Cantillon about his time in Ireland, leaving out his extracurricular activities with the Defenders. The lawyer seemed pleased that he'd chosen a career in jurisprudence, although he appeared less impressed by St. Patrick's College in Maynooth. Justy remembered his father telling him Cantillon was a Yale man, although he had been forced to pretend he was an Ulster Protestant to get into the prestigious college. Not an easy thing to do when you're christened with an Irish saint's name. But he managed it somehow.

As Cantillon refilled their glasses, Justy examined the painting that hung above the fireplace. It depicted a plump, cheery woman of about twenty years, dressed in a pink dress that flattered her figure and clashed appallingly with the long locks of red hair that fell over her bare shoulders.

Cantillon was staring out of the window. His glass was slack in his hand.

"Is everything all right, Mr. Cantillon?" Justy asked.

"Oh yes, quite." Cantillon's voice was brittle. He cleared his throat. "So, now you are back in our fine city, how can I be of service?"

"My father always talked about you with great affection, Mr. Cantillon. He said you were a man he could trust."

Cantillon gave a glassy smile. "Thank you."

"I've come back to New York to make my start as a lawyer, but I know so few people here." Justy paused. "In this part of town, anyway."

Cantillon winced, and Justy cursed himself for his clumsiness. He had no wish to make a point of his relationship to the Bull. Cantillon may have distanced himself from the waterfront, but he would almost certainly be well informed about what went on there. Every Irishman in New York knew Ignatius Flanagan had clubbed and stabbed and intimidated his way to the top of the city's Irish gang hierarchy. He owned or protected most of the waterfront, and it was common knowledge that every hellion who worked the wharves between Dover Street and Maiden Lane paid the Bull a tax or risked a cracked head followed by a dip in the East River.

Justy decided to deal with the issue head-on. He looked Cantillon in the eye. "I have nothing to do with my uncle. Nor do I want to in the future. I want to make my own way."

"Very admirable." Cantillon folded his hands in his lap.

Justy felt a sting of frustration. Budding attorneys apprenticed themselves to older lawyers. It was how the system worked. And it was part of a lawyer's portfolio of responsibilities to act as a mentor to those who needed it. Given Cantillon's connection to Justy's father, it was entirely reasonable for Justy to expect the lawyer to take him on as a clerk, or at the very least to help find him a position. But for some reason Cantillon was reluctant to volunteer his help.

Justy looked up at the painting of the plump woman. "A relative?"

"My mother. She passed away a few years ago."

"I'm sorry."

Cantillon gazed at the painting. "I know people say this about their mothers, but she really was a remarkable woman. She came here from Ireland in 1750. Pregnant with me. And alone. My father was washed overboard on the crossing. Fortunately, she had some money, which she used to buy this place. She rented it out and used the money to send me to school." He paused, looking wistfully at the portrait. "This was painted just after I was born. She hated it. I found it in the attic after she died."

"She has a lovely smile."

Cantillon beamed. "Doesn't she? It is the one redeeming feature of this otherwise appalling daub."

"You could find someone to paint her dress a different color. A shade of green, perhaps."

Cantillon cocked his head on one side. "Good Lord. What an excellent idea. That would improve things."

Justy felt the thaw. "What kind of lawyering do you do these days, Mr. Cantillon?"

"Why do you ask?"

"I wondered if there was any way that I might be of assistance to you."

Cantillon gave him a hawkish look. "What do you know about securities law?"

"I know what my father told me about stocks and bonds and the like. But as for the law? I didn't know there were any laws."

Cantillon smirked. "Well said. There aren't. Which is why we're writing some."

"We?"

Cantillon placed a hand on his chest. "I am part of a small group of reformers. We base ourselves at the Tontine. The new coffee house on Wall Street. I am the secretary. I arrange the meetings, help set the agendas, keep the minutes and draft the bill that we shall soon send to Congress."

"It sounds exciting."

"It is a great deal of work."

"What I mean is, you are at the beginning of something."

Cantillon bobbed his head. "Yes. We are. We are not popular, however. Most brokers and auctioneers would have no rules governing the trading of stocks and bonds, but we have seen the results of that kind of anarchy. Last year land speculators caused a panic that ruined a great many people. Although that was nothing compared to '92, of course."

He stopped.

An image flashed in Justy's mind. His father, hanging. The gold signet ring on his right hand. Justy remembered touching it. How cold and stiff his father's fingers were.

Cantillon's face sagged. "Forgive me."

Justy looked him in the eye. "I'd like to be a part of what you are doing."

Cantillon said nothing.

Justy leaned forward. "I am a quick study and hard worker, Mr. Cantillon." He glanced towards the window. "And perhaps I can be of service to you in other ways. Beyond the usual clerk's duties."

Cantillon's face was blank. "I don't know what you mean."

"I'm merely saying, I have a full portfolio of skills that I'd be willing to place at your disposal." He filled Cantillon's glass.

The lawyer drank half the water in a single swallow. He paused to catch his breath. "Perhaps I could use an assistant. It is not intellectual work, by any means, but it requires considerable discretion."

"I can keep a secret."

"It may also require long hours."

"I'm not afraid of hard work."

"It's an unusual arrangement. I have no office, to speak of. I work in the Committee Room at the Tontine, and keep my records here."

"I'm comfortable working wherever I'm needed. Just tell me what to do, and I'll get it done."

Cantillon gave him a sharp look. "Yes. I do believe you would."

There was a long silence.

"I must warn you that people will ask about your relationship with your uncle," the lawyer said.

"And I will respond by saying there is no relationship. He paid for my tuition, but I shall not be beholden to him for that. He will be paid back."

"With what? You're a clerk."

Justy reached for his glass. "I have some money. Not enough to pay him back yet, but enough to sustain me for a while."

"Indeed?"

Justy smiled. "I developed some facility with games of chance while I was in Ireland."

"Cards?"

Justy shrugged. "Anything that required a stomach for high stakes."

Cantillon raised his eyebrows. "Very well. But remember, at some point you are going to have to ask people for favors. They may want your help dealing with the Bull in return. God knows how that might end."

Justy shook his head. "I can't live like that. I can't be compromised."

Cantillon shifted in his seat. "We're lawyers. Compromise is our business."

He looked away, but not before Justy saw something in his eyes. Not fear, this time. Something else.

Guilt?

Almost before the thought was in his head, the words were in his mouth. "What can you tell me about the partnership William Duer created with my father?"

Cantillon's eyes were wide. "What are you talking about? What partnership? Why are you asking me this?"

"I'm just curious. I met a man named William Constable in London. He told me a few things, but he said you might know more."

"You met Constable? What did he say?"

"Just that my father worked with William Duer, and a fellow named Isaac Whippo. Some things about their business."

Cantillon's face was pale, except for two red spots burning high on his cheekbones. He pulled the lapels of his dressing gown closed at his throat. "What did he say about me?"

"Just that you were one of my father's closest friends. And that you might know more. About the nature of the partnership. I want to get a better understanding of what happened."

The lawyer jumped to his feet. He paced to the window, then back again. "At the risk of upsetting you, Justice, I must tell you that your father was not a good speculator. He went into business with William Duer against the advice of several of his associates, including William Constable and me. I am a lawyer, not a financier, but it was clear to everyone at the time that Duer was taking tremendous risks with borrowed money. But your father would not listen, even when the market kept moving against him. He was besotted with Duer."

Cantillon smoothed his hands down the front of his dressing gown. The touch of the silk on his palms seemed to soothe him. He glanced apologetically at Justy and sat down again. "Forgive me. Your father was very dear to me. I feel his loss acutely, even now."

"I understand."

Justy was telling the truth. He understood perfectly. Cantillon felt some kind of guilt about his father's death. And he was lying. Or at the very least, not telling the whole truth. Justy felt a tingle of hope. Duer might be dead, but there was still a way to find out what had happened to his father, and why. But he knew he was in danger of pushing Cantillon too far.

He stood. "Forgive me for coming unannounced, Mr. Cantillon. I'm grateful to you for receiving me. And I'm indebted to you for offering to include me in your work."

Cantillon stared at him.

Justy hid his smile. "When would you like me to start?"

SEVEN

It took Cantillon nearly an hour to change. When he came down the stairs, he was dressed for business in black coat, breeches, hose and shoes, but under his coat he wore a flamboyant yellow waistcoat, embroidered with designs in black and gold. It fit like the skin of a sausage around his portly frame.

"Let's be off." He stepped down into the street, and Justy caught the scent of wax and rose water. The lawyer had tried to tame his hair, pulling it back behind his head and tying it with a black ribbon. But the unruly orange curls were already working their way free.

Cantillon led, tossing questions at Justy over his shoulder. "I called your father a speculator, earlier. Do you know what that is?"

"Someone who makes a wager on the future value of something."

"Very good. You paid attention to your father, then."

"He once told me everyone's a speculator. Whenever you buy something or sell something or lend somebody money, you're placing a bet."

They flattened their backs against a wall to make way for a handbarrow loaded with bright green apples.

"Your father was right. We're all speculators. We all take risks. The problem arises when we take risks with other people's money."

The man handling the cart nodded gratefully to Cantillon as he eased his burden past. The lawyer leaned forward. "Excuse me, my good fellow."

The carter stopped. "Sir?" He wore a long hessian smock and a wide cap, and his face was burned red.

"Are these your apples?" Cantillon asked.

"Yaas." The man had a broad Dutch accent. He had probably risen at four in the morning to wheel his cart from the orchards up at Kip's Bay.

"Do you grow them yourself?"

The man grunted a laugh. "No. The farmer grows. I pay the farmer to pick. Some my wife uses to make apple pies to sell. The rest I bring to the market."

"May I ask where you get the money to pay the farmer?"

The man frowned, and Cantillon held his hands up. "I'm merely curious."

The man shrugged. "Sometimes we have money. Sometimes I borrow from the farmer. He is my wife's brother."

Cantillon dug a coin out of his pocket. "Thank you, my good man. Here."

The coin disappeared, and the man selected two large apples. He handed one to Cantillon and the other to Justy, then carried on his way.

Justy sniffed his apple. "The brother-in-law sounds like a sharp one."

Cantillon shrugged. "He still takes a risk. But at least both the farmer and the carter know the apple business." He started up the hill. "But imagine if the carter is more ambitious. He decides to buy every apple in the orchard. And instead of just borrowing from his brother, he borrows from every person in his village. And the people in the village don't just lend him a few coins, but give him all the money they have."

"Why would they do that?"

"Because they think he's going to sell his apples for lots of money and they'll get a nice return, of course. The question is, what happens if those apples don't sell. Or they're pilfered. Or lost."

"Everybody loses their money."

"Everybody loses everything. The whole village is ruined. And all because they put too much trust in one man, who made too big a bet." He handed Justy his apple and hurried on up to Wall Street.

The Devil's half mile. A narrow, cobbled corridor, flanked with tall, gray stone buildings that ran steeply downhill from Trinity Church to the East River wharves. It thronged with traffic. The sidewalks were crammed with people: messengers and clerks in their black coats; delivery boys in their shirtsleeves; shoeshine men with their boxes; crossing sweeps with their brooms and shovels. The noise was deafening: men shouting extravagant greetings or colorful abuse; merchants calling out the cost of their wares. And everywhere, all the time, the clatter of iron on stone, like a thousand hammers, as carriages and jigs of all shapes and sizes hauled up and down the hill, disgorging well-heeled men who hurried into the grand-looking buildings.

Cantillon peered at the traffic, waiting for an opportunity to cross the street. "Speculation on a large scale is dangerous. It has pushed us to the brink several times in the last decade alone." He launched himself into a gap between two carriages, stepping left and right to avoid the pools of urine and piles of dung. He reached the other side, breathing heavily, and smoothed the lapels of his coat.

"And that's why we need rules, you see? To be sure no single reckless individual can endanger the entire system. Ah. Here we are."

The Tontine Coffee House was an imposing building of gray granite, three stories high, that took up half a Wall Street block. A staircase of blackened teak beams led up to a wooden entrance platform, head height above the street.

A sleek black carriage was drawn up under the platform, and two men stood beside it, making sure that none of the passing carts scratched the cab's brass fittings or immaculate paintwork. The bigger of the men stared. He was about six feet tall, almost the height of Justy himself, but he had the bulk of a cart horse. He was well dressed, all in black, and wore his greasy hair long, but not long enough to conceal a King's regulation brand on his forehead, a letter *D* for deserter. The man swung a big blackthorn stick up onto his shoulder and said something to his companion. The second man was a foot shorter, but almost as wide. He too was dressed from head to toe in black. Both of his ears had been cropped—the punishment for thievery—and his head was shaved. He stared at Cantillon and Justy, his eyes like two black stones in his wide, pale face.

Cantillon glanced at the carriage and hurried up the steps. Justy followed him up onto the platform, through a pair of wide oak doors and into the Tontine's lobby.

As he walked across the wide room, Justy's eyes were drawn upwards. A chandelier hung from the roof, as large as a mill wheel and bristling with three tiers of candles. But the sky-blue ceiling was so high and the room so big that the chandelier looked small. The room was lit by four high windows, one in each wall, below each of which hung a single enormous painting depicting people at work, in a field, in a shipyard, in a forest.

A dull roar, like rain on a cheap roof, came from a room on the left side of the lobby. Justy followed Cantillon to the entrance and stood for a moment, stunned by the noise. The room was long, perhaps a hundred feet, with ceilings as high as the lobby. The floor was made of oak, and the walls were whitewashed. Light streamed in through a number of high windows and reflected off a highly polished mahogany table. It ran the entire length of the space and was dotted with dozens of tiny white coffee cups, like the first scattering of snow on a ploughed field.

The room was crammed with men, all shouting, arguing, laughing, scribbling, gesticulating. Justy had the impression of a hundred mouths, red throats, flushed faces, white teeth, chewing up business, mangling it, swallowing it, washing it down with cup after cup of the coffee that they poured out of tall white jugs into the tiny white cups.

Cantillon forced his way through the crowd. They passed close to a group of seven or eight young men, all expensively dressed, who were gathered around a tall, big-bellied man of about thirty. He wore a bright green jacket edged and frogged with gold material. His hair was teased into a white pompadour that bobbed and swayed as he talked.

". . . a fabulous return. Sixteen percent. How could I say no?"

He caught sight of Cantillon and tapped the side of his nose, eyebrow raised. His companions laughed. The lawyer ignored him and pushed past to the table. He slumped into a chair.

"Bloody man," he muttered.

A waiter appeared at his side. He was a big man, taller than Justy, but with heavy shoulders that strained a jacket that was so pristinely white that it made his skin look as dark as the mahogany table.

Cantillon glanced at him. "Rolls please, Thomas. And coffee, of course."

The man nodded and disappeared into the crowd.

An enormously fat man in a long white wig appeared at the door. His face was caked in powder, and there were two red circles painted on his cheeks. He was immaculately and flamboyantly dressed in the French style: a rose-colored long-tailed coat, frogged and embroidered with thick gold thread, matching breeches, white silk hose and black shoes adorned with large silver buckles. A hush fell over the room.

"Good morning, gentlemen," he said in a high voice.

The men broke into a spontaneous round of applause. The fat man beamed and pushed his way into the crowd, as the shouting and bargaining began afresh.

Another figure appeared in the doorway to the room. He was tall and thin, with a lined face. He looked about fifty, but his hair was jet-black. He wore it pulled sharply back from his face and tied with a black ribbon. He was soberly but expensively dressed, entirely in black.

He watched as people rushed to get close to the fat man, to slap him on the back and squeeze him by the hand. Suddenly, as though he had felt Justy watching him, his head turned. His gray eyes stared. He started across the room.

Justy turned to see the waiter easing through the crowd, holding a tray on one hand above his head. He placed a plate of rolls, a coffeepot and two cups with saucers on the table. Suddenly the thin man appeared beside him. Thomas froze as the man placed a hand lightly on his shoulder.

"The same for me, please, Thomas, if you would be so kind." An English voice, but with none of the plummy, inbred overtones of the aristocracy.

Thomas kept his eyes down. "Right away, Mr. Colley, sir."

Colley looked at Cantillon, who had given all his attention to pouring coffee.

"Good morning, Carrots."

Cantillon's jaw tightened. He stood slowly, adjusting his necktie. "Good morning, John."

Colley's cold gray eyes looked him up and down. "I do admire your waistcoat, old man."

Cantillon flashed a grin. "Thank you. May I present my new assistant, Justice Flanagan? Justice, this is Mr. John Colley."

Colley extended his hand. "A pleasure."

His eyes dropped to take in Justy's cream breeches and boots. "Dressed for hunting, I see. Very appropriate for a trader. We eat what we kill here."

"I'm not a trader."

Colley tilted his head back. "Do you even know what a trader does?"

Justy ignored the tension in his guts. "Buys low. Sells high. And makes sure he gets a sniff of the fish before it's wrapped. That's what my mammy taught me." He paused. "When I was a wean."

Colley's eyes flashed. "You've got a spine, I see."

He stood aside to let Thomas pass. The waiter's hands trembled, and the cup rattled against its saucer as he placed them on the table.

Cantillon cleared his throat. "Mr. Flanagan has just returned from college in Ireland. Complete with a bachelor's in law."

"Indeed?" Colley glanced down at the bulge made by the knife in Justy's right boot. He lifted the coffeepot and poured a long stream of the steaming black liquid into his cup. "So, what do you have planned for your new protégé, Carrots?"

"Mr. Flanagan will help me in my preparations for the conference next week," Cantillon said. "Drafting the bill . . ."

"Oh yes, the bill." Colley glanced at Justy over the rim of his cup and raised an eyebrow. "New rules to keep us all in our places. Heaven forfend that anyone should actually be allowed to make any money."

Cantillon reddened. "I would have thought, John, that after the last panic, you of all people would recognize the need to curb excesses of speculation."

"Yes, yes. You're right, of course." Colley let his cup and saucer clatter on the table. "It's just all this rule making is so incredibly dull. Perhaps you'll let me take Mr. Flanagan to lunch tomorrow. I can give him the traders' view of things."

"We have a great deal of work to do."

"Oh for heaven's sake, Carrots. It's just lunch."

Cantillon scowled. "Very well."

"Good. Until tomorrow, then, Mr. Flanagan. One o'clock, in the lobby."

He tossed a contemptuous glance at Cantillon. "And I promise not to poison his mind."

EIGHT

Securities law was every bit as dull as Colley had promised. Even Cantillon seemed only able to bear it for a few hours, and at half past four he packed up his papers and asked Justy to escort him home.

Once the lawyer was safely in his house, with the bolts on his door in place, Justy went back up to the debtors' prison. He found a shadowy alleyway on Chatham Row that gave him a good view of the prison door. He waited.

People came and went. Most of them were women who went in with their heads held high and came out with handkerchiefs pressed to their faces. It was nearly six o'clock when Drummond left. In the softening light, the jailer looked older and shabbier than he had inside the prison. He walked slowly down the Row, his shoulders hunched and his head down. Justy followed on the other side of the street until he was certain which way Drummond was going, and then he quickened his pace. He turned up a lane that ran parallel to the street Drummond had taken, then down another that would put him ahead of the jailer. He leaned on the wall, his nose full of the reek of stale piss, listening for the sound of footsteps on the cobbles.

Too late, he sensed someone behind him. Before he could turn, he felt the sting of a knife point below his ear.

"Thought you could get one over on me, did you?" Drummond's

voice sounded clotted. "Well, I didn't come up the Clyde on a fucking banana boat."

Justy held his hands up. "My name is Justice Flanagan, Mr. Drummond. We met yesterday. I came to the jail. I just wanted to talk to you."

Justy could feel the jailer hesitate. Then the knife jabbed again. "Aye, it would be just like a fucking Flanagan to start a conversation with an ambush."

Before he even knew what he was doing, Justy had doubled forward, stamping down hard. Drummond howled as the heel of Justy's boot raked down his shin and hammered his foot. Justy spun to the right in a tight circle, smashing his right elbow into Drummond's solar plexus so that the jailer jack-knifed forward. He kicked Drummond's hand and the knife skittered across the alley.

"How's that for a fucking Flanagan, you bastard?" he shouted.

Drummond dropped to his knees, an old man, wheezing and retching. Justy felt shame flood through him. He waited until his hands had stopped shaking, then knelt and put his arms around Drummond's shoulders. "Come on, now."

He helped the jailer to his feet. "I'm sorry, Mr. Drummond. I didn't mean to hurt you."

Drummond coughed. "So why sneak up on a man?"

"Because I knew if you saw me following you, you'd run."

Drummond doubled over again. Justy went to pick up the knife and waited until the jailer had caught his breath. "Let's find somewhere to sit."

He took Drummond's elbow, and they walked back down to the Row to one of the benches scattered in the small park north of the jail.

It was a few minutes before Drummond stopped wheezing. He pulled a grubby handkerchief out of his pocket and wiped his face.

Justy handed him his knife. Drummond glared at him. "How is it you know my name?"

"The Bull told me."

"And how does he know?"

Justy shrugged. "He makes it his business."

Drummond's eyes flickered. "So what do you want with me?"

"The Bull told me you've worked in the prison a long time. He said you would have known William Duer."

"And if I did?"

"Then maybe you can tell me a few things."

Drummond rubbed his thumb on the blade of his knife. He unbuttoned his coat and slid the knife into an inside pocket. "So you're the Bull's nephew. Francie Flanagan's lad."

"How do you figure?"

"I know Francie had a son who was raised by the Bull after he died. I know that boy went away to college a few years ago. You'd be about his age. And you've the hack of a man who's studied the law."

"Did you know my father?"

"A little." He gave Justy a steady look. "I'd say you've more of your uncle's air about you than your old man's."

"Is that so?"

Drummond held up his hands. "Easy now. I'm only saying, you've the look of a man who'll do what needs to be done, and not turn a hair about it."

Justy felt the warmth in his face. "You have me wrong, Mr. Drummond."

The jailer's eyes flicked down to the bulge in Justy's boot. "If you say so."

A sharp whistle made them both look up at the street. A drover was standing on a cart pulled by a pair of oxen that had veered into the center of the street. The man whistled again, hauling hard on the hemp ropes attached to the animals' yoke.

"So did you know Duer?" Justy asked.

"I did. I was a constable when they put Duer in here, back in '92. I was a guard up on the third floor where he had his rooms. I heard every word spoken up there until '98, when I moved up front. Duer talking to his lawyer. His lawyer talking to other lawyers. They do love to conjobble, God knows."

"Anything about my father?"

The scarring on Drummond's face turned his smile into a leer. "Maybe. What's it worth to you?"

"I suppose that depends, doesn't it? But why should I believe you know anything? You might just spin me some ditty."

"So test me." Drummond sat back and folded his arms.

Justy thought for a moment. "All right then. The partnership my father had with Duer. Who else was invested?"

The jailer cracked his lopsided grin. "I'll tell you what. You give me some names, and I'll say whether they were or weren't a party to it."

Justy gave a wry smile. "Fair enough. William Constable."

"Aye. He was one. Duer was forever sending him letters. He lives in London now."

Justy thought of one of his classmates in Maynooth. "Henry McLaughlin."

"Never heard the name."

"How about Isaac Whippo?"

"Oh aye. Izzy the Whip. A sharp one, for sure."

"I was told he died in Hispaniola."

"I heard Ohio."

"Well, either way, you're right. Whippo was a partner, but Constable wasn't. I met him in London. He told me he tried to keep my father away from both Duer and Whippo."

Drummond scowled. "Constable said that? Well, maybe he wasn't their partner, but he was certainly up to his neck in their business. He was in and out of here visiting Duer all the time, the first few years. Him and two others you've not named yet."

"Who?"

Drummond's eyes were beady. "Small fry back then, but coming men in the Tontine today."

"The Tontine?" Justy couldn't keep the excitement out of his voice.

Drummond smirked. His eyes slid over Justy's shoulder to look at the city skyline beyond the spread of the green that surrounded the jail. Justy's mind was spinning. Two more partners? Constable had said nothing about two more names. But he told Justy he had been unsure of what Francis was up to. He had kept everything secret, even from his old mentor.

"What are the names?"

"You want 'em, you pay for 'em."

A humming sound made him look up. A line of young women, all in long black dresses and matching bonnets, walked past, led by an old nun. They were humming a hymn of some kind.

Justy watched them pass. Drummond seemed plausible, but how could Justy tell if he was telling the truth? He looked at the blotch on the jailer's cheek. It looked like a deserter's mark, but whoever had branded him hadn't used a regulation stamp but had simply burned the letter in with a hot knife, or a bayonet.

"How did you get your love bite?" he asked.

The pupils of Drummond's eyes shrank into tiny points. "What kind of question is that?"

"It's the question I'm asking. You want me to pay for information about Duer, you tell me how you got your stamp."

Drummond closed his eyes for a moment. A breeze set the trees around them rustling. The air was warm, but the old soldier huddled in his coat. "New London. I stole an officer's horse, and his sword. Did a runner with them the day before the attack."

"Theft and desertion. You were lucky not to lose your ears."

Drummond gave a short laugh. "Aye, I got off easy, I suppose. The bastards were in a hurry. They needed every man jack of us, so they couldn't have me sick on the big day."

"Why'd you scamp?"

Drummond looked Justy in the eye. "I fell for a local girl. She lived in the town. I was the quartermaster of the Thirty-Eighth, under Benedict Arnold, and when I heard his plan was to burn the town to the ground, I took off and warned her. Gave her the sword and the horse and told her to bolt. A good thing I did, too, after what they did to the place."

He looked pale with the memory. "Anyway, on the way back, I ran into a patrol, and that was that. They busted me to private, gave me fifty lashes, carved my face and put me in the front rank of the assault on Fort Griswold."

Drummond fell silent, looking into space. His blue eyes were glassy. Justy imagined the thump of the guns, the crackle of rifle fire and the screaming of wounded men. He shivered.

"What happened to the girl?"

"She made it to New York. I came and found her after the war. Sixteen years married last August." His smile reached his eyes, but Justy sensed a sadness there.

"How much for the names?" he asked.

Drummond's purple scar twitched. "There's more than just the names. I've papers. And letters."

Justy looked at him, his chest fluttering. "What letters?"

"All sorts. From Constable. Alexander Hamilton. Aaron Burr. And a whole clutch from Isaac Whippo."

"How did you come by them?"

"Duer didn't die in jail, did you know that? He was mortal sick, so the Marshal let him go home to his missus. He died a few weeks later, but he left boxes of papers behind. I was supposed to burn them, but I didnae."

"Why not?"

Drummond leered. "Because where there's lawyers there's gold. And after he died there was flocks of 'em, like vultures, all going through what was left, all asking for the papers, the papers. So I tucked 'em away. But that's not where the real gold is."

"Oh?"

"No." Drummond tapped his temple. "What you really want is up here. Six years of memories. Conversations had, people seen. You meet me in a quiet place and give me an eagle and I'll answer any questions you've got."

"Ten dollars? You're cracked."

Drummond shrugged. "Suit yourself. But I know a lot more about what went on than you'll read in those papers. An eagle's a fair price."

"And how much for the papers, then?"

"Another eagle."

Justy scoffed. "You're just after telling me they're not worth that much. I'll pay you a quarter eagle."

Drummond glowered. "All right then. Done."

The line of black-clad nurses was disappearing into a grand building made of black stone on the north side of the street. Justy watched as the last nurse pulled the heavy glass-paneled doors closed behind her, then took up her post in the window, her face like a white smear against the darkness of the stone.

He looked at Drummond. "When can you meet me?"

"Tomorrow. Do you know the Counting House? It's down on Gold Street."

The Counting House was a small tavern, frequented by old soldiers. Drummond would have it packed with his pals.

"I know it."

"We'll meet there at ten in the evening. And bring all the money. Or I'll make a wee fire and burn the lot in front of ye."

76

Drummond stood up. It was nearly dark, and the city seemed to sparkle under the empty sky.

"Drummond," Justy said.

"Aye?"

"I heard Duer had his own wine cellar up there. Is that true?"

The jailer thought for a moment, as though weighing the value of the information and deciding how much he should charge.

He shrugged. "Aye, it's true. All them stories are true. Except the privy. Duer had plenty of influence and lots of rich friends, but he had to pish in a chamber pot, just like the rest of us."

NINE

Justy lay on the narrow bed in his plain room at Mrs. Montgomery's, thinking about the two other men Drummond had said were in the partnership with his father. He felt the excitement of giving chase, and then he remembered the fear in Drummond's eyes when he had mentioned the Bull. So much for not exploiting his relationship with his uncle. He wished he hadn't hit the old man quite so hard.

The hubbub of Canvas Town filtered into his consciousness. Shouting and laughing. The scrape of a violin. A scream.

And then a sharp whistle blast. And another. He jumped up and looked out to see two big men in long coats, running down the hill and turning the corner.

He hurried down the stairs and into the street. People in groups of three or four, some carrying lanterns, were walking quickly in the same direction the watchmen had gone. Justy followed the lanterns for a few blocks, until he ran into a small crowd. He pushed through to the front to find five watchmen in a loose circle at an intersection, swinging their long billy clubs to keep the people back. A lantern, placed in the middle of the street, threw light over what looked like a rough heap of blankets, but as Justy pushed closer he could see it was a body, lying on its side, covered with a coat.

Justy looked at the faces around him. Most were black, and all were grim. A muttering came from the back of the crowd, and Justy could feel the press of people against him. He thought about what the Bull had said about the tension between the Negroes and the Irish. That the city might burn. The watchmen spread their arms and braced themselves.

A short man in a long red coat pushed through the crowd on the other side of the street. He stood in the intersection with his legs apart, his hands on his hips.

"There have been complaints that the Watch has not been responsive to the wants and needs of all of the people of New York," he said in a loud, nasal voice that echoed off the walls of the new townhomes. "Well, I am Jacob Hays, Mayor's Marshal, and I say that is not true."

He spread his arms wide and turned a quarter circle. The light from the lantern illuminated a high forehead, deep-set eyes and a thin owl's beak of a nose. "I am here. We are here. Hear me when I say to you that the Watch serves all the people of New York, regardless of color or creed." He turned and looked down at the body. "Or profession."

A murmur rippled through the crowd.

Hays pointed at the body. "Murder cannot be allowed to go unpunished. It is my duty to pursue the perpetrator of this abominable act. And I shall. But I remind you . . ." He raised a finger like a baton and looked around. "The man who did this lives among us. He conceals his evil in ordinary clothes and in an ordinary profession. That is his strength, but it is also his weakness. Because if we are vigilant, we will see through his disguise soon enough. His evil will seep out, like the smell of a dead rat."

He paused.

"So help me," he said, quieter now. "Help us. We are only a few men. We cannot be everywhere. But you can. So be vigilant. Watch. Listen. Sniff the air. And when you smell him, even the faintest whiff, come and see me. Come to Federal Hall and ask for Jacob Hays."

He paused and looked around at the crowd of dark, sullen faces.

"Perhaps you need more incentive," he said. "So know this: any man that gives me information leading to the arrest of the monster that did this will be rewarded."

"How much?" a man shouted from behind Justy.

Hays smiled slightly. "More than you make in a week."

The crowd murmured.

"Hays pays!" the same man shouted, and the murmur became a ripple of laughter.

Hays nodded, his hands on his hips. "That's right, gentlemen. Hays pays. Remember that, and come and tell me what you know."

There was a buzz of conversation, and people began to drift away, talking excitedly to one another. The watchmen relaxed, letting their clubs fall by their sides as the crowd dissolved.

Someone whistled, and two burly men in round hats came down the street with a stretcher, their shirts white in the gloom. Justy took a step forward, but one of the watchmen poked him hard in the chest with his club. "You'll stay where you are if you don't want them to make a second trip."

Justy stepped back. A small, neat man with dark hair and a pale, narrow face hurried past him.

The watchman lifted a finger to his cap. "Marshal."

There was a white flash as the man gave a brief salute in acknowledgment. His hand was wrapped in a thick bandage. "Where's Marshal Hays?"

The watchman pointed with his club, and the man stepped quickly towards the knot of watchmen that had gathered around their commander.

Hays nodded as he approached. "Marshal Turner will give you your orders, gentlemen," he announced.

Justy leaned on the railings of one of the houses, watching as the narrow-faced Marshal with the bandaged hand directed the watchmen. Two of them hefted the body onto the stretcher and carried it to a cart. Another threw handfuls of sawdust on the ground. The rest marched away in pairs, swinging their clubs.

"You there!"

Justy turned to see Hays striding towards him, like a seaman crossing a rolling deck.

"Move along now," Hays ordered.

Justy pushed himself off the railings. "That was quite a speech. That bit about the dead rat played well."

Hays stopped a few yards short of him. He put his hands on his hips. "Move on, I said. Unless you wish my stout fellows to induce you."

Justy smiled. "Would you deny me the privilege and immunity to walk the streets of my own city?"

Hays narrowed his eyes. "Don't parrot the Constitution at me, sir. Or I'll borrow a billy from one of my lads and crack your canister myself."

Justy held up his hands. "No need for that, Marshal. I just have a question."

"You're trying my patience."

"The victim. Was her throat cut? Like the girl they found at the docks?"

"Who says it was a woman?"

"I saw your men lift her. She was too light to be a man."

Hays' face showed nothing. "Perhaps it was a child."

"Not the way they were handling the body. They were too careless. They think she's a whore, don't they? And so do you. The way you talked about her profession just now. Her face is marked, isn't it?"

Hays said nothing.

"Take another look at her face," Justy pressed. "I'll bet the cut is fresh."

"Everything right, Marshal Hays?" The narrow-faced Marshal strode towards them.

"Quite right, Marshal Turner," Hays said without taking his eyes off Justy. "This young man is giving me a lesson in civic order."

Turner stood beside Hays and examined Justy. His eyes were small and quick, like a bird's, darting back and forth in his pale face beneath a sharp widow's peak of dark hair. The bandage on his right hand looked yellow in the lamplight. His coat and breeches were made of a dark cloth, obviously expensive, and meticulously tailored to his lean, compact frame. He had the air of a tightly coiled spring. If you lifted the lid, he would lunge at you.

Hays was rounder. Softer. He was padded with a layer of fat and his red coat was flamboyant, but his eyes were as hard and as calculating as Turner's.

"The mark on the girl's face," Hays asked Turner without looking at him, "was it a fresh cut, or an old mark?"

Turner stared at Justy. "Hard to say." He had a strong Yorkshire accent. "There was blood all over her. Who's asking?"

"What's your name, sir?" Hays asked.

"Justice Flanagan."

Turner snorted. "There's two words you don't often hear in the same sentence."

"Any relation to our old friend the Bull?" Hays asked.

"My uncle."

Hays raised an eyebrow. "Did we know Ignatius has a lawyer for a nephew, Marshal?"

Turner hesitated. "We did not."

Hays nodded thoughtfully.

"You have a sharp eye, Mr. Flanagan. It's a shame to think that you'll be placing your skills at your uncle's service."

Justy reddened. "You presume too much. I'm my own

82

man, not some cow to be kept in a pasture until the occasion requires."

Hays smiled. "Well, that's very good. Very good indeed."

He looked at Turner. "Are we finished here?"

"We are."

"Then let us leave Mr. Flanagan to his evening walk."

He glanced at Justy. "And we'll take a closer look at those bodies."

TEN

Justy watched them go.

"You weren't codding about what those Frenchies taught you, then."

Kerry was sitting in the shadows at the top of the steps of one of the townhomes. She had a grim look on her face.

"How long have you been there?" he asked.

"Long enough."

She walked down the steps and across the street to the place where the body had been. The south side of the street on both sides of the alley was bordered by an old, high wall. The alley itself was a narrow tunnel, made even darker by the branches of a tree growing out of a garden behind the wall.

The ground was the usual mess of horse droppings, dried mud and straw. Sawdust was scattered in a wide swath, over the sidewalk and onto the street.

He stepped into the alley and sniffed.

"He cut her throat."

She gave him a sharp look.

"How do you know?"

He pointed. "The blood. Look at the sawdust. If he'd hit her on the head, or stabbed her, there would have been a big pool of it. But you can see it sprayed out here. That means he cut an artery. Her throat, most likely."

He stepped into the alley and pressed his back to the wall. "He hid like this. In the shadow. Which means she was coming from the north, walking on the pavement on this side of the street. He waited until she passed. Then he attacked from behind."

He wrinkled his nose. "And then he went back this way, after."

"How do you know all that?"

Justy pointed at the sawdust. "He must have come at her from behind. You can tell by the blood. If he'd been in front of her, it would have gone all over him. And I know he came back here afterwards because he vomited. You can still smell it."

"That could have been anyone."

"It could. But why do people puke? If it's a rotten oyster they'll take to bed first and throw up in a bucket. If it's from too much drink the vomit smells of booze. There's no smell of liquor here."

"So all killers shoot the cat after their doings, do they?" Her voice was heavy with sarcasm.

"Some do. Especially if they're new to it. Even a lot of veterans puke after they kill with a knife. It's bloody and messy, and it's hard, physical work. You have to hold the victim close while you're killing them. And hold them tight until it's done."

She gave him a long look, her face shadowed by the moon behind her.

His mouth was dry. He sucked some spittle into it and rolled it around his tongue.

"Anyway, I'd say he came back here, puked and then took off."

"Where to?"

Justy looked down the alley. "Who knows? Canvas Town, maybe. He followed her from north of here, that's certain."

"You said he was waiting for her here."

"Yes, but it's not likely he'd have been waiting for just anyone to come along at this time of the evening. There were still people about. I'd say he spied her walking this way, hurried along Greenwich Street to get ahead of her, then up the alley to here. He was bold, that's for sure."

He made a last slow turn. Out of the corner of his eye he saw the moonlight catch on something shiny on the ground beside the curb. He used the toe of his boot to scuff through the filthy straw. "Maybe he left something behind."

It was a slim piece of light-colored leather, longer than his hand was wide, studded with rivets that looked as though they might be silver. "It's a knife sheath. A hunting knife, most likely. Long and thin, for skinning game." He pointed. "You see the top of it's loose, here? That's where the leather wraps around the handle. It means there's no guard to stop your hand slipping. And this hole at the end here? It's like a buttonhole. The knife this belongs to will have a knob at the end that this slides over. Probably brass or silver."

Kerry peered at the sheath. "Looks like you paid attention during your lessons."

"It's not a black art," Justy said. "It's mostly keeping your eyes open for the unusual, and using your common sense to work out what happened."

Kerry was looking at him, an unreadable expression in her eyes.

He colored and shrugged. "It's only so useful. They catch most people through interviews with witnesses."

Kerry made a face. "That won't happen here, then. Nobody gives a damn about a bunch of dolly-mops. And they care even less because of the color of their skins."

━━━━━◆━━━━━

They walked back to the boardinghouse. Kerry's shoulders were hunched, her hands thrust deep into her trouser pockets. Her face was tight. Justy watched her out of the corner of his eye. "Did you know that girl, Kerry?"

"No. How would I?"

They passed a stable yard. There was the musty smell of wet straw. A horse muttered in the darkness.

"It's just you seem vexed about something," he said.

She stopped. Her eyes were full of tears, but her voice was hard. "You mean, that some bravo can run about the city milling young Negro girls and no one gives a black joke?"

He had the hot feeling of being slapped in the face. She started off and he let her go, head down, wiping her cheeks roughly with her sleeve.

She stopped on the sidewalk. "Sorry."

"No. I'm the one should apologize."

She shook her head. "You already apologize too much."

They were outside the boardinghouse. She jerked her head back the way they had come. "I'm away this way."

"You're not going home?"

"To O'Toole's? In this rig?" She shuddered. "No. I'll stay at my cousin's. He's up near the Collect."

Justy felt stung. "You're staying with Lew Owens? You told me he tried to put you on the street."

She smiled. "Believe it or not, he meant well. That's just who he is. And it's better than staying with my old man. At least with Lew I can be myself."

She gave him a frank look, and he felt himself redden.

She grinned. "I'll catch up with you later, then."

"You will? When?"

"Whenever I decide."

She touched her fingers to the brim of her hat and winked, and then slipped away into the darkness.

ELEVEN

Wednesday

He was at Cantillon's house at nine the next morning. They walked to the Tontine, where the lawyer instructed him on the way the trading system worked and the plans the reformers had to create a framework of rules. Justy nodded his head and made encouraging noises, but all he could think about was what Drummond might tell him and what he might find in Duer's papers. After a few hours, the lawyer dismissed him, warning him not to be late for lunch with Colley.

Justy sat on a padded bench in the Tontine's lobby, listening to the din coming from the dining room, looking at the huge paintings on the walls and wondering what the tall, gaunt trader wanted with him.

"Do you mind if I sit?" Colley folded his long frame onto the other end of the bench. He looked around, as though seeing the lobby for the first time. "I saw you looking at these dreadful daubs. I don't suppose Carrots has explained them."

"No."

He pointed. "That's tobacco, that one is furs and that one indigo." He turned around and nodded upwards. "This one is rice. It's new. It replaced a painting of Whitney's cotton gin. Do you know why they switched it?"

"No."

"Because it depicted the people who pick the cotton and work the gin."

"Slaves."

"Slaves, indeed. The traffic in Negroes is no longer so much in fashion, you see. And the members were offended by the sight of such a repugnant trade."

"It *is* a repugnant trade," Justy said, feeling a little warm. "And the sooner all the states fall behind us and ban it, the better."

Colley sat up. "Do you have a handkerchief?"

Justy reddened. "I do, Mr. Colley, but I must tell you that I've already suffered through a long lecture this morning. I don't really want another one from you explaining why slavery is justified because it keeps cotton prices low."

Colley laughed. "Very good. You saw through me. You're probably wondering why I asked you to luncheon, too."

"I'm fairly sure it wasn't to eat."

"It never is, young man. But we'll eat anyway."

The Tontine Club Room had the same high ceilings and windows as the lobby and was about the same size. Royal-blue curtains made of velvet hung from the ceiling every few feet, and there was a luxurious carpet of the same color on the floor. Pairs of large leather armchairs, each one flanked by a small side table, were spaced across the room. Some of them were occupied with people talking quietly or, in some cases, sleeping. Colley led the way to a table set with a large plate, heaped with sandwiches. He flopped into one of the armchairs, which creaked and wheezed like a set of broken bagpipes. Justy perched on the edge of the seat of the other chair, his back straight and his hands between his knees.

Colley raised his eyebrows. "You look as though you're preparing for a lesson."

"You don't intend to school me on the benefits of slavery to the economy?"

"I feel I would be wasting my time. Your loyalties are quite apparent. Will you be attending the Manumission conference this week?"

"I hadn't planned to."

"Well, good. The pamphlets they've been putting about the place are calling for a boycott of all companies that still use slaves in any capacity."

"I've read them. And I'm glad people are speaking out, at last."

"You'll be glad to see the economy collapse, too, then, I suppose. And see your own people starve."

"My people?"

"The Irish. You have more to lose than anyone if the trade is abolished wholesale. Thousands of Negro workers, newly freed? They'll sell themselves cheaper and drive your entire community into the poorhouse."

"My community, as you call it, is already in the poorhouse. It would be difficult for things to be much worse." He looked Colley in the eye. "I thought you weren't going to give me a lesson."

Colley held his hands up in mock surrender. "Forgive me. I just wanted to point out our particular brand of New York hypocrisy to you. Here."

There was a decanter of red wine and two glasses on an occasional table beside his chair. Colley plucked the stopper out of the decanter, filled the glasses and leaned forward in his chair to examine the sandwiches. "Now let's see. Roast beef, by the looks of it."

The beef was thinly sliced and slathered in horseradish sauce that made Justy's eyes water. He relaxed, sliding back a little on the warm leather of the chair, then looked up to see Colley watching him.

He waited. Colley ate and drank, watching him the entire

time. Minutes passed. Justy knew he was being tested. He had used the same technique himself, a few times.

Colley put his glass down. "It's unusual to meet someone so comfortable with silence."

"I don't believe in talking for the sake of it."

Colley smiled. "And yet you wish to be a lawyer."

Justy shrugged. "It's what I studied."

"Of course. And it is a noble choice of career. But if you really want to make something of yourself, I'd suggest an alternative."

"Trading?"

"Indeed. Lawyering is all very well if your aim is to become a powdery politician or an inky-fingered bureaucrat. But if you want adventure . . . if you want excitement . . ."

"If you want money."

"Of course. But don't lawyers want money, too?"

Justy drank his wine and felt a pleasant tingling in the tips of his fingers. He allowed himself to sink back into the chair. The leather cushions molded themselves around him.

He had a sudden memory of a house in Dublin, owned by a lawyer in the emancipation movement. It had the same smell of leather and cigar smoke and the dark scent of good cognac. Justy had gone there to deliver a message for the Defenders. It was late, and the lawyer had given him dinner and a bed for the night. He remembered sitting at breakfast the next day, being waited on by several servants and feeling deeply guilty about it. The lawyer had looked at him over his newspaper and caught the look on his face and smiled. It was possible to do good and to live well, he had said. Justy felt the same sense of guilt now. Only the wine had dulled its edge.

"Buy low, sell high," he said.

"And be sure you get a sniff of the fish before it's wrapped." Colley raised his glass. "You see? You've already begun."

"What do you want from me, Mr. Colley?"

Colley raised his eyebrows. "Why should I want anything?"

"How often do you pay this much attention to lawyers' clerks?"

Colley smiled. "Fair enough." He leaned forward to refill Justy's glass. "I wanted to talk with you because I knew your father."

Justy felt the warmth drain out of his body.

"Carrots didn't tell you?" Colley asked.

"No."

"Well, I can't say I knew him as well as Carrots did. Enough to say how d'ye do."

Colley's eyes were blank. Justy wondered if he should ask what he knew about his father and the business with Duer. But there was something about the tall black-clad trader that told him it would be like trying to squeeze venom out of a snake.

"Did you ever work with him?" he asked.

"We may have traded paper once or twice. He had a reputation for being an honest broker. Rare, in this business." Colley smiled his thin smile. "I wonder if you're cut from the same cloth."

TWELVE

Cantillon was waiting in the lobby, his case clamped under his arm. He gave Justy a cool look. "I've done all I can here today. Would you be so good as to accompany me home?"

"Of course."

They walked down onto Wall Street. It was the middle of the afternoon, and couples were enjoying the late summer warmth. Cantillon glanced at him. "So what did Mr. Colley want with you?"

"He suggested I abandon the law and learn how to trade."

Cantillon made a face. "By the look of you, I'd say he has you halfway convinced. I did not think you'd be quite so susceptible."

Justy felt the heat in his face. "I didn't say yes."

Cantillon stepped quickly across the street, then turned on Justy and jabbed a finger at his chest. "Be careful of who you associate with in this business. Not everyone is what they seem."

"What do you mean?"

Cantillon stepped back to let a strolling couple pass. "Did you hear that foppish fool Tyson yesterday? The man with the spout of white hair? Boasting about the fabulous return he's getting on his money?"

"Sixteen percent."

"Sixteen percent. Precisely." Cantillon swerved to avoid a pile of horse shit that had somehow found its way onto the sidewalk. "No one does the kind of business that generates a sixteen percent return for investors. No one."

"Well, clearly someone does."

Cantillon sighed. "Yes. That fat fellow Harry Gracie."

"The man in the pink suit?"

"Yes, that crusty-faced clown. His venture has been paying out between sixteen and twenty percent a year for the past two and a half years."

"No wonder he's so popular."

"He is now. Just five years ago he didn't own a single security, let alone a decent suit of clothes."

They both stepped into the road to allow two women to pass. They were modestly dressed, but one wore a wide-brimmed hat with a tall plume of royal-blue feathers. Cantillon ducked his head, flashing a nervous smile, and the plume dipped and wobbled as the lady returned the compliment.

"What kind of business does Gracie do?" Justy asked as they walked on.

Cantillon scowled. "That's the point. Nobody knows. He claims to operate an import-export venture, which means it can do almost anything. And he won't tell anyone who his partners are. No law against it, of course. Not that anyone seems to care. They hear sixteen percent and they hand over all their money."

He glanced over his shoulder. "That woman with the ridiculous hat, for instance. You may have heard of her. Maria Reynolds."

"Alexander Hamilton's paramour?" Justy turned for another look. Two years before, a journalist had published papers detailing an affair between the then Secretary of the Treasury and Reynolds, whose husband had blackmailed Hamilton for nearly three years.

"The same. No doubt she's in town for the Manumission conference. A good excuse for her to meet Hamilton in public without attracting any more scandal. You know she received a considerable settlement in her divorce."

"Yes, I read about it."

"What you won't have read is that she invested a large proportion of it with Harry Gracie. All her rich friends have followed her in. I've heard of politicians, bankers, sober men who've been seduced by Gracie's malarkey. Even Hamilton himself, although he was more likely seduced by the Reynolds woman than by Gracie, I expect."

"Why do you care?"

Cantillon stopped again. They were immediately opposite his house, but the lawyer appeared too agitated to notice. "Haven't you been listening to a single thing I've been saying?" His face was scarlet. "That fat gull Gracie has convinced some of the wealthiest and most powerful people in the country to hand over their money, in return for the kind of interest that can only be generated either by a venture of a dangerously speculative nature, or by fraud. Now imagine what happens if his venture, whatever it is, fails. The most powerful men and women in the country will lose their principal. They will question the integrity of the system. They will stop investing. They will stop lending. The money, in other words, will dry up, and the entire economy will collapse." The lawyer stood, red faced, clutching at his cravat.

Justy waited until Cantillon's breathing had slowed. "You said Gracie's venture might be a fraud. What did you mean?"

The color drained out of the lawyer's face. "I spoke hastily. I did not mean that." He stepped quickly across the street to his door.

Justy followed. "Is everything all right, Mr. Cantillon?"

Cantillon waved him away. "Quite all right. Thank you. I am merely passionate about such things."

Justy waited until Cantillon had opened the lock on his

door. "Forgive me for exciting you. I'm just curious to know what form a fraud might take."

Cantillon's eyes bulged. "Didn't you hear me? There is no fraud. I never said such a thing. Do not mention it again, I implore you." He backed into his house, clutching at his tie. "Now please be so kind as to leave me. I'm quite tired. We can continue tomorrow. Good day."

And he slammed the door in Justy's face.

THIRTEEN

Dutch Street was one of the few streets in the city that hadn't changed since the colonists built its stone-walled, gambrel-roofed houses a hundred years before. It had survived fires, floods, riots, even the rapacious developers who seemed to want to turn every building in the city into a tenement. Perhaps it was because the street was so short and easy to miss, running as it did for barely a hundred cobbled yards between the licentious hurly-burly of John Street and the commercial grit of Fair Avenue.

The street had no markings and its entrances were as plain and as narrow as an alleyway, barely wide enough to allow a hansom cab. It was easy to miss the turn, but once you were past the corner it was like walking into an old walled garden. The sounds of the city fell away, and the air filled with the smell of herbs and flowers. The narrow gables of the houses loomed above the street, so that it seemed the apexes of their doglegged roofs might touch each other, three stories up. The ground floor windows of the houses were fronted by wide flower boxes, brimming with herbs and blooms. It was so quiet that the sound of dripping water was loud on the cobbles, and Justy found himself stepping lightly, careful to keep his weight off the noisy heels of his boots.

The house was three-quarters of the way down, on the north side of the street. The red stone had been scrubbed, and the wooden cornices above the windows had been whitewashed. The door had been painted a glossy black. The leaded windows glittered in the afternoon sun.

Justy stood, looking up at the single third floor window, high up under the apex of the roof. He heard the scrape of a footstep behind him, but he didn't turn around.

"They painted the door," he said.

Kerry stood beside him. Their shoulders touched. "I preferred it green."

"That was the Bull's idea. He said Father should fly the flag in the midst of the enemy."

"That sounds like the Bull, all right."

He turned to look at her. "What are you doing here?"

"Just keeping an eye on you." Her eyes were cool and green and amused.

"You followed me?"

"I saw you up on Wall Street. I thought I'd see what you were about."

"You were forking, were you?"

A shrug. "A girl's got to make a living."

"Well, I'm sorry if I queered your pitch."

"No fear." She smoothed the empty pockets of her coat. "Slim pickings today."

She pointed her chin at the window on the third floor and leaned against him slightly. She smelled like olive oil, warmed in the sun. "I used to sit up there, on that padded bench you made, do you remember?"

Justy smiled. "It took me months to make that thing. I could never get the horsehair to stop poking through the velvet."

"It was like sitting on a hedgehog, right enough. And it wobbled."

"I never was much good with my hands."

"Plenty of time for that."

Her fingers brushed the back of his hand, and his whole body seemed to vibrate. He felt the heat in his face and the thump in his chest, and he pulled away, walking towards the door.

"What are you doing?" Her voice was sharp.

"I have to see inside."

"Justy!"

But it was too late. He rapped his knuckles on the thick paint. There was the sound of a firm tread on a wooden floor, deep in the house, and he counted to himself, recalling how many paces it was from the scullery to the front door.

The bolt clicked, and the door swung open. A big, bald man with a ruddy face stared at him. He wore black breeches and a tight black waistcoat. A long club was propped against the wall behind him.

"What's your business?" the man demanded in a strong Dublin accent.

"Justice Flanagan. Attorney-at-law. Is the master of the house in?"

"A lawyer?" The man's eyes flicked over Justy's shoulder. "So who's this?"

Justy glanced at Kerry. "My clerk."

"He doesn't look like no clerk. Looks like he should be heaving spuds."

"Nevertheless. Would you let your master know I am calling on him?"

The man scowled. "My master's not in. And even if he were, he wouldn't be troubling himself with the likes of youse."

He went to slam the door, but Justy stepped into the doorway.

"Get on out of it," the man snarled.

"Don't worry, Terrence." The voice echoed down the hallway. A man shuffled into the light. He was bent over a cane, long white hair spread over his shoulders like a nun's wimple.

Terrence stood aside as the old man made his way to the door. He brushed away a wisp of white hair and peered up at Justy.

"Young Justice Flanagan. You look just like your father." The old man's voice showed no sign of age. It was deep and mellow, and Justy felt the jolt of recognition.

"Mr. Kimball?"

The old man tapped his cane on the floor in appreciation. "Very well met, Justice. How long has it been?"

Justy knew exactly how long. The last time he had seen Jeremiah Kimball was at his father's memorial service. The priest had refused to bury a suicide in consecrated ground, but Kimball, then Chief Judge of New York, had threatened all sorts of jurisprudential retribution. They had compromised on a cremation and a scattering of ashes, followed by a memorial in the church.

Kimball had mentored Justy's father. He was a staunch Protestant of English stock, but he saw the value in training Catholic Irish lawyers who could represent their people properly in the new America. He was disappointed when Francis turned away from the law and towards Wall Street, but he had remained a mentor and a friend, comforting him when his wife died and acting as a grandfatherly presence in Justy's life, with gifts on birthdays and invitations to his mansion on Broad Street each Christmas.

"What are you doing here, Mr. Kimball?"

"Why, I live here, of course." The old man smiled at Justy's confusion. "Why don't you come in and I'll explain."

"May I bring my clerk, sir?"

Kimball's eyes were watery, but still sharp. They looked Kerry up and down, lingering on her face. "As you wish."

He shuffled in a half circle and led Justy and Kerry to a small room that was made smaller by the four heavy armchairs that took up most of the floor space and the books that lined all four walls. Every square inch of wall was occupied by shelving, all the way to the ceiling, and even the spaces above the door and below the window were heavy with books. A thick rug covered most of the floor, dampening the sound and making the room feel womb-like.

Kimball eased himself into a chair. "Do you remember what this room was used for when you lived here?"

Justy glanced at Kerry. She shrugged.

He tried to picture the room as he had last seen it. "Storage, I think. I remember bare floors and walls, and piles of dusty boxes full of papers. Very little to interest a boy who chafed to be outside, running about. It's much improved."

Kimball waved his cane. "Please sit down. Terrence will bring us some refreshment presently."

They sat, and Kimball leaned forward in his chair, both hands on the knob of his cane. "Do you remember Mrs. Kimball, Justice?"

Justy had a sudden memory of a tall, severe woman with pale eyes and a faint mustache. "Of course, sir."

"She died two years ago."

"I'm very sorry."

Kimball flicked the sentiment away. "She was a good woman, but I can't say it was much of a marriage. Once it became clear we weren't going to be blessed with babies, we occupied our time in separate ways. I in the law and she in her missions. Ah. Here we are. Thank you, Terrence."

The big Dubliner came into the room, carrying a tray of glasses. They each took one. Kimball stared into his for a moment.

"Mrs. Kimball," Justy prompted.

"Ah yes. Well, once she passed, I found myself rattling around in that place on Broad Street like a marble in a magician's hat. So I sold it to some Wall Street chap with far more money than sense. I could have rented it out, of course, but where's the fun in that?"

"But how did you manage to end up here?"

"Simple. I owned the place."

Justy blinked, and Kimball thumped his cane on the carpet. "Yes. I thought that might surprise you. I bought it after your father died. No one else would, you see. Thanks to the Panic, no one was buying anything, and then there were the circumstances of your father's death." He glanced away. "Makes a house hard to sell, that kind of thing. And there was a mortgage. That didn't sit too well with your uncle."

"The Bull likes to be the one owed, not the one owing," Kerry said.

Kimball laughed. "Just so. Yes, Ignatius wanted rid of the place, so I bought out the mortgage, along with a small premium for the rightful heir."

He smiled, and Justy felt his eyes fill with sudden tears. "I didn't know. He never said."

Kimball flicked the sentiment away. "But now it's your turn. I heard you tell Terrence you're a lawyer."

"Yes, sir. My uncle sent me to study at St. Patrick's, in Maynooth."

"The new Catholic college? Excellent! And you graduated?"

"I did, sir."

The cane thumped. "Damn good show. Well done. I'm proud of you!"

Justy's nose tingled, and he had to blink hard again. "Thank you."

Kimball beamed. He took a long sip of his wine. "So why come back? And why come here? Not to see me, I'm sure."

"I just wanted to see the old place, sir."

"You seemed pretty determined."

Justy felt his skin prickle.

"Come on, lad. Out with it." Kimball's voice was sharp.

Justy looked at his hands. "I found him, sir. Out there. In the hallway."

Kimball glanced at the door. "I thought your uncle . . ."

"The Bull cut him down. But I found him." He kept his voice low. "I've been thinking about it a lot these past few years. I have dreams."

"I see."

"I thought that coming back and looking at the place again might help."

Kimball leaned on his cane. He tapped a fingernail on the polished wood. "There are those who believe that the unspeakable events of the past should remain in the past. After a lifetime at the bench, I cannot say that I agree. My experience is that the truth will come out, eventually." He glanced at Kerry. "Better for us all to confront our past and live in the truth, wouldn't you say, young fellow?"

Kerry was trembling. She looked away. The room was silent.

Kimball stirred. "This was your house once, Justice. I'd like you to treat it as your house again. Take your time. Go where you need to go."

The soft evening light streamed into the hallway through a window at the top of the stairwell. Motes of dust turned in the still air. Justy stood at the bottom of the stairs, looking up at the landing.

Kerry stood behind him. "Are you all right?"

Justy thought for a moment. "I'm fine." He looked at her. "What about you?"

She shook her head. "Who is he?" She kept her voice low.

Justy smiled. "He used to be a beak. The terror of the state bench, they said. My father told me there was no lie that Jeremiah

Kimball couldn't sniff out. So don't feel bad about him twigging you."

She said nothing, and he turned back, looking for the banister that his father had been found hanging from. The heavy rope had chafed and splintered the wood, he remembered, but now all the banisters looked the same. Perhaps the Bull had it restored, before putting the house on the market.

He felt detached. There was a picture in his mind of his father hanging, but there was no sense of horror or despair. Instead, he looked carefully around the space, recalling every detail. He walked under the landing and stretched his hand up. The ceilings of the house were unusually high, twelve feet up, and impossible for him to reach.

He walked carefully up the stairs to the landing, then leaned over the railing and looked down into the stairwell. Carefully, he climbed over the railing, so that he was suspended over the hallway; then he let go.

He landed hard on the wooden floor, and the sound of his boot heels echoed through the house.

"Jesus Christ, Justy!" Kerry's face was white.

The door to the library swung open, and Kimball shuffled into the hallway. "What's going on? Where's Terrence?"

"I'm sorry about the noise, sir. And I'm not sure where Terrence is. But I've finished looking around."

Kimball's watery eyes were unwavering. "Some help to you, I hope."

"Very much so, sir. Thank you."

The old man tapped his cane on the floor. "Well, I hope you'll come and see me again."

"I shall." Justy paused. "Before I go, may I ask you one question?"

"Of course."

"You said you paid more for the house than the mortgage

was worth. Why didn't the money go to pay off my father's creditors?"

Kimball thought for a moment. "I'm not aware that there were any. Certainly none ever made themselves known to me. The only loan I was aware of was the mortgage on this house."

"My father didn't borrow money to buy securities?"

"He may have. Many do. But if he did, he never told me about it."

"And no one ever called at the house?"

"Never."

Justy looked into the library, at the books lining the walls.

"What about his papers, sir? That room used to be full of them. Do you know what happened to them?"

"I would assume your uncle took them, when he cleared out the house and put it on the market."

Justy nodded. "Thank you, sir. I won't trouble you any further."

"It was no trouble at all, Justice. I'm delighted to make your acquaintance again after all these years." He smiled. "You have made an old man very proud. I hope you will come and see me again, before long. And that you will consider this place a home."

FOURTEEN

The setting sun had transformed the tiny street. The windows of the houses reflected the honey-colored light, softening the brickwork and the cobbles and the lines of the steep-pitched roofs. Justy stood with his back to the door, thinking.

"What was that about?" Kerry asked.

"Answers."

"And did you get any?"

"Some. But I have more questions now, too."

"For the Bull?"

"Him as well."

Kerry sighed. "Well, he'll be ready for you. Your man Terrence will have told him by now."

"How do you know him?"

"He used to work with O'Toole. He was a right head cracker, until he caught a twelvemonth in stone jug for thieving, a few years back. I heard he went into service after he came out, but I had no idea he was a fart catcher for a lambskin man."

Justy smiled. A valet was so called because he was required to walk close behind his master. "So you think he went to my uncle?"

Kerry nodded. "Or sent word."

Justy sighed. "I suppose I should go to him."

She looked over his shoulder and pursed her lips. "No need."

It was a trick of the light, but the Bull seemed to take up almost the entire width of the street. The two Galwaymen Justy had seen at his house walked behind him, the right sleeves of their coats stiffened by the long clubs they kept hidden there, ready to slide into their hands at the first sign of trouble.

Justy waited.

The Bull came close. "What are you doing here? This isn't your house anymore."

Justy ignored the tightness in his belly. "It's not yours, either. Mr. Kimball told me he paid you more than the mortgage to get it off your hands."

The Bull seemed to swell up. "It cost a pretty penny to feed you and clothe you and send you to your fancy school."

"I'm not questioning you, Uncle. I know you spent a great deal more on me over the years than you got from selling this place."

The Bull's eyes searched Justy's face. They shifted to look at Kerry. "What's she doing here?"

"She's helping."

"Is that what she calls it?"

Justy reddened. "What does that mean?"

"It means you shouldn't trust people you don't know."

"I've known her since we were weans, Uncle."

The Bull shook his head. "No. You knew her *when* she was a wean. That's not the same thing. She's not a wee girl anymore. Are you, lassie?"

Kerry's face was white.

The Bull smirked. "Away on with you. Unless you want me to tell O'Toole you're still gladding about dressed like that. He may be my man, but I'll not be able to stop him whipping the skin off you."

Kerry turned to go. Justy grabbed her arm. "Don't listen to him. Stay with me."

She snatched her arm away. "Get your hands off me. I'm not some piece of property to be pawed at."

Justy stepped back, confused by the rage in her eyes. "I'm sorry."

"Touch me again and you will be."

The Bull watched her walk away. "You're well rid of her."

"She's a friend."

His uncle gave him a neutral look. "If it's a little rantum scantum you're after, I can help fix you up, and no complications after."

"I don't want a whore. And I don't want your nose in my business, either."

"You're happy to stick your nose in mine, though, aren't you?" The Bull's shout reverberated off the walls of the quiet street. A face showed pale in a window and then disappeared.

"Come on." The Bull jerked his head. He led Justy back down the quiet street and out onto the commotion of the main road. The noise was like a slap in the face. The clackety-clack of carriage wheels on cobblestones, the rhythmic calls of the night market stall owners advertising the prices of their goods, the screeches of men and women getting an early start on the night's drinking.

It was as though an invisible herald were walking ten yards ahead of them as they descended the hill. People stepped out of the way and onto the road, fear on their faces as the Bull bore down on them. One vendor picked up his entire stall and moved it back on the sidewalk to let them pass. A drunk man tried to get out of the way but slipped on the ground. He rolled desperately to the side, directly into a pool of manure. The Bull ignored him.

It wasn't until they reached Front Street that the Bull spoke. "So. What else did that old skinflint say?"

"Did he cheat you?"

"Depends on how you call it. He paid market value. But the market was a wreck back then, which means he was able to beat me down like a piece of warm copper. He got the place for a song. A lot less than what it's worth now."

"Sounds like good business."

The Bull grunted. "I just wanted the debt off my books."

The rutted street was slick with runoff and spillage. Pools of fouled ale and dirty water reflected the flickering lights from candles in windows and the braziers and grill pans on the street, so it looked as though the ground itself were on fire. This was the heart of the waterfront, and the Bull's home turf. People waved at him from windows and doorways and called out "good evening." He replied every time. He knew everyone's name.

"I'm sorry my father didn't leave me with any means of support," Justy said.

"You didn't need support. You're my kin. My responsibility."

"What happened to his papers?"

"Why?"

"I thought there might be something of value in them. Share certificates, perhaps."

"You think I wouldn't have sold them myself if there were? No. There was nothing like that."

"What about debts?"

He shrugged. "The only debt I cared about was that damned mortgage. Your father put my name on the contract, so some puffed-up pettifogger of a lawyer came around from the Bank of New York, threatening to have me before the beak."

"Any other creditors?"

"No other banks. There were all sorts of tales about the money Francis owed around Wall Street, but none of those huffs ever had the bounce to try to collect from me. I'd have tied them to a post and used the papers as kindling to light them up, if they had."

"Did you burn the papers?"

"Read them. Burned them. Forgot them. Until you started whiddling on about them."

They walked in silence for a while, the two big Galwaymen close behind them. Even with the noise of the street, Justy could hear them breathing.

They passed a two-story tenement that had been converted from a warehouse. Like most of the waterfront, it was built on landfill, but the foundation here hadn't been packed in hard enough and the decrepit building slumped at a distinct angle, like a drunk leaning on a lamppost. Harsh laughter came from inside. A woman screamed.

The Bull stopped. "Get in there, Duffy. See what's what."

The big Galwayman with the broken nose walked into the tenement. There was a sound like a hammer hitting a nail, and a moment later two men stumbled out into the street. Duffy was hard behind them, his club in his hand.

"It was Fat Bridie screaming, boss," he said. "There was a fella trying to tup her, so I cracked him on the swede. These two were waiting their turn."

The two men stood in the street, their eyes on the ground.

"Do you know who I am?" the Bull asked. They nodded.

A short, plump woman ran out. She wore a too-tight cotton dress with a deep décolletage. The dress was threadbare and stained. She threw herself at the Bull. "Oh Jesus! Ignatius Flanagan! Bless you!"

Her head barely reached the Bull's chest. He pushed her away gently. "What happened, Bridie?"

She spat on the ground. "Three of 'em. They just came in and started at me. First they said they want a room for the night; the next thing I know they have me tripped up and they're hauling away at my drawers. Look!"

A small crowd of onlookers had gathered. They gasped as Bridie showed a long tear in the back of her dress.

The Bull ignored the gawkers. He stared at the two men. "Is this true?"

They were dressed like farm laborers, in long woolen trousers and cotton smocks. The taller of the two shook his head. "We paid a half-dollar for the room. Then she said if we gave her the whole coin, we could have her, too."

"Bridie?"

The woman scowled. "I didn't mean then and there. And they never paid me. These two just jumped me and held me down while that son of a bitch in there dropped his breeks."

The Bull's face was hard. "Did you pay her?"

The man who had spoken looked at the ground. His companion was cringing, almost folding in on himself.

"Well, pay her now," the Bull growled. "And not the half-dollar, either. The full coin."

The men looked at each other. The taller man shuffled his feet. "We don't have it."

The Bull shrugged. "You'll pay in broken bones then. Knees and elbows. Duffy?"

The big Galwayman smacked his club into the palm of his hand. It sounded like a fish being slapped on a rock. The tall man cowered. "Him inside. He has our coin. In his drawers."

Duffy went back inside. A moment later, he reappeared, shaking his head.

The tall man gasped. "He had it, I swear. We sold fifteen barrels of apples today. Fifteen!"

The Bull folded his arms. "Bridie?"

"I don't know nothing about it." She tugged her dress, avoiding his eyes.

The Bull waited. The crowd murmured. Someone laughed.

Bridie sighed. She reached into the deep V in the front of her dress and pulled out a grimy woolen purse. She handed it to the Bull.

"This your friend's skin?" the Bull asked.

The tall man nodded.

The Bull took out a coin and flicked it to Bridie.

"Your man inside there, Duffy. Is he dead?"

"No, boss. He's still breathing," the big Galwayman said. "He's leaking a bit, mind."

The Bull took another coin from the purse and spun it towards Bridie. "That's for the mess."

"Ah, Mr. Flanagan. You're a topping gent. Thanks for saving me." She tucked the coins into her bodice.

The Bull looked around at the crowd.

"It's not about saving you, Bridie. It's about making sure everyone knows their place. You follow?"

She ducked her head. "Aye, sir."

The Bull tossed the purse to the taller of the two men. "You come to my part of town, you pay your way. In advance. Get me?"

The man nodded.

"Fetch your pal and be on your way, then." The Bull glanced at Bridie. "And I'll see you at the end of the month, girl. Same as always."

She nodded and scurried back inside the tenement.

The Bull looked at Justy. "Right then, lad. I'll leave you here. Unless there's anything else you want to ask me?"

Justy shook his head. He stood aside and watched as the Bull walked on, the crowd melting away in front of him, the two big Galwaymen falling in behind.

FIFTEEN

Justy's conversations with his landlady had so far been short and transactional, but he was curious to know more about the tall, wide-hipped woman who had married an English officer and was childhood friends with Kerry's father, O'Toole. So when she asked him if he would join her for an early supper, he readily agreed.

Clodagh Montgomery's dining room was decorated with the same whitewash and plain jute carpet as the rest of the house. But it was dominated by her dinner table, a flawless oval of polished walnut, surrounded by six delicate chairs. The ensemble seemed to glow in the evening light.

"My late husband's," she said, spooning vegetable and barley soup into Justy's bowl.

Justy was on the point of asking what had happened to him when there was a knock at the door. When he opened up, he saw a familiar red coat.

"Good evening, Mr. Flanagan." Jacob Hays stood on the bottom step, his hands clasped behind his back.

Three men stood in the street behind the Marshal. Two of them were big watchmen dressed in long black coats. It wasn't until the third man turned, his small, bright eyes gleaming in the candlelight, that Justy recognized the other Marshal, Turner.

Hays stepped forward. "Forgive the intrusion, but may we come in?"

Justy heard Mrs. Montgomery come into the hallway behind him. She looked over his shoulder. "Police?"

"How did you know?"

She made a face. "Only a lawman would have the spunk to walk about dressed like a lobster in this city."

Hays smiled and made a slight bow. "You speak with the verve of a soldier, madam."

"My husband was one, so I shall take that as a compliment."

"I meant it so."

She looked at Justy. "Are you in trouble?"

"I don't think so."

"Then show them into the parlor."

The room smelled of damp and wood polish. A large painting of a white horse on a green field hung above the empty fireplace. Four armchairs were arranged around a low table in the center of the room.

Justy lit a candelabra and placed it in the center of the table. Hays sat in the chair facing the door. "You're probably wondering how I found you."

Justy said nothing.

A smile twitched at the corner of Hays' mouth. "Marshal Turner and I hold the same rank. But we occupy different positions in the city administration. I am, for want of a better term, the chief of police. Marshal Turner is our head of intelligence."

"Your spymaster."

Hays ignored the comment. "Marshal Turner has considerable experience in the gathering of information. He was a scout in the war, and he has kept his skills sharp since, recruiting agents all over the city. They see a great deal. For example, they observed you taking up residence here. And they saw you meet with a Mr. Drummond yesterday afternoon."

Justy waited. His palms were suddenly slippery with sweat. Drummond was either badly injured or dead. There would be no other reason for the Marshals to visit him in person.

"Do you deny meeting him?" Hays asked.

"No." He knew the drill. Answer simply and precisely, don't elaborate, don't volunteer information. Wait for them to tell you what they know, not the other way around.

"What did you discuss?"

"The weather."

Hays frowned. "Don't toy with me, Mr. Flanagan."

Justy thought for a moment. Hays would doubtless speak with Drummond's chief, Desjardins. If he hadn't already.

"I went to the jail to see William Duer earlier this week, but I was told he had died. I wanted to ask Drummond if he knew much about Duer's affairs and his dealings with my father."

"And did he?"

"No."

The candles flickered as the door to the parlor swung open. Turner nodded to Hays, then lowered himself carefully into a chair, his black, birdlike eyes fixed on Justy.

Justy stared back as Turner settled himself. The Yorkshireman looked about fifty, but it was his clothes that made him move stiffly, not his age. His coat and breeches were fitted so tightly to his lean, spry frame that it took him a few moments to adjust them and get comfortable. He ran a hand lightly over his widow's peak, smoothing a stray hair into place. He was wearing gloves, and he tugged at the cuffs of them, pulling the leather tight over his fingers. Justy remembered the bandage he had been wearing the night before.

Hays cleared his throat. "You and Mr. Drummond parted ways at Chambers Street. Which way did he go?"

"I don't know. North."

"Did he say where he was going?" Turner asked.

"No."

Hays placed his hands carefully on the arms of the chair. "I have to tell you that Mr. Drummond was found dead about an hour after you parted."

Justy exhaled slowly, feeling the pulse in his temples. He saw the candles in the corner of the room flicker and smoke a little, and he wondered if Mrs. Montgomery was standing at the door, listening. "Where was he found?"

"Little Ann Street."

Justy frowned. "Did he live there?"

Little Ann Street was one of the network of stinking, muddy lanes around the southern end of the Collect Pond. Much of the city's freshwater still came from the pond, even though the sewage from abattoirs, tanneries and breweries had turned it into little more than a cesspool rimed with bright green scum. The streets around it were not much better, breeding grounds for yellow fever and cholera where only the most desperate lived.

"Mr. Drummond lived on Fisher's Street," Hays said.

Fisher's Street was the other side of the Bowery, nowhere near the Collect. Which meant there was no obvious reason for Drummond to be on Little Ann. There were no taverns in that area, and Drummond didn't seem the type to go leching after the kind of dangerously cheap doxies who plied their trade in that quarter.

Hays smiled, as if reading his thoughts. "It's a mystery, isn't it? Normally I would ask what time you left Mr. Drummond and the time he was killed, but we have a witness who saw you part ways."

Justy recalled the white face in the glass door of the almshouse. "The nurse."

Turner tugged at his gloves again. "There's nowt to say you didn't double back and kill him."

Justy grinned. He felt a sudden rush of clarity. "Except Mrs. Montgomery just told you what time I got here. And without a spot of blood on me."

Turner's black eyes stared. "A good killer knows how to keep his cuffs clean."

"I still wouldn't have had time. I would have had to walk all the way down Chambers, then double back, kill Drummond by the Collect and then get here. It would be hard to do, even if I was running fit to bust the whole way."

A muscle twitched in Turner's jaw. "Who says he was killed by the Collect?"

"He must have been. It's the only part of Ann Street where there's places to take a man in broad daylight."

"You talk like you've had some experience."

"I didn't kill him. And you know it."

There was silence. Turner and Justy glared at each other. Hays stood up and walked to the fireplace. He peered at the painting of the horse. "You have a fine deductive mind, Mr. Flanagan. And you are very cool, if I may say."

"Shouldn't all lawyers be so?"

"Of course. But you appear to have been given some unique training."

Justy said nothing.

Hays leaned on the wooden mantelpiece above the fireplace. "I went to the morgue today, to take a second look at that unfortunate young woman who was murdered last night. You were right about the mark on her face. It was a fresh cut. Someone had rubbed dirt into it, to stop the blood and make it look old."

Justy nodded. "I saw the same mark on a woman pulled out of the harbor on Monday. She had her throat cut in the same way, too. And I've heard the same happened to two other girls."

Hays frowned. "You speak as though you believe it's the same man."

"Don't you?"

"It's not the kind of thing we want to hear spoken of. A man, walking the streets, killing women. The city is restless enough, what with the yellow fever outbreak and these labor disputes with the Negroes. We nearly had another riot earlier this week."

"Yes. I saw you down at the docks."

"And no doubt you got the feel of the crowd last night. The city is like a box of tinder." He stared. "But perhaps you don't think any of this concerns you."

Justy sighed. "What do you want, Marshal?"

Hays smiled. "Why, your help, of course."

"So I can spy on my uncle and report back to you?"

Hays waved a hand. "Good heavens, no. Marshal Turner has more than enough people in that quarter of the city."

"What, then?"

"I would like to make you an advisor. Unofficial, of course."

"And unpaid."

"I told you he'd want money." Turner's voice was dry. "I told him you're nowt more than a waterfront rat with an education, and the idea of civic responsibility would be a mystery to you. And so it proves."

"That's enough," Hays snapped.

Turner sat back in his chair, smiling slightly. His eyes were as black as pitch.

"That may be Marshal Turner's opinion of you, but it is not mine," Hays said.

Justy felt a pulse in his throat. His mouth was dry. He controlled himself.

"But the Marshal's right," he said. "I am a waterfront rat. The Bull is my uncle. So what makes you think that I would want to help you?"

"Your actions say so. Why did you even engage me in conversation yesterday, if not to offer your help?" Hays looked serious. "You have trained in the law, and not just as a lawyer. You appear to have received an education in police work as well, in London or Paris, perhaps. You are here, not as your father's son, or as your uncle's nephew, but in your own right. As a man of the law. And I need men of the law. Particularly those with the kind of unique skills that you appear to have acquired."

"Perhaps I have other aims."

"On Wall Street?"

Justy tried to hide his surprise. Hays smiled. "I am not suggesting that you derail your ambitions, merely that you lend me some assistance."

Turner had sat back in his chair, so that his face was now cast into a deep shadow. But Justy could still feel the contempt in his gaze. He fought down the urge to step across the room and punch Turner in the face.

"When do I start?"

Hays beamed. "Immediately."

SIXTEEN

There was no morgue in the city. Corpses were almost always claimed by a family member within a day and buried or burned within a week. But no one had claimed the Negro girls' bodies, and Hays needed somewhere to store them. He had pressed the almshouse into service, and it was only a short carriage ride to the imposing black granite building that Justy had seen the black-clad women walk into the day before.

Turner waited in the carriage. Hays led Justy up a shallow flight of steps and hammered on the door. After a few moments, he hammered again. "If that damned guard is asleep, he'll regret it," he muttered.

There was the scraping sound of a bolt being drawn. A barefoot man with a potbelly and a heavily jowled face opened the door. He was wearing a coat that was too small for him. Wax from the candle in his hand dripped on his bare wrist.

"Where have you been?" Hays snapped.

"Sorry, sir. I was caught short. Just went round the back for a piss." The man's voice was thick with sleep, and his thin hair was sticking up at the back where he had failed to smooth it into place.

"Not sleeping?"

"No, sir." The man avoided Hays' eyes. His wide feet looked like two dead fish on the dark wood of the almshouse floor.

Hays wrinkled his nose. "Take us down."

The man led them down a long flight of brick steps to a large chamber. The air was cold, and heavy with the smell of dust, brine and lavender. Justy remembered how the attendants at the Paris morgue used baskets of the fragrant flowers to combat the smell of decay.

The guard went around the room, lighting candles until Justy was able to look up and see a high vaulted ceiling and several niches, each of which was finished with four stone tables. The walls were brick and the floors made of huge flagstones. It reminded him of an old church.

On the brief ride over, Justy had told Hays a little about his time with the Paris police. Now the Marshal turned towards him. His eyes were two dark sockets, making his face look even more grim. "Time to see just what you learned on your travels, Mr. Flanagan."

Justy swallowed. Hays had told him that at least one of the bodies was nearly two weeks old, and likely in an appalling state of decay.

"How did you find this place?" Justy asked.

"The Mother Superior of the convent told me about it. It was built as a storage cellar for wine. It's still well above the water table, so it's cool, it's dry and the temperature is constant. Perfect for a wine cellar. And for a morgue."

The potbellied man shuffled towards them and held out a three-taper candelabra. Hays took the light. "Where are they?"

The guard nodded towards one of the niches. Justy followed, braced for what he was about to see. The terrible wounds and the mutilation would be the least of it. The oldest corpses would have swollen up, despite the cool of the room, and the stone slabs. Fluids would be leaking from the ears and noses; the skin would be green and blistered. The stench would be heart-stopping.

Hays stopped. He turned left and right, then leaned forward into the corners of the niche. The four stone tables were lined up together but placed far enough apart from each other that a person could walk between them. They were made of blocks of iron-colored granite, and the flecks of quartz in the gray stone sparkled in the candlelight.

"God damn it." Hays' voice was soft.

The tables were empty.

———◆———

The potbellied guard was sweating, despite the chill. He kept his eyes on the floor and seemed to shrink inside his too-tight coat as Hays loomed over him, the candelabra still in his hand.

"Where the hell are they?"

"They was there yesterday, sir."

"Yesterday? Aren't you supposed to check every eight hours?"

The guard said nothing. His arms were straight at his sides, and his hands were fists. Justy watched him closely.

"When did you last do your rounds?" Hays demanded.

"Five this evening, sir."

"But you didn't check the bodies. You're supposed to count them, aren't you?"

"Yes, sir." The guard's jowls shook slightly. There was a mean look on his face. "I didn't think it would do any harm. I mean it's not as though they was going to walk off on their own, was they?"

The candelabra in Hays' hand shivered as he fought to control himself. "Except that they apparently have walked off on their own, you damned fool. Now get to your post."

Hays and Justy stood in the center of the chamber, watching as the guard shuffled up the steps, the scraping of his bare feet echoing off the brick walls.

"Only one way in and out of this place?" Justy asked.

"Out of the morgue, yes. But once you're in the almshouse, who knows."

"But no one reported a break-in."

"Not to my knowledge." Hays watched as the guard disappeared out of sight. "You think he was telling the truth?"

Justy nodded. "He admitted to not doing his rounds. I don't think a guilty man would have done that."

"A clever man might."

"True. But he didn't strike me as too clever. You?"

Hays shook his head. "No. I think he was probably fast asleep when some rogue broke in last night and took the bodies away."

"But who steals the bodies of four unknown women? And why?"

The candles guttered as Hays sighed. "I have no earthly idea."

Justy tugged a handkerchief out of his pocket and blew his nose. "I won't pretend I'm not somewhat relieved."

As he stuffed the linen square back in his pocket, he remembered the knife sheath. It was folded in the inside pocket of his coat. He handed it to Hays.

"I found this in the street, right beside where the last girl was murdered."

Hays rubbed his thumb on the soft leather. "It's a well-made piece. For an expensive knife. Hardly the sort of blade a common killer would use."

Justy looked at the empty niche where the girls' bodies had been. He could just make out the four granite tables, lined up in a row, like fresh tombstones in a graveyard.

"Perhaps this killer is not as common as we think."

SEVENTEEN

Thursday

When Cantillon's front door opened to his knock the next morning, Justy thought for a moment that he'd come to the wrong house. A plump, rosy-cheeked woman of about thirty-five stood in the doorway, her hands on her hips. She wore a housekeeper's apron and she had crammed a generous headful of dark curls into a white bonnet. The bonnet was pushed back on her head, to reveal a high forehead and a pair of quick, dark eyes with long lashes.

She looked him up and down, and a smile twitched at the corner of her mouth. "Well, then? State your business."

Justy knew his face was bright red. "I'm sorry, I didn't know Mr. Cantillon had a housekeeper."

"Well, now you do. So what do you want?" Her voice was broad cockney.

"I'm Mr. Cantillon's clerk."

"Since when?"

"Since Tuesday. You can ask him, if you don't believe me."

She snorted. "Not likely, not today. He's in a crinkum of a humor. Slammed his study door in my face without even a 'good morning.' So I left him there." She looked Justy up and down. "If you're his new dogsbody, you can deal with him."

She stood aside, leaving just enough space for him to brush past.

"Any idea what might be bothering him?" Justy asked.

"Lack of sleep might have something to do with it. Some cove was round bangin' on his door in the small hours. Made a devil of a noise."

She pushed a panel in the wainscot to reveal a small space full of cleaning supplies. A broom clattered on the floor. Justy picked it up and handed it to her. "How do you know there was someone at his door, if he hasn't said a word to you?"

"'Cause I live next door, don't I?" She pouted. "Don't look so surprised."

"I'm sorry. I just assumed . . ."

"What, that I'm just a housekeeper?" She folded her arms, exaggerating her décolletage.

"I really am sorry," Justy said. "May I start again?"

He made a small bow. "I'm Justice Flanagan. I work with Mr. Cantillon, as a legal apprentice. I'm pleased to meet you."

The woman bobbed a small curtsey. "Mrs. Sarah Boswell, if you please." A lock of her dark hair wriggled loose from her bonnet. It accentuated the creamy color of her skin. She brushed it away. "My 'usband left me the house next door when he died, ten years ago. But he didn't leave me any money along with it, so now I look after 'alf the houses on this street. Keeps a roof over my 'ead and keeps me from getting bored, too, if I must be truthful."

"You must see a lot."

She winked. "I see everything round 'ere."

She bustled into the parlor and began wiping down the surfaces with a cloth she pulled from her apron.

"Tell me about last night," he said.

"What about it?"

"What did you see?"

She bent to dust the legs of a small table. "I don't know what time it was, but I was already awake. I don't sleep well this time of year. But I 'eard the knock, and I thought it was an odd time to come calling, so I poked my 'ead through the curtains. There was a tall cove in dark clothes with a long staff walking across the street. He leaned on the railings of the house opposite and just stood there, watching this place, like it was the middle of the day."

"Did you see what he looked like?"

"Nah, 'e was too far away, and the lantern was out. Dark 'air, and dark clothes, like I say."

❖

Cantillon looked up from the pile of papers as Justy entered his study. The lawyer's face was pale. His waistcoat was relatively sober, a dark green with gold edging and buttons. He had clearly dressed according to his mood. The room was small, dusty and unkempt, with stacks of papers piled on the desk and two armchairs. A bookshelf, crammed with dusty tomes, took up one wall. The largest of the stacks of paper was weighed down by a large rock.

Cantillon sneezed and blew his nose. "Mrs. Boswell let you in?"

"Yes. She seems a spirited woman."

A snort. "That's one word for it."

"Handsome, too."

Cantillon raised his eyebrows. "If you say so."

Justy reddened. "She says she was woken in the night by someone knocking on your door."

"Indeed?" Cantillon concentrated on his papers.

"Is someone trying to intimidate you, Mr. Cantillon?"

The lawyer frowned. "Don't be ridiculous."

Justy picked up the rock and found it had been cut in half.

126

Inside it was hollow, filled with dark, spiky crystals. It looked like the maw of a strange beast. "You'll forgive me, but I know a frightened man when I see one."

Cantillon's face darkened. "Don't be impertinent."

"I don't mean to be. But the last two days I've seen you jumping at shadows and twitching at noises, and I don't think it's because you have a naturally nervous constitution."

He turned the strange stone so that its interior caught the light, and he was suddenly dazzled by a rainbow of pinks and purples, reflecting off the crystals.

"Surprising, is it not?" Cantillon said.

"It's beautiful."

"Not everything is as it seems to be at first glance. You for example."

"Me?" Justy replaced the strange gray stone on the top of the stack of paper.

Two spots of color burned high on Cantillon's cheekbones, and there was perspiration on his upper lip. "While you were at the trough with John Colley yesterday, Henry Desjardins came into the Tontine. You remember him? He told me you went to the jail, to meet William Duer. Why?"

"I wanted to find out about my father."

"Find out what?"

Justy shrugged. "I've already told you. I'm curious about his business. What he did. And who he did it with."

"I ask again. Why?"

"Do I need a reason?"

"Don't take that tone with me, damn you." Cantillon jumped to his feet. He paced back and forth in the tiny space behind his desk. He stared at Justy, his eyes wild. "I object to being taken advantage of. I give you a position, and then I find out you've sung me a fine taradiddle about learning the law, when it's clear you're interested in something else entirely."

Cantillon closed his eyes and pressed the heels of his hands against his temples. His voice was almost a whisper: "What is it you want to know?"

"I want to understand why my father did what he did. Why he killed himself."

Cantillon let his hands drop to his sides. He looked as though he was about to cry. "There's a simple enough explanation. He lost money. He was ashamed."

"So I keep hearing. But I still don't understand what it was that he was involved in. And why he may have risked everything. But I suspect that you know, Mr. Cantillon."

He kept his eyes fixed on Cantillon's face. The lawyer looked like a cornered animal. He stood, slightly hunched, as though he was waiting for a blow, tiny drops of sweat on his long upper lip. His eyes flicked back and forth, from the papers on the chair beside him, to the door behind Justy, to the ceiling above.

"I shall tell you what I know," Cantillon said. A loud thud came from above them. Mrs. Boswell was cleaning the room upstairs. Dust spiraled down from the ceiling, turning in the wan light that came through the dirty window. "But first I need a drink."

———•———

The Seagull was a tiny alehouse, tucked into the network of alleys that ran behind Broad Street. It was dim inside, the only light coming from the windows that faced the alley. There were perhaps thirty men and half as many women crowded into the tiny space. Most were drunk, and the smell of stale sweat and spilled beer was overwhelming. Cantillon pointed him towards a corner of the room. The bench was wet, and Justy grimaced as he sat down, feeling the moisture soak the leather seat of his breeches. Cantillon shouldered through the crowd, a tankard of dark ale in each hand. The mugs sloshed as he placed them on the table.

Cantillon settled onto the bench. He took a long draught of his ale. "Your father and I talked often, but he didn't tell me much about the specifics of his business day to day."

He lined up his tankard on the table so that it was exactly in front of him. "He had several steady clients, as you may know. It was enough to make a reasonable living, but he was ambitious. He wanted more, but the only way to make money in that business is to wager large amounts. And he didn't have large amounts. Which is why he needed partners."

A large man with a heavy black beard that reached almost to his eyes slumped down on the bench beside Cantillon. He wore a woolen coat that was sodden with spilled beer. He reeked of dried blood. He tossed back a glass of clear liquor and belched loudly.

Cantillon flinched and sucked at his mug of ale. He spoke to the table. "You recall our conversation yesterday, about Harry Gracie's venture?"

"The sixteen percent? Yes, what about it?"

Cantillon drank again. "Your father and Duer were involved in such a venture. Huge returns for investors. Irresistible. And empty."

"What do you mean, empty?"

"I mean the point of the venture is not the venture itself, but the returns it produces. The partners start by convincing a handful of people to hand over their money; then they use them to spread the word about this fabulous venture that pays a twenty percent return. Soon the Mrs. Reynolds of this world are lining up to invest, and the partners use their capital to pay interest to the original investors. Then they use the next investor's capital to pay Mrs. Reynolds. And so on and on. If the returns are high enough, nobody dreams of withdrawing their capital. The money keeps flowing. And nobody bothers to look to see what the underlying business is."

Justy felt the ale turn sour in his stomach. "So there is a fraud after all?"

"Yes and no. There is no law against such a scheme, but if the investors knew what was afoot they would consider themselves victims of a fraud. And they would certainly withdraw their investments. But no one knows. I have suspected for some time, but only managed to find proof of it recently."

"And you're saying my father was involved in such a venture? That he was a fraud like Harry Gracie?"

Cantillon nodded, his eyes on his tankard. "It wasn't your father's fault. Duer was in debt up to his neck. He badly needed capital to keep his other schemes afloat. He convinced your father to help him find investors, and created a scheme to draw them in. Raising the wind, it's called. There was a real business at the heart of the whole thing, but it was never going to make the kind of money that Duer needed, or to pay the investors the returns they were owed."

"What was the business?"

Cantillon seemed not to have heard him. He stared miserably into his tankard. The crowd ebbed and flowed in front of them like a rough sea. A man slid senseless to the floor, beer spilling out of his tankard and soaking his breeches. A woman groped between an obese man's legs and the man laughed, gin spilling out of his broken mouth.

Cantillon closed his eyes. "When the Panic came, there was no way out. So many investors had given them money. Duer had borrowed thousands himself, not a penny of which he could pay back."

"And my father?"

Cantillon nodded. "He must have borrowed, too. When the price fell, he would have owed a tremendous amount, and had no way of raising the money. No one would have lent a penny to him then."

"Who did they owe the money to?"

Cantillon looked at him blankly. "What do you mean?"

"You say my father must have owed a great deal of money. But to whom? If he had creditors they would have tried to collect from his estate, surely. But no one seems to have asked for a penny."

"And who would they ask? The Bull? Can you imagine the likes of Tyson or Gracie running the gauntlet down on Dover Street to beg for their money back?"

"I suppose you're right," Justy conceded. He leaned close. "So who else was involved in the business?"

Cantillon refused to look at him. "I don't know."

"I know you know, Mr. Cantillon." Justy let the anger put an edge on his voice. "And I know something else. My father did not kill himself. He was murdered."

The lawyer cringed. He put his hand over his eyes, bent forward and let out a low moan. Justy felt a shock of realization. Cantillon knew.

The rage was like something alive in Justy. He felt his pulse writhe in his throat. His fingers twitched. He could have the knife out of his boot, the point slipped between the lawyer's ribs, slicing into his heart, before he could draw breath.

No. He blinked, focused on his hand, lying on the sticky table. He clenched his fist, digging his fingernails into his palm, waiting for the pain to clear his head and drain the tension from his shoulders.

He watched Cantillon, bent double, his face in his hands. The lawyer knew his father had been murdered, Justy was certain. But the man was petrified. There would be no scaring the truth out of him.

He put his hand gently on Cantillon's shoulder. The lawyer flinched.

"It's quite all right, Mr. Cantillon. I'm not here to hurt you. I want to help."

"You can't help me."

"I think I can, sir. If only by making sure that you're not left alone."

Cantillon said nothing.

"But to keep you safe, I need to know who is threatening you. Can you tell me?"

Cantillon turned in his seat and stared at him, his eyes like dinner plates. "I can't tell you. That man last night . . . I've asked too many questions. And so have you."

Justy frowned. "About my father?"

"Yes." Cantillon's voice dropped to a whisper. "I mean no. Not about your father."

"About who? About my father's associates?"

Cantillon nodded slowly.

Justy put his arm around the lawyer's shoulder. "You said we've both been asking too many questions. Why are you asking about them, too?"

Cantillon's hand trembled as he picked up the tankard. He took a deep draught, then stared into the mug. "Because they're doing it again."

EIGHTEEN

Cantillon stared into the middle distance. Justy waited. He knew how effectively silence could work on a frightened man. The crowd milled around them. The man on the bench beside Cantillon fell asleep, his head lolling back, and a skinny woman in a torn woolen dress began rifling through his pockets. She caught Justy looking at her and winked, her tongue sticking out, a flash of pink between her blackened teeth.

Cantillon gulped his ale, wiped his face, fiddled with his cravat. He kept his eyes lowered. He took another swallow and placed the mug on the table with the exaggerated care that a man takes when he knows he is drunk.

Justy leaned close and murmured into the lawyer's ear, "Tell me, Jarlath. Who are they? Who was in on the scheme with Francis?"

In the gloom of the tavern, Cantillon's face looked as white as a fish's belly. His hair was a thicket of red weeds. His eyes were wide and brimming with tears. He took a single deep, shuddering breath.

"What the good heavenly fuck?" The drunken man had woken up and was searching inside his coat for the money that the skinny whore had stolen. He glared at Cantillon. "You!"

He lunged, and Cantillon shrank away from the man, crowding Justy, who was trying to get to his feet but could not. The mix of spilled gin and yeasty beer that had soaked the leather seat of his breeches had dried and glued him to the bench. He forced himself upwards, feeling the stitching give way, and as the drunk man threw a wild haymaker with his left fist Justy forced Cantillon flat on his back on the bench.

The man's swing missed, and Justy caught him by the elbow and pushed, so that the momentum of the punch carried the man off balance. He crashed to the floor, landing on his back, bringing the table and the empty mugs with him. The crowd scuttled backwards. Justy was vaguely aware of Cantillon wriggling along the bench behind him, but before he could turn, the bearded man was back on his feet again, and this time there was a knife in his hand.

There was silence in the alehouse. Every eye was on the knife, four inches of weathered steel with a curved spine and a rounded point. A cheap skinning knife, but one with a glittering edge that spoke of daily use and frequent sharpening.

Justy stood his ground, his eyes on the man's face, waiting for him to look down. An inexperienced knifeman will always glance at his blade before he swings, as if he needs to check his weapon is really there and pointing in the right direction. But the bearded man held the skinning knife easily, as though it were an extension of his arm.

Justy stepped back and raised his hand. "We didn't take your money."

"The fuck you didn't." The man's voice was a croak. His black beard was flecked with spittle.

Justy took another step back. He dropped his hand to his waist, keeping his palms towards the man. He bent his knees a fraction, keeping his weight above his heels. "I don't want trouble."

"Too fucking late, you flash molly bastard Irish madge."

The man shuffled his feet, and Justy knew they were done talking. The man swung fast, and Justy let his knees collapse underneath him so that he fell backwards, catching his weight on his left hand. The blade hissed in the air a foot above his face, and he shoved himself back upwards into a crouch, his right hand reaching for the knife in his boot.

The bearded man was a fast learner. He checked his swing and recovered quickly, bending forward, his blade held out in front, ready to stab or swing at Justy as soon as he stood up. But Justy didn't stand. He kept his knees bent but rocked forward and then exploded upwards. His right hand swung hard outwards, catching the man's forearm and sending the skinning knife wide. At the same time, the full power of Justy's legs drove his body upwards at a sixty-degree angle, so that his forehead connected with the bearded man's chin. For an instant Justy had a faceful of greasy beard, and then the man was down, clutching his mouth, blood running between his fingers.

Justy kicked the skinning knife under the bench and stepped back. He tucked his own unused knife back into his boot and looked around. The crowd was staring at him. Cantillon was gone.

There was no answer at the house on William Street. Justy ran around the block and up the lane to the back entrance, but it was locked. He hammered on the door and pressed his ear to the gap in the frame, but no sound came from inside the house.

"What are you doing?"

He looked up. Sarah Boswell was leaning out of the second floor window of the house next door.

"Mrs. Boswell! Have you seen Mr. Cantillon? Did he come back just now?"

She peered down at him. "What's that on your face? Is that blood?"

He wiped his hand on his forehead. His palm was red. "Mr. Cantillon is in trouble. We were at a tavern. There was a fight. I lost track of him. I hoped he'd come home."

"Go around the front." Her face disappeared from the window.

By the time he had retraced his steps to William Street, Mrs. Boswell had left her own house and opened Cantillon's front door. She shook her head and clucked as Justy hurried inside. "Men. Always drinking and fighting."

"That's not what happened, Mrs. Boswell."

"It's 'Sarah,' if you please. 'Mrs. Boswell' makes me sound like some old harridan." She put her hands on her hips and frowned. "You were down the Seagull, I suppose."

"How did you know?"

"It's where Jarlath always goes when he renounces the pledge." She spun him in a half turn. "Blow me. Look what you've done to your farting crackers. They're a right mess."

The leather seat of his breeches hung down behind him, like the flap of an old man's long johns. "I can't bother about them now. I have to find Mr. Cantillon."

"Well, you can't go running about the place looking like that. I can stitch 'em up with Mrs. Cantillon's sewing kit. It's upstairs in 'er old bedroom."

Justy hesitated, and she sighed. "Don't worry so much. 'E does this every now and then, gets an 'ot stomach and runs about for a day and a night. But 'e always slinks back in the end and sleeps it off. Sometimes with company. Male company, if you get my meaning."

Justy said nothing.

She smirked. "Don't look so pious. It's not so unusual, nowadays. Anyway, you may as well wait for old Carrots 'ere as run about the town looking for him. 'E could be anywhere." She clicked her fingers. "Now come on. Off with 'em."

She was right. He couldn't run about in a pair of tattered trousers. His first stop would be the Tontine, and they wouldn't let him in the door dressed like that.

He sat on a chair by the door and pulled off his boots. Her eyes widened when she saw the knife, but she said nothing, and he tucked it quickly into his coat pocket. He pulled off his trousers and handed them over.

She recoiled. "Good Miss Laycock! What is that reek?"

Justy grinned. "Cheap gin and heavy stout, I think. Maybe some other things."

She took the soiled, ripped breeches at arm's length. "Well, I'll give 'em a scrub as well."

Justy frowned. "I'm supposed to just sit here until then?"

"Well, you need to give your face a wash, but it won't take me a dicky. I'll be back quicker'n you can say 'spank.'" She glanced down at his bare knees and gave him a frank smile. "You don't have to stay down here on your ownsome if you don't want. Unless you and Mr. Cantillon are birds of the same feather. . . ."

She winked and bustled along the hallway to the stairs, leaving Justy in the dim hallway with his face burning.

NINETEEN

An hour later, he was hurrying up the steps to the Tontine. It was the hour before luncheon, and trading was in full swing. The noise in the lobby was deafening, as groups of men spilled out of the dining hall. Each group had a nucleus, a single tense-faced man who listened intently as the others shouted at him and waved rolled-up sheaves of paper to attract his attention. Every few moments, the man in the middle would point at one of the other men and shout something back, at which point the chosen man would rush away, red faced and panting. None of it made any sense to Justy, but he was only interested in finding Cantillon. He shouldered his way into the dining room and towards the high white door that led to the kitchens.

The crowd seemed to ebb and flow as men rushed from one group to another, trying to get the best bid or offer for whatever it was they were selling. Before Justy had made it halfway across the room, the tide ran against him, and a short man with a crown of silver hair cannoned into him, shoving him against the long table. He upset a pot of coffee, and the hot black liquid spilled into the lap of a man in a shabby purple coat who was scribbling in a tattered ledger.

The man jumped to his feet, screeching in pain. "You goddamned slubberdegullion! Look what you've done!" He gestured at the crotch of his grubby white breeches, now stained with coffee.

"Sorry!" Justy pressed on. He reached the doorway. Thomas stood there, dressed in his immaculate white jacket, watching the mayhem in the crowd.

"Good afternoon, Mr. Flanagan," Thomas said, as though Justy had strolled in for a light lunch.

"Good afternoon, Thomas." Justy was breathless. "Have you seen Mr. Cantillon?"

Thomas gave him a steady look. "Not today, sir."

"You there." The man in the purple coat thrust his way through the crowd. He stopped and pointed at Justy. "You've damned well ruined my kicks, laddie. And you're damned well going to pay for a new pair. What d'you say to that?" The man had thrown off his wig, and his hair stuck out in sweaty white wisps. His face was flushed red, and his pale blue eyes were watery. His nose and cheeks were pitted with pox scars. He looked like an old boar, spoiling for a fight.

Justy gave him a cool look. "It was an accident. I have apologized."

The man screwed up his face and leaned forward. Spittle sprayed from his wet lips as he spoke. "These cost me five pounds in London, laddie. Five. Now they're ruined. So, accident or not, you owe me."

Justy drew himself up to his full height and stared down at the man, who was a good foot shorter and at least twenty years older. The man frowned and swayed back. "Don't you threaten me."

"I didn't say a word."

The man's pink face turned red. "I'll call you out, you young pup."

Justy grinned. "Any time, old toast."

There was a ripple of laughter. Several traders had taken a sudden interest in the spat. They whispered among one another, and then one of them, a skinny man with sunken eyes and a hawk's beak of a nose, called out, "'Ware, Ramage.

That's Francie Flanagan's boy. If you're not careful, you'll end up getting fleeced again!"

The men laughed, all except the purple-coated man, who flinched as though he had been struck. "Is this true?"

"True as the corns on your fizzog. He's working with Carrots now." The hawk-nosed man winked. "It's just like the old days."

The purple-coated man made a low noise in his throat. He spun on his heel and stared at Justy. His face was ivory white, his eyes now shiny with anger. "You filthy bog-landing madge. You dare show your face in here, after what your father did?"

Justy hesitated. He knew the man had come after him the first time to gull him out of a few dollars. His anger had been fake, and his aim had been to intimidate. But this was different. Justy looked into the man's eyes and saw rage, the kind of unthinking, uncaring fury that drove men to kill. He was certain that if this man had a knife or a sword he would have been looking for a place in Justy's guts to slide it home. He glanced about. The men gathered around them looked pink-cheeked and prosperous. Some were smiling at the theater playing out before them. But they all had the ruthless, dispassionate eyes of the professional deal maker.

The man called Ramage jabbed his finger at Justy's chest. "Your money-grubbing foister of a father ruined me. Me and a thousand others. And if he hadn't hanged himself, I'd have gutted him, like the filthy coward that he was."

Justy grabbed Ramage by the throat. The man's jowls were loose, stubbled with unshaven bristles that scratched at the skin of Justy's hand. It was like gathering up a burlap sack, but as he tightened his grip he felt the familiar sensations of tendons, muscle, the ridges of the windpipe.

He squeezed, his whole body like a taut wire, the frenzy like a burning fuse. Ramage scratched at his hand, but Justy was oblivious.

"Justice!"

He let go. It was a moment before he realized where he was. The purple-coated man was lying on the floor, clutching his throat. A tall, dark-haired man was looking into Justy's face. John Colley.

"Are you right?" Colley said.

"Aye." He heard his voice, a long way away. He looked down at the man on the floor, who was staring up at him, eyes wide, trembling. He looked at the bloody scratches on his hand. "He called my father a thief. And a coward."

Colley glanced around at the crowd. He put his arm around Justy's shoulders. "You'd better come with me."

———•———

The Club Room was empty. Colley led Justy across the soft blue carpet to the far corner of the room. The heavy door and thick drapes on the walls muted the sound of the crowd in the dining room to a faraway rumble.

Justy felt quite cool. Quite still. As though he was not quite part of the world around him.

"You had me worried there," Colley said.

"I can look after myself."

Colley smiled slightly. "It's not you I was worried about. Another few seconds and you'd have killed that slug Ramage."

"It takes a lot longer than a few seconds to strangle a man."

Colley's eyes were steady. "And where did you learn that?"

"In Ireland."

They watched each other for a while. Justy broke the silence. "He said my father ruined a thousand men."

Colley waved his hand. "Ramage is a broken-down Smithfield bargainer. He's a pamphleteer who puts out a rag once a week that prints the prices of securities and fills the blank spaces with idle gossip. He hasn't the wit to make his living from trade, so he just writes about others who do."

"He was very specific about my father. And very angry. You don't get that bent without a good reason."

Colley walked to a long, low cabinet that ran along the back wall of the room. He opened one of the doors and took out a pair of small, fine-cut wineglasses and a decanter of a pale golden liquid.

"Sherry," he said. The glass he handed to Justy reflected the sunlight, and it looked for a moment as though each panel had an individual rainbow painted on it. Justy drank off the glass and felt the warmth spread out from the pit of his stomach. "Is it true? About my father?"

Colley refilled Justy's glass. "I told you before that your father had a reputation as an honest man. That was the truth. Everybody knew him as a plain dealer, and a man to be trusted. Everyone including William Duer." He gave Justy a sharp look. "You know who Duer was?"

"Yes."

"Well, Duer needed to raise capital. He had lost a lot of money buying shares in the Million Bank, and his creditors were restless. He needed cash, lots of it, and quickly. That's where your father came in."

"Raising the wind."

Colley was very still. His eyes were like glass. "Raising the wind. Exactly."

He poured Justy another drink. "Have you ever wondered why your father struggled to do well on Wall Street?"

Justy shrugged.

Colley sipped his sherry. "It's not that he wasn't intelligent. He was. Fiercely so. His problem was that he wasn't ruthless."

"And that's a bad thing?"

"On Wall Street? It's not called the Devil's half mile for nothing. When you have a man on the hook to buy or sell, the last thing you want to do is make him think twice. But

142

that's what your father did. And too many men wriggled free. That's why your father failed to find partners. Everyone knew he wasn't a closer."

"But Duer went into business with him."

"Duer was desperate." Colley stroked the sumptuous leather upholstery of his chair. "He needed money, so he created an investment opportunity. That was the easy part. His problem was raising the wind. For years Duer had been a master at it—he'd start rumors, put on great presentations, promise the earth. And it always worked. People would empty their bank accounts for him, because his ventures almost always paid off. But by the beginning of '92, everything had changed. Everyone on the Street knew he was in debt up to his hairline. He couldn't raise a fart, let alone the money he needed to break even."

Justy's glass was empty. He forced himself not to glance at the decanter on the table beside Colley. But he could feel the flush of the wine beginning to ebb. His head ached and he felt suddenly weary. "So Duer used my father."

Colley nodded. "As I said, Francis had a reputation for honesty. Duer coached him in his presentation skills, and taught him how to resist his generous impulses, to go in for the kill." Colley smiled and drank his sherry. "Their timing was perfect. There was a kind of stock fever on Wall Street back then. If you told the right story, men would fight each other to get a piece of your deal. A lot of people made a lot of money. But Francis raised a whirlwind. More than a million dollars. Much more than Duer needed."

"So what happened?"

Colley shrugged. "The Panic. All of a sudden, everyone wanted their money back. Some got it, but a lot more didn't."

"Like Ramage?"

"Like Ramage."

Justy thought for a moment. He remembered seeing less and less of his father in the days before his death. He would come home late at night, but instead of going to bed, he would pace about their new echoing, empty house on Dutch Street. Justy would lie in his bed and listen to his father's footsteps, wearing circles into the floorboards of the rooms that he had never got around to furnishing. "What was the venture?"

Colley swilled his sherry in his glass and watched the viscous liquid slide down the crystal. "The rumor was Brazilian gold. Duer claimed his scouts found a seam of it in a place called New Lima, and that he contracted with the Portuguese officials to bring it out of the ground."

Justy frowned. "You said it was a rumor? Was it real?"

"Who knows? Duer certainly had people all over the Southern Colonies looking for opportunities. But whether this was a real venture or just a way to raise money to cover his debts we'll never know. Either way, the money disappeared, and, as Ramage said, a thousand people lost their savings."

Justy looked away. He stared across the room at the door, over the ocean of blue carpet, the islands of comfortable leather chairs and carved tables. The image of his father seemed to hover at the edge of his vision. He couldn't quite see it, but he knew it was there, waiting to overwhelm him as soon as he closed his eyes for more than a moment. His stomach was sour, and he felt the sweat under his arms. "Who else was in the deal?" His voice sounded hoarse.

"What do you mean?"

"The partners. Duer, my father, Isaac Whippo. Who else?"

Colley sipped his sherry. "Yes, Whippo was part of it. He was part of everything Duer ever did. But he was merely a whipper-in. Do you know the term? It's the huntsman who calls the hounds together. That was Isaac. Your father sold them; Isaac made sure they paid. He had no money of his own."

"Who else?"

Colley looked surprised. He put down his sherry. "Why, Carrots of course."

Justy felt a cold sensation. "Cantillon was a partner?"

"He didn't tell you? I'm surprised. Who do you think did all the legal work and the conveyancing?"

Justy swallowed, but his mouth was dry. His throat ached. "How do you know this?"

"There's not many that didn't know, I'd say. He and Francis were knotted so tight; they may as well have been spliced. Duer brought them on as a package." Colley frowned and cocked his head on one side. "He really didn't tell you?"

Justy said nothing. There was a dull ache in his guts. He realized he'd put nothing in his stomach all day, other than the mouthful of ale he'd swallowed at the Seagull. But he knew that wasn't what was making him feel ill. He thought about Cantillon's evasiveness. Justy knew he'd been lying when he claimed not to know about his father's business, but he hadn't expected this. And he knew he should have. His father had trusted Cantillon. They had been old friends. There weren't many Irishmen connected to the investing community, after all. Justy knew all this, and yet he hadn't seen the truth. Hadn't wanted to see.

He pushed himself out of his chair. "I have to find him."

"What d'you mean?" Colley put down his glass. "He's not here?"

Justy shook his head. "We were together earlier. At his house. He was . . . upset."

Colley sighed. "Was he drinking?"

"A little."

"Poor Carrots. Well, if the past is any indication, he'll dust it away through the wee hours, then crawl back to his house in the morning. You'll be lucky if you find him before then."

"I have to try."

Justy made his way across the lush carpet to the door. He could hear the sound of men shouting in the lobby. As he opened the door he looked back to see Colley staring at him thoughtfully from across the room.

TWENTY

Justy walked down to the waterfront. His head was reeling. Cantillon was his father's partner, of course. And he had been about to unburden himself in the Seagull before that bearded fool had started a fight. Justy paused at Pearl Street. Which way to go? The waterfront catered to every taste and every class. But he realized he had no idea what class Cantillon considered himself to be, and only a vague idea of what his tastes were. It dawned on him that after four years away he was a stranger to New York. He would never be able to find Cantillon on his own.

He stood on the sidewalk, staring down towards the water, trying to think where Lars Hokkanssen would be. The *Netherleigh*'s mate wasn't a New York native, but he had sailed there many times. Many of his crew came from the city, and Justy was sure Lars would be able to muster a small team of searchers for him.

He walked across the road, stepping sharply sideways to avoid a drunk, who spilled out of an alehouse and vomited in the street. A pair of ragged hounds ran out of an alley and began licking away at the ground.

Justy aimed a kick at one of the dogs, but it was too quick, and it skipped aside, snapping at his boot.

"You shouldn't be cruel to animals."

He spun around to see Kerry leaning on the entrance to

an alleyway. She was still dressed in men's clothing, her old-fashioned hat tilted over her eyes.

"Jesus, Kerry! What are you, following me again?"

"I wouldn't say 'following.' I was looking for you, though."

"Why?"

"Do I need a reason?"

He said nothing.

She shrugged. "All right then. I wanted to say sorry. For yesterday. For being short with you."

He felt a warmth in his chest. "It's all right."

She grinned. "Friends again, then. That's good. Where are you headed?"

"I'm looking for another friend of mine."

She made an ironic bow. "Perhaps you would allow me to accompany you, good sir." Her eyes twinkled, and he couldn't stop himself from smiling.

He pointed at her pocket. It was bulging with what looked like a man's wallet. "Busy afternoon?"

"Busy enough. So where's your pal?"

Justy made a face. "Good question. In some tavern somewhere. He shouldn't be too hard to run down, mind. He's six and a half feet tall with a badly-shaved head and a beard as red as the Pope's slippers."

She laughed. "I'll try not to miss him. What's his name?"

"Lars Hokkanssen."

"Norwegian?"

"Half of him. The rest is civilized."

She laughed again, and then her eyes skipped over his shoulder and her face changed. She took a long, fast step back into the alley.

He followed her. "What is it?"

"Thieftakers. I have to go. I'll see you later."

"Wait!"

But she was gone.

Justy looked back. Halfway down the hill were the two men he had seen outside the Tontine, two days before. A big man, built like a cart horse, with a deserter's brand on his forehead. And a smaller man, bald, with two black pebbles for eyes. His ears had been cropped, the purple scraps of skin on the side of his head making it look as though they had been torn from his head by hand. Both were dressed entirely in black.

The two men walked slowly up the hill, looking left and right, scanning faces. The bigger of the two carried a long blackthorn stick that he swung back and forth as he walked. His eyes met Justy's and he stared. The smaller man caught sight of him then, and the pair stopped and watched as Justy walked all the way down the hill to the waterfront, his heart pounding and his skin tight across his back, as though he expected to be stabbed there at any moment.

He made a fast turn onto Front Street. A man was selling pastries from a small stall with a wooden bench. Justy realized he was starving. He bought two mutton chonkeys and stuffed them into his mouth.

He leaned on the wall and thought about the two men as he ate. Thieftakers were freelancers, often former criminals, who arrested pickpockets and housebreakers and handed them over to the law for a reward. It was no surprise that Kerry would be frightened of them. But why had those two been guarding a carriage on Wall Street the day before? That was hardly the kind of business that thieftakers usually did. He thought about the mad glint in the eyes of the big man with the deserter's mark, and the way he had swung his gnarled blackthorn stick back and forth as he walked. He remembered what Cantillon's neighbor Sarah Boswell had told him, that a big man, dressed in dark clothes, with a long staff, had been watching the lawyer's house. He twisted around to look back up the street. But the thieftakers were gone.

A big man, dark clothes, a long staff. A perfect description for a hundred men in New York City. But why had the big huff given him such a hard stare, as if he knew him?

Justy dismissed the thought. He didn't have time to think about some deranged bouncer. He had to find Lars. The big sailor had eclectic tastes in drink and women, which didn't narrow the field much. There was no mileage in checking every alehouse and tavern along the waterfront.

He stopped in the middle of the street.

Justy and Lars had been firm friends since a grim day in June, the year before. They had lifted a pot together here and there but never gone on a real guzzle-run, as Lars liked to call it. The big sailor had some hair-raising drinking stories but swore that he was always as upright as an alderman the next day, thanks to a unique Norwegian hangover cure called lutefisk.

Justy had no idea what it was, but he knew only Norwegians had the courage to eat it, which meant only a Norwegian would sell it.

"How's about a coin for a poor old campaigner?" A ragged, bearded man with no legs dragged himself on a wooden pallet across the pockmarked street from a doorway. He held up a hand. Thin hanks of gray hair hung over a face that was lined and mottled with drink. Cloudy eyes sized Justy up. "Forget that," the man said, showing a pair of blackened gums. "Gi's an eagle!"

Justy smiled. "I'll give you a half dime if you tell me where I can find a Norwegian who sells lutefisk."

The man grimaced. "Whit d'ye want wi' that reeking fish danna?"

"That's my business. Do you know where I can get some or not?"

The man showed his gums again. "A quarter dollar?"

"A dime."

"Hallam's Wharf," the man said, and Justy took a coin from his waistcoat and spun it in the air. The man leaned to the side, stretching, and slid off his pallet. He sprawled in the street, cursing as his legs slipped out from their straps and gave his game away.

It was a short walk, down a dank, stinking lane between two tanners' shops. The lane was rutted and pooled with urine, the runoff from the tanning process. There was a wide dip where the lane met the wharf and the landfill that extended the shoreline into the East River had subsided. A long, narrow two-story building with a steeply pitched roof abutted the wharf, and Justy could see from the candlelight flickering through the windows that it was a tavern of some sort, although an unusually quiet one.

Inside, the tavern was not like any Irish alehouse. The floor was swept clean, and there was a single long bench that went around the room. There was no bar, just a hatch in the wall, through which the pots and bottles were passed. The half-dozen men in the room sat alone, drinking steadily, not talking. A few puffed at long pipes. One had fallen asleep in the corner, his head tipped back, a small glass of clear liquor on the bench beside him. Opposite the entrance was another doorway, and Justy could see an adjoining room, well lit by a large chandelier. As he walked into the room, he saw it had been divided into a series of snugs, each with its own door. He made his way along the line, looking over the tops of the doors and murmuring apologies as men cursed and women giggled.

Lars was in the last one on the right, sitting at a table littered with empty pots and glasses. Kerry sat opposite him. "About time," she said.

Justy looked at Lars. The big man shrugged. Kerry smirked. "You said you were going looking for a half-Irish, half-Norwegian sailor with a big red beard. If you'd have asked me, I could have told you this is where he'd be."

Lars grinned. "Gave me a turn when I heard some fella was asking for me. Gave me an even bigger turn when I got close and saw the fella was a beour."

"They call him the Irishman here," Kerry said. "I'm not sure how they can tell, with that beard on him."

"I know you ladies find it irresistible," Lars replied. Kerry snorted.

"I'm glad you two are getting on," Justy said.

The snug was smaller than those in most New York taverns, but there was an impression of airiness and space. The wall was whitewashed, and the owner had used varnished pine, rather than stained oak or mahogany, to make the benches and table. The whole place glowed, reflecting the candlelight that radiated from the chandelier.

"Lars was just about to tell me what you and he got up to in Ireland. During the Rebellion," Kerry said.

Justy glared at Lars. "What did I tell you about running your mouth?"

The big sailor raised his hands. "She's a friend, isn't she? I didn't think it would be any harm."

Kerry was looking at Justy. He shook his head. "I don't want to talk about it."

Her face flushed. "Jesus, Justy! You have to tell me! You fought the English! You were a revolutionary!"

"I hardly did much in the way of fighting."

Lars snorted. "Don't you believe him. You should see this fella with a knife. Quick, silent. The bloody lobsters had no chance."

Kerry sat back. "So that's how you know so much about what happened to them girls. It's not because of some learning you did in France. It's because you've done it yourself."

"So he has." Lars lifted his tankard. "And a fair few times, too."

"Shut up, Lars."

The big man shrugged. "It's something to be proud of, in my opinion." He tipped his tankard back and took a long swallow.

"No one's asking your opinion."

There was a soft tap, and a tall, severe woman appeared in the doorway. She wore a long black dress that buttoned from her neck to her ankles. Lars spoke to her in Norwegian.

Kerry was staring. "How did you get into all of that?"

He shrugged. "I went to a meeting my first year. In Dublin. The Catholic Emancipation people invited an English lawyer called Charles Butler to speak. It was the usual bollocks, but there was a fella there name of Napper Tandy who asked me and a few of my college mates to go for a drink."

"Old Napper." Lars raised his tankard. "He captured an English ship. Sailed it to Norway."

"Aye, and then got captured and thrown in Lifford Jail. He was a fool, like the rest of us, but he spun us a wild tale that night, about revolution and freedom and all the rest. He said Wolfe Tone himself was on his way to save Ireland and free its people."

The waitress reappeared, carrying a tray. She placed three large pots on the table, loaded the tray with Lars' and Kerry's empties, wiped the table and left, as quietly as she had come.

Justy looked at his beer. He suddenly realized he had a raging thirst. He took a long drink. The beer was crisp and cold, and he belched softly as the bubbles fizzed in his nose. "Anyway, I swallowed all of Napper's gammon. Every slice. Signed up then and there."

"Signed up with who?"

"The Defenders. It was small stuff at first. I'd go into Dublin on the weekends and follow people around the town. Make notes of their movements, watch their houses, that kind of thing. But as things warmed up, I was doing riskier work. Running messages, mainly."

"And all the time you were still at school?"

"I never missed a lesson. I'd take off to Dublin on Friday afternoons and get back by Monday. I did it for more than a year. Until the Rebellion."

He looked down at the table. He had the sense that there was a box inside him that, if he opened it, would let all the evil of the world come pouring out. The wise part of him wanted to keep the box closed, and locked and buried. But Kerry was looking at him with her big green eyes. He felt the overwhelming urge to open the box and to hell with it.

Lars made a rumbling sound in his throat. He stood up. "Lise forgot to bring the aquavit. Anyone want anything?"

Kerry and Justy shook their heads.

Justy waited for a moment after Lars was gone. He looked around the small, neat space. Kerry was watching him carefully. He avoided her eyes. "Lars is from a wee village in Wexford, called Gorey. Spring of '98, he was away at sea. An English regiment, the North Cork, came to the town. They were commanded by a Magistrate-Captain named Hunter Gowan. A brutal bastard."

He glanced at Kerry. "They were looking for rebels. They arrested a dozen villagers, none of whom had anything to do with anything. They hanged three, and the rest got the lash and a pitchcap."

"What's that?"

"It's a paper hat, lined with melted tar. They press it on a man's head, then leave it to cool. Then they tear it off, so the hair and the skin come away."

"Jesus!"

Justy looked at his beer. His mouth was dry, but his stomach was sour now. He rubbed his hand over the table. It had been meticulously sanded, was perfectly smooth under his palm. "Lars' mother kept a small tavern. Everyone knew Lars was a sailor, so no one was looking for him, but when she refused to serve a soldier for free, the bastard kicked off and started accusing her of harboring a rebel. That was that. They dragged her into the street and started tearing the clothes off her. The captain heard the noise and came to see, but instead of stopping them, he told them to keep on."

He rubbed his hand over the wood, round and round. It was so smooth it hardly made a sound. "They raped her. One after the other. I don't know how many of them. And then they tied her to the door of her house and whipped her until her bones showed."

Kerry was pale. "What happened to her?"

"She died."

He put his hand in his lap. A murmur of conversation filtered through the door. He could hear Lars speaking to the waitress.

He took a drink. Forced himself to swallow. "Martial law. The bastards could do anything they liked. They were beasts, and Hunter Gowan was the worst of them all. I heard he liked to stir his drinks with a finger that he cut off a woman's hand. Whether it was true or not I don't know, but after two months of that kind of treatment, the people had enough. We started fighting back."

"We?"

Justy nodded. "I didn't get involved until the end of May. There were a couple of big scraps close to Maynooth, but the English whipped us at Kilcullen and half the Defenders in Kildare surrendered. I was still in the college at the time and I couldn't get out, and the whole thing looked hopeless anyway. But then those lobster-backed bastards massacred all the lads who surrendered. Five hundred of them, shot down dead on the Curragh."

He stopped. The curtain twitched open and Lars came in. He placed a bottle of oily liquor on the table with three glasses and sat down. Justy nodded to him. "That's when I got in. I got out of the college that same night and made my way down to Wexford. It took me a couple of days. I went through Dublin and down the coast to Carrigrew. Lars was already there. He'd been trying to get into Gorey, but the whole county was full of soldiers, so he teamed up with the Defenders."

Lars filled the glasses. The oily liquor made a thick glugging sound as he poured. "I remember Justy coming into the camp. It was a Friday afternoon, and the sentry thought he looked like a gent. Reckoned he was an English spy. And that gave John Murphy the idea to use him to reconnoiter Gorey. The crazy bastard wanted to capture it, you see. So he sent Justy and three others out to look at the approaches to the town, and see how many sentries they had."

He fell silent.

Kerry frowned. "What happened?"

Lars looked at Justy. "It's your story, *a chara*." His voice was soft.

Justy leaned back and looked up at the window. His eye caught a tiny movement. A spider was swinging on the end of a thread of silk in the corner of the frame. He took a breath.

"We stopped a quarter mile out of the town. We found a small wood overlooking the road. We left this young lad, Patrick, to watch the road. The rest of us split up to look around the edge of the town. I don't know if he made a noise, or what, but Patrick was caught by an English patrol. I heard him screaming from about a half mile away. I knew they were trying to draw us out, so I came around in a wide loop behind them."

He was aware of a tremor in his voice. "There was four of them. Three were supposed to be watching out while the sergeant did the work. He had stripped Patrick naked and tied him to a tree; then he lit a fire. He had two bayonets heating in the flame. He was using them, one after the other, to brand the boy."

He cleared his throat. The spider had completed the main-stays of its web and was moving smoothly back and forth between them.

"Of course the bastard English are all sadists, so the sentries couldn't resist turning around to watch. I hardly knew what I was doing. All I knew is, I had my knife out in my hand, and as soon as the first of them turned his back, he was finished. I used his rifle to shoot the next one and rushed the third with the bayonet. He was so surprised, he didn't even have the chance to aim."

He stopped.

"And the sergeant?" Kerry asked.

"The fool panicked. He tried to pick up one of the bayonets out of the fire, but forgot to use a rag. He burned his hand and then he tried to surrender."

"What did you do?"

Justy's smile didn't reach his eyes. "I cut Patrick loose and gave him my knife. He was half-dead by then with the pain, but it didn't take much."

Lars swilled his aquavit. "He carried the lad back to us. I've never seen burns like them, not before or since. He should have died, but he didn't. Not then, anyway."

He refilled his glass. "The next day, we moved on the town. We were lucky, because they were marching out to find us, after what Justy did. Their blood was up, and they weren't paying attention. We caught the bastards in an ambush and cut them to pieces. Killed their officers and set the rest of them running. The bloody cowards. They quit Gorey, the whole garrison, and hightailed it to Arklow."

He nodded at Justy. "It was a good day."

Justy said nothing. He looked up at the window. The spider had finished and was sitting in the corner of the web. It might be a long wait in a room as clean as this, Justy thought.

"Anyway," Lars went on. "After that, we used Justy to reconnoiter all our targets. Which meant he had to use that knife of his more than a few times. Until we all got snared up in that mess in Ovidstown."

"What happened there?" Kerry asked.

"We lost," Lars said flatly. "The bloody English whacked us and we had to run for it. We ended up in the bloody Bog of Allen of all places, me with a hole in my leg the size of your fist."

He smiled at Kerry. "I was sure I was going to die in that damned place, but your man here found a way out, through the marsh. He carried me the whole way. He had to put me down now and again, to deal with the odd sentry, and then there was that officer."

He nodded at Justy. "If you hadn't held it together there, I'd be dead, or in an English bastille."

"Don't be so dramatic."

"I wouldn't call it that." Lars turned to Kerry. "We ran into a redcoat rag carrier. An ensign. We surprised him. He was out hunting or some fool thing. Anyway, he'd already fired his barking iron at a rabbit, so we thought we had him. But then he produces another one. He points it at us, and I freeze solid, but Justy runs at him like a demon, drags him off his horse and pinks him." He picked up his glass of liquor and threw it back. He coughed. "I won't forget that in a hurry."

Kerry stared. "You're mad."

Justy made a face. "Not at all. I could see the fool had only half-cocked his weapon."

"Meaning what?"

"Meaning I knew that when he pulled the trigger, nothing would happen. Then all I had to do was tip him off his prancer."

"And knap his boots," Lars said. "Don't forget that."

Kerry grinned. "I was wondering where those fancy beaters came from."

Justy frowned. "You think I couldn't afford to buy them myself?"

"Affording's one thing. Willing to pay up's another."

"What are you saying? That I'm scaly?"

"Well, maybe not scaly. Thrifty, let's say." She winked at Lars.

He laughed. "She knows you well, *a chara*."

"She knows nothing."

"I know where you learned to steal, Justy Flanagan," she snapped. "I watched you, remember?"

"A thief?" Lars gasped in mock horror. "Justice! You never said you had such a checkered past."

"Lifting a few apples from a farmer's stall hardly makes me a thief." Justy glanced at Kerry. "Not compared to some."

Kerry folded her arms. "You still winning at cards, Justy?"

"What if I am? I win fair and square."

She smirked. "Aye. Keep telling yourself that."

Her words hung in the silence of the snug. Lars smiled to himself and poured another slug of the aquavit into his glass.

Justy sighed. "All right. Now we've all confessed our wicked pasts, maybe we can press on with the matter at hand."

"Which is?" Lars asked.

Justy picked up his glass and drank. It was like being punched in the face and the stomach at the same time. He coughed and wiped his eyes. "Jarlath Cantillon."

Lars refilled his glass. "Who's he?"

"A lawyer. An old friend of my father. I need to find him. We were together this morning, but I got in a bit of a tilt and he ran off."

Kerry frowned. "He didn't go back to his libben?"

"No. His housekeeper says he usually takes the pledge, but

every now and then things get the better of him and he goes carousing for a day or so."

Lars shrugged. "So let him away and suck the monkey. He'll be back to his house when he's had enough, and no harm done, except to his purse."

"No! I need to speak to him now!"

Kerry and Lars looked at him. He held up his hands. "Sorry. It's just he's been lying to me. About my father. I heard some things today. . . ."

He let his voice trail off.

Lars squeezed his shoulder. "We'll find your man for you. What's he look like?"

"He's a wee gundiguts of a fella," Kerry said. "Curly red hair. About fifty years old. Likes to wear flash waistcoats."

"Aye, but not today," Justy said. "Today he's wearing green."

Lars chuckled. "Hoping to blend in with the locals, is it?"

"I don't think he planned it."

"Aye, well, never worry. We'll find him. I'll put some of the lads on it. There's a few fellas from New York in the crew, and they all owe me a favor or two. Let's all meet back here after sundown. Drunk or sober, we'll have your lawyer friend in the bag by then."

TWENTY-ONE

Justy pushed open the door to the Counting House and waited until his eyes adjusted to the light. The tavern was one long, narrow room, with a counter along one side and a line of benches and tables that ran the length of the opposite wall. Light came from candles burning in sconces on the white-washed walls. Regimental pennants and old weapons hung from the beams of an unusually high ceiling that was darkened with smoke from the drinkers' pipes and cigars. There was a large brass spittoon, halfway down the counter, in the middle of the floor.

It was still mid-afternoon, and the tavern had just one patron, a small, thin-haired man, dressed in a dark blue military coat that had been patched and stitched many times. He raised his glass to Justy, grinned a set of toothless gums, then spat with pinpoint accuracy into the spittoon.

A tall man stood behind the counter. A mismatched pair of cavalry officers' swords hung on the wall behind him, their handles downwards, their curved blades crossed close to the tips, just above the man's head. The man looked to be in his early fifties. Candlelight gleamed on a long, brutal scar that wound its way from his right eye and around the back of his shaven skull.

"What'll it be?" the barman asked.

"Calibogus."

"Flicker or bumper?"

"Flicker."

Justy settled himself on a stool.

The barman poured a small measure of rum into a half-pint glass, then filled the glass up with a light spruce beer from a black bottle.

Justy sipped the fragrant mixture. It had a warm, sweet taste. "It's good."

"Aye, well, this be a soldiers' stop. Can't get away with flogging balderdash or pug cider. Either it's quality tipple or it's stingo, or I'm out of business."

There was a door to the back of the premises at the end of the counter. It swung open a little, and a small fair-haired boy in a pale green waistcoat and black breeches poked his head through. "I've finished the mugs."

"Good lad," the barman said. "Away down to Mrs. Rose and get the towels."

The boy disappeared. Justy took another sip. "I was supposed to meet a fella here yesterday. Name of Drummond. He's a warden up at the jail."

The barman's face was expressionless. "Was a warden, you mean."

"You heard the news, then."

"The cossacks were in here. Said he'd been milled, up by the Collect. They wanted to know when he was last in."

"What did you tell them?"

"Why should I tell you?"

The challenge hung between them.

Justy's eyes flicked to the scar that bisected the man's eyebrow. "Toasting iron?"

The man's eyes were cold. "What makes you think so?"

"I've seen a few sword cuts. You were lucky."

"Lucky I've got a hard head."

Justy nodded at the crossed swords on the wall. "Was one of those two the doer?"

The barman gave a faint smile. "Aye. Redcoat bastard cut me deep. I thought the top of my head was off. Then one of the lads put a ball through his swede and I filched his poker. Just as well, with the rest of the lobsters scuttling through the gate like rats. Hundreds of 'em. And not inclined to stop their slaughter, even though we'd surrendered."

He looked up as two men came into the tavern. They were both tall and lean, about forty, with hard faces and watchful eyes. One of the men held up two fingers and the barman nodded. The men removed their hats and walked quietly to a corner.

The barman took two tall bottles from a shelf under the counter and two mugs from the wall and carried them over.

"Bleedin' shoulder-clappers," the toothless drinker said. "This used to be a place you could escape from the cossacks. Not anymore."

"Shut up, Sharky." The barman took up his place behind the bar again.

Justy nodded at the swords. "What about the other poker there? Where'd you get that one?"

"My brother-in-law."

Something clicked in Justy's head. He remembered his conversation with Drummond. "I heard Fort Griswold was a hard day."

"What do you know about it?"

"Only what Drummond told me. He told me he stole an officer's sword and shab'd off to New London to warn his sweetheart. Your sister, right?"

The barman was about to reply when the back door swung open again, and the small fair-haired boy's face appeared. "I got half the towels, Da. Mrs. Rose says she won't have the rest until tomorrow. They're still drying."

The barman nodded. "All right then. Sit and do your letters until supper."

The boy disappeared, and the man turned his attention back to Justy. He dropped his voice. "Callum told me he was going to meet some young lawyer here. I suppose that'd be you."

"It would."

"He said he was going to sell you some papers."

Justy nodded. "I still want the papers. I was hoping you'd tell me where to find his wife. I'd like to speak to her about it."

"Sure. Go up onto the Broad Way and turn left into town. You'll find her right at the northwest corner of Lombard Street and Thames Street."

Justy was halfway off his stool before he realized he'd just been given directions to the Trinity Church cemetery. For a moment he was about to snap at the man. Then he remembered Drummond's wife was his sister. "When did she pass?"

"Last September. Yellow fever."

Justy remembered Drummond's slow, sad smile and felt his own chest tighten. "I'm sorry for your loss."

The man gave him a careful look. "I do believe you are."

"My own mother was taken by the fever. In '83."

The barman nodded sadly. It was a common enough tale in New York. "Sorry I can't help you."

"Will you tell me where Mr. Drummond lived, at least?"

"You know the big building up at Fisher's and First Street? He has a room in there. Not that it'll do you any good. The crushers'll have stripped the place to its beams and boards by now."

———•———

Justy stood outside the tavern, blinking in the late afternoon sun. It was that time of the day when all the smells of the city seem to congeal in the air, ripened all day by the heat. His throat felt as though he had swallowed a teaspoon of sand. A horse clopped past, its tail high in the air, and he blinked as the hot smell of fresh manure clogged his nose.

The barman was right; Turner's men would have torn Drummond's place apart by now. His landlord would have plundered his possessions for anything worth selling. The rest would already have been thrown into the street, to be picked over by all comers. Justy's only hope was that no one would have seen any worth in a bunch of old papers.

As he passed the alley that ran down the side of the Counting House, he heard a whistle. He stopped and peered into the gloom. The small fair-haired boy was halfway down the alley, beckoning.

The alley appeared to double as the tavern's latrine. Justy followed the boy, breathing through his mouth. They made a left turn around the back of the tavern, and Justy found himself face-to-face with the barman. He had a worn leather infantryman's satchel slung over one shoulder. "Sorry to drag you down here. I just don't want the crushers knowing my business."

"Those two men who came in?"

"Nah. They're old campaigners. Mates of mine. It's Sharky Ward, that scrawny little weasel. He's a mounter. Thinks we don't know he tells anything he hears to the law, but everyone's wise to him."

He ruffled the boy's hair. "Good lad. In you go and study your letters. Don't shirk. I'll not be long."

Justy waited until the boy had gone. He glanced at the satchel on the barman's shoulder. "Are those the papers?"

"Aye. Callum left them with me after Rosalie passed and he sold their house." The man clamped his arm around the bag. "He said you'd pay."

"And I will. A quarter eagle, we said."

"That's not what Callum said. He said five quarters."

Justy shook his head. "The deal was an eagle for him to answer any questions I had and a quarter for the papers. Now that he's dead . . ."

The man's face darkened. Justy took a step back, opening the distance between them. He could see the man deciding what to do. He could use the bag as a weapon, it was heavy enough, but swing wrong and Justy might just grab it and run.

The barman's shoulders sagged. "A quarter eagle?"

"That was the deal."

"Damn it." He thought for a moment. Then he scowled. "Go on, then."

He swung the satchel halfheartedly. It scraped against the wall of the tavern, and Justy had to bend forward to catch it before it landed in the muck. He slung the bag over his shoulder. "You said Drummond sold his house?"

The barman sighed. "Aye."

"To provide for the boy?"

Something changed in the man's face. His eyes softened. "Aye. He's mine, but my wife died a year after he was born. Callum and Rosalie looked after him much of the time. A tavern's no place for a lad that age. But when Rosalie passed . . ." He shrugged.

"You've got a tutor for him?"

"Aye. And we're saving to get him schooled properly." He looked suddenly lost. "Or I am, I suppose."

Justy unbuttoned his waistcoat and fumbled in his money belt. He held out the coins. They gleamed dully in the dim light of the alley. "Here. Five quarters."

The barman looked at the coins. He frowned. "That's not the deal, you said."

"Here's a new deal. A quarter for the papers, an eagle to keep your eyes open on my account. I'll be back."

The barman gave him a long look. Then he nodded. "Fair

enough." He tucked the coins into his waistcoat pocket. "So where did you get your licks?"

"What do you mean?"

The barman smiled. "Your phiz may not be marked like mine, but don't think I can't see your scars. I can see you know what it's like to stand in the line while the bees buzz about your head and men drop around you. It's in your eyes."

Justy nodded. He knew exactly what the man meant. "Ireland. The Rebellion. More than a year gone now."

The barman nodded slowly. "We heard the news. A bad time."

"A small affair compared to what went on here."

The barman rubbed the scar above his brow. His eyes glittered. "The size of the stage don't mean much to them has to play on it."

"You're right about that."

TWENTY-TWO

The papers were a random collection of poems, cuttings, letters, lists, and sketches of plans and ideas. Some dated back more than a decade, others just a year. Drummond had clearly grabbed a stack of whatever was at hand and jammed them into a box and hurried away.

Justy sat in the snug of the Norwegian tavern and sorted the papers into two piles. On his left, a large heap of papers that meant nothing to him. On his right, a shorter stack of Duer's correspondence.

The sound of men talking quietly in the bar area of the tavern was reduced to a low hum by the stout pinewood walls. There were three candles set in a sconce high on the wall, and the small space was filled with the honey-like smell of colza wax. The flames flickered slightly whenever Justy turned a page or placed a paper on one of the piles.

The more recent of Duer's letters showed that while he had fallen hard, he had maintained contact with some of the most important men in the country, right up until his death. Thomas Jefferson and William Bradford, the former Attorney General, were among his correspondents, and his relationship with Alexander Hamilton appeared to be warm, despite Duer's misdeeds. But no one, it was clear, was prepared to offer him anything much more substantial than moral support.

It was in a dozen letters from Duer's principal securities salesman, Isaac Whippo, that Justy found what he was looking for. The letters were dated between the summer of 1791, before the Panic, and March of 1793, after Duer had gone to jail. The later correspondence was focused on Duer's legal position. It detailed lists of creditors and debtors and descriptions of securities of various kinds.

The earlier letters were what Justy wanted. Whippo's poor command of the written word made the letters hard to read, but they clearly showed he had spent several months in the Carolinas, purchasing goods that were due to be shipped back to New York by sea. He considered a land journey too risky, as the roads through Virginia and New Jersey were plagued by highwaymen, whereas a sea voyage that kept close to the coastline was less likely to be intercepted by pirates. It wasn't clear what the goods were, but they were clearly high-priced items. There was to be a single voyage, with all the goods aboard, and Whippo was warehousing the cargo until the calmest coastal months, in mid-summer, when a voyage would be least risky.

The letters referred to two other partners in the venture. *FF*, presumably Francis Flanagan, was responsible for encouraging investment in the venture. *JC*, he assumed, was Jarlath Cantillon, who had a long list of responsibilities that included legal advice, accounting, providing warehousing and security for the cargo on its arrival in New York, as well as arranging the sale of the goods to the public. There was no mention of another partner.

August 12, 1791

Charlotte a brutal place, but I have considerable progress obtaining the collateral for our venture. Product from our first supplier expensive, but of excellent quality. Am pleased to hear from JC that FF has progressed in raising the funds I need. Seems the work that JC has done in preparing our warehouse facilities excellent. Gurney's Wharf ideal for our purposes. It be further from the town indeed but discreet and has good access for loading.

I am unlikely to be present when you next assemble all the partners, but I have attached invoices for JC^ that detail the expenditure of capital contributions, as pledged. As FF did not request a specific investment, I have not included an invoice. Please inform him that if he changes his mind he will need to write quick with the specifics.

* * *

September 4, 1791

Arrived Charleston last week. An even more miserable place than Charlotte. Hot damp and full of flies. Midsummer must be hell. I received reports from the JC^ but have heard nothing from FF. Please inform as to his progress. Negotiations here have gone poorly. Supplier not as described, nor his produce. He is as sharp a shaver as any to be found on the waterfront in New York, and the commodity he has for sale is poor quality shows rough handling and other damage. There will certainly be no market for such in New York. Not at the prices we shall be seeking.

I am in search for a more reliable supplier, but now I am told that the unit price of goods may be higher. Therefore I shall need more capital when JC makes his next foray south, once he has completed work at Gurney's Wharf and at the house on Bedlow Street.

* * *

September 28, 1792

Dismayed to read your last letter. Under no circumstance must our investors become aware of the status of the ven-

ture. Strongly urge action with FF by you either JC,^ who-
ever is more convincing. The poor weather here and the
failure of our partners is conspired to delay us but I can
and will find alternatives. I need time, and I need capital,
and you must stiffen FF's spine, and convince him to dis-
semble when asked for situation reports by the curious.
Persuade him to use his loquacious charm. His people are
famous for it after all!

The candles on the table guttered. Lars stood in the entry to the snug, a tankard in each hand. "I took the liberty." He put the mugs on the table and sat down opposite.

Justy took a long, grateful drink. "Any sign?"

Lars shook his head. "I have the lads out looking. They'll tell me when they find him. What do you have there?"

"Duer's letters. Some of them, anyway. They mention my father."

Lars flicked through the sheets of paper, his eyes darting back and forth as he read. "FF is him, right? And JC?"

"Jarlath Cantillon."

"Jarlath and Francis. A saintly pair."

Justy grunted a laugh. "If thieves can be saints, maybe."

"How do you mean?"

"Cantillon told me they gulled people into investing with some tall tale, and paid them a high interest rate to stop them from asking for the capital back. But you can see from these letters that the venture, whatever it was, made no money at all."

"So how did they make those grand interest payments?"

"Simple. My father kept recruiting new investors, and Duer used their principal to pay the interest to the others. Principal amounts are big. Interest payments are small. Duer channeled some of the leftover money into this venture. The rest he kept for himself."

Lars laughed. "Jesus, that's brazen. They can't have hoped to get away with it for long, can they?"

Justy butted the large stack of papers into a neat pile. "I don't know. So long as you can keep enough money coming in, and people don't ask too many questions, you might be able to keep a scheme like that going for years."

"There's no underestimating the foolishness of a fat cull, I suppose."

"Don't mock. Plenty of sensible people got caught up in it."

Justy's stomach growled, and Lars looked up. "When did you last eat?"

Justy thought about it. "This morning."

The big man rolled his eyes. He shouted something in Norwegian, and from somewhere in the tavern a woman called back what sounded like a curse.

Lars winked at Justy. "She loves me, that one. She just doesn't know it yet." He returned his attention to the pile of letters. "What was it they were after buying down there, do you suppose?"

Justy shook his head. "I don't know. And that's what I'm confused about. These letters come from Georgia and the Carolinas, but someone else told me the venture was to mine gold in Brazil."

Lars grunted. "I heard talk of prospectors looking for gold in the hills near Savannah once, but never more than that."

"I was trying to think what kind of commodity fits the bill in these letters. I thought cotton or timber, but there's a mention of poor handling and other damage, which doesn't seem to fit. Could be bales of silk."

Lars swilled a mouthful of beer. "Could be. Or deerskins." He glanced up at Justy. "Or slaves?"

Justy felt his guts writhe. His father a slaver? New York had an active slave market when he was a boy, but the city also had a large free black population, so Justy's father had dealt with Negroes both free and enslaved. Justy couldn't remember his father making any kind of comment about slavery. And he had treated Kerry like a daughter.

Lars shook his head. "No. Can't be slaves. These letters say whatever he was looking for is hard to find, and if there's one thing that's easy to come by on the coast down there, it's slaves. There's markets every day." He made a face. "Filthy bloody business."

"Cantillon'll tell us what it is."

Lars raised an eyebrow. "You look like you're getting ready to chain him up and make him kiss the gunner's daughter."

Justy realized how tense he was. "Don't worry. I won't whip him. I won't even touch him." He forced himself to smile. "Besides, there's no gun to lash him to."

"There's a couple of big yins down on the battery. Maybe the mayor will let us borrow one."

They both laughed, but Justy felt the coldness inside him. *There was something bigger here. Something ugly. He could feel it.*

The tall, austere woman appeared with a tray carrying a half loaf of bread and some cheeses. Lars smiled and said something to her in Norwegian. She gave him a look of pure contempt and left.

Justy smiled. "I've never seen you so successful with the ladies."

Lars tore off a piece of bread. "She's not my type anyway." He tapped the letters. "Your man Cantillon was the lawyer, right? And the accountant, too?"

"That's right."

"Seems strange he'd be handling the warehousing as well, don't it? It's a lot of work for one man. And dealing with the hectors and bouncers what do business on the waterfront takes a certain type of character. And by that I mean not the lawyerly type."

Justy nodded slowly. "You're right. Cantillon's not the fellow you'd send to deal with longshoremen."

"Maybe there's two JCs." Lars pointed. "Look, on this one there's a squiggle by the *C*. And on this one . . ."—he shuffled through the papers and pointed—". . . there's no squiggle. And here he says 'the JC' and there's a squiggle. Like there's more than one. Maybe that squiggle is an *s*, or a squared symbol. Maybe there's two JCs."

Justy stared at the letters. Lars was right. Whippo's splotchy, poorly punctuated scrawl was hard enough to make sense of, and Justy had ignored the seemingly random blots and marks that appeared here and there around his writing. JC was sometimes referred to in the singular and at other times in the plural, which Justy had blamed on Whippo's ignorance of grammar. But now that he looked closely, he realized they weren't errors of grammar at all.

He nodded slowly. "I think it's more likely an *s* than a squared symbol, but yes. You're dead-on." He looked at his friend. "I didn't know you knew algebra."

Lars looked offended. "And why wouldn't I? I learned me letters and me mathematics at the same time. Father Michael at the Christian Brothers took a shine to me. Not like that, thank God. There was plenty of fumble-fingered slubbers there, but Father Mick wasn't one of them. He was a solid man for the learning and that was all."

There was a thumping of hurrying footsteps, and the door to the snug slammed open. A boy in a heavy woolen shirt pushed inside. Justy recognized him. One of the cook's lads from the *Netherleigh*. The tall waitress stood behind him, a frown on her face.

"This one says he knows you," she said in a singsong Norwegian accent.

Lars nodded. "It's all right, Lise. He's with me."

She folded her arms across the front of her plain black dress. "He is damned rude. Running in here, making a big noise."

Lars put his hand on his chest. "I'm sorry, my love."

She rolled her eyes. Lars grinned and eyed the boy. "Well, Sandy? What do you have for me?"

"I found 'im, Lars!" The boy's face was bright red, his eyes shining.

"So sit down and stop fizzing."

The boy eyed the plate of bread and cheese.

Lars smiled. "Go on, then. Tell us while you eat."

Sandy tore a hunk of bread off the loaf and stuffed it in his mouth, followed by a slice of cheese. The words spilled out of him, muffled by the food. "I was up on Water Street, near where the death hunter gets his coffins made. I seen a jarvie there, he said he picked up a short gundiguts with a froth of red hair on him, and took him to the Fair Lady, down near the market."

"Aye, I know it."

"So I gan there, but 'e's left already. A doxy down there telt me 'e was set up there for a few hours, drinking swizzle. They tried to get him to tumble, but 'e'd have none of it, pushed 'er away and runs off down Dab Lane. I went into all the 'ouses thereabouts, but the only one what saw him was the landlord at the Judge."

He stopped and eyed the tankard. Lars sighed and pushed it into his hand. The boy drank greedily and let out a huge belch. "That's the clicket!"

The waitress rolled her eyes. Lars grinned. "Was he at the Judge then?"

"Nah, 'e was long gone. The landlord said he reckoned he was Irish on account of his red strommel and that 'e ordered a six and tips. That being a boglander's favorite tipple, an' all. But he fell asleep afore he could drink it. Slept for more than an hour, then 'e wakes up and asks for a coach to take him to Bedlow Street."

Justy leaned forward. "Are you sure it was Bedlow Street, Sandy?"

"Course." The lad was indignant. "I went up there, didn't I? There's no alehouses up there, so I asked a jarvie where a half-seas-over cove might go if he had a few coins in his pocket, and he points to a rum-looking kip, four floors high. 'What's in there?' I ask, and he winks and tells me I'm too young to know, not that I could afford it anyway, so I know it's a knocking shop."

Lars laughed. He pointed at Justy's tankard. "Anything left in there for the lad?"

Justy pushed it across towards Sandy, who drank it off in a single swallow. Lars patted him on the back. "Well done, son. Now, tell us more about this bawdy house you saw."

Sandy belched again. "Four windows on the ground floor, and four floors high. A big pointy roof. A high black iron fence out front, as high as a man's head."

"I know this place," the waitress, Lise, said.

Lars blinked. "You do?"

"Yes. At Bedlow Street and Cullen Lane. It is a Negro house. All girls."

It was a moment before Lars spoke. "And how do you know this, my love?"

She gave him a sharp look. "I am not some pet, locked in this box for you to take out. I know things."

He reddened. "Of course, Lise. I'm just surprised you know such a place exists."

"Because I am so pure, I suppose."

Lars' face was now as red as his beard. He opened his mouth and closed it again.

Lise smiled. "My friend Silve is a maid in one of the big houses in Cherry Street. I went walking with her one afternoon a few weeks ago. She showed me this house. She told me what goes on there."

"But how does she know?"

"Because one of the servants from her employer's house was hired there this year and they have remained friends. He told her all. And made her swear to tell no one."

"Was your friend sure it was just girls at this house, Lise? No boys?" Justy asked.

"Yes. Only girls. Only young girls, she said. It is a very exclusive place."

Justy nodded. "Thank you."

Lars cleared his throat. "Yes. Thank you, Lise."

"You are welcome." She gave him a sour look. "I shall be in the front, if you need anything."

She turned smartly on her heel and left. Justy tried to smother his grin. Sandy paid closer attention to the plate of food. It was a moment before Lars had gathered himself.

"So, Sandy. How close were you to this place? What did you see?"

"I were across the road. I seen two men walk by when I were there, which is how I know how high that fence were. And those coves weren't passersby, either. Looked like they were on watch, walking back and forth like they were guarding the place."

"Many people coming and going?"

"A few carriages. They go in the back, down an alley. Some looked like hackneys, and some looked like private coaches, well dressed. No one on foot."

Lars looked at Justy. "What do you think?"

"I think I want to know what Cantillon's doing in a Negro whorehouse."

"Every man's entitled to his appetites."

"Aye, except those aren't Cantillon's appetites. His housekeeper told me he prefers men to women."

"There's plenty of other things go on at whorehouses. Drinking. Gambling."

Justy shook his head. "He's already had a skinful. And if you'd heard him talk for five minutes about the evils of speculation, you'd know he hates gambling."

Lars shrugged. "Means nothing. There's plenty of gamblers rail against the evil of the dice. And no matter how much you've had to drink, there's always room for another."

"Maybe." Justy stood up. "But I still want to see for myself."

TWENTY-THREE

Lars decided Sandy should lead them along the route that Cantillon had taken. "In case they gave him the boot for being too plastered. A cove who's three sheets to the wind usually goes where he's familiar, in my experience."

It had been four years since Justy had seen the waterfront in its full sleazy, desperate glory. It was far worse than he remembered. By day, the rickety wooden buildings looked drab and worn. By night, lit by flickering torches and the occasional barrel fire, the place looked like the entrance to hell. The streets were crammed with people, most of them drunk, spilling from taverns and alehouses. The usual stink of the street was spiced with woodsmoke and the smell of roasting meat from the open grills that street vendors had set up on the sidewalks.

Lars led them through the crowd. "Sharp elbows, lads!" Sandy ducked his head and followed, and Justy kept close behind, as they shoved through the crush of screeching, laughing men and women.

Something tripped Justy. He stumbled and went down on one knee, and when he recovered himself he saw Lars, his scrub of red hair gleaming like hot iron, just as the big sailor disappeared around a corner.

He cursed. He had no idea where the taverns that Sandy had talked about were. At least he knew how to get to Bedlow Street.

He was about to step off the sidewalk, into the melee, but he was suddenly shoved hard sideways into a wall.

"Got you, you green laycock! Now it's my turn!"

A knife flashed in his face. Justy threw his arm up and spun sideways, feeling the blade catch on his sleeve. The delay gave him the time he needed to grab his attacker's wrist. He twisted it, hard, and the man bent over with a howl of pain. He dropped the knife. Justy shoved the man into the wall, turned him and grabbed him by the throat. The blood was hammering in his face. He had no memory of reaching for his knife, but it was there, in his hand, his thumb on the catch of the blade.

"Don't kill me!" The man cringed. His face was shadowed by a wide-brimmed hat. He smelled strongly of cheap spirits. He began to cry.

Justy let go. The man snatched the hat off his head. His face was wet with tears. "You goddamned madge. How dare you do that to me? How dare you?" His voice was a screech. He wore a purple coat. His breeches were stained.

Justy stared. "Mr. Ramage?"

Ramage's chin trembled. "Isn't it enough for your father to ruin me? Wasn't that sufficient? I have spent near ten years trying to rehabilitate my reputation, and then you come along and burn it to the ground, by treating me like a dog."

"You insulted me, sir."

"And deservedly, after what your father did. He was a dirty trickster, but at least he had the courtesy of a gentleman. You, on the other hand, responded not with words, but with violence." He drew himself up. "But what should I expect from a filthy boglander."

Justy fought down the desire to punch the man in the face. His knife was slippery in his hand. Several people had stopped to watch them. A man in a battered tricorn hat was chewing on a chicken drumstick, his eyes bright in his face at the prospect of having his evening of drinking further enlivened by a show of violence.

Justy took a deep breath, folded the knife and put it carefully in his pocket. "You took me by surprise, sir. I apologize. I reacted badly. My treatment of you was inexcusable."

Ramage swayed back an inch, a puzzled expression on his face. Justy reached out and took Ramage by the elbow. "It would be small comfort to you, perhaps, but would you allow me to buy you a cup of something?"

The man in the tricorn hat cursed them in German and threw his gnawed chicken bone at them. It hit Ramage on the chest, but he didn't seem to notice.

"Mr. Ramage?"

Ramage looked up, his eyes bright, and his face seemed to crumple. He nodded, and Justy guided him around the corner and up towards Water Street.

Ramage was quiet, his hat in his hand, his wig awry, his head down. Justy recalled what Colley had said, that having failed as a trader, he was now making a living selling a newsletter that quoted the prices of securities. The lapels of his purple coat were shiny with use, his cravat was grubby and his hose was threadbare and torn at the shins.

Justy led them into a well-lit eating house. It was only a block from the chaos of the waterfront, but it may as well have been another country entirely. A large chandelier threw a warm golden light across the room. Silver and glass glittered on the oak counter and matching tables scattered around the room. The place smelled of roasting game and cedar, from the sawdust sprinkled over the floorboards.

As they entered, a man behind the counter tapped a large ship's bell that hung from a beam. It gave off a mellow ring and swung slightly, glowing in the candlelight. A waiter appeared and led them to an empty table near the back of the room. Justy sat facing the door. Ramage slumped into the chair opposite. His eyes were red rimmed and bloodshot. His chin was gray with stubble.

Justy nodded at the waiter. "Bread and cheese. And some tea, if you please."

The waiter frowned. "Tea?"

"You can't see my friend has had enough to drink? Tea. And make it strong."

They sat in silence until the waiter had returned with a plate of soft bread and hard cheese, a jug of hot tea and two cups. The tea was scalding hot. Ramage blew on the liquid, sipped, and color came into his cheeks.

Justy watched him. "How did you know where to find me, Mr. Ramage?"

He sighed. "I followed you. To that Norwegian place. I waited by Callan's slip; then I followed you onto Front Street."

"You planned to kill me?"

Ramage smirked. "No. I could have done that in the crowd. I was behind you the whole time. I just wanted to scare you. And to mark you a little, perhaps."

"To cut my face?"

"You have no idea what it is like to be humiliated so," Ramage hissed. "First by the father, then by the son. In public. In full view of my peers."

Ramage's face was beet red. Justy felt a prickle of shame. He leaned over the table.

"Again, Mr. Ramage, I apologize. For the insult and the injury. I knew nothing about my father's business dealings. I always thought he was square. It's a shock for me to hear otherwise."

Ramage grunted. "He was square, before. Until Duer got his claws in him." He tore off a piece of bread and chewed, then washed it down with the tea.

They ate for a moment in silence. Justy eyed him over the rim of his cup. "I'm told you have a newsletter."

Ramage looked at him suspiciously. "I used to trade in securities. Now I trade in information. It's a commodity like any other. People pay to know things."

Justy sipped his tea. It was a good brew, fragrant with bergamot. "It seems to me the problem with a newsletter is that only one person need pay for it. Then it can be passed around, and the information gotten for free."

"Just so. But only a fool writes down all he knows. A clever man gives the reader a taste, and those who wish to know more can buy the whole story bespoke. That's where the profit lies." He nibbled at a piece of cheese.

"You must know a great deal about Wall Street and its goings-on," Justy said.

"It's my business to be well informed." He glanced at Justy. "And to be paid for being so."

"Of course."

Ramage leaned forward to spear another slice of cheese. The candlelight glittered on the silver tines of his fork. "Perhaps there's something you'd like to know."

"Perhaps there is."

"About your father, for example?" Ramage's teeth were stained dark with red wine and coffee. His clothes looked worn, he was unshaven and unwashed, but he suddenly looked like a different man, calculating and controlled, and no longer even half as drunk as he had seemed.

Justy nodded. "That's quite a disguise you're wearing."

Ramage smirked. "It's a useful thing, to be unseen and underestimated."

"You've done well by it."

"As I say. Information is a commodity like any other. Except that, unlike most commodities, it is always valuable." He sat back, hands folded over a round belly. "So what is it that I can tell you about your father?"

Justy poured himself another cup of tea. "Nothing. I want to know about you."

"Me?"

"Yes. If my father's venture with Duer was so risky, why did you invest in it? I would have thought a man like you would have made sure it was sound before putting your money in."

Ramage shrugged. "They were paying twenty percent."

Justy laughed. "So you were gulled. Did you even know what the venture was?"

Ramage scowled. "I learned my lesson, Flanagan."

"I'm sure you did. So what was the venture?"

Ramage stared at him for a moment. "That's a simple question with a complicated answer."

"It seems straightforward enough to me."

"Tell me what you've heard."

"That Duer had men in Brazil, looking for gold."

Ramage said nothing.

"But I also know that Isaac Whippo was in the Carolinas. And in Georgia. And it wasn't gold he was looking for."

Ramage grinned. "So you do want to know about your father."

"Do you know?"

"Of course I know."

"Then tell me."

"What's it worth to you?"

"What's your price?"

"A thousand dollars."

Justy coughed. A thousand dollars. An unimaginable price. A budding lawyer would be happy to make that in a year. A manual worker might make the same amount in ten.

"That's absurd."

"So make me an offer."

Justy frowned. "What?"

"Come on!" Ramage's face was bright red. "Make me an offer."

"Very well. Five dollars."

"Ha!" Ramage's eyes gleamed. "Five hundred."

"Ten."

"Four hundred!" Ramage let out a yelp of laughter. "Such sport!" He rubbed his hands together, his face flushed.

The ship's bell chimed, and Ramage glanced up. The blood drained from his face. Justy spun in his chair to see two men weaving towards a table in the far corner of the room. And, behind them, a third man, small and neat, in a tightly tailored coat, leaving the tavern. He had his back to the room, but as he stepped into the street he turned slightly and Justy glimpsed a pale face and a sharp widow's peak of dark hair.

Turner.

He turned back. Ramage was staring at the table. He looked like a puppet whose strings had been cut.

"Mr. Ramage? Are you quite all right?"

Ramage's cup clicked against his teeth as he drank. "Of course."

Justy twisted around in his seat again, but the doorway was empty. "Was that Marshal Turner I saw there?"

"Turner?" It looked as though it was painful for Ramage to swallow. "I do not know him."

The tavern was loud around them, raucous voices and the clatter of cutlery. Someone shouted for a bottle of porter. Justy waited.

"I must apologize." Ramage's voice was hoarse.

"What for?"

"I have misled you. I do not know anything about your father's business with William Duer. I was gulled, as you say. Like everyone else."

"What?"

Ramage stared into his cup. "Forgive me. It was a childish ruse. I wanted to pay you back for your assault on me earlier. But I know nothing. I apologize."

Justy felt as though his face had been dipped in cold water. "You have me mistaken, Mr. Ramage."

Ramage's eyes opened wide. His head seemed to withdraw into the collar of his coat. "What do you mean?"

"I mean I am not some wooly-crowned milestone just back from the old country. I can tell a lie as sure as I can smell a turd. And you're as full of shit as a bishop's bedpan."

"I am not. I know nothing about your father's business."

"Liar."

"I am not a liar!" Ramage's voice was a squeak.

"You lied about Turner. You do know him. You only glimpsed the man and your face went as white as a nun's knickers."

"I don't know him. I saw nothing. I swear it." Sweat trickled down the newsletterman's temples.

"You see nothing; you know nothing. You're not much good at your job, then."

Ramage looked as though he was about to cry. Justy leaned across the table. "You have information that I want, Mr. Ramage. And you have no idea what I might do to get it."

"You don't frighten me." Ramage's jowls wobbled.

Justy smiled slightly. He could hear his own breath in his ears, like waves on a beach. "In Ireland, fighting the English, I would lead patrols to capture redcoat soldiers. We would take them into the forest, and I would . . ." He paused, and let the smile fall from his face. "I would question them."

Ramage was pale. "I don't see what this has to do with me."

"I'm merely telling you a little about myself, Mr. Ramage." Justy's voice was a murmur. "It's always a good idea to know as much as possible about the person you're negotiating with.

Especially when the item under negotiation is considered by one of the parties to be of the utmost value."

He paused for a beat. His eyes never left Ramage's face. "The soldier would be gagged and tied to a tree. We had to move fast, of course, but there was always room for a little finesse. We would have a fire ready. The soldier would watch me put my knife into the hot coals. If he was soft, he'd spill his guts before the metal was even glowing. The harder cases would wait until the tip on the blade was white-hot. I would hold it up, right in front of their right eye, so that they could feel the heat. Most gave up then. Those that didn't? Well, the lightest touch of the blade, and the eyeball would simply . . ."

He mimed a bubble bursting with his fingers. Ramage shuddered and Justy felt a thrill of power. "This is something I have never told anyone before, Mr. Ramage. I'm telling you because I want you to understand just how valuable that information is to me. And how determined I am to get it. Do you understand?"

Ramage swallowed. He looked as though he was ready to crawl under the table. "I don't know anything, I told you."

He pushed back from the table. Justy reached out and grabbed Ramage's wrist. It was slick with sweat. He looked up into the man's eyes. They were wide with panic. Justy tightened his grip.

"What was Whippo looking for in the Carolinas?" he snapped.

Ramage shook his head, and Justy realized the man would rather stay silent and risk losing an eye than talk and lose his life. He thought of Cantillon and remembered the look on the lawyer's face. The naked fear. He let go of Ramage's arm, shame curdling in his guts.

"Keep your secret, Mr. Ramage. But tell me one thing." He took an eagle out of his pocket and placed the heavy ten-dollar coin carefully on the table. "There were five partners in the venture. Duer, my father, Whippo and Cantillon were four. Who was the fifth?"

Ramage rubbed his wrist. "I thought you knew."

"So tell me."

Ramage's eyes darted left and right. "You seemed so thick together. I thought you must know."

"Who?" But Justy already knew.

Ramage darted forward and snatched up the eagle, a mean smile on his pocked, sweaty face. His eyes gleamed.

"John Colley."

TWENTY-FOUR

Bedlow Street was south and west of the Bowery, in an area of the city that had only been developed in the last twenty years. Justy remembered walking there as a child with his father, through open fields along the headland, to the lookout on the hill at Crown Point. Since then, the Rutgers family had sold their brewery and the land around it to the city, and the green fields that had stretched the length of the coast were now elegant, paved boulevards, lined with grand town houses in the English style.

Bedlow Street and Timber Street had the high ground and the views, while Cherry Street had the seafront promenade, but the maze of lanes and alleys that tumbled down the hill and connected them was something else entirely. Much of the land there was marsh, and the work to drain the soil and fill in the incline had not gone well. The lanes were sunken, and the buildings on them flooded in the fall, froze in the winter and attracted mosquitos in the summertime. The mysterious fevers and sicknesses that plagued the city seemed to center on those sinkholes, so that only the poorest and most wretched lived there. But the rents were cheap, and as a result they were overflowing with newcomers seeking a fresh start in the growing city.

Justy avoided the sump of Charlotte Street and Cheapside and took the long way around, up the wide avenue of Pearl Street to the Bowery. It was the middle of the night, so Bedlow Street was quiet, lit by the moon and the new street lanterns. Justy could see one house whose upper windows were all brightly lit. He was a block away when he saw a carriage turn across the road and stop in the driveway to the side of the house. A man stepped out of the shadows and onto the running board of the carriage, stuck his head briefly through the window, then stepped off and waved the carriage on.

The street was quiet. Justy leaned on the wall to wait. His mind turned to what Ramage had said. And what he had not said. Colley was the fifth man. He thought about the tall trader, lounging in his overstuffed chair in the Club Room, reaching for a sandwich. The pale eyes. *I knew your father. . . . I can't say I knew him as well as Carrots did. Enough to say how d'ye do.* A smooth lie, as smooth as the sherry he had poured, and Justy had swallowed them both down.

He felt sick. He had no idea how much he could trust Ramage, but something told him the newsletterman was telling the truth. About Colley, at least. He saw again the blood draining out of Ramage's cheeks. And then Turner's long, thin nose and his sharp widow's peak, black and glossy in the light from the tavern. Ramage had lied about not knowing Turner, he was sure, but why? And what was Turner doing in the tavern in the first place?

A movement on the sidewalk pushed the thought from his mind. Two men were walking slowly along the pavement. Both wore caps and carried cudgels. Neither looked much like a gentleman. They reached the driveway that ran along the side of the house, and the guard who had checked the carriage emerged from his hiding place in the hedgerow. They conferred, and the two men turned and walked back down the sidewalk again, swinging their sticks, deep in conversation.

The moon was half-full. It hung high in the sky to the east and cast long, deep shadows down the lanes and alleyways that led off the main streets. Justy stood for a moment in the shadows, scanning the street, then went back down the hill. He walked quietly along Cherry Street, until he came to a narrow, crooked lane between two grand houses. The alley was not much wider than his shoulders, and Justy felt hemmed in as he slipped up the hill, ignoring the squelching under the soles of his boots.

Lars was standing in the shadows at the top of the lane, looking out over the wide avenue of Bedlow Street at the house. He smiled at Justy. "Still got the touch."

"Just like old times."

The house was exactly as Sandy had described it. A wide, four-story townhome, built with white stone. It had a wide frontage, with two large windows either side of an oversized door and three windows on every floor thereafter. The front door was painted red. The curtains behind the ground floor windows were drawn. An iron fence, head high and topped with spiked railings, ran around the frontage of the property.

Justy rolled his head around, easing the tension in his neck muscles. "Where's Sandy?"

"Sent him back with a coin, and orders not to spend it on neither punch nor judy."

"Good luck with that." Justy used his chin to point across the street. "Did you try to get in?"

"I did. You saw the fella in the driveway? He stopped me. Big lad. Polite enough, though. He told me it's a private house. I said I'd heard about a Negro knocking shop, but he told me I was mistaken. Then there's these two charlies out front."

The two men patrolling the front of the house strolled past the gate set in the middle of the iron fence. They were deep in conversation, their weapons over their shoulders. They reached the end of the property, marked by the high fence, and turned and ambled back again.

Justy made a face. "Sloppy."

Lars grinned. "Easy meat, if we happened to be hunting."

A carriage clattered past, slowed to turn into the driveway and stopped. It rocked as the sentry there climbed aboard, and then it clattered down the lane. A few moments later it reappeared and turned to drive back into town.

"They must have a turning space in the back."

Lars nodded. "No one can see who's coming or going. Clever. But it's all a bit much for a vaulting school, wouldn't you say?"

"Depends on the ones doing the vaulting."

The two sentries had stopped outside the high iron gate. A third man was striding quickly from the driveway. He was big and a careless man would have called him fat. He had a cap pulled down low over his eyes.

"Here's the gaffer come to teach these two sapsculls a lesson," Lars said.

The boss looked unhappy. He pushed one of the guards in the chest and pointed down the street, then snapped at the other man. The guards separated, walking in the opposite direction, swinging their cudgels purposefully.

Lars whistled softly. "Your man's been in the wars."

The boss had turned to scan the street, and even though the peak of his hat obscured his eyes, Justy could see his badly broken nose, squashed across the right side of his face. The man's mouth hung open slightly as he breathed.

Justy felt his heart in his mouth. "The devil!"

"What?"

"I know that man. His name's Duffy. He's one of the Bull's men."

"So?"

Justy felt the panic, fluttering inside him. "He was inside the house, Lars. He's one of the Bull's trusties. And here he's a guv'nor. Which means whatever this is, the Bull's part of it."

"So what? The Bull's got a piece of half the knocking shops in the city. Why's this one such a big blow?"

"Because this one's on Bedlow Street. The same street that Whippo mentioned in his letter to Duer. This was part of the scheme that did for my father. I know it. Which means the Bull . . ."

He sagged back against the wall, suddenly light-headed.

God damn the Bull. God damn him.

A scraping sound came from the end of the alley, and they both turned quickly, Justy with his knife in his hand. There was just enough moonlight for them to see Sandy's white face, his eyes wide and his mouth like an O at the sight of the long, wicked blade.

He held up his hands. "It's only me!"

"I thought I told you to go back," Lars hissed at him.

"And so I did." The boy's voice was a hoarse whisper. "But then I seen that jarvie again, the one what told me about this place. And he says they've pulled a body out of the river, down by the shipyards. Normally I'd pay no mind, but 'e says it was a gent got topped, a puff guts with carroty hair. I thought it sounded like the cove you're looking for, so I came right back."

Justy was past him before he finished speaking. He ran down the alley, his heart pounding in his ears, barely aware of the sound of Lars and Sandy behind him. The alley carried him in a rush down to Lombard Street. He ran out into the moonlit road and hurtled over the cobbles to the next alley. It was a midden, filled with filth and garbage, but he ignored the muck that splashed his boots and breeches, the stench of rotting food and the sound of rats trying to get out of his way.

Cherry Street was another still life, bright under the moon, empty of traffic and people. His boots hammered on the stone. His lungs burned. As he made the turn down to the shipyard slips at Catherine Street, he could see a line of black carriages and, closer to the water, a small crowd held back at the shipyard gate by several tall men in long coats and leather helmets.

He pushed through the gawkers, until he felt the hand of one of the crushers on his chest. Fifty feet away, at the end of a slip, a group of men stood around a low shipyard trolley. Justy could make out a body on it, a short, plump shape, clad in dark clothing made darker still by the filthy water. The face was pale and flat in the light. Its hair was sodden, slicked back from its forehead, but despite the weight of the water, it was still curling here and there at the temples.

One of the men at the end of the slip turned, his cape revealing a scarlet coat. Justy tried to push past the watchman. "Marshal Hays!"

Jacob Hays squinted in the dark. "Who is that?"

"Justice Flanagan."

"What do you want, Mr. Flanagan?"

"That man." It was an effort to control his voice. "I know him."

"Let him through," Hays ordered, and Justy shouldered past the watchman, his legs like jelly underneath him, the sound of his breathing loud in his ears.

Hays took him by the arm. "Steady now." He guided Justy to the end of the trolley and sat him down slowly. He pushed Justy forward, so that his head fell between his knees. Justy closed his eyes, feeling the blood surge into his head. He breathed low and deep, acutely aware of the corpse on the trolley beside him.

He sat up slowly, and looked at Cantillon. If it weren't for the water that soaked his clothes and hair, the lawyer might have been asleep. His face was slack, the skin falling back off the bones. The moonlight gave it a bluish cast. He hadn't been in the water long, Justy could tell. The skin didn't have the bloated, puffy look that came from prolonged exposure.

Hays touched him on the shoulder. "Take your time."

Justy nodded. He took a deep breath. "His name is Jarlath Cantillon. Attorney-at-law."

"Ah yes." Hays' voice was a sigh. "I thought I recognized him. Do you have any idea what he was doing down here?"

Hays' face was serious. Justy wondered what he knew. "He'd been out drinking. Along the waterfront."

"Anywhere in particular?"

"The Fair Lady. The Judge. I only know because I was looking for him."

"May I ask why?"

"I wanted to ask him something." Justy narrowed his eyes. "You don't think I did this."

Hays gave a wry smile. "Of course not. I was merely curious." He looked down at Cantillon. "The poor man obviously had too much to drink, then came down here and fell into the water."

There was a slopping sound in the slipway behind him, and a strong smell of sewage. This had been the original drainage channel for the water that had been pumped out of the marshland to the north. The outlet had been left in place to act as the main sewage line for the area, and an entire neighborhood's effluent dumped out into the yards, sucked in and out by the tides. Hays grimaced and looked around. The hulk of a half-built ship in the slip to the east loomed over them, throwing tangled shadows over the oily water and the barrels and boxes and piles of timber that were heaped around the yard. "But what in God's name was he doing down here at all?"

Justy felt suddenly weary. "As you say, he was drunk."

"Drunk? He must have positively mauld to have come close enough to this goddamned sewer to fall in." Hays leaned over the corpse and sniffed. As he swayed forward, he lost his balance and put his hand onto Cantillon's chest to steady himself. Cantillon's mouth fell open, and Hays pushed himself up hastily, wiping his hand on his cloak and grimacing. "He's reeking of whiskey."

Justy frowned. He stood and pushed Hays aside.

"What the devil are you doing?" Hays snapped.

Justy pressed down on the dead lawyer's chest. Cantillon's mouth fell open again, and Justy bent to look down his throat. "He didn't drown."

"Don't be a fool, man. Of course he did. Look at him."

Justy shook his head. "There's still air in his lungs. When you pushed down on his chest, the air was forced out, which is why you smelled whiskey. If he'd drowned, you'd hear gurgling in his windpipe, and there'd be water coming out of his mouth, not fumes."

Hays stared at Justy. "What are you saying?"

"I'm saying he was dead before he went in. If he was alive, he'd have breathed in water and drowned. But he didn't."

The crowd of onlookers at the gate had thinned. Lars stood patiently in the shadows of the gateway, watching. Behind them, a carriage clicked slowly down the street. It pulled to a halt, and a slight, neat figure stepped down into the street. The wan lights on the corners of the cab made Turner's face look jaundiced. His small black eyes flicked back and forth as he walked quickly past the guards onto the slipway.

Hays nodded to him. "News travels fast, Marshal."

"Always does, Marshal, when a rich cove comes a cropper." Turner's flat Yorkshire accent was like a rasp on a nail. His eyes flicked to Justy. "What's he doing here?"

"Mr. Flanagan is a friend of the deceased. Jarlath Cantillon."

Turner said nothing.

"Mr. Flanagan believes that Mr. Cantillon was dead before he went into the drink. No water in the lungs, you see."

Turner's laugh was as dry as kindling catching fire. "Oh aye? So he's turned a drunk falling into the harbor into a murder, has he?"

"Nobody said anything about a murder," Justy said.

"So what killed him, then, Lord Sly-Boots?"

Justy shrugged. "He might have fallen and knocked his head hard enough to kill him, then rolled into the water."

Hays snorted. "That doesn't sound particularly likely."

"No. It doesn't, does it." Justy knelt on the trolley and put his hands to Cantillon's head. The hair was slimy under his fingers and he had to fight to keep his gorge down.

"What the bloody hell do you think you're doing?" Turner's voice was harsh.

"Checking to see what killed him." He ran his hands gently down the back of Cantillon's head, then turned it side to side. "There are no bumps or contusions. His neck isn't broken. Let's turn him."

Hays snapped his fingers, and two of the watchmen stepped up and rolled the body onto its right shoulder. Justy examined the back of Cantillon's coat for tears or signs of a knife wound, then ran his hands under the coat and up the back of the lawyer's waistcoat. He examined his hands in the moonlight, then nodded at the watchmen to roll the body back into position. He pulled Cantillon's sodden coat wide and looked at the barrel of his torso. No marks, no cuts, no blood. The lawyer looked peaceful.

Turner smirked. "Fancy yourself a right whipster, don't you? Are you satisfied now?"

Justy stood over Cantillon. Something nagged at him. There was nothing unusual about Cantillon's clothes. He wore the same dark green waistcoat, black breeches and coat, the same white hose and well-made but subtle black shoes. But something was off.

Justy closed his eyes and remembered Cantillon in the Seagull, the panicked look in his eyes, the nervous tic when he clutched at his throat, adjusting his neckband.

Justy's eyes snapped open. Cantillon's cravat, normally perfectly arranged, was a twisted mess. He bent forward and examined it. It was a common enough garment, a yard of ivory silk, wrapped once around the neck and then tied in a loose knot and folded over to show a smooth sheet of white at the collar. But the knot was twisted to the side, and when Justy pulled at the smooth silk he saw it had been shredded. He tugged the silk away from the throat and saw a livid blue bruise line that ran across the windpipe.

"Look here."

Hays leaned over. "My God! Again?"

"It looks like it." He reached over Cantillon's face and used the tips of his fingers to gently open the lawyer's right eye. The pupil was tiny, the iris like a dark bruise. The white was covered with tiny red dots. "Do you know what these are?"

Hays leaned closer. "As a matter of fact, I do. My wife's brother is a physician. He theorizes that if one puts enough pressure on the blood in any area of the body, it will be forced to the surface of the skin. In the case of the head, this includes the whites of the eyes." He looked up. "Such marks are often seen in cases of asphyxia or strangulation. And garroting. Am I correct, Marshal Turner?"

Turner said nothing. He glared at Justy.

Hays waved to one of the watchmen. "Cover him up. Clear away these people and get the body to the morgue." He clasped his hands behind his back, pulling back his cloak so that his scarlet coat seemed to shine in the moonlight. "Two men killed in the same way in as few days. One a jailer, the other a lawyer. This doesn't seem the usual gang dispute or drunken squabble gone badly, now does it?" He looked steadily at Turner. "Do you think it could be the same man?"

"It's too early to make a jump like that." Turner's voice was harsh. "There's plenty of old soldiers in this town know how to mill a man with a wire."

"Perhaps, but not so many that actually would, surely."

Hays' face was pale. He drew a deep breath. "We must explore the possibility. Have some of your men put the word about that we're looking for a rogue who kills in this way. But discreetly. I don't want the Mayor reading about this over his breakfast."

"I'm sure the Marshal's connections are good enough to keep the story out of the newspapers," Justy said.

Turner did nothing. He said nothing. He simply stared at Justy for a moment, his two black marble eyes quite still in his face. And then he turned on his heel and walked away.

"How long have you worked with Marshal Turner?" Justy asked.

Hays thought for a moment. "Nearly three years."

"He has a knack for being in the right place at the right time."

"He has a knack for this kind of work. Knowing things. Finding them out. He did something similar in the war, running spy networks among the English at Trenton and Germantown. The man who recommended him told me if it wasn't for Turner's knowledge of the English dispositions, Valley Forge might have been an even greater disaster than it was."

The watchmen had wrapped Cantillon in a large tarpaulin, then rolled the trolley to the shipyard gates. Ahead of them, Turner climbed into his carriage. It was a private cab, black with brass fittings, not one of the plain boxy carriages used by the leatherheads. The coachman hauled hard on the reins, pulling the horses around, clicking his tongue, then clapped his hat on his head, an absurd beaver stovepipe hat that gleamed in the moonlight as the horses carried the carriage up the hill.

TWENTY-FIVE

The Counting House was closed, its windows dark. Lars tapped gently on the door, and after a few moments a small viewing hatch snapped open. There was a brief pause, followed by the sound of bolts being drawn, and the door opened just enough to let them slip inside.

The tall bald man with the scarred skull greeted Lars like an old friend. He nodded to Justy. "If I'd known you were shipmates with this big damber, I'd maybe have given you them papers for nowt."

Justy smiled. "Just as well for your boy, then. How come you know each other?"

"You're rookin' me, aren't ye? Every publican in the town knows this cove."

Lars looked uncomfortable. "Not every publican."

The barman laughed. "Near as dammit. Come on and have a drink."

He lit candles at each end of the bar. The scar on his head looked deep and brutal in the light. "What's it to be?"

"Ale," said Lars.

"Water," said Justy.

The man pushed a bottle at Lars and filled a tankard from a barrel behind the bar for Justy. The water was cool and tasted slightly mossy.

"Thanks. What's your name, by the way?"

"Rafe Durcan. Them's are my friends call me Dirk."

He pointed them to the opposite corner of the tavern.

"You can talk over there. There'll be no one else in tonight."

"Well, there might be one more," Lars said. He glanced at Justy. "I sent the lad to ask after Kerry."

Justy felt a stab of resentment. "Why did you do that?"

"Because she asked. And I can tell by the look on your face that we're not done for tonight. I figure the more heads we have together on this the better."

Justy shrugged. They settled in the corner. Lars took a long drink from his bottle.

There was a soft knock at the door. Dirk went to open the hatch and, after a brief conversation, drew the bolts. Kerry slipped past him to where Justy and Lars sat.

She slid onto the bench beside Lars. Her eyes were large and bright in the candlelight. She reached over the table and touched Justy's hand. "Sandy told me about Carrots. The poor clunch. He was a starchy wee bounce, but no one deserves that."

Justy's throat was tight. His tongue felt as though it were made of lead. He nodded and looked down. She pulled her hand away.

"Where's Sandy now?" Lars asked.

"Back at my cousin's house, being stuffed full of leftovers. One of the cooks took a shine to him. He said he'd be away back to the ship, after."

Lars nodded. "He's a good lad."

Kerry hadn't taken her eyes off Justy. "It's been a long night for you. Are you all right?"

He coughed out a dry laugh. "If being caught in a nightmare is all right. I talk to Drummond about my father and he's killed. Then Cantillon. I find out my father was up to his ears in some filthy swindle before he died, and now it turns out my uncle's involved as well."

She frowned. "How do you mean?"

"I dug up some old letters between William Duer and Isaac Whippo, talking about some property they were going to buy on Bedlow Street. So we went up to take a look. And what do we find, but a fancy whorehouse, with a brace of solid-looking charlies out front, being bossed by a big Galwayman with a busted nose. Duffy's his name. He's one of the Bull's bodyguards. So you know what that means. The Bull's in it up to his neck."

"That's a bit of a stretch, isn't it? Some letters from nearly ten years ago? It might not even be the same place."

Justy felt himself redden. "It's the same goddamned place. I'm sure of it. It's too much of a coincidence. The letter said John Colley had already bought the place in September of '91, and was renovating it. Six months later was the Panic, and we know how hard it was to sell property then, so I don't think he did sell it. I think he held on to it. And now it's a whorehouse, run by the Bull, it seems. I don't know the details, but something ties all of this together."

There was silence in the room. Kerry and Lars were staring at him. The flames from the candles in the holders on the bar seemed to lengthen in the still air until they almost touched the ceiling.

Lars broke the spell. "Did you say John Colley?"

"Aye. What of it?"

"Black Jack Colley? Pompey Jack?" Lars' voice was urgent. "Tall, dark-haired mackerel-backed cove, about forty-five years? Wears everything black?"

Justy shrugged. "Sounds like him. But I never heard him called those names."

"So he's the other JC, in the letters. John Colley."

"Aye. A man called Ramage told me."

Lars sat back on the bench and exhaled in a whistle. "Well,

strap me. Black Jack." He glanced at Kerry. Her face seemed sickly, but whether it was just the candlelight Justy couldn't tell.

"Do you know him?" Lars asked Kerry.

She shrugged. "Everyone's heard of Black Jack."

"Jesus, the two of you! Who the hell is he?" Justy's voice was tight.

Lars tipped his bottle back and placed it carefully on the table. "The story goes Black Jack was born in Pompey. Portsmouth, in England."

"I know where Pompey is, Lars."

"Course you do. Right. Anyway, he was hired on to a ship there when he was sixteen, came on board as a topsail monkey. The ship was loaded to the gunwales with an expensive cargo. French wine. They was off the Canaries when a privateer came alongside and boarded them. The captain was killed, but in the melee Jack somehow gets across into the privateer and sets a fuse in its powder room. Then he gets back on his own ship and relieves his recently departed skipper of a pair of barking irons. The privateer goes up like a plum pudding at Christmas, then goes under, faster than shit through a goose. Jack then pots two of the privateers' boarding party, and the crew follows his lead and takes back the ship."

"Impressive." Justy imagined a young Colley, coolly aiming and firing his pistols.

"That's not the half of it. He ties one of the privateers to the mast and goes to work on him with a marlinspike. The fella tells him the whole thing was a swindle. The first mate had arranged the rendezvous. The mate denies the whole thing, of course. He goes for his sword, but Jack's too quick. He stabs the mate to death with the spike, right through the eye, then takes command of the ship. Sixteen years old! Anyway, he sails it all the way to New York, and hands it over to its owner, contents untouched, save one barrel of Bojeley to keep the lads happy. The owners gave him a fat reward, and he was made. Went into business on his own. Baccy, rum, sugar, furs."

"Slaves?" Justy asked.

"Aye, that too. Like most of 'em. I was never on any of his crews, but I heard he runs a tight ship. Bristol fashion."

"That's a poor joke." Bristol had been the main slave port in England before slavery was outlawed on the British Isles. The city's slavers had been famous for making their ships as efficient as possible, cramming as many men, women and children into their holds as they could, but not so tight as to increase the death rate beyond an acceptable percentage.

Lars made a face. "I'm not joking. Once he was in business, he got a reputation for being a hard bastard, the kind you don't cross if you value your puff. Nothing proven, like, but now and again you'd hear about folk just disappearing."

Justy sipped his water and thought about John Colley. A ship's boy, a trader and now a topping man on Wall Street. It wasn't so unusual. One of the reasons so many came to America was to become wealthy. A few did it overnight, thanks to a combination of luck and good timing. And there was a direct road from the docks to the Tontine. Commodities like coffee and sugar were traded in the same coffee houses as securities like shares and bonds. It wouldn't take much for a trader as sharp as Colley to make the leap. And why shouldn't he? There was nothing wrong with becoming rich.

But if John Colley was one thing, Black Jack was another. A ruthless man. A slaver. Justy remembered the look Colley had given him in the lobby of the Tontine as he defended the trade in human flesh, his cold eyes the color of the sea in winter.

Kerry was leaning back on the bench, her feet up on a chair, her face in shadow. "So, what's next?"

Justy shook his head. "I need to speak to Colley, that's all.

He's the last person alive who was in on that deal, which means if anyone knows what happened to my father, he does."

"What are you going to say to him?" Her voice was cautious.

"I'll show him the letters. I'll tell him what Cantillon told me, about the fraud that Colley and a bunch of Wall Street coves are cooking. About some secret business they've got going. I'll tell him that if he doesn't stop lying to me about what happened to my father, I'll go to his investors and bring this whole thing down. And him with it."

They agreed to meet at the Norwegian tavern at five o'clock the next day. Lars went back down to the ship, and Kerry and Justy walked together up to the boardinghouse. Nothing stirred in the city, no carriages or carts, and the Broad Way looked vast in the moonlight as they walked north along the middle of the street.

The wind gusted hard off the East River, carrying a yeasty smell up the hill from the Coulthard brewery. Without looking at Kerry, Justy reached out his hand. It was like taking hold of a bird. His skin bumped as she slid her long, slim fingers across his palm. He felt the pulse in her wrist.

And then she made a fist and pulled her hand away.

"What's wrong?"

"Nothing. I'm just cold." She thrust her hands deep into her pockets and walked on, swaying away from him, her head down, her eyes on the ground.

"I'm sorry, Justy." Her voice was small.

"Sorry for what?"

"For everything."

"You mean Carrots?"

Her eyes were luminous, wet with unshed tears. She sighed. "Aye. For Carrots."

Justy frowned. "I didn't know him so well. It's just that he was set to tell me something about this business with my father."

"Right." She looked away. "So what did he say?"

"Not much. He was a mess. Scared stiff of something. Or someone. The woman who lived next door told me a man was watching the house last night. A big hackum, dressed all in black. When I asked him about it, he got angry. He said my father was tangled up in some scheme, and that it was happening all over again. He didn't give me any details. And I knew he wasn't telling me the whole story. I knew he felt guilty about something, too. So I pressed him. Maybe too hard."

Kerry said nothing.

Justy turned on her, anxiety like a hot coal in his chest. "I know, I botched it. Jesus! Have you never made a mistake?"

"Oh, I've made mistakes all right. Like you wouldn't believe." The weight of her voice stopped him. "What happened, Kerry?"

"Nothing you want to hear about."

He had to hurry to catch up to her. He grabbed her elbow. "Tell me."

She shook her head, her hands in fists by her sides. She shuddered once, and he wrapped her in his arms. They stood in the middle of the Broad Way, her forehead pressed into his shoulder, her body shuddering with the sobs.

After a moment, she sniffed hard and pushed him away. She tried a laugh. "Now it's my turn to snot all over you."

He held her by the shoulders. "Will you tell me, Kerry? I want to help."

She shrugged free, then wiped her face with her sleeve. "You're a good man, Justy. But you're too late for that."

He felt the breath go out of him, as surely as if she had punched him in the guts. She squeezed his arm. "I'm not blaming you, *a chara*. It's my life, and my mistakes. Not yours."

"I don't understand. Are you talking about . . . what you do?"

"What, you mean thieving?" She stepped back, spread her arms wide and turned in a full circle in the center of the street. "Dressing up like this?"

"I suppose."

She laughed. "Jesus no, boy. This is freedom!"

He frowned.

"You've no idea what I'm talking about, do you?" Her laugh was caustic. "That's because you're a man. All your lot sit around and blather about freedom, and how you won it from the bloody English in the war, and how it's enshrined in your Constitution and all of that shit. Well, let me tell you, all of that trumpery might sound great, but it means nothing to a woman, and even less than nothing to a woman whose skin isn't lily-white. We're not free, Justy. We can't do what we want or say what we want, like you can. All the world's a stage, right? Except we're not players. All we are is the fucking furniture."

Justy said nothing. He had heard Kerry curse before, but her anger was so white-hot, it was like being slapped in the face.

Kerry plucked at the lapel of her coat. "That's why I dress up like this. So I can be a player, at least for a few hours a day. So I don't have to sit in some dank libben, waiting for my fat madge of a father to come home for his tea." She thumped a fist into her chest. "These clothes give me freedom. The gelt I knap from rich folk gives me a life. Can you twig that?"

She stood in the middle of the street, the moon behind her, her eyes bright in the shadow of her face. Her head was up, her chin out; her hands were on her hips. He felt a surge of warmth that made his face flush.

"I can," he said.

She scoffed. "You're stuffed with it."

"I am not. Be a whore or be a servant, you said your choices were. This is better than either; I see that. I wish it was different, but I understand."

She was very still. A rustling sound came from the gutter behind him. Litter being blown in the light breeze pushing up from the docks. Or a rat.

She shrugged. "Well, then."

"But that's not what we're talking about, is it?"

She said nothing.

He took a step towards her. "Please, Kerry. Whatever it is. Will you let me help?"

She hesitated. And then she swayed backwards slightly, as though something scared her. "I will not. It's in the past and none of your fucking business anyway."

He felt as if the ground had suddenly opened up like a chasm between them. She gave him a fierce look. "Don't go sticking your nose in, Justy. Not unless you want it cut off."

And then she was gone, quick across the way and into the darkness. He stood in the road, the moonlit cobbles like a dangerous sea around him, the ache in his chest making him feel as though she had cut out his heart and taken it with her.

TWENTY-SIX

Friday

When Justy awoke, his head ached and his mouth felt as though it had been stuffed with feathers. The drink, he supposed. It had been a while since he'd taken so much. He lay on his back, a pulse in his temple, and a hollow feeling in his guts as he thought about Kerry, about the rage in her voice and the warning she had given him.

Think about something else, he told himself, and forced himself out of his bed and onto his feet. He drank as much water as he could, washed in the basin on the cupboard and dressed in a new shirt. From a distance away, he heard the church bells ring nine o'clock. For a moment he thought he would be late, and then he remembered Cantillon's body, slack and dripping on the dock trolley, and the thin blue scar around his neck.

He sat heavily on his bed. Colley would not be at the Tontine yet. He had plenty of time. He thought through all that he knew. Drummond and Cantillon murdered, the jailer because of the papers he had stolen from Duer, Cantillon because of what he knew about a new fraud that replicated the venture Justy's father had been in with Duer eight years ago. A business deal that had included Whippo, Cantillon and Colley, who had bought a property on Bedlow Street. A property that was now an exclusive brothel, run with the help of Justy's uncle, the Bull. He felt as though he had the frame of the puzzle almost complete, but there were huge holes there, too.

His hand was shaking. He made a fist. Colley had the pieces. He was at the heart of all of this. Colley had cooked up a lie, sugared it and fed it to him, and he had swallowed it whole. The shame ached like a stone in his gullet. He would not prove so gullible this time around.

A carriage was parked in the road outside the boarding-house. The glossy black paint and brass trim looked familiar, but it wasn't until the big thieftaker with the brand on his forehead jumped down that Justy recognized the cab.

The big man opened the door to the carriage. He pointed with his gnarled blackthorn stick. "Get in."

Justy didn't move. "Who are you?"

The man grinned. His teeth looked like a burned forest. "I'm Mr. Campbell," he said in an Ulster accent. The stick swung up to point to the top of the carriage. "That's my associate, Mr. Fraser."

The man with the moonlike face and the cropped ears looked down at him. He held two pistols. Both guns had the dull sheen of instruments that were often used and well cared for. Both had their hammers fully cocked.

"I'd rather walk," Justy said.

Campbell tapped his stick on the ground. "Come on now, and get in the carriage. I don't want Mr. Fraser turning you into a Swiss cheese and rousting the neighbors."

"Can I at least know who it is I'm going to see?"

Campbell laughed. "I'd have thought you'd have worked that out by now, Mr. Lawyer."

Justy's mind raced. How did Campbell know he was a lawyer?

"Come on, now." Campbell gestured at his clothing. "Black uniforms, black horse, black carriage?"

Justy cursed himself for a dupe and a fool. *Of course. Black Jack.*

Colley had spent a lot of money equipping his cab. Every inch of the interior was covered in black material. Silk on the walls, velvet for the curtains, leather on the seats and stained mahogany on the floor. The padding on the walls and the stuffing in the cushions muffled the clatter of the iron-clad wheels on the cobbles. It was like being wrapped in a cocoon. Or laid in a coffin.

Justy sat facing forward. Campbell and Fraser sat opposite, staring, saying nothing as the carriage rocked and lurched through the traffic. The cab stopped in a quiet street, lined with tall gray-walled houses. Campbell knocked at a bright blue door. The man who opened it was at least a foot taller than Justy. He was dressed in an old-fashioned military coat, dark blue with red facings. It was a moment before Justy recognized the dress uniform of the old Continental Army that was disbanded after the Revolutionary War. The doorman's head was shaved close to his dark skin, and he sported a neat, square beard.

Campbell flashed his rotten teeth. "Step aside, darky. I've brought a visitor for Mr. Colley."

The man in the uniform coat barely glanced at Campbell, but it was a look so full of contempt that the Ulsterman's face went red with anger. He lifted his blackthorn. "Step the fuck back, you black bastard, or I'll break my stick over your skull."

The doorman ignored him. He looked at Justy. "Mr. Justice Flanagan?"

Justy almost smiled. The man's voice was deep and soft, with a rich Galway accent. But his eyes were as hard as a frozen pond.

Justy nodded. "That's right."

The doorman stepped to the side to let Justy enter, then slammed the door in Campbell's face. There was a hammering sound as Campbell battered the door with his blackthorn, but the man paid no attention. Instead, he led Justy through a foyer and up two flights of stairs to a long, polished hallway. He pointed to an open doorway. Sunlight streamed through it. Spirals of dust turned in the light.

Colley sat, reading a book, in one of a pair of armchairs under a high, narrow window. As usual, he was dressed entirely in black. The armchair he sat in was upholstered in red velvet. The carpet on the floor was the same shade of blue as the doorman's coat.

Colley put down his book. "Welcome to the Firecake Club."

"Fire cake?"

"Hardtack, you might call it. Or brewis, in Ireland. It's what we lived on during the winter at Valley Forge."

There was a framed Continental Army flag on one wall. Justy noted the scorch marks on the edges. Something snagged in his mind. "You were there?"

"For my many sins." Colley gestured to the empty armchair.

Justy sat. The velvet was hot from the sun.

"You know, I was on my way to see you, Colley. You didn't need to send your grunters."

"Charming fellows, aren't they?"

"Just about the kind of slubbers I'd expect to be working with Black Jack."

Colley steepled his fingers. "I've been keeping an eye on you, Justice. You have a bit of a temper. But a sharp mind, too."

"Not sharp enough to see through you, it seems."

"Oh, I don't know. In just three days you've managed to turn over quite a few rather important stones."

"I've certainly seen a few creatures crawl out from underneath."

Colley sighed. "I didn't ask you here to fence with you."

"You didn't ask at all."

"Bring you here, then. I want to answer your questions. About your father. That's what you want, isn't it?"

Justy waited. The warm silence of the room was slowly displaced by the sounds from outside. The window looked out on to a building site on the waterfront of Hudson's River. Developers were constructing warehouses and tenements along the waterline, and he could hear hammering and the voices of laborers shouting orders and encouragement.

It was several moments before Colley spoke. "I apologize for misleading you, before."

"Lying, you mean."

Colley conceded the point with a curt nod. "Your father came to us. He had approached William Duer before, but never with anything worth considering. This time was different, as I told you before. William was in trouble. He needed capital. A lot of capital. And he saw an opportunity to employ your father's facility in certain areas."

Colley brushed at a speck of dust on his breeches. "Francis may not have been much of a success on Wall Street, but he was an acute observer of the type. He saw that once a man has committed himself to an investment, the higher the return he receives, the less inclined he is to ask questions about the business."

Justy felt the heat in his face. "I already know about the swindle my father cooked up for you."

"It was not a swindle. There's no law against what he did."

"That doesn't stop it being theft."

Colley shrugged off the insult. "It's an investor's responsibility to determine the validity of an opportunity, not the venturer's responsibility to prove it."

Justy gripped the arms of his chair and forced himself to calm down. "What was the venture? I know it wasn't Brazilian gold, as you put about."

"It was real, if that's what you're wondering. It had a real balance sheet, import documents, shipping manifests, bills of sale. We needed those things, to convince our more curious investors. And it's fiendishly hard to create them out of thin air, believe me. But we didn't need to create them, because our business was genuine."

"Imports. From the Carolinas and Georgia."

Colley smiled. "Very good. You see, you have done well."

The sun had moved, and the light that came through the narrow window was now falling on the shoulder of Colley's chair and onto his left thigh. He crossed his legs. "Your father had nothing to do with the real venture, of course. His job was solely to raise the wind, to tell whatever story he needed to bring in new investors. The new money was split into three. Some went to pay existing investors their returns and some went into the operations of the real business. But the bulk of the money was spent by William. He was heavily invested in bank shares, but investors were losing confidence in the banks, and beginning to sell. To safeguard his considerable exposure, he had to keep the market up. The only way to do that was to buy huge quantities of stock."

"So this was all about protecting Duer?"

"Not at all. We were genuinely committed to creating a working venture. But William was the principal investor, and he saw an opportunity to both participate in a lucrative investment, and protect his interests at the same time. Of course, the entire scheme required vast amounts of capital to succeed, and because the venture itself failed to make money, your father's role, bringing in new funds, was vital. And he did very well."

Justy flushed. "Don't patronize me."

"I don't mean to. You may not like what he did, but I would say it was the pinnacle of his career. He showed an outstanding ability to raise capital, and his scheme allowed us to bridge a frustrating period of insolvency. The venture would have made a staggering amount of money, eventually. But it became very clear, very quickly, that it was going to take a lot longer to become profitable than we thought."

He reflected for a moment. "Of course, there was a degree of mendacity involved. We had to fiddle the figures significantly. Or Carrots did, poor fellow."

Justy thought about the look on Cantillon's face in the Seagull. The panic in his eyes. "Did those dogs of yours kill Cantillon?"

"Certainly not."

"You're a goddamned liar. You sent that dunghill Campbell to intimidate him. People saw him standing in the street, swinging that stave of his. And it worked. Cantillon was scared. 'They're doing it again,' he told me. He said fools are throwing their money at that fat princock Harry Gracie, in exchange for fat returns. Except that it's not Gracie's venture, is it?" He pointed at Colley. "It's yours."

Colley was silent. His chair was bathed in sunlight. He shifted, uncomfortable in the warmth.

Justy leaned forward. "What was it? What was Whippo looking for down there, eight years ago? What are you buying down there now?"

"A rare and expensive commodity. One that became even more expensive on the fourth of July of this year."

Justy frowned. The fourth of July was Independence Day. Nothing unusual there. So what made this year special? He thought back to his conversation with Lars, about what was exported from the Carolinas and Georgia. Timber. Cotton. Skins. Tobacco. Crops. Nothing particularly expensive. And nothing that had become more expensive recently.

It struck him like a slap in the face. *Slaves*. The Manumission Society had passed its bill for the gradual abolition of slavery in March. The children of slaves were to be freed. The loopholes in the law that still allowed trafficking in human flesh had been closed. The law became effective on Independence Day.

His stomach was hollow. "You're buying people."

Colley's eyes were blank. "We're buying a commodity. Entirely legally. But not just any commodity. The cream of the crop. Exquisite specimens that command the highest price."

Justy shook his head. "But why? You can't sell slaves in New York anymore. It's against the law."

Colley waved his hand. "A fig for the law. We shall import them, sell them and make a very pretty penny keeping them thereafter."

Justin's head cleared. He felt like a craftsman, slotting one perfectly carved piece of wood into another. "Keeping them. In your whorehouse on Bedlow Street. You were building it in '91. Whippo was looking for the women in the South. You commandeered a special wharf where they could be landed close by, in the shipyards on Catherine Street."

"How did you find out about that?"

"Duer's letters. Drummond took some of them."

Colley sighed. "Of course he did. I suppose they told what a difficult time Whippo had procuring the goods. You'd be surprised how hard it is to find good specimens. Scars, deformities, broken bones. It's rare to find a jewel. Much rarer than we thought. And that makes them expensive."

Justy felt breathless. It was as though a giant fist were squeezing his chest. He had come back to find out about his father and found himself wading in a river of filth. Fraud. Slavery. Prostitution. He thought about Francis Flanagan, attorney-at-law, in his sober clothes and his old-fashioned wig, the lectures he used to give about integrity and uprightness. His father. A pimp. A swindler. A goddamned thief.

He felt the tears stinging behind his eyes. He remembered the fawning look on his father's face when he had met William Duer at the Merchant's Coffee House. Duer had recognized Francis Flanagan for what he was. Desperate. A dupe. He felt the pulse in his temples. These filthy bastards. They had seduced his father and dragged him down into the gutter. And then they had killed him.

Colley was staring at him, a strange look on his face. Justy looked down. He had no idea how, but his knife was in his hand. His throat was tight, his face burning. He felt the smooth nub of the catch under his thumb. It would take him a single stride to reach Colley. He imagined himself smashing the heel of his hand into Colley's face, breaking his nose, driving his head back against the chair. Then burying his knife in Colley's neck, feeling the warm gush on his hand.

There was a sticky, coppery taste in his mouth. "How much did my father know about this? Not the swindle. The business."

"At first, nothing. In the end, everything. He was never quite satisfied with the idea of Brazilian gold. And he became less satisfied and more persistent the longer things dragged on. In the end I had to tell him. Or rather confirm what he already knew."

"What did he say?"

"He was every bit as squeamish about the business as you appear to be. Perhaps that's why he killed himself."

Justy looked down. His fingers were white, wrapped around the knife. "Except he didn't kill himself, did he?"

He looked Colley directly in the eye. He felt a sudden calm. "The rope used to hang him was a heavy thing, brought up from the docks. A ship's hawser. Not the kind of thing a man kept about the house. Especially not a man like my father."

"I fail to see—"

There was a snap, like a dry branch breaking. Justy held the long blade in the sunlight.

"You shut your fucking mouth, Colley. I'll tell you when it's your turn."

Colley said nothing. His face was as white as bone.

Justy's rage was like a cold river flowing through him, making his fingers numb. He stared into Colley's eyes. "When I was in

Paris, the *police militaire* brought in a suicide. A sergeant major had been found hanging from a ceiling beam in the *caserne*. He used a tent rope, a thick hawser, two inches across. He had a huge, dirty abrasion running diagonally across his neck, from his right collarbone to his left ear." Justy pointed with the tip of the knife. "It looked quite obvious. Self-murder. But when the man's body was washed in the morgue, an attendant discovered that the dirt and the abrasions concealed a second mark, a thin, purple line that ran directly across the throat, like this."

He tilted his head back and used the tip of his knife to draw a line across his own throat. The cold steel scratched his warm skin. He felt his flesh bump. "The sergeant major had been murdered, then hanged posthumously, to cover up the crime. I read case notes, then went to see the body in the morgue. It was like going back in time to the day I found my father. The same marks, almost exactly."

"And you suspect me?" Colley's eyes showed nothing.

"Why not? My father starts asking awkward questions about your business and is strangled to death with a garrote. Now I come asking questions about his death and your business, and the men I speak to are found killed in the same way. First Drummond, then Cantillon. Coincidence?"

Colley made a dismissive gesture. "This is absurd. I had nothing to fear from your father knowing what kind of venture I was running. It was entirely legal."

"Legal or not, it wasn't the kind of business a gentleman would want to be associated with. Slavery? Prostitution? I saw the names of your investors. Robert Troup. John Jay. Alexander Hamilton. All Manumission men. They would have run for the hills had they found out, and taken every other enlightened citizen with them."

Colley laughed "You think so? Half of those fine gentlemen still own slaves, you know. I suspect most of them would have taken one look at their dividend notes and swallowed their mis-givings."

He let his head loll back on the velvet headrest, a smug look on his face. Justy was acutely aware of the knife in his hand. It would be so easy. But Colley's men were outside, ready to take him. He would never get away. And Colley's words rang true. John Jay had founded the New York Manumission Society, but it was common knowledge that he still kept household slaves. And then there was the money: a 16 or 20 percent return was more than enough to make most men ignore their morals and look the other way, even if they were strong for Manumission.

He felt suddenly weary, beaten, as though he had reached the end of a long road and found it led to a high cliff face, with no way over or around. The memory flashed in his mind again, his father, laughing, dancing through the house in his long black coat, the powder from his wig floating in the still air and the eve-ning sun. His stomach writhed, and he tasted acid. Part of him had always feared it, and now it was clear: he had no real proof. No proof that his father was murdered. No proof that Duer or Colley had anything to do with it. Cantillon knew, he was sure. But Cantillon was dead. The door was closed. He had failed.

He folded the knife and slipped it back into his boot.

Colley slapped his hands on the arms of his chair and heaved himself upwards.

"Come with me."

Justy did nothing for a few moments. He had the feeling that his anger had drained through the soles of his feet and taken his spirit with him. His head buzzed slightly, as though he had drunk too much and stayed too long in the sun. He could have sat there forever, in that comfortable chair, in that warm room, looking out of the window at the clouds.

"Come on," Colley's voice came from behind him, and Justy stood up. Numb, he followed Colley along the hallway and down the first flight of stairs to the landing. An ornate clock on the wall read ten thirty. One side was a large dining room, with the same blue carpet, dominated by a polished table surrounded by a dozen ornate chairs. On the other was a taproom with a worn wooden floor. A group of men stood drinking quietly at the bar. Colley called out a good evening, and a barrel-chested man with a bald head and a long brown coat raised his glass.

Colley led Justy into the dining room and half-closed the door. They stood beside the table. "Did you recognize that man?"

"No."

"His name is Robert Barnes. He is the private secretary to the Governor of New York. A powerful fellow. An investor in our scheme, like so many of the rich and powerful in this city. Also a client of my establishment on Bedlow Street, although he has no idea the two are connected, of course."

Justy sighed. "Your point?"

"My point being that I am doing nothing more than trying to build a business here. Providing a service to men like Mr. Barnes, of whom there are many. It may not be the most socially acceptable enterprise, but prostitution is not illegal in this state, and there is no law that says I cannot profit from it."

Justy felt a flash of anger. "There is a law against trading in human beings. Here, at least."

"Indeed, but is slavery any worse than prostitution? I'd argue it was better. What woman would not prefer to be owned and kept and cared for by a wealthy man, rather than being rented by the hour, to be used and used again, until she is used up, and thrown away? Ownership is far more humane. And besides, our patrons prefer it."

He leaned back against the table and folded his arms. "Now, when our shipment arrives in a few days, its contents will be smuggled to Bedlow Street. Soon they will be sold to the highest bidder, in an exclusive, fabulously luxurious auction. The buyers will receive a notice of ownership, and their property will be housed with us. In return for that accommodation, the owner will enter into a contract that allows us to share his property with other members. The degree of sharing will be determined by the level of membership. The higher the level, the more exclusive to the member the property will be. That way the house makes money on both ends, by charging membership fees, and user fees."

"Good holy Christ." Justy's voice curdled with contempt. "How do you sleep at night?"

"I sleep perfectly well." Colley's voice was like ice.

Justy's lethargy had evaporated. His heart pounded, and he felt like a ship's spar reefed tight in a storm: one tiny gust and he might snap. "You wear the clothes of a gentleman, Colley, but you may as well be rolling about with the rats in the Portsmouth gutter you were born in. You are filth."

Colley gathered himself. A muscle twitched in his jaw. "I am doing my very best to control myself here."

Justy clenched his teeth. "I would rather you let yourself off the leash."

Colley hammered his fist into the table. "Good God, man. Don't you understand what is happening here? This venture is a partnership. I am only one of the partners. There are others involved who are not so understanding as I, who do not hold you in the same regard. Were it not for me, you would have been found facedown in the docks a long time ago."

"That's a lot of cock," Justy snapped. "If there's any reason I'm still alive, it's because of the Bull."

Colley was silent. Justy sneered. "That's right. I know he has a spoon in the stew. I'm assuming he's a partner. I can't see him running this close to the law without taking a stake."

Colley nodded. His face was tight. "Very well. You have me. Your uncle has indeed been watching over you. There are those who would have had you killed the moment you started asking questions about William Duer. But your uncle forbade it. And I have supported him."

"Why?"

"Because I value you. You are an intelligent man. I saw that the first time I met you. You're hungry, you're determined and you have as steely a spine as any young man I've seen since the war. My God, when you had that knife of yours out earlier, I was sure I was done for. But it was your restraint that really impressed me. You're that rare breed, a man of action who uses his brain. That's the kind of man I need with me."

Justy laughed. "You want me to join you? Let's say for one moment that I decide to believe that you didn't have a hand in my own father's murder, why would I want any part of this dirty business of yours?"

This time, the smile reached Colley's eyes. "For the money."

For the money. Justy felt dizzy. He put a hand on the table to steady himself. Portraits of men looked down at him from the walls. The table, he realized, was made from a single piece of wood. The tree it came from must have been enormous, he thought. The wood was cool under his hand, the carpet soft as newly picked cotton under his feet. The chairs were luxuriously padded and upholstered in leather. The room smelled of wood polish and leather soap and fresh cigar smoke and old brandy. It smelled of money.

Colley's eyes gleamed. "My agents tell me the cargo is of exceptional quality. When it arrives, in just a few days, a week at the most, the money will begin to flow like a river. More auctions will follow. And our little scheme, what you choose to call a fraud, will end. We will have no need for new investors. The dividends we pay our shareholders will be genuine proceeds, from a real business. And we will become very wealthy men. You too, if you join us."

Justy tasted a sticky bile on his tongue. "Fuck you, and your filthy trade. I call your bluff, Jack. I'm going to your investors.

They're all in town for this Manumission conference, so it'll be easy. I'll go to Hamilton. And Burr. They may hate each other, but they'll hate what you're doing a good deal more. I'll tell them what their money is really buying, and I'll burn you to the goddamned ground."

Colley laughed. "Why not spill a barrel of whale oil down the steps of Federal Hall and set it alight while you're about it? You say you'll burn me to the ground, but all you'll end up doing is putting a torch to the city. Perhaps even the country."

"You overestimate your own importance."

"Do I?" Colley's smile was as thin as a razor cut. "Think about it. Some of the most influential men in the country have their money with us. You mentioned Hamilton and Burr. And Troup. Well, here are some other names to think of: Clinton. Van Buren." The smile widened slightly. "Adams."

"You're lying."

"Indeed I am not. The President came on board just before the election in '97. A paltry investment, I grant you, but the weight of his involvement is worth far more than the actual sum."

Justy's head spun. There was no way to tell if Colley was lying, but, as usual, he sounded utterly plausible. Justy desperately wanted to sit down. But he was determined to stay on his feet. He leaned his hip against the edge of the table. "Even if you've managed to kimbaw some topping men into your dirty sham, that doesn't mean you've got New York by the nutmegs. And it doesn't make you any less of a gammon-hawking, bully-trap madge."

Colley raised a hand to his mouth. "Good heavens, Justice! Such colorful language!"

"Well, you grew up in the gutter, Jack, so I reckon you're flash."

Colley's eyes flickered. "Yes. I speak cant well enough. And I may as well tell you, I object to being referred to as a woman's fundament."

Justy leaned over him. "I call a spade a spade, Jack. And I call you a cheat and a liar. I wonder what your investors will call you, when I spill."

"You'll be taking a pretty risk if you do, kiddy." Colley's accent had slipped now, and his words were edged with the Portsmouth dockyard. "Because if you turn conk and sell me to those coves, think what'll happen next. They'll cry beef and sell, and they'll do so hard."

"So what? That'll put you in the ground, and that's what I want."

Colley sneered. "You ain't learned much, have you, chub? That's not how things work on Wall Street. When one venture goes down, if it goes down hard enough, it brings everything with it. The whole lot. That's what happened in '92, and if you snitch, it'll happen again. Coves won't just sell out of our scrap; they'll sell out of everything. Some because they'll feel like they can't trust any investment, others because they'll have borrowed money to invest in our venture and they'll have to sell everything they own to pay those loans back. Either way, it'll be a bloodbath."

"You look scared, Jack."

"Any sensible man would be." Colley plucked at his cuffs, restoring his composure. "I can see you think I'm overegging the pudding, but I can assure you I am not. Investors do not act as individuals. They're like a herd of sheep. They go where their leaders go. It doesn't matter how small their investments are, if Hamilton or Adams sells his entire holding, the other investors will do likewise. It will spur another Panic."

He stopped. He touched a finger to his lips. "Your mother died of fever, did she not?"

Justy said nothing.

Colley smiled his thin smile. "Well, perhaps you will understand me when I tell you that a Panic unfolds in exactly the same way as a fever, and it can be every bit as quick and deadly. As soon as anyone with means gets wind of a bad outbreak of fever, they leave the city, do they not? To stay in the city risks death. Investors react in the same way. They start to sell up, and for the same reason, because to stay in the market risks ruin. They remember what happened in '92, how so many were wiped out, and they get out. The more of them that sell, the further prices fall. The hardheaded ones stay on for a bit longer, hoping prices will pick up after a few days, but as the ink gets redder, those men sell up, too. Now fear takes hold, and fear is like the worst fever that ever swept through this city. And it can take many more lives. If fear is allowed to sink its fangs into the market, trust and confidence will disappear. All investment will stop. Not just here, but right across the country. Ships won't sail, coal won't be dug, cotton won't be picked and workers won't be paid. Hunger. Disease. Destitution. War." The smile was gone. "And you, Justice Flanagan, will be responsible."

He let his words hang in the quiet of the room. The sound of laughter drifted from the taproom through the half-open door. He lolled back in his chair and crossed his legs. "Do I look scared to you now, boy?"

Justy's mouth was dry. "You look damned."

Colley's eyes crinkled. "Damned. That's rum. Perhaps I am." He examined his fingers. "You certainly will be. If you do as you have threatened. I'm not talking for myself here, but for my partners. If they suspect that you might start to raise a hue and cry against us in the coffee shops, with our investors or with the Manumission people, then you will be stopped, and violently so."

"I'll take my chances."

Colley closed his eyes for a moment. "I want you to remember that you pushed me to this point, Justice. I had no wish to take things this far."

Justy felt a chill in his guts. "What are you talking about?"

"Timing is everything in trade. Had you started your investigations a month from now, I would be paying you no more attention than I would a fly buzzing about my head. This, however, is a most delicate time. You have knowledge that in a month would have no effect, but which disseminated today could upset plans that have been carefully laid and require precise execution. I cannot allow anything to go awry, not least because I have so much of my own fortune at stake in this. Which is why I am now upping the stakes for you."

Justy frowned. "I have nothing at stake in this."

"Oh, but you do. By threatening what is precious to me, you force me to threaten what is precious to you. Your friends."

Justy smiled. "Lars can look after himself."

"Your sailor friend? I don't doubt it. Would you say the same for Kerry O'Toole?"

Justy held his breath. The blood sang in his ears, a long, high-pitched whine. He heard the clock tick in the hallway, and the sound of the men carousing in the taproom.

"Leave her out of it."

"I cannot. You seem to care little for your own life, so I need something else. The look in your eyes confirms how much you care for Kerry."

"You wouldn't dare. Kerry is O'Toole's daughter. And O'Toole is the Bull's right hand."

Colley laughed drily. "Your uncle is a businessman, and this partnership represents a great deal of money to him. And O'Toole is eminently replaceable."

Justy thought of Kerry taking off her hat, her long, dark hair falling over her shoulders.

"What if I promise to say nothing?"

"You know that's not enough. My partners will need firm assurances, as do I. You will need to bind yourself to us."

"Bind myself?"

"Join us. Join me."

Justy felt breathless. His laughter was a dry croak. "You're insane."

"If it makes it easier for you, you may think so." Colley's lips were a bloodless slash. "Your choice, Justice. Join me, or lose her."

Justy gripped the top of the chair. He sat down slowly. His mind turned. He remembered saying good-bye to Kerry, the day before he left New York, four years before. It was a hot day, and she was helping with the laundry. She wore a long blue dress, but she had rolled her sleeves up to her elbows. She had pinned up her hair, but wisps still hung about her face, and there was sweat on her upper lip. She was tall and gangly, with huge green eyes that had filled with tears when he said good-bye, and she had hugged him hard, refusing to let go, refusing to let him see her face. And now she was a woman, and he remembered how she looked when he had seen her last and how the pulse that had leapt into his throat felt when she had touched his hand.

"How?" he asked.

"You'll sign some papers. We'll have a small induction ceremony. To welcome you."

To incriminate him. To drag him down into hell. Well, at least he would meet his father there. Justy swallowed the bile on his tongue. "I need time to decide."

"Time is a luxury neither of us can afford in this instance."

"Nevertheless. You cannot expect me to just abandon my principles here and now."

Colley stood. "Very well. You have until six this evening. Come to my house. Number Twenty-Eight Cherry Street. And I should warn you. We'll be watching."

TWENTY-SEVEN

Justy felt eyes on him, the whole way down to the docks. His mind whirled. He needed to warn Kerry, but he had no idea how to find her. She was unlikely to be at her cousin's house until evening, and there was no point at all in going to O'Toole's. She'd be on the streets somewhere, picking pockets, he supposed. But where? And how to get to her without leading Colley's men there, too?

Lars put two men on the *Netherleigh*'s gangway, with orders to stop anyone boarding. He and Justy sat in the fo'c'sle of the ship, on a pair of waterlogged pallets. The space smelled of wet wood and raw wool, but as far as Justy was concerned, it was the safest place in New York.

"Colley's dogs'll be watching the ship. Is there another way off?"

Lars shrugged. He picked his teeth with a sliver of wood pulled from the pallet. "We could lower a boat over the far side and row over to the next wharf. They might not have thought of that."

"That might work."

"So you're going to tell Colley no, then?"

"Are you joking? I'm not going to tell him a goddamned thing. I'm not going anywhere near the bastard, or his dirty scheme. I'm going to find Kerry and scour off."

"You might have your work cut out, convincing her."

"She'll see sense."

"All right, then. Say she does. How will you get out of the city? You can't hide her on the ship."

"I know." The naval ships of the line were big enough to hide stowaways, and sailors often smuggled whores on board. But on a small ship like the *Netherleigh*, without the knowledge and cooperation of the crew it would be impossible. Once the sailors discovered her, all hell would break loose, and Lars would never work on board a ship again.

Justy shifted on the sodden pallet. The leather seat of his breeches stuck to the wood. "Maybe her cousin Lew can help us."

"What about your uncle?"

"Jesus, no. I don't want anything from that madge."

Lars pulled a fresh sliver of wood loose from the pallet. "You think he knew about your da being kilt?"

"I don't know. I don't even know for sure if Colley knew. He denied it, but he would. I know he's lying about something, but I don't know what."

Justy rubbed his face with both hands. His head ached. He had made so many mistakes. Colley and his partners must have been watching him almost as soon as he arrived and started asking questions about Duer. That fat warden, Desjardins, must have told them. He was probably a member of the Tontine or the Firecake Club, perhaps even a client at the brothel. Justy cursed himself for being a fool. He had set a pretty trap for Drummond and put them on to Cantillon as well. There was no way he was going to do the same to Kerry.

"Can you send a couple of your lads around the alehouses? See if we can get a message to her?" he asked.

"Surely. What are you going to do?"

"I'll look, too. There's one place I think she might be. And it's the last place Colley would expect."

The ruse worked. Lars rowed him over to Spice Island Wharf, and Justy worked his way up the alleys, checking behind him every few paces, doubling back and calling on his sixth sense until he was sure he hadn't been followed.

Eventually he reached Nassau Street. He waited in the shadows cast by the setting sun, watching the people walking up and down Wall Street. The Trinity Church bell struck the half hour. Four and a half hours to go, after which the hounds would be let loose and he'd be running for his life. Colley might already have people watching the docks and the roads. Justy's best hope was to get Kerry and hide out somewhere they couldn't be found, where Campbell and Fraser wouldn't be welcome. Canvas Town. Kerry would know people, or her cousin might help. They could wait until Colley thought they had slipped the net, and then find a way out of the city. Hide in a crate of smoked fish. Or a wagon of night soil.

A carriage drew up sharply to the curb in front of him. A big man in a long brown dustcoat jumped off the cab and opened the door. A gentleman in his late fifties stepped down into the street. He was dressed in a lovat-green coat and buff-colored breeches. His thinning gray hair was brushed down over his forehead. He had a sharp, intelligent face, with a long nose and a pointed chin. He was carrying a small black bag, and as he stood on the sidewalk, blinking in the sunlight, he looked every bit like a country doctor just arrived in the city.

"Mr. Hamilton! Mr. Secretary!" A man in a black tricorn hat shoved past Justy, brandishing a roll of paper in his hand. Justy stared. He had seen Alexander Hamilton once before, ten years ago, at George Washington's inauguration, right there on the steps of Federal Hall. Justy remembered a youthful, ruddy-faced, twinkle-eyed man, with a slight double chin and a coat that strained against his middle. This Hamilton looked twenty years older. The plumpness had melted from his face and body, his eyes were ringed with dark circles and his cheeks were pale, hollow and veined and patched with red.

Hamilton held up a hand. "I am no longer the secretary of anything, sir," he said to the man in the hat. "I am a private citizen. I cannot help you."

The bodyguard in the brown dustcoat steered the man in the hat away. Hamilton pulled a watch out of his pocket and frowned at it.

Justy felt as though his feet had grown roots. He could not move. His mouth was dry. All he had to do was take two steps forward and speak, and it would be done.

Hamilton snapped his watch shut. His head turned, as though he could feel Justy watching him. His blue eyes were sharp, quizzical. He watched Justy for a moment, and then he nodded once and walked away, down Wall Street, to the Tontine.

Justy watched him go, Colley's words thumping in his head. *Join me, or lose her.*

Hamilton reached the steps of the Tontine Coffee House. He shook hands with another man, short and moonfaced, with a button nose and a scurf of fair hair. Together they climbed the steps, Hamilton holding tight to the railings.

Join me, or lose her.

A prickling sensation along Justy's spine made him freeze. He was about to spin on his heel, but he was stopped by the feeling of something sharp and pointed, pressed against his neck.

"Don't move a goddamned finger." A whisper. A familiar voice. But one with a steely edge that made the blood thump in his forehead.

"Kerry?"

"I told you. Don't move. Keep your eyes on the street. And keep your fucking mouth shut, or I'll cut you."

"Jesus, Kerry . . ." He felt the sting of the knife piercing the skin under his ear, and then a trickling sensation. "Christ!"

"I told you," she hissed. "Eyes on the road. Mouth shut."

He went very still. He kept his eyes front, not seeing, aware only of the blade a fraction of an inch from the artery in his neck.

"I'm only going to tell you this once." Her voice was louder now, harsher. "Stop following me. I don't care what you want, or what you have to say. Just stay away. Leave me be."

If you cut a man once, even slightly, he will lose sensation around the area of the wound for a time. So, if you have a blade resting on his neck, he will not notice immediately when you take it away. Justy wondered who had taught Kerry that little trick, because as soon as he had the feeling that the blade had lifted and had turned to catch her, she was long gone.

He slumped against the wall, feeling the sweat trickle out of his armpits. A couple passing by on the street gave him an odd look, and he straightened up, pulling at his coat. He put his fingers to his neck. A tiny cut, not much more than a pinprick. He sucked blood from his fingertips and pulled up his cravat to cover the wound. He felt a sneaking admiration. She was as quick and stealthy and deft with a knife as anyone he had ever met.

Leave me be. Well, that was plain enough. Except that he could not leave her be, not now. Not yet. Not with Colley after her.

He sighed. Perhaps Lars would have an idea of how to convince her to hear him out. He stepped into the street, dancing between the carriages, avoiding the heaps of shit-caked straw until he was safe on the other side. He used a curbstone to scrape something off the sole of his boot and joined the flow of people heading down the hill, towards the docks.

He only saw her by chance. She must have known that he would keep an eye out, so she had removed the bright green caubeen hat and tucked her hair into the collar of her coat. It was a risky play, but slouching along, head down, she could still pass for an apprentice boy too slovenly or lazy to cut his hair.

And Justy would have missed her, had she not been jostled by a careless tradesman hefting an empty barrel. She was making the turn on Broad Street when the man cannoned into her, turning her shoulder slightly and revealing her profile. It was less than the blink of an eye, but it was enough. Justy saw the green eyes, the tea-colored skin, and he shoved his way through the crowd and onto Broad Street, ignoring the carriages that sped past. A coachman roared curses at him and struck at him with his whip. Justy barely heard him. He reached the other side, steadied himself with a hand on the wall, stood on his toes and looked down Broad Street. It was bustling with shoppers, less well-heeled than those on Wall Street. Smoke rose from braziers and the air was loud with tradesmen's cries. He craned his neck, his eyes skipping back and forth over the heads of the throng of shoppers. She was gone.

And then she was there, a half head taller than the people around her, despite the slouch, sunlight touching the head of straight, glossy hair as she passed Beaver Street and ducked into an alley. Justy followed, using his shoulders to drive through the crowd until he reached the narrow lane.

It was strangely silent. High stone walls, less than an arm's span apart, seemed to shut out all the noise of the street. Justy's ears whined in the quiet and he felt the tension in his shoulders. He stepped forward, cautiously, half-expecting her to jump out from a doorway, but there was nothing.

The alley was rough underfoot, paved with odd pieces of stone. Water trickled down a gutter in the center of the lane. Justy walked carefully, his boot heels grating on the loose stone, following the line of the gutter as it curved downhill. His eyes caught a movement, a door closing a few yards away. He stepped quickly down the hill and pushed the door.

It opened on to a long, narrow room, empty except for a line of ale barrels stacked against the left wall. There was no plaster on the walls, the bricks were exposed and everything was covered with a thick layer of dust. A single narrow window above the door provided the only source of light.

The room was quiet. There was a musty smell of stale beer and rat droppings. Justy felt more than heard the man behind him. He spun around, but the man was already on him. Silent. Heel scraping down his calf, hand reaching for his mouth. It was a textbook attack from behind. One that he had practiced and executed many times himself.

His half turn wasn't much, but it was enough to put his attacker off balance. Justy jerked his head back, feeling the soft crunch of the man's nose against his skull. He pushed hard off his left heel, shoving the man into the wall, and pivoted away, reaching into his boot for his knife.

The man leaned back, his left hand pressed against the bloody mess of his nose. Justy recognized the narrow shoulders and the tight green coat.

Turner wiped his face and flicked the blood away, then pushed himself off the wall. In his right hand, he held a long, thin knife.

The Marshal sniffed hard and spat a lump of bloody phlegm onto the dusty floor. Then he dropped into a crouch, his knife held out in front of him. He slid his right foot forward, so that he almost turned to the side.

Justy stood still. Turner was a foot shorter than Justy, which meant he was at a disadvantage when it came to reach, but he looked fast and lithe, despite his age. Justy knew that a lower center of gravity could help a shorter man in a knife fight, and he could tell by the way that Turner crouched, making his profile as narrow as possible behind the point of his knife, that Turner had plenty of experience with a blade.

The Marshal shuffled forward, and what light there was glimmered down the long curve of the knife. There was no guard on the smooth wooden handle. Turner wore gloves. Justy remembered the bandage he'd seen on the Marshal's hand. "My God! It was you!"

"Me what?"

"You killed those girls. The ones with the marked faces."

Turner sniffed and spat again. "Who says?"

"The cut on your hand says. You should have used a chive with a guard. And you forgot to wear gloves."

Turner sneered. "Is that the best you can do? A bloody finger? Who says I didn't do it cutting a piece of cheese?"

"Did you?"

Turner gave him a steady look. "No."

Justy nodded. He pressed the catch on the handle of his knife and the blade snapped out.

Turner smiled, and Justy felt the tightness in his chest, the fear like a pot of bubbling pitch. He was not much of a knife fighter. He had learned how to kill a sentry and survive a desperate tangle with a soldier in the heat of battle. But a cold-blooded duel with a professional was something else entirely.

Turner's eyes were hard and watchful. He was waiting for Justy to drop into the fighter's crouch, to start the ritual of circling, jabbing and sounding each other out.

Instead, Justy ran. Straight at Turner, exploding off his left foot, driving hard across the room. At the same time, he swapped the knife from his right hand to his left, slicing the blade down at Turner's own knife as he lunged forward.

It broke every rule of knife fighting, and it took Turner by surprise. Justy felt the shock in his hand as the two knives clashed. He ignored the pain in his fingers and drove his head forward, aiming at the pulp of Turner's nose.

Turner was quick. He stepped back and ducked his chin, then forced himself upwards, so that Justy's forehead hammered against the solid bone of the top of Turner's skull. It was like running into a wall. Everything went white for a moment, and Justy felt his knees wobble under him. He closed his eyes, wrapped his right arm tight around Turner and drove him backwards into the wall. He dropped his knife, grabbing for Turner's right arm, but he missed, slamming his own hand into the bricks. He was aware of a blur of movement as Turner swung his knife blindly upwards, and then there was a searing pain in the back of his head as the knife slid across his skull.

He slammed his left shoulder into the wall, trapping Turner's arm. He heard screaming. The knife jabbed at his head, again and again, as Turner tried to get his arm loose for a killing stroke. Justy forced his left hand up, his knuckles scraping themselves raw on the coarse bricks and uneven mortar. He grabbed Turner's left elbow and squeezed his thumb hard into the soft tissue below the joint. Turner grunted. Justy knew he had hit on a pressure point, a nerve that led all the way up to Turner's hand. All he had to do was squeeze tight and the Marshal would be forced to drop his knife.

It took ten seconds, but it felt six times as long. Turner jerked his knee upwards, again and again, but Justy angled his thigh to deflect him. Turner's face was slick with sweat and blood, his breath rasping as Justy hugged him as hard as he could, his thumb and fingers like a vice on the nerve in Turner's arm.

The knife bounced off Justy's shoulder and made a tinkling sound as it fell to the floor. Justy pushed Turner back and drove his own knee hard into the Marshal's groin.

Turner let out a sound, somewhere between a wheeze and a screech, and doubled over. Justy shoved him hard, sticking out his foot so that Turner tripped and went down like a felled tree, both hands clutching at his balls. Justy stepped around him and kicked him hard in the face. The Marshal went limp.

Justy stood over Turner, his chest heaving, his vision darkening around the edges. He staggered back against the barrels and leaned forward, his head between his legs. There was a roaring in his ears.

He felt a hand on his shoulder and he swung wildly and spun away. Where was his knife?

"Steady on there, big fella."

He looked up at the familiar voice. The big sailor seemed to fill the room.

"Lars. What are you doing here?"

Lars grinned. "I followed you up from the wharf. I wanted to keep an eye on you. I lost you in the alley out there, but then I heard you squawking like a butchered hen."

"That was me?"

"Aye." Lars grabbed him by the shoulders. "Now come on. We have to get out of here."

Justy shook his head. He was still breathing hard. "We have to question him."

Lars stared. "You're mad."

Justy used his boot to roll Turner onto his back. He was unconscious. Justy picked up his knife, wiped it on Turner's coat, folded it and tucked it away. He walked to the end of the room. The door opened on to a large room, a warehouse floor, empty and dusty.

He turned back. "We're going to have to be creative."

"Don't do this, Justy."

Justy picked up Turner's knife. The handle was sticky with blood. The fingers of his left hand throbbed, like a burn from a hot iron. Turner had cut them deep, down to the bone.

"Your head as well, lad," Lars said softly.

Justy put his hand up. It came back sticky with blood. "We have to be quick then. Wake him up."

Lars looked at him, something in his eyes.

Justy pointed the knife. "He's the one killed those Negro girls, Lars."

"So tell the law."

"He is the law. And he's in it with Colley. I don't know how, but Colley warned me he couldn't keep me safe from his other partners, so I reckon he's one of them. He must have followed me up from the wharf."

Lars looked skeptical. "Can't be. I was following you, remember. No one saw you come off that ship."

Justy looked at him. Something writhed inside his head, a truth he didn't want to face. He pushed it away.

"Get him up."

Justy shifted one of the barrels into the center of the room. Lars knelt beside the unconscious Marshal and put his hand over his mouth. The blood in his nose bubbled, and Turner's body convulsed. His eyes sprang open. He flailed an arm, but Lars held him tight.

"Easy now," Lars said gently. He stood Turner up and pushed him back against the barrel. Justy unwrapped the silk scarf from around Turner's neck. He used the knife to notch one end, then tore it lengthways in two. He knotted the two pieces of silk together and used them to tie Turner's arms behind the barrel.

Turner stood straight, his face tight, his eyes blazing.

"I am a Marshal of this city."

Justy stepped up to him. "I know exactly what you are, you murdering bastard." He waved the knife in front of Turner's face. "You spent your time on the line, so you know how this goes. Interrogate the enemy soldier as soon as possible after capture."

Turner said nothing. His eyes flickered.

Justy nodded. "Usually, I'd start with your fingers. I'd just keep breaking them and pulling out the nails until you spilled your guts. But I haven't got time, and it'll be too noisy anyway. So we'll move straight to the main event."

He slid the knife under the fold in Turner's waistcoat and

slid it upwards. The buttons skittered away across the floor as he cut them loose. Turner's waistcoat hung open.

"Good to see you keep your chive sharp." Justy reversed the blade, pushing it into the top of Turner's shirt and cutting downwards. The linen opened easily, revealing Turner's chest, pale and covered in black hair. There was a puckered scar above his left nipple.

Justy placed the tip of the knife on the scar. Turner's eyes opened wide. He shuddered and Justy felt nausea and shame twist his guts. He took a long, deep breath and separated himself from the horror of what he was about to do. It was like looking through a window at a version of himself, leaning close to Turner, the knife in his hand.

He used the tip of the knife to draw a circle around the scar. "Where'd you get this?"

"Valley Forge." Turner's voice was hoarse. The sweat was fresh on his forehead. It beaded and rolled down the side of his face to mingle with the blood from his nose.

"So you and Colley were comrades-in-arms, then?"

Turner nodded.

Justy used a finger of his left hand to pull the band of Turner's breeches away from his belly. He slipped the point of the knife in and sawed gently downwards. More buttons popped and the breeches came loose, falling and pooling around Turner's knees. Justy cut the rest of his shirt open to reveal the Marshal's underdrawers. Turner's breath was coming fast now, his chest heaving in short bursts.

"Turner. That's not a Jewish name, is it?" Turner blinked rapidly and Justy felt a coolness wash over him. "You'll still have the twizzle on the end of your tool, then."

He held the knife up in front of Turner's right eye. "The Romans used to circumcise their enemies. It was an alternative to castration. If you take a man's tallywags, he can bleed to death. But snipping the old foreskin is rarely fatal, unless it gets infected." He leaned closer. "Bleeds like a waterfall, mind you. And hurts like a swive with Satan himself."

Turner's face was gray, his legs shaking. Justy's voice was a whisper. "You don't believe I'll do it, do you, Turner? You don't believe I've got the sand to cut off the end of a man's cock, to make him bleed like a stuck pig and scream like all the devils in hell are jabbing spears into his pipe."

His nose was almost touching the bloody mess on Turner's face now, the tip of the knife a hair's breadth from his eyeball. He pushed his fingers into the top of Turner's drawers and pulled gently. Looked hard into Turner's eyes. "You'd better hope my hand doesn't slip."

"No!" Turner's voice was hoarse, clotted with the blood from his broken nose. His eyes rolled in his skull like a frightened horse's.

Justy didn't move. "Who sent you after me?"

"No one."

"Not Black Jack?"

Turner's head shook fractionally, his eyes locked on the blade. "He wanted to protect you. Him and your uncle. They said they'd get you to join us and stop with your questions. But I knew you'd have no part of it."

"How?"

Turner's eyes flashed. "I know your type. You think you're better than the rest of us. Pure. Just like your father."

Justy felt his pulse quicken. "You knew my father then?"

"Oh aye. Billy Duer's pup, I used to call him, because he was always rolling over to have his fucken' tummy tickled."

Justy ignored the jab. "How did you know Duer? Were you one of his partners?"

Turner choked out a laugh. "No. I wasn't a partner. I worked for him. Did his dirty laundry, you might say."

"Whose dirty laundry are you doing today? Killing Negro girls and marking them up to look like whores?"

Turner spat. "They were whores."

Justy leaned in closer, cheek to cheek. "You're wrong, Turner. I'm not like my father at all. You see, I used to think I was pure. But you English bastards cured me of that."

He swayed back and held the knife up, twisting it so that it caught the light. Then he pointed it at Turner's groin.

Turner's knees sagged. He looked drained, his face pale.

"Why did you kill the girls?" Justy asked.

"They were from the kip on Bedlow Street." Turner's voice was dull. "We bought twelve girls from the Frogs in Louisiana. Set them up in the house a month ago. Those four ran away. They pretended they knew no English, but I saw them listening when we talked about the plan. They understood rightly. So they had to be stopped."

"Did Colley know?"

"Aye. I told him."

"And my uncle?"

"Him too."

Justy felt a sudden flare of anger. He grabbed Turner by the throat and squeezed. Turner made a gagging sound. His face turned red, then purple.

And then Justy was on the ground, his head ringing. He rolled onto his back. Lars stood over him.

"That's enough," the big man said.

Justy groped for the knife. Lars kicked it away. "Enough, I said."

"But I'm not finished."

Lars' face was like thunder. "Yes, you are."

TWENTY-EIGHT

Lars dragged Justy out of the warehouse by the collar. Then he followed, grim and silent, as Justy led the way through the network of alleys to Cantillon's house. The gate was open, but the door was locked, and as he tried to use Turner's knife to lift the latch it was opened from inside.

"Jesus Mary!" Sarah Boswell leapt backwards. The broom she was carrying clattered to the floor.

"Sarah! What are you doing here?"

"Me? I work here, remember?" She clapped a hand to her breast. "Sweet Christ! What you done to yourself?"

Justy touched his head. His fingers were sticky with blood. "Don't worry about me. Did you know Mr. Cantillon is dead?"

"Yes. Some crusher name of Turner came round this morning and told me. He said he got drunk and fell in the East River. Poor Jarlath. I didn't know what to do when I 'eard, so I just kept cleaning. Been cleaning ever since." Her eyes brimmed.

"I'm sorry, Sarah."

She brushed a hand over her face. "Don't mind me. What about you?"

There was a large ewer of water and a wide, shallow basin on the table in the middle of the room. Justy picked up the jug and poured water over his head. A wave of pain made him stagger. He felt hands grasping him, and he let Lars sit him down. Sarah pulled his coat off. She gasped. His shirt was soaked in blood.

"Not all mine," he muttered.

"Off," she ordered.

Lars stood in the corner of the room, leaning on the wall, watching as Justy stripped and Sarah Boswell washed him down, examining him for cuts. She tore the shirt into strips and used them to bandage his hand, then made him lean forward as she washed his head.

She winced. "These cuts are deep, Justice. You need a surgeon to sew them. There's one lives two doors down from here. I'll get him."

Justy shook his head. It felt twice its normal size, throbbing. "Just wash them clean, then brush the hair back. I'll get them seen to later."

She pressed her lips together and poured the water over Justy's head. He gritted his teeth. Looking down, his head between his legs, he saw the water run scarlet into the white bowl and onto the tiled floor.

He dried his hair carefully with a towel. "I need to borrow one of Carrots' shirts, Sarah. It'll be too small, but I'll roll up the sleeves."

"You're cracked. You need those cuts stitched and into bed, right away." She stood beside the table, her hands on her hips, her bonnet tipped onto the back of her head. Her white apron was streaked and spotted, like a butcher's.

"A shirt, please, Sarah. And no arguments."

She rolled her eyes and walked out of the scullery. Lars was looking at him, expressionless.

"What?" Justy snapped.

"What was that? Back there . . ."

"That was me questioning a prisoner, Lars. That's all."

"Questioning? You damn nearly killed him!"

"Not even close. I wanted him to think I'd kill him, so that he'd tell me the rest of it. Who killed Drummond. And

Cantillon. And my father. And he would have, if you hadn't stopped me."

Lars shook his head. "I saw it, Justy. In your eyes. You were like . . . someone else."

"Don't be soft!" But Justy felt the shame crawling over his skin as he remembered the sense of power he had felt at Turner's helplessness. Cutting open his clothes. Pressing the knife against his groin. He felt a wash of relief that Lars had stopped him from doing what he might have done.

They sat, looking at the floor, listening to the sound of Sarah's footsteps coming down the hallway. She bustled into the scullery and tossed a shirt to Justy. The sleeves stopped in the middle of his forearms and the shirt bloused around his waist. He tucked it in tight and rolled up the sleeves.

"How do I look?"

"Like a sorry shag-bag, I'd say." Lars' eyes crinkled at the corners, and Justy grinned like a fool, his skin prickling with relief.

"So what now?" Lars asked.

Justy struggled into his coat. "Now I go up to Federal Hall."

Lars snorted. "Jesus, your woman here has it right. You are cracked."

"No, I'm not, Lars. I have to get the law involved. It'll make sense when this is over. You'll see." He held out his hand. "Give me the knife."

Lars took Turner's knife from his pocket and dropped it in the basin. Justy washed the blood off, dried the long blade with a piece of his ripped shirt and wrapped it in the linen. "Where are you meeting your lads?"

"The Norwegian place. At four."

"I'll see you there. If you find Kerry first, bring her." He touched the tiny cut under his ear. "She may not want to come, but try and persuade her."

"Persuade? How hard?"

"Just do your best."

Sarah looked indignant. "Who's this Kerry?"

Lars winked. "Don't you worry, *a chara;* it's a friend of his, not of mine. I'm fancy-free."

"Ignore him," Justy said. He reached for Sarah's hand. "Thank you."

She brushed him away. "You nearly 'ad me in an early grave, coming in like that. Don't think I'm going to forgive you in a hurry."

"I'm sorry. I'll make it up to you. I promise."

"I'll believe that when I see it." She glanced at Lars. "Promise me you'll make him see a surgeon about those cuts."

The big sailor put a hand on his heart. "On my honor, sweet lady."

She snorted. "Don't mistake me for someone who falls for a lost cause." There was the faintest touch of color in her cheeks.

Lars grinned. "Don't worry, *a chara.* We're a long way from being lost just yet."

TWENTY-NINE

Jacob Hays sat at a wide desk in his office, writing in a ledger. The only other furniture in the room was a single wooden chair in front of the desk. The Marshal looked up as Justy walked in. Hays' face gave nothing away, but it was a moment before he spoke. "I'm told the reason the British wear red is so soldiers in the line can't see their fellows bleed. Perhaps I should lend you my coat."

Justy made a face. The trickling sensation at the back of his neck told him the collar of his shirt was slowly turning pink with bloody water. The rest of his shirt was clean, but blood had soaked through the bandage around his hand, and his forehead was livid with an angry bruise where he had connected with Turner's skull. He decided to be direct.

"I had a fight with Marshal Turner."

Hays stared. "Turner? Where is he?"

"I left him tied up in a warehouse off Broad Street."

"Is this some kind of a joke?"

"No joke. Those four girls who were killed and marked? Turner did it. He confessed. And Drummond and Cantillon? He may have killed them, too."

Hays' face was red. "This is preposterous."

Justy unwound the strip of linen from Turner's knife. "Do you still have that knife sheath that I found up on Church Street? I gave it to you at the morgue."

Hays gave him a blank look. After a moment, he pulled open a drawer. He laid the piece of leather on the desk. Justy placed the knife carefully beside it. "I took that knife from Turner. I think you'll find they're a match."

Hays picked both items up. The steel of the knife slid neatly into the leather pouch. There was a loose piece of leather at the hilt end of the sheath. Hays pulled the leather over the handle of the knife. A smooth brass knob at the base of the knife's handle slipped snugly into a buttonhole in the sheath.

He placed the knife carefully back on the table. "And?"

Justy sat down in the plain wooden chair. "William Duer."

"What about him?"

"Turner used to work for Duer, back in '91. Did you know that?"

Hays frowned. "No."

"It will be easy enough to check. Duer was running a scheme with Colley and Isaac Whippo. And my father. It was a fraud and an immoral business, laid one on top of the other. Turner was their bagman."

Hays' chair creaked as he leaned back. "A fraud, you say?"

"Nothing strictly illegal. But a massive swindle, just the same."

Hays snorted a short laugh. "Like so much of the goings-on on Wall Street. And the immoral business?"

"It was a kind of bespoke brothel. They told investors they were prospecting for gold in Brazil, but really they were procuring Negro girls from plantations in the South. The idea was to ship them to New York, then sell them at auction to rich New Yorkers. They built a house on Bedlow Street, where the clients would be able to warehouse their property, for a fee. Sparing them the inconvenience of having to house them in their own homes. Something their wives might object to, I'd imagine."

"So, slavery and prostitution. Which would certainly make it an immoral enterprise. But not an illegal one. Not in '91."

"No. Not strictly. And besides, the scheme never really got going. Procuring the women proved harder than they expected. And then the whole scheme fell apart in the Panic, when the money ran out."

The sound of singing wafted up from the street below. Hays got up to peer out of the window. "Bloody Quakers," he muttered. "I'm all for Manumission, but these damned boycotts will be the death of the city."

He spun around, his hands clasped tight behind his back. "So. Duer, Colley and Whippo. No surprise there: those three were up to all sorts of flummery before we sent Duer away. But a slave brothel? That is an unexpected low, even for them."

He walked slowly back to his desk and picked up the knife. "What any of this has to do with your assault on Marshal Turner, however, I fail to see."

"Well, I'll tell you." A door slammed somewhere in the building, and there was the sound of someone hurrying along flagstone floors. "They're doing it again. And this time, Turner is in on it."

"Preposterous," Hays said again. But this time his eyes were sharp and Justy could see he was interested. "What do you mean?"

"Colley is replicating the venture. And this time, Turner's one of the partners. The Bull, too. Do you know who Harry Gracie is?"

"Fat fellow. Loud clothes."

"The same. He's the front man for Colley's venture. And he's attracting a lot of capital. His investors don't know where the money goes, but they don't really care, because he's paying sixteen percent returns."

"I've heard." Hays settled back in his chair. "I've also heard he has recruited some big names to back him."

"You heard right. I saw two of them earlier in the street. Alexander Hamilton and Robert Troup."

"Here for the conference, I should imagine."

"No doubt, except I saw them just down the street from here, going into the Tontine together. That made me think they might be meeting to discuss their investment with Mr. Gracie."

Hays steepled his fingers. "Hmm. And being Manumission men, they wouldn't take kindly to the notion of their money going to buy female slaves, would they?"

"They would not. Especially not if they knew what will happen to the women, once they've been sold off and ware-housed in the house on Bedlow Street."

Hays grimaced.

Justy could feel his cuts leaking. He needed to move. He stood up, his chair grating on the floorboards as he pushed it back. He paced in a circle and rested his hands on the back of the chair. "You're worried about the political aspect."

"Of course I am," Hays snapped.

"Well, I don't wish to make you feel any worse about this, but Colley claimed that John Adams is an investor, too."

Hays was very still.

"I threatened Colley," Justy went on. "I told him I'd tell everyone I could what he was up to. He said if I did that, I could spark another Panic. I could bring the market down, and the country with it."

"You could," Hays muttered. "You could very well."

"I could have told Hamilton today. He was right in front of me. I could have walked up to him and told him everything."

"We can thank heaven that you did not." Hays was pale. "Are you absolutely sure about all of this?"

Justy shrugged. "About Adams? I don't know. Colley is capable of any kind of lie. But I believe what he told me about the venture. He boasted about it. He said it's a precise replication of what they planned to do ten years ago. Only this time they've managed to succeed. And Turner confirmed it. He told me the house is already operating. They started with a dozen girls, brought up from Louisiana, but four escaped. Turner hunted them down, killed them and marked them to look like waterfront doxies."

"Turner." Hays reached out and picked up the knife. He turned it over in his hand.

Justy sat down. "Remember the night you found the girl on Church Street?"

"Of course I do."

"Turner was late, if you recall. Half the Watch made it there before him. And his hand was bandaged. Now look at that knife. There's no guard on the handle, so if you're not wearing gloves, and your hand gets slippery with blood or sweat, you're liable to cut yourself. Just like Turner did."

Hays put the knife down. His eyes were hard.

"You say he confessed to killing these women."

"He did."

"What about Drummond and Cantillon?"

"I didn't get a chance to ask him. I was . . . interrupted."

"But you believe he may have killed them. Why?"

Justy sat up straight and rubbed his face. "Because of me. Because of the questions I've been asking about my father."

"Your father?"

"As I said, he was part of the original partnership, with Duer and Colley. He was murdered. That's why I came back to New York, to find out who killed him, and why. I started up at the jail. Someone must have told Turner, and when he heard I'd met Drummond the next day, he decided not to take any chances."

Hays looked skeptical. "Why stop there? Why not kill you, too?"

"The Bull. He was looking out for me. He told the others that he could convince me to join them."

"And Cantillon? Why kill him?"

"Like my father, he was part of the original scheme. But he wasn't involved this time around. He invested in Harry Gracie's venture, not realizing Colley was involved. I think he was happy enough to take the returns at first. He was probably reassured by the sight of people like Hamilton investing as well. But then he got suspicious. He didn't believe Gracie could make that much money honestly. He must have noticed the similarities to the scheme they cooked up in '92. So he started asking questions, although he was a good deal more subtle than I was."

"But not subtle enough, you think?"

"No. He found out what Colley and Turner and their partners were up to. And Turner killed him for it."

Hays stood up, bumping his desk so that a pile of papers spilled across the wood. He looked down his nose at Justy. "Marshal Turner is a trusted and valued member of this administration. What you're telling me is unthinkable. I should have you locked up."

"What for?"

Hays snorted. "What for? You have just admitted to assaulting a Mayor's Marshal!" His eyes were hard and there was a set to his mouth, but Justy had the impression that Hays was playing a part.

"It's strange that Marshal Turner is not here to accuse me, isn't it?" Justy said. "You'd have thought that he would have set up a hue and cry by now."

"Perhaps he is still where you assaulted him. Perhaps you killed him."

"Is that what you think?"

Hays gave him another of his long looks. "No."

He walked to the window, the nailed heels of his glossy shoes clicking on the parquet tiles of the floor. He looked down into the street, his hands clasped behind his back.

"There's a substantial hole in your thesis, Mr. Flanagan. As we both know from our studies, assassins tend to favor a single weapon. If Marshal Turner did indeed kill the women, that makes him a knife man. But both Drummond and Cantillon were garroted."

Justy nodded. "That's true, but if you want to make a murder look like just another waterfront milling, you don't use a specialist tool like a garrote. Before Drummond, when was the last time you saw anyone killed with a wire?"

Hays said nothing. Justy nodded. "I thought so. One doxy killed with a wire would have stood out. And four? That's why Turner had to use a knife. Knife killings happen all the time in this city, and time was, Turner could have filled up the harbor with dead molls and no one would have minded a mote. Turner didn't reckon on these causing such a stir, especially with you."

Hays drew himself up stiffly. "They were human beings. The murder of any citizen is an outrage, regardless of color, or social standing."

Justy smiled slightly. "And if you ignored these killings, the Negro community would be up in arms. And the city would burn."

Hays said nothing. He turned to look out over Wall Street.

Justy could hear the clatter of carriage wheels and the whistle of pastry sellers. He took a deep breath. His head was beginning to ache again, and he could feel a prickling sensation as the blood dried in the cuts. "There's one more thing. The bodies. How could they disappear from the morgue like that?"

Hays shook his head. "The almshouse is lightly guarded. Anyone with half a wit could break in."

"Yes, but why? Why steal the corpses of four unclaimed, unnamed prostitutes? It must have been to prevent you examining them further. Which means the person who stole them, or ordered them stolen, must have known your plans to do so. And how many people knew your plans, Marshal?"

Hays said nothing.

"You're right about the almshouse: a one-eyed monkey could have got past that guard of yours, but you said yourself there was no sign of a break-in. Nothing was disturbed, which means the taker knew his way around the place. Which makes him one of your people, wouldn't you say?"

Hays lowered himself into his chair. Justy could see the conflict in his eyes.

"You told me Turner was a scout in the army, remember?" Justy said.

"What of it?"

"Well, I know what scouts do. They sneak about. They get into places no one else can get into. And they kill. Quick and quiet. And they get a reputation for it. Ask Turner's old comrades. I'm sure there are one or two in the Watch. I wager they'll say he was just as good with a wire as he was with a blade."

Hays nodded. His face looked bone white against the collar of his scarlet coat. "Very well, Mr. Flanagan, you have made your case. Now leave me to look into it."

THIRTY

He checked the warehouse, found Turner gone, then went to the Norwegian alehouse. He arrived a few minutes after the four o'clock bell. Lars was in the same snug with three of his crew. The three sailors looked dirty and ragged in the clean space.

"Any luck?" Justy asked.

"Charlie saw her." Lars nodded at one of the sailors.

"Did you speak to her?" Justy asked the lad.

"Aye. I said she was tae be here at four o' the clock, just like Lars telt me."

"And what did she say?"

The sailor's face reddened. He reached out to pick at the pool of wax on the table. "She telt me to go box maself."

Justy smiled. "Well, that sounds like Kerry, all right. Where was she?"

"The Bowery. South end. Near McGillivray's dance hall."

Justy reached in his pocket and took out a handful of coins. He gave one each to the other two sailors and an extra one to Charlie. He was rewarded with a wide grin.

Lars cuffed Charlie gently around the back of his head. "Don't spend it all in one shop." He jerked his head towards the doorway. "Curfew's at nine, remember."

The three young sailors scrambled their way out of the snug, as quick and lithe as ferrets. Lars waited until their chatter had faded. "I'm only going to say this one time, and then I'll not say any more about it."

Justy rolled his eyes. "Don't tell me you're still cooking about Turner."

Lars slapped his palm on the table. "I don't give a goddamn about Turner."

"What then?"

The pine bench creaked as Lars leaned back. "We did some bad things in Ireland, lad. Terrible things. All of us. Me included." He gave Justy a long stare. "But we didn't enjoy it."

"You're saying I did?"

"I saw that look in your eye."

Justy looked down at the table. The back of his head throbbed. He felt dirty, as though he had fallen into a sewer. As though he stank. Lars was right. A part of him, deep inside, had thrilled with the power he had held over Turner.

"What's wrong with me?" His voice was a whisper.

Lars reached across the table and took him by the shoulder. "Look at me."

The big man's beard bristled, golden in the candlelight. His eyes looked like the open sea. "No one comes back unbroken from what we've seen and done. No one. Some are broke so badly that they can't stand to live no more. But of the ones that live, there's two kinds. There's those who find a way to mend themselves and live out their lives. And there's those that stay broken inside, so that the horror and the pain and the evil takes over. Those men turn into something else. Something you don't want to be. So you have to find a way to mend. If you stay broken, you die inside."

The waitress, Lise, appeared at the door of the snug. She placed two brimming pots on the table. "A boy came. With a message for the red giant." Her mouth twitched. "I told him the giant is not such a big man as he seems."

255

Lars snorted. "Norwegian women are an acquired taste, Justy. The kind of thing you can go off pretty quick, if you wit."

He glared at Lise. "So what's the message? Or are we to be treated to more of your jesting?"

She matched his stare. "You'll be treated to nothing unless you behave with some grace."

There was silence in the snug. Lars stood. He placed his right hand on his chest. "Forgive me, my bird, for speaking to you so."

The slightest incline of her chin. "You are forgiven."

Lars beamed like a small child.

Lise glanced at Justy. There was a triumphant look in her eyes. "The boy said you can find your friend where she first met your father."

She picked up the empty mugs and left.

Justy placed a hand on his chest. "I promise not to tell anyone your secret," he mocked.

Lars smirked. "I believe that's what the financial folks call a hedge."

He took a long drink and wiped his mouth. "Now, come on. You've an appointment to keep."

THIRTY-ONE

The sound of their boot heels echoed off the black flagstones of the church, carrying all the way to the high ceilings, where forbidding-looking saints looked down on them. They walked quickly, side by side down the center aisle. In front of them, the altar was covered in a white cloth, decorated with a long runner of bright green silk.

"Are you sure this is the right place?" Lars whispered.

Justy nodded. "Remember I told you that story about when Kerry was born? After her mother died? O'Toole brought her down here and left her on the steps of the sacristy. The priest asked my father to look after her while the Bull went after O'Toole to calm him down."

Lars looked around. "A good place to meet."

St. Peter's was set a block back from the Broad Way, close to Federal Hall and a long way from either the waterfront or Cherry Street. Neither the Bull nor Colley would look for Kerry there.

The church was empty, but as they reached the altar, the door to the sacristy opened, and a small man in a white surplice appeared.

"Well, well. Justice Flanagan." His voice was surprisingly deep.

"Father." Justy stepped forward and shook the priest's hand. "It's been a long time."

The priest had thinning black hair that he had cropped close to his skull. His face was wrinkled and sunburned, and his eyes were a startling blue. He looked solemn. "I think the last time was when we buried your father."

Justy nodded. "This is Lars Hokkanssen. He's a friend of mine. Lars, Father Michael."

The priest shook Lars' hand. "Norwegian?"

"On my father's side. My mother was from Wexford."

"Beautiful country."

He led them towards the back of the church and down a dark hallway. A door opened into a plain room. The paint on the walls was peeling, and there were holes in the plaster. Against one wall was a table, littered with the remnants of a meal for two: a half loaf of bread, cheese rinds and a small bowl of wizened apples.

Kerry was leaning back in a plain wooden chair, her hands in the pockets of her breeches, her legs thrown out carelessly. But Justy could see the tension in her face, and her eyes were quick and restless.

She gave a half smile. "You remembered then."

"Hard to forget. It was one of my father's favorite stories, coming down here and being presented with you. Wrapped in a piece of green silk, wasn't it, Father?"

"The very same that's there today." Father Michael smiled. "You should have heard her squeal. I thought she'd bring the place down on our heads."

Justy rubbed the tiny cut under his ear. "You'd never have thought she'd turn into such a quiet wee thing, would you?"

They all worked a little to laugh. The priest cleared his throat. "I'll leave you alone, then. I'll be in the church if you need me."

The door closed. Lars leaned against it and folded his arms. Justy sat down and stared at Kerry for a moment. "What are we doing here, Kerry?"

She shrugged, avoiding his eyes. "You said you wanted to meet."

"You didn't seem to want to meet earlier."

"It wasn't safe."

"Safe from whom?"

"Who do you think?"

The cuts in his head burned. "Colley."

She nodded slowly, her eyes on the ground between them.

He reached out and took an apple from the bowl. It had been picked too early and left too long. It would taste bitter. "What do you know about Colley, Kerry?"

"I know he's dangerous. I know he's killed people. I know he'll kill you if you don't do what he wants."

"And how is it you know all this?"

She folded her arms. "I just know."

The room was quiet. Justy turned and looked at Lars. The big man shrugged.

"What else do you know? Do you know about the house on Bedlow Street?"

"Aye. It's a bawdy house. So what?"

"You know Colley owns it? Him and the Bull and some others?"

"Aye."

He felt the anger flare in him again. "You know it's not just a brothel, right? You know he keeps slaves there. Slaves, Kerry. Young Negro girls. Girls like you."

She hugged herself tight and kept her eyes on the floor.

Justy sighed. "You said he'd kill me, but it's not me he threatened."

Her eyes were suddenly sharp. "What do you mean?"

"He wants me to join his scheme. He said if I don't commit to him tonight, he'll kill you. That's why I needed to meet you. To get you out of the city."

"I don't need your help."

He threw the apple, hard. Her right hand plucked it out of the air. She used her thumbnail to slice through the skin and sniffed it. She wrinkled her nose. "How long before you have to give him an answer?"

"Six o'clock."

"Not long, then."

"No."

Her eyes were hard. "You should run."

"Didn't you hear what I said?"

"He won't kill me."

"You said yourself. He's killed men before. Or had them killed, by those hounds of his. He's a slaver, Kerry. And a cock-bawd pimp. You're nothing to him. He wouldn't think twice."

She shook her head. He looked at the apple in her hand. She had driven her thumb up to the hilt into the fruit.

"Kerry."

She looked up. She looked suddenly tired, as though she had resigned herself to something inevitable. He restrained the urge to touch her.

"Why won't he kill you, Kerry?"

She blinked and her eyes were shining with tears.

His voice was soft. "How do you know what you know?"

She gritted her teeth, tears rolling down her cheeks. She wedged her other thumb into the same hole in the apple. "Remember I said I'd made some big mistakes?"

He thought about the weight of her head on his chest, the trembling as she cried.

She sighed, and he could hear the break in her voice. "It was two years ago. I'd been tooling for a half year or so. I was coming home, down Dover Street, and all I see is a drunk gent in a black coat wandering up the hill. Easy pickings. I bumped him, and lifted his mackerel, and then he had me."

She rubbed her wrist. "It was Colley. He'd been at the Bull's house, for a meeting. He pushed me agin the wall and put a blade up by my eye. He said he'd cut both my glimms out, and that's when my hat fell off and he twigged me. He said he'd seen me at the Bull's house once, with O'Toole. He let me go, but he said if I didn't come to see him at his house on Cherry Street the next day, he'd tell the both of them what I was up to."

There was a dull crack. She looked down at the two halves of the apple in her hands, the pale flesh of the fruit and the black pips.

"I did like he said. I went up to Cherry Street. I was scared, you know. If O'Toole found out what I was up to, I'd be sunk. But Colley was nice. He sits me down, asks me if I want something to drink. I'm canny, so I ask for yarum. I figure I'll taste it if he puts rum or anything in it. But it tastes just like regular warm milk, so I drink it down. And at first I'm fine. . . ."

She stopped and squeezed her eyes shut. Her cheeks were wet. Justy leaned forward and took the pieces of apple from her hands.

She hugged herself and took a deep, shuddering breath. "I woke up in his bed." Her voice was a wail. "He was on top of me. He was . . . inside me. I could feel the pain, and the blood. But I couldn't move. It was like I wasn't there and I was there at the same time."

Justy felt like ice, as though he had frozen from the inside. And yet his head was burning, an intense pressure stoking inside his skull. He thought his temples might burst. It was an effort to reach forward, but she shook her head and shrank back, hugging herself even more tightly.

"When it was over, he told me I was his now." Her voice was soft. "He said I had to keep coming back or he'd tell O'Toole and the Bull and then I'd be meat for the street."

"He said that? Meat for the street?"

"Aye."

Justy could hear the sound of his own breath, loud in his ears. "So you went back?"

"What choice did I have?" Her voice was sharp.

He held up his hands. "I'm not saying anything. I'm just asking."

She stared at him. Her eyes were hard. "Aye. I went back. It was either be his whore or everyone else's."

"Why didn't you run?"

She laughed. "Run? Easy for you to say. You've got white skin and a cock, so you can go anywhere and do anything. But if you've got dark skin and a madge, you can only go one place and you can only do one thing, if you're to survive."

Justy felt the shame burning his face. He knew she was right. He looked at the floor and felt the shame curdle into anger. He remembered how carefree she had been. How easily she had laughed. And now Colley had used her up.

"So run with me now," he said. "You're right. On your own, you'd have no chance. But together we can get away. We'll go west, to Ohio, or even further. We can start again."

She smiled faintly. "Will we get married then, Justy?"

He felt the warmth wash over him. "Why not?"

She examined her thumb. There was apple flesh under the nail, and she put her thumb in her mouth to clean it. She made a face. "Father Mike gets them from a fella at the market. But he only gives him the ones he can't sell, so they're never ripe. Or they're rotten. But when you're a beggar you don't have no choice, do you?"

"You have a choice now."

She shook her head. "No. I don't. I can't go with you. Even if I thought you'd do right by me. I can't run."

"Why not?"

262

There was a long pause. Justy could hear Lars breathing behind him, slow and steady. Kerry had a faraway look in her eyes.

"Colley made me go back every day. I hated it at first, but then I got used to it. He let me do what I wanted otherwise. I felt almost free. And he was nice, you know, except for . . . that. He would tell me things. About his business. And then one day I woke up sick as a dog. I knew straight off I was up the duff, and I didn't know what he'd say if he knew. Probably send me to some back-alley finger smith to have the child broke out of me. I've seen what happens to morts when that goes wrong."

She fell silent. Justy waited, light-headed, holding his breath. She went on, her voice toneless now. "Seven months I kept it a secret. He liked me to keep my duds on when we did it, so even when I got big I could hide it. But he clocked me soon enough. It was too late to do anything by then, so he had me spin a story to my cousin and to O'Toole about going to stay with a friend in Greenwich, and then he set me up in Bedlow Street with a midwife. The kinchin came in August of last year. The fifteenth."

Justy leaned back in his chair. He felt sweat under his arms and on his upper lip. "Where's the child now?"

She looked at him, her eyes black. "Cherry Street."

Justy said nothing.

"He took him away, and gave him to a wet nurse. I'm allowed to see him once a week." Her voice wavered.

Justy reached out again, but she stood up abruptly. "That's why I can't run. He'll kill him if I do."

"Surely not. The child's not even a year old—"

Kerry slapped her hand down onto the table. "You don't know Colley. There's a reason they call him Black Jack. If you fall on the wrong side of him, you're lucky if he only kills you. He's carved women into ribbons for talking back to customers.

He's had those dogs Campbell and Fraser beat people to death for spilling a drink. He wouldn't think twice about killing Daniel."

She spun away and faced the wall. Justy watched her as she hugged herself, a trembling curtain of dark hair falling halfway down her back.

Trinity Church was only a few hundred yards away, but the thick walls of the church muffled the sound of the bells as they struck six.

Justy turned in his chair and looked at Lars. "Time's up."

Lars said nothing. His eyes were like flint.

Justy reached over the table for the half-eaten loaf. He tore off the end and tossed the rest to Lars.

Kerry sat back down, wiping her face. Lars offered her the bread. "You need to eat. We've a long night ahead of us."

She shook her head. "Jack's men will be all over looking for you. And forget going to your ship. You'll never make it on board. You can't get away."

"Who said anything about getting away?"

She frowned, and Lars grinned. "First rule. Never do what the bastards expect you to do. Your man'll be looking for us, sure enough. But we'll be where he least expects us."

"Where's that?"

Lars looked at Justy. "You thinking what I'm thinking?"

Justy nodded. "Cherry Street."

THIRTY-TWO

It took him nearly an hour to get to the Bull's house. A long, circuitous route took him along the Hudson River docks and up through the new developments near Rhineland's Quay. He walked carefully up the unpaved streets, his feet squelching in the churned mud, ignoring the women who called out to him from doorways and alleyways, showing their breasts as he passed.

He thought about the plan. He would talk to the Bull, to persuade him to trade Justy's silence for safe passage out of the city. Lars and Kerry were on their way to Cherry Street, to watch the house until the small hours, to see what Colley would do. If he went out to join the hunt for Justy, Lars would break in and take the child. If he stayed in, Lars would set a diversion, to draw Colley out and give Kerry the chance to take her baby. Once they had the child, they would go to Kerry's cousin's house. Lew Owens might be a gang leader and a criminal, but, Justy figured, he was a Negro and unlikely to be well disposed towards a man who trafficked in black flesh.

The Bull's men were out in force at the top of Dover Street. Big lads, dressed in shirtsleeves and flat caps, like a crew of farm laborers just in from the fields. Standing quietly on the corners. Watchful eyes.

Justy had sneaked out of the Bull's house many times at night when he was young. He used the same route now, up the side of Callahan's bread shop, along the beams of the stables and from there over the rooftops to the small window at the top of the house.

His old room. He peered inside. It was dark, and the window was shut tight, but he slid his knife up the gap in the wood and lifted the latch.

The window creaked a little as it opened, and he stopped and waited, crouching on the tiles of the roof, listening for the sounds of the house. It was silent inside. Nothing moved. He wondered where the Bull was. At Colley's perhaps. Or the house on Bedlow Street.

Never mind. He would wait.

He grabbed the top of the window and swung his legs inside, over the desk. It was a tight squeeze, but after a few moments he was standing on the floor of his old room, breathing hard.

He put his knife on the desk.

"I don't know why you didn't just break the feckin' thing open, the amount of noise you're making." His uncle's voice came from the shadows in the corner of the room. Justy turned, slowly. The Bull was sitting in a chair, his hands on his knees.

"I didn't hear you," Justy said.

"Of course you didn't. I know how to be quiet." The Bull's face was in shadow, but Justy could hear the smirk in his voice. "Unlike you. I heard you were some kind of scout, over in Ireland. I can't say I see it."

"Who told you that?"

"I've got tongues everywhere, boy; you should know that. I know what you did, and when you did it. I know everything."

The Bull leaned forward, so that his face was lit by the last of the daylight that filtered through the window into the room. "I knew you'd come in this way. You think I don't know how you came and went when you were a pup?"

Justy said nothing. He sat down on the bed.

It was a moment before the Bull spoke. "You've made a

dangerous enemy out of John Colley, Justice. He won't think twice about slitting you open and airing out your puddings."

"I don't intend to die at his hand. Or anyone else's. Not today, anyway."

"Perhaps you learned some of that old country magic while you were away, then. I don't know what else is going to save you. He gave you a chance and you snuffed it. Now he's got no choice but to fillet you."

"He could just let us go."

"Us?" The Bull chuckled. "Ah right, the lovely Kerry. She has her hooks in you, then. Just like he said."

Justy felt himself redden. "It's not like that."

"Is it not?" He took Justy's knife from the table. The blade snapped into the air. He grunted his approval. "I heard you got pretty handy with this thing."

"Not as handy as your pal, Turner."

The Bull turned the blade in the half-light. "You mean those runaways? He had no choice. If they'd tooken rattle, they might have talked, and that would have crabbed the whole scheme."

"Your slave brothel."

Justy put all the contempt that he could into his words, but the Bull just laughed. "Don't make out you're any better than me, boy. You've got plenty of blood on your paws."

"That was war."

"Enjoyed it, though, didn't you? Taking men's lives. Torturing. That's what Turner said. He reckoned you picked up a taste for it. I thought I saw something in your glimms the other day. And I should know."

Justy's skin prickled, the shame and the revulsion curdling inside him. He swallowed down the sharp taste on his tongue. "At least I did what I did for my country."

"Of course you did, lad." The Bull's eyes glinted. "And now you can come and do it for me."

267

Justy stared.

The Bull shrugged. "This city's full of lawyers. But there ain't many coves know how to get a man to open up without breaking him in two. That's a skill I can use."

"What are you saying?"

"I'm saying I'd pay you well, boy. Better than those hicks on Wall Street."

Justy felt as though his face were on fire. "Money? You want me to burn and gouge and bleed men for money? You think that's who I am?"

"I don't judge, Justice. We are who we are."

Justy rocked back. *We are who we are.* His stomach was a hollow void. His skin was damp and clammy. "I am not that man," he whispered. "I am not you."

"What's that supposed to mean?" The Bull's voice was sharp.

"It means that the only person you care for is yourself. You cheat and lie and steal. You enslave, and you kill. For money and for power. That is who you are. It's why you still live down here, in the gutter with the dogs and the rats. But you will not drag me down here with you."

"The gutter? God damn you!" The Bull threw the knife. It stuck in the boards between Justy's feet. "Who took you in when your father died? Who educated you and sent you to your precious college? I did."

"Guilt." Justy spat out the word. "You knew he was murdered and you did nothing. You were too set on trying to get a piece of Colley's business. That's why you took me in. Because you felt guilty."

"Guilty of what, now? There's nothing to prove Francis was murdered, no matter what you or I might think otherwise. The man lost a lot of money, more than he could ever have paid back. Everyone knows that. He was broken and ashamed. He died of his own hand."

"That is a lie!" Justy was on his feet now. "You keep saying everyone knew he had debts, but you told me yourself no one ever came to collect. Not one person, apart from the bank. And there were no records. You read his papers. But did you see a single creditor's note?"

The Bull said nothing. Justy sat down again. "You asked me the other day what I was doing at the house on Dutch Street. I've had this picture in my head all these years, and there was one thing about it that I had to check. You remember how Father was hanging, before you cut him down? He was a good four feet off the floor. His head was just below the ceiling. It's just not possible that he could have hanged himself that way. The rope was too short. I even tried climbing over the banister and lowering myself down, to see if it could be done. It couldn't. And if he didn't lower himself down, it means someone else pulled him up."

There was silence in the room. Justy leaned forward.

"He died because he found out what Colley and Duer were up to. Yes, he was corrupted. Yes, he came up with a way to dupe investors out of their money. I won't deny he was a fraud. But he hated slavery; you know he did. And when he found out their venture wasn't to buy gold in Brazil, but slaves in the Carolinas, he planned to tell the Manumission Society. Hamilton, Jay, Burr. All of the big investors. They would have pulled out, and the whole thing would have collapsed. Duer was already in trouble, but that would have been the end of him, and Colley too. So they had him killed."

"Your arse."

"You know it's true. I look in your eyes and I see it. You've always known there was something wrong about what happened. It was Colley's will. And Turner's hand." Justy bent and tugged the knife free from the floorboard. "And I can prove it. If you'll give me the chance."

It was several minutes before the Bull spoke. They sat in the cool gloom, a breath of wind coming through the open window. Justy watched the Bull's face. It was like a piece of dark stone, the eyes glittering like granite. He felt strangely calm. His uncle wouldn't kill him, he was sure. But there was still the chance the Bull might hand him over to Colley.

The Bull's chair creaked. "You know the only reason you're still breathing is because of me."

"I know. I saw Duffy and some others up on Bedlow Street yesterday. Colley needs your men to secure the kip."

"It's more than that. There's only a few girls at the house now. The rest are coming in by ship, tomorrow or the next day. He has to smuggle them off the docks and up to the house, and he can't do that on his own. I own the waterfront. From the Battery to the Bowery, nothing illegal moves without my say. And the gangs on Cherry Street tithe to me. I told him if anything happened to you, he'd have neither my help nor my protection."

"So you are his partner."

The Bull smirked. "If you call it that. I've put no money into it, except what it costs to give Colley protection and some strong arms. In return I get a cut, when the profits start to roll in. If they ever do."

"And if he shirks?"

The Bull shrugged. "If he shirks, he burns."

"Then make him burn." The blood thundered in Justy's temples. "I know you don't give a damn about anything or anyone but yourself, but the bastard had your brother killed. Your own blood."

"So you say."

"And so I can prove. Turner will get what's coming to him for what he did, but it was Colley pulling his strings. I want that blackhearted bastard, and I want him tonight." He stood up, trembling, like a man struck with a fever. "Now are you with me?"

THIRTY-THREE

The house on Bedlow Street was built back to front. Colley had bought the land behind it to make room for a sweeping driveway, with a turning circle for carriages and a stabling bay. In front of the driveway was a grand entrance, flanked by tall columns. A pair of heavy teak doors opened on to a high-ceilinged hallway that glowed in the light thrown by three chandeliers.

Colley stood halfway up a wide staircase that started at one end of the hall and swept up to a mezzanine. He watched, a smile on his face as Justy and the Bull approached.

"I expected you at Cherry Street."

Justy said nothing. Colley gave a small smile. "No matter. I see you have seen reason nonetheless." He nodded to the Bull. "Have you explained to him how things work?"

The Bull gave Colley a long look. "It was *he* explained a few things to me."

"About what?"

"Not here. The library."

Colley nodded. The Bull led them across the hall to a high pair of double doors. They opened on to a long room, one entire wall of which was lined with books. The floor was flagged with large black and white stones, so that it looked like an angled chessboard. A number of deep leather chairs were clustered around a fireplace in the middle of one wall. A small fire was dying out in the grate.

Colley pulled the doors closed behind him. He strode over to the fireplace, took a poker and thrust it into the coals. "We're slow tonight. Just two upstairs. But you know we can't get properly started until the shipment arrives. Those runaways cut our stock down to nine, and it's been hard enough to break them in. Only a handful are fit for trade as it stands."

"A round mouth to all of that." The Bull was holding on to the back of one of the armchairs. His knuckles were white and his face was red. "Did you have my brother killed?"

Colley looked startled for a moment. Then his eyes narrowed. "What on earth are you talking about?"

"Don't swive about, you sharping bastard. Answer the damned question."

Colley glanced at Justy. "Is that what he told you? He's been galumphing up and down Wall Street like a drunken matelot, asking questions that are set to ruin us, and now he's come up with this? Ridiculous."

"Is that so?" The armchair made a loud cracking sound as the Bull bore down on it. "Remind me then, why Francis hanged himself."

Colley shrugged. "Debt. He borrowed to invest in our venture, and he borrowed to buy public stock in the banks. He borrowed too much. When the bank shares fell, he had no way to make his margin payments, and because of the Panic, no one would buy his shares in the venture. Money dried up. He had no way out. There were many others like him. They decided it was better to end their lives than submit to the endless disgrace of debtors' prison."

"William Duer didn't think prison a disgrace," Justy said.

"William was an unusual man. Moreover, he had wealthy, influential friends. Francis was not so well supported."

Justy's head ached. He could feel the open cuts in the back of his scalp burning. "This is horseshit. Get Turner in here.

Whether it's me that works on him, or a couple of my uncle's men, he'll tell us the truth."

Colley's eyes were cold. "Yes, I've heard about your enthusiasm for the fine art of interrogation. And I imagine the Marshal would tell you whatever it was you wanted to hear. But he is not here."

"Another lie," Justy snapped. "You have him upstairs in some boudoir, licking his wounds."

"Or having them licked for him." The Bull bared his teeth. "But don't worry. My lads'll ferret him out."

Colley didn't move. He held the poker lightly in his hand. "You'll ruin our business, Ignatius."

"What business? Near a year I've been sending lads to watch over this place, and I haven't seen a soft cent so far."

"I said at the outset you would need to be patient. The procurement process is . . . challenging."

"Christ above, man. You're more full of shit than the Pope's privy."

"I'm full of shit?" Colley's face was tight. He jabbed the poker at Justy. "He's the one making up stories. Rewriting history. He has concocted all of this in his head. And he has not a shred of proof."

There was a knock at the door.

"Come." The Bull's voice sounded like raking gravel.

Duffy filled up the doorway. The shadow from the candles in the nook made his broken nose look like a hole in his face. "We found him in O'Grady's, boss. Up to his nuts in guts. We had to pull the dirty skelp off the poor doxy."

"You paid her, I hope."

"I did, aye. And then we went to his office for the papers, like you said. He has them now."

"Wait there." The Bull still had his eyes on Colley. "All right then, Jack. You say Francis lost his head with all of the rest of them during the Panic. What started it?"

Colley shrugged. "There was no one thing. People had been nervous for weeks. There were all sorts of rumors flying about. One day shares were up; the next they were down. Then they were up again. As shares are wont to be."

"You said Francis bought shares in some public companies. Which ones?"

"Banks, I believe. The Bank of the United States and the Bank of New York. They were the stocks that collapsed and triggered the Panic."

"And what was the date of the collapse?"

Colley winced. "For heaven's sake, man. It was nearly eight years ago. How can you possibly expect me to remember the exact day?"

The Bull turned to Justy. "What day was it you found your father, do you remember?"

"I remember." Justy stared at Colley. "It was the second of March. A Friday."

The Bull turned back to Colley. "So if Francie killed himself in the Panic, the selling must have started before that."

Colley nodded. "Yes. It did. The week before, as I recall."

The Bull nodded. "All right then, Duffy. Bring him in."

The big Galwayman stepped aside and jerked his head.

Ramage stumbled in, shoved from behind, his shoes skittering on the checkered flagstones. He had a heavy satchel over his shoulders that threatened to unbalance him, and it was a moment before he could gather himself. He looked around, smoothing his long, greasy hair with his right hand.

The Bull glared at him. "Do you know who I am?"

The newsletterman looked pale. His knees were shaking. "You're Ignatius Flanagan. The Bull."

"And you know these others?"

Ramage glanced at Justy and Colley, his head twitching like a panicked chicken's. "Yes."

Colley's face was a hard mask. Ramage flinched away and glanced back. Duffy stood like a fleshy wall, the door closed firmly behind him.

Ramage looked back at the Bull. "Why am I here?"

"To give us a history lesson. Sit down."

The Bull patted the armchair, and Ramage crabbed across to it, clutching his briefcase, his head twitching, his eyes wide, doing everything they could to avoid looking at Colley. He slid into the seat.

The Bull looked at Justy. "You said he has proof. Let's hear it."

Justy clasped his hands behind his back, ignored the churning in his stomach and looked down at the newsletterman. "I'm sorry about the way you were brought here, Mr. Ramage. But I do appreciate your assistance. And I can assure you, you will come to no harm. All I need is for you to clarify a few things for me."

Ramage nodded hastily. "Of course."

"Did you bring your papers from '92, as Mr. Duffy asked?"

Ramage nodded. He hugged the satchel. "Everything I published, yes. And my notes."

"Good." Justy smiled. "First, can you tell me when the Brokers' Board began keeping records of securities trades?"

Ramage's eyes glanced at Colley, then back to Justy. He cleared his throat. "The Board? Well, I suppose it began immediately it was formed. In May of '92."

"Just after the Panic, then?"

"Yes."

"So there are no formal records of trades before that date."

"That's correct."

"But you kept records."

"Well, yes. Of what I heard. And what I published, too, of course."

Justy nodded. He could feel sweat on his palms. "Did you hear of, or publish news about, any big purchases by William Duer after the New Year?"

"Oh yes. Mr. Duer told me himself, in fact. He was keen for as many people as possible to know." Ramage scrabbled in the satchel and pulled out a yellowing fold of paper. "Ten thousand dollars of Bank of New York shares on the tenth of February. Another ten thousand on the twenty-fourth. Twenty thousand on the twenty-eighth, and forty thousand on the first of March. His last purchase."

"Big amounts."

Ramage nodded. "Very substantial."

"And do you have the share prices for those same dates?"

Ramage frowned. He hunched over his satchel and dug inside, a hank of greasy hair falling over his forehead. He pulled out a pamphlet. "One of my competitors. *The Gazette*." He leafed through the pages. "Here we are. Prices. For the tenth of February, twenty-seven shillings."

"And the following day?"

"Um . . . twenty-nine shillings."

"So the price went up after Duer made a big purchase. Did that happen every time?"

The strand of greasy hair whipped back and forth as Ramage compared the newspaper in his left hand with his own pamphlet in his right. "Yes. Every time. Bank of New York stock was twenty-five shillings on the first of March, when he bought, and thirty shillings the next day. The peak price, as I recall."

Justy glanced at Colley. He was standing by the fire, quite still, the skin drawn tight over his pale face. He was listening intently.

"Just one more question, Mr. Ramage," Justy said. "When did the Panic begin?"

Ramage sat up, pleased to share his knowledge. "Well, that's an interesting question. The coffee houses were buzzing with rumors, and you can see some people had already begun to sell. That was why Duer was making such big purchases, to keep the share prices high and protect his own investments. And it might have worked, if he hadn't run out of money."

"And when was that?"

"Oh, just a few days later." He pulled another of his yellowed pamphlets from his satchel. "I wrote about it. Friday the ninth of March. Duer announced that he would stop paying interest on a number of his loans. He claimed it was to investigate their provenance, but everyone knew he had run out of funds. And that was that."

"Panic."

"Indeed." Ramage crossed his arms over his satchel.

The Bull leaned over the back of the chair and spoke into Ramage's ear. "I'm not a Wall Street shyster like Jack here, so clear something up for me."

The newsletterman cringed. "Of course, sir."

"If a man had bought shares in the Bank of the United States and the Bank of New York in January or February, what would the state of his accounts be on the second of March?"

Ramage swallowed. He kept his eyes on the floor. "Well, it depends on what price the shares were when he bought. But, as I said, peak price for all bank shares was the first of March. So any buyer would be in the black when the market closed that day, and possibly a very wealthy man."

"Not an unhappy man, then. Not indebted, or disgraced or despairing. Not of the mind to top himself."

"Quite the reverse, I'd say."

The Bull stared at Colley. "What do you say to that, Jack? If Francie had bought as much as you claim he did, he wouldn't have been bushed the day he died. He'd have been as rich as mad King George."

There was a creaking sound as his massive hands squeezed the back of the chair. "That's if he'd bought stock at all. The thing is, there's no record of him ever buying shares in the banks, or borrowing to do so. I never found a single certificate among his things, and no one ever came and asked me for a penny. I always thought that was queer, but I told myself it was because no one fancied coming down to Dover Street to collect. Now I'm thinking it's because there were no shares, and no loans neither."

Colley looked down at the poker in his hand.

"Don't even think about it," the Bull snapped. "You might give me a wee dub o' the hick, but then my lads would break you in half."

Colley glanced at Duffy, blocking the door. He seemed to deflate. "He wasn't supposed to kill him," he said.

"Who?"

"Turner. I told him to keep your brother quiet. Intimidate him. Lock him away. Get him out of the city. Anything. I didn't mean murder him."

"But he did murder him."

"I'm sorry, Ignatius. Truly. It was not my intention, but your brother was about to bring down the whole castle about our ears. Just as your nephew is about to do now."

Justy felt numb. After eight years, he knew. He had pictured this moment, thought about how he would feel when he had proved what really happened. And now he had no idea how he felt at all.

The Bull was staring at Colley, his eyes blank. Justy knew that look. His uncle was trying to control himself, to stop himself from snatching the poker from Colley's hand and beating him to death where he stood.

"Don't do it, Uncle."

"Don't tell me what I should and shouldn't do."

Colley held a hand up, as though he was fending him off. "You should listen to your nephew, Ignatius. If you kill me, you'll lose everything you've invested."

"It's a good thing I've not invested much then, isn't it?"

Colley's eyes flickered. They landed on Justy. "There's Kerry to think of, remember. And little Daniel."

Justy's throat tightened. "You weren't fast enough, Colley. I got to her first, and she told me about the child. And while we've been standing here, Lars has broken into your house and taken the boy back. By now the three of them will be safe, somewhere you or your dogs will never find."

He hoped to God it was true.

There was a tap at the door. One of the bodyguards stuck his head in the gap. He was a round-faced, red-cheeked man of about twenty. He nodded at the Bull. "I've rounded them up, boss. Want to take a look?"

"Do you have your barker, Sean?"

"I do indeed, aye." The red-cheeked man pulled a pistol from his waistband.

"Get in here, then, and keep it pointed at that blackhearted mackerelback there. If he moves, pop him."

Sean pushed his hat back on his head and sauntered into the room. He cocked his pistol and aimed it at Colley's chest.

"I'll be back," the Bull said.

They stood in a half circle around the fire. Ramage had sunk deep into the armchair, clutching his papers to his chest as though he were trying to disappear into the upholstery.

Sean stood on Justy's left, his pistol arm straight and steady as a ship's spar.

"You'll be Justy Flanagan, then," he said, his eyes fixed on Colley's face.

"That's right."

"I'm Sean O'Faolain. You know my cousin Patrick. He said

you were with him in Wicklow. Said you saved him from being tortured to death once."

Justy frowned. "Patrick? I thought he was captured, and shot at Kilkeel."

"He was not indeed. He scowred off and hoofed it up to Newmarket. He came over last year, to Boston. He's working up there as a snakesman for Tip O'Riordan." Sean glanced at Justy and grinned, and Colley saw his opening.

He struck, whip fast, lashing out with the poker at the pistol. There was a deafening crack and a cloud of smoke as Sean fired, and Colley dropped to the floor. For a moment Justy thought he was hit, but then Colley was back on his feet and running for the window. Justy followed, but his foot slipped on the polished floor and he went sprawling. There was a loud crash as Colley hurled himself through the window, and before Justy was up, Colley had crossed the narrow strip of grass in front of the building and swung himself up and over the railings. Justy watched as Colley ran hard across the road and into the same alley he and Lars had stood in, watching the house just a few days before.

"Don't worry." The Bull's voice was thick with anger. "He won't get far. We'll have every Irishman in the town out after him."

Justy pushed past him. "We can't wait. He'll go to Cherry Street first, to check on the child. We can trap him there, if we're quick."

A dull thud made him turn his head. Ramage was slouched in the armchair, his chin on his chest. The satchel had slid out of his hands onto the floor. His face was the gray-white color of fish guts.

"Jesus." Sean looked at his pistol.

"Not your fault, Sean." Justy pointed to a small, neat hole in the plaster above the fireplace. He put his hand on Ramage's neck. He could feel no pulse. The newsletterman's skin was clammy. His tongue had slid obscenely out of his mouth.

The Bull grunted. "What, did we frighten the poor bastard to death?"

"Looks that way."

Ramage's hands were folded over his potbelly. His greasy hair fell over his face. He looked just like a man taking a nap after a heavy meal. Justy looked down at him for a moment. He felt nothing.

"Let's go."

THIRTY-FOUR

It was quicker to run. Justy followed the route Colley had taken, across Bedlow Street and down the alley. There was no moon, and Justy tripped over the detritus that was strewn about the dark, narrow passage. A dog ran at him, snarling, and Justy slipped again. Lights burst behind his eyes as the back of his head collided with the brick of the alley wall. He lay for a moment, wedged against the stone, his head ringing, blood running down the back of his neck. He gritted his teeth and pushed himself up off the ground. His breeches were soaked.

He forced himself on. Down the alley, left on Cherry Street and hard down the sidewalk, his breath loud in his ears, ignoring the looks on the faces of the few passersby on the street. He was vaguely aware of the sound of a carriage hammering past him, but he drove himself on until he reached Colley's house.

It was an ordinary London-style town house, three stories high with a narrow frontage. But it had the same high railings as the house on Bedlow Street. Justy leaned against the iron bars, his legs weak and his chest heaving. The cuts on his scalp burned like fire. The carriage that had passed him was drawn up outside. One of the Bull's men held the reins.

Justy closed his eyes. He felt a hand on his shoulder. The Bull's face floated in front of him.

"There's no one here, lad."

God damn Colley. But at least Kerry and Lars were safe. Justy grabbed the railings and hauled himself to his feet.

The Bull surveyed him, hands on his hips. "You look like a bucket of afterbirth."

"Thanks."

"Don't worry. We'll hunt the dog down. Like I say, I'll have every Irishman in the city on him. And when he's in the bag . . ."

Justy waved his hand. "I don't want to know."

They stood awkwardly for a moment. There was a rushing sound as the wind suddenly picked up, and the light from the streetlamp above them flickered.

The Bull made a fist and punched Justy gently in the chest. "I can see now my money was well spent. I've never seen a man so mad for the truth. Your father would have been proud."

Justy felt his breath catch, as the anger surged in him. "My father was a cheat and a thief. That's the truth for you."

The Bull frowned. "There was no law against what he did."

"Jesus! How many times am I going to hear that? It doesn't mean what he did wasn't wrong!"

He stared into his uncle's eyes. It was a moment before the Bull looked away. "We need to get you cleaned up."

"No. We need to get Lars and Kerry."

The Bull paused. Then nodded. "Right you are. You can go in the carriage. I'll have a few of the lads go with you, just in case. Where are they?"

"Lew Owens' place."

The Bull blinked. "Owens? You're codding me."

Justy felt something twist inside him. "What's wrong?"

The Bull coughed out a dry, mirthless laugh. "Owens is a partner, Justice. He's one of them." His jaw tightened. "One of us."

Justy reached behind him for the railings. "But Owens is . . . he's . . ."

"He's a Negro? You think that means he's not a slaver? By all that's holy, lad, are you that much of a gull? Owens is the biggest beard splitter in New York. It's not much of a step from pimping black girls to slaving them, now is it?"

The Bull grabbed him by the front of his coat. "Get in the rattler. We'll drive over and see what's what. Maybe Kerry was fox enough to stay clear of her cousin's."

But Justy knew better.

———◆———

It was a short ride to Owens' house on Leonard Street, but long enough for Justy to recover his wits. The Bull had sent one of his men to raid Colley's scullery, and Justy had just enough time to fill his belly with cold chicken and a half-pint of weak white wine. The Bull insisted on trying to clean out the cuts on his head, but he didn't have Sarah Boswell's finesse, and by the time the carriage pulled up at the Owens house Justy's scalp felt as though it were on fire.

But his head was clear enough.

The Bull stepped down first. "Look who's here."

The moonlight glittered on the black paintwork and brass fittings of Colley's coach. Fraser was perched on the running board, watching them, and Campbell stood in the road, swinging his knotted blackthorn. He grinned, showing his rotten teeth. "I heard we missed all the fun."

The Bull nodded to his men, who had hitched a ride on the roof and sides of his carriage. They jumped off, one by one, and arranged themselves in a half circle around Colley's coach. The Bull looked at Campbell. "There's still plenty of fun to be had, if you fancy."

Campbell glowered and said nothing.

The Bull sneered. "I didn't think so, you cowardly northern cunt."

He stepped to the door of the house and hammered on it with his fist. After a few moments it swung open.

A tall, silent man with a long scar across his face led them through the hallway to a large room. There was a brightly colored carpet on the floor, and odd pieces of expensive-looking furniture were scattered about at random. The room was a blaze of candlelight, with a candelabra on every table and a chandelier hanging from the ceiling.

A small fire burned in the grate. Colley sat on one side of the mantelpiece in an ornately upholstered chair. There was a glass and a decanter full of a honey-colored liquor on a small table beside him. A tall man with a gleaming cannonball of a head leaned casually on the wall on the other side of the fireplace. He wore cream breeches and a linen shirt so white that it made his skin look the color of ink. The glass in his hand looked like a thimble. He nodded to the Bull. "Ignatius."

"Lew."

"How's business?"

"Can't complain. You?"

The man chuckled. He had a faint Welsh accent. "Nothing like a Manumission conference to bring in the ducats. Those coves may not like slavery, but they do enjoy their dark meat, regardless."

His eyes swiveled in Justy's direction, like a pair of cannon shifting aim. "This must be the nephew I've heard so much about. I'm Lew Owens. Kerry's cousin."

Justy stared back. "And where is Kerry?"

A perfect set of teeth flashed white in Owens' face. "No idea, bach. Probably dipping her fingers into some drunk cove's pocket up Broad Street way."

"You haven't seen her tonight, then?"

"I have not." Owens looked at the Bull. "You didn't come here to inquire after my wayward cousin, did you, Ignatius?"

"I did not."

"So how can I be of service?"

The Bull jerked his head at Colley. "You can hand over that bastard so I can open his throat for him."

"Can't do that, I'm afraid, boyo."

"The madge killed my brother, Lew."

Owens pushed himself off the mantel and crossed the fireplace. He poured himself a glass from the decanter beside Colley and sipped delicately. He stopped, a look of concern on his face.

"Forgive my poor manners, Ignatius. Can I offer you a drink?"

"My balls in your drink, Owens. Hand him over."

Owens sat down slowly in a small chair that looked as though it might collapse under him. "I'm sorry about your brother, Ignatius, but Jack tells me it was just business."

"Business? He had that rat Turner strangle him and dress it up to look like self-murder. He didn't even get a proper burial."

"Well, that's what you get for trying to blow up a going concern. You'd do the same thing, I daresay, if one of your schemes was about to go down with all hands." Owens looked meaningfully at Justy.

The Bull took two long strides across the room. Colley sprang out of his chair.

The Bull barked out a laugh. "Don't worry, Jack. You're safe for now." He grabbed the decanter. "Where are the glasses?"

Owens waved a hand towards a cabinet on the far side of the room. The Bull walked over, selected a large tumbler and filled it. He drank it off and belched loudly.

Owens looked offended. "That ain't your cheap grapple, boyo. That's Armagnac brandy. All the way from Frenchieland."

"Pricey, I suppose."

"By heaven, yes."

"I'll have another, then." The Bull topped off his glass. He paced up and down in front of the fire.

"I know what you're thinking, Lew." The Bull stood in front of the grate, feet planted wide. "You don't want a war, but it could be worth fighting me, to keep this affair up. You've got enough chink sunk in it, God knows. But I'll tell you two things. First, you won't win. I've got double the men you can muster, and even if you do manage to put me in the ground, my lads'll spill so much black blood that you'll never be able to keep your schemes running after. Second, you can't run this racket without me. You can't staff the house on Bedlow Street with your own folk. Your clients would run a mile. They may want black tail in their beds, but they want white faces opening the doors and guarding the gates. Last, you need access to the ports. If I'm not on board, you won't even get your ships unloaded. They'll sit at anchor, and your cargo will starve."

Owens nodded his head slowly. He looked at Colley. "He makes some good points, Jack. I may have to trade you."

The Bull swallowed a mouthful of brandy. "You don't need this madge anyway, Lew. The supply lines are working fine. You just take 'em over. Same with the house. No one'll miss Black Jack. And there's plenty will thank us for hushing him."

Owens smiled faintly. "Except Jack's our man on Wall Street, bach. He's a sharper, I grant you, but we need him and that fat fool Gracie to keep the ducats flowing until we get self-sufficient, don't we? How else are we going to raise the chink to pay for product in the meantime? Not to mention bringing in the members. The quality, remember. Jack's the only one of us who can move about in that world."

Colley slammed his glass down on the table. "I remind you, gentlemen. I am here in the room."

The only sound in the room was the fire crackling in the grate. The Bull gave Colley a long, empty look. He swiveled his head to look at Owens again.

"We have my nephew."

Justy felt the air go out of him, as though he had been punched in the chest. He wanted to shove his uncle into the fire and run out of the room.

But something stopped him. He thought about Kerry, sitting in that small, whitewashed room in the church, telling them what Colley had done. The look in her eyes, the sound of her voice. Desperate, like a trapped animal.

Everyone was looking at him: Owens, lounging in his chair, smiling slightly; the Bull, half-turned towards him, his face blank, his eyes cool. And Colley, leaning on the fireplace surround, a sneer twisting his thin lips.

A cold rage seemed to filter out of Justy's guts and through his veins. He felt the sweat, like ice on the back of his neck. His fingers twitched. He imagined Colley underneath him, his knee in the trader's throat, the point of his knife prizing out his eyes, the blade widening his smile. He felt his skin bump, the hair rising on his legs and his neck and the back of his arms. Black Jack would not get away with what he had done. To his father. To Kerry. To the dead girls, lying on the cold slabs in the grim morgue under the almshouse. Murderer. Rapist. Slaver. It was time to give Colley a taste of his own poison.

And there it was.

Just an idea, at first. An idea so vicious, so repellent, that his mind recoiled from it, like a man backing away from a venomous snake. But the idea would not stay away. It came back to him, like a dog with a stick, and part of his mind, the cool, objective, unfeeling part of him that knew how to threaten, where to cut and what to ask, began to explore the idea.

The idea was so simple, it was less like arranging a puzzle and more like fashioning a key. He thought the idea through, and the key turned, smoothly, the tumblers falling into place, one by one. A simple solution, pristine in its logic. Perfect. And unspeakably evil.

The breath caught in his throat. He felt like a child standing over an ants' nest, holding a heavy stone, watching the creatures scurrying back and forth. He glanced up. The Bull was watching him, the broad slab of his face cracked by what passed for a smile.

In Justy's mind, the stone fell. He imagined the sound of it hitting the ground, the vibration through his feet, the nest crushed, the bodies mangled. He swallowed the acid on his tongue and felt his stomach turn.

"Aye. You have me."

The smile on Owens' face was wider, but it still hadn't reached his eyes. "I heard you were morally opposed to this venture of ours. Not to mention you're a lawyer and what we're doing likely wouldn't sit too well with the beak, if we landed in court."

Justy could feel Colley's wine bubbling deep in his guts. The chicken had tasted good going down, but now he felt he was about to bring it right back up again. He thought of Kerry, her hair falling over her face, like a blackbird's wing. He thought of his father, the way his fingers had felt when he touched them. Like a clutch of sausages pulled from an icebox: swollen, cold, obscene.

He swallowed.

"You are right on every count, Mr. Owens. I do find this venture objectionable. Deeply so. And yes, I am a lawyer. As such, I can reassure you that your scheme, as described, is legally questionable in a number of areas. Nevertheless, despite all of that, I could be persuaded to assist you, as my uncle has described. And, indeed, to put you right in the eyes of the law."

"Really?"

"Really. And it won't cost you a penny."

"But it will still cost me." Owens' laugh was as dry as the ash in the fireplace. "So what do you want?"

Justy's mouth was sticky. "Payment in kind. I want Colley, I want Turner and I want Kerry."

Owens' lips twitched. "Ah yes, sweet cousin Kerry. Of course." He paused for a moment. "That all sounds a bit expensive to me, if you don't mind my saying."

"You'll find it's worth it. For my silence. And my skills."

Colley laughed. "This is ridiculous. The boy has no connections in the city, none. He has no access to capital, or to the kind of clients we need. He is useless."

Justy ignored him. He kept his eyes on Owens. "My father showed me how to raise money, and you all know how good he was. He invented this scheme of yours, remember. And you don't need Colley to make it run now, anyway. The network is already in place. All you need is Harry Gracie to keep on fronting it, to keep it ticking over until you're making enough capital from Bedlow Street. As for bringing in new clients, you don't need Colley there, either. If the product's as good as you claim, word will travel fast."

Colley's gray eyes were like flint-tipped spears. Justy smiled. "But above all of this, as I said, there's the legal issue. And that's something Jack here can't help you with."

"Go on."

"This whole plan of yours, to smuggle women into the city and then sell them to the highest bidder? It's madness. Not only is it against the law; it's almost certain to be found out. A slave auction on Bedlow Street? There's no way you're going to be able to keep that quiet."

"You'd be surprised what we can keep quiet, boyo," Owens said.

"Really? You already had four women slip away. You had to kill them to shut them up. What happens when you have twenty-four? Mass murder? If you do this, word is going to come out, eventually, and when it does, the Manumission Society will be up in arms, your investors will drop you like a hot coal, your clients will run like rats and all the connections you have won't be enough to keep you out of clink."

He paused, and stared at Owens. "Unless you do things my way."

"And what way is that?"

"Take Colley out of here, and I'll tell you. Then you can bring him back and ask him what kind of a solution he's got."

Owens jerked his head, and the scarred bodyguard strode across towards Colley. He stood over him until Colley stood up and followed him, mutely, out of the room.

Owens waited for a moment. He walked over to where the Bull had placed the decanter. He filled his glass. "Before you write us off as a bunch of drumbelos, you should know we did think about all of this."

"And what did you come up with?"

Owens smiled. "We were still mulling on it." He sipped his brandy. "Go on then, boyo."

Justy glanced at his uncle. The Bull was watching him, impassive. His glass was still half-full. Justy walked over to him, took the glass from his hand and drank a mouthful. The liquor was sweet, but it scorched the back of his throat. It was an effort to stop himself from coughing.

"Leases," he said.

Owens frowned. "What do you mean?"

He took a deep breath. "If you sell these women to your clients or your partners or whatever you call them, you'll be breaking the law. But if you lease them, you're not selling them. In the eyes of the law, there is no transfer of ownership. You will still own them, but you'll sell their labor for a certain period, and selling someone's labor is entirely legal. The lessees, your clients, could either pay a lump sum or installments. All other parts of your contract, the fees and sharing agreements, all of that could remain the same. All it requires is some paperwork."

"What kind of period would the lease be for?"

"Anything more than a life-span should do. Say ninety-nine years."

Owens nodded thoughtfully. "So if the woman dies before the lease ends, we don't have to worry about taking her back. And if the client grows tired of her, he has to pay a fee to break the lease and return her to us." His teeth flashed in his face. "Bloody brilliant! You think this could really work?"

Justy swigged another mouthful of brandy. It burned in his guts. "It would make you safe from prosecution under the law." He looked at the Bull. "It doesn't remove the moral question."

Owens made a dismissive gesture. "That's the least of our problems."

"The Manumission Society is strong. And getting stronger. Look at how many are in the city for this conference. From all over the country."

Owens grinned. "As I say, don't worry about them lot. You'd be surprised how many anti-slavery saints have shown interest in membership in our little club."

Justy felt as though his tongue were covered in a dirty slime. He couldn't quite believe what had just come out of his mouth. Needs must, but it didn't take away the shame. He took another drink.

Owens' man opened the door, and Colley strode back into the room. He looked feverish. His hair had pulled loose from the tie at the back of his head, and there were two red spots high on his cheekbones.

"So, what fantasy has Mr. Flanagan dreamed up for you?"

"Sorry, Jack. No clues." Owens winked at Justy.

Colley scowled. "I warn you, gentlemen. Without me, this venture will sink like the *Mary Rose*. Those contacts in the Carolinas and the French territories are mine, carefully cultivated and dependent on a personal connection."

"Fadge." Owens flicked his fingers dismissively. "I'll take a bimble below the Line myself. Then we'll see whose contacts are better. What about our little legal problem?"

Colley's face was tight. He was very still, but his gray eyes flicked around the room, as though he was looking for a way out.

Owens grinned. "Looks like young Justice here has the jump on you, boyo."

Colley shuddered. "So that's it? You're going to cut me out?"

Owens shrugged. "I can't see as how I've much of a choice, bach. I don't want a war, I can't run this racket without Ignatius here, and he wants you fitted for an eternity box. As for the lad, he's green, true enough, but he's got more sand than the beach at Turtle Bay. And he has a solid plan to make us legal, which is more than what you've got." He paused, and the corner of his mouth twitched. "I'll not send you away empty-handed, mind. I'll give you a fair price for your share."

Colley turned on Justy. "You don't chouse me for a moment, Flanagan." The two red spots burned on his cheekbones, and his dockyard accent grated like a burr on the edge of his voice. "I ken what you are, even if these cod-headed sapsculls can't see it. You're a purehearted Manumission man, like that simkin Hamilton. You've got no stomach for any of this. Your plan is to sink the whole scrap, not save it."

Justy stood up, his face burning. "You're right, Colley, this scheme makes me sick to my stomach, but I'll do what I have to do to get what I want. I'll remove all legal impediments, and then I'll wash my hands. By then it won't matter who knows what kind of business it really is. It'll be just like any one of the hundreds of brothels in this city. It'll be turning a profit, and it won't need any more Wall Street money. Word'll get out, sure, but investors who don't want to be connected to an immoral business can just sell their stakes." He turned to Owens. "You'll more than likely be able to buy most of them out at a steep discount."

Owens smiled and toasted him.

Colley sneered. "So you just throw all your principles over-board? Just like that? You're more cheaply bought than I expected."

"Not so cheap, Jack. Unless you value your life so poorly, yours and Turner's."

"And the precious Kerry's, too." Colley's sneer turned into a hard smile. "You have a good brain, Justice; I'll give you that. But like most arrogant young men, you miss what's right in front of you."

"What are you talking about?"

"Kerry, of course. You know that whatever happens to me, she won't be going anywhere with you."

Justy said nothing. Colley walked back to his chair, picked up his glass and threw what was left of it into the fire. It flared, and he waited until it died down. He turned and looked at Justy, grinning like a skull. "How do you think Turner found those runaways? He didn't do it without help, you know."

Justy felt his mouth go dry.

Colley was almost laughing now. "You were a scout in that little conflagration over in that member mug you call a country, weren't you? Searching out the enemy and leading your soldiers in for the kill? Well, the good Marshal had a scout of his own, looking for those girls. And it wasn't one of those lumbering long-shank leatherheads. No, he needed someone a good deal more discreet, someone used to blending into the undergrowth of this city. And into the world of womankind, of course."

There was a sick feeling in the pit of Justy's stomach. His mind uncoiled to the first time he'd seen Kerry, down at the docks, looking at the dead girl who had been pulled out of the water. Turner must have sent her to check that the girl was dead. And the next night Kerry had suddenly appeared on the street, where the other girl's throat had been cut. He remembered wondering how she had arrived so quickly, but she must have been there all along, covering for Turner while he cleaned himself up, and bandaged his cut hand. She probably helped him get the bodies out of the morgue.

It explained her reticence, her anger, her refusal to meet Justy's eyes the last time they'd talked. She knew that she and Lars would be walking into a trap, either at Colley's house or at Owens'. She knew, because she was the one who had set it.

Lars.

"Your sailor friend is quite safe," Colley said, reading his mind. "Mr. Campbell and Mr. Fraser are looking after him." He peered into his glass. "So I propose a further trade. His life for mine."

Justy looked at the Bull. There was no question. Justy wanted to see Colley dangling from a rope, but Lars was his friend. Colley for Lars was an easy trade for him to make. But he couldn't speak for the Bull.

His uncle looked at him for a moment and then nodded slightly. His eyes were dark, and Justy knew the Bull would hunt Colley down eventually. All Black Jack was buying was a little time.

"What about Turner?" the Bull asked.

Colley sniffed. "He's yours, if you can find him."

"Oh, I'll find him." The Bull stared at Colley. "I'll find him, and fillet him and feed him to the gulls, piece by piece. And then I'll come for you."

"But what about our deal?"

The Bull's face was hard. "You're a trader, Jack, so you know how it works. Your deal's with my nephew. Not with me."

Colley gave him a sour look. "Well, I hope you'll give me a sporting chance to flee."

"Oh aye, Jack. I will. But only so I can enjoy the hunt."

THIRTY-FIVE

Lars was in Colley's carriage. He looked up as the door swung open and shrugged ruefully when he saw Justy in the street. Lars' hands were secured with a thick leather strap that was tied around the doorframe. The strap was scored and ragged where he had tried to gnaw through it with his teeth.

Fraser cut him free, and Lars stepped out of the carriage. His beard bristled as he brushed past Colley, but he said nothing.

The Bull was standing with his men in front of Owens' house, his hands behind his back. The light from the streetlamp shadowed his face. Colley faced him. "I consider this a betrayal, Ignatius."

"Do you, Jack?"

"If you think this is over between us, you're very much mistaken."

The Bull made a sound, deep in his throat. "It'll be over when I've given you an earth bath, you cunt."

Colley's eyes flickered. "How long do I have?"

"You walk free from here tonight. But tomorrow's a new day. If I even get a sniff of you anywhere near New York after first light, you're fair game."

Colley looked at him for a moment, then stepped up and into the cab. He slammed the door behind him, then lowered the sash and looked out. His face was taut with anger. "I'll burn you to the ground, Flanagan. You and your goddamned nephew."

"I'm looking forward to seeing you try, Colley." The Bull bared his teeth. "Now fuck off."

Colley knocked twice on the door of the carriage. The driver snapped his reins and the carriage jolted forward.

Justy watched it pull away. "Where will he go?"

The Bull shrugged. "Boston or Philadelphia, I'd say. He has plenty of friends there. Or he might go south, below the Line. We've not heard the last of him, that's for sure."

"I thought you might kill him, right there."

"Did you want me to?"

"I don't know. Maybe." Justy gritted his teeth. "I just wanted him to answer for what he did."

The Bull clapped a hand on his shoulder. "And so he did, Justice. He answered to us. To me."

"It's not the same."

"It's as good as any court. He pled guilty, and he had his sentence commuted." The Bull squeezed. "But not for long, I promise."

Justy shook his uncle's hand away. "Damn Colley. You can do what you like with him. It's Turner I want now."

"Don't fash about that wee bastard. He'll pike, but I'll run him down, eventually. And when I do, I'll peel the fucker's skin off. With the edge of a spoon."

"No."

"No?"

Justy shook his head. "No. I want him in a box, in front of a judge."

A chuckle. "On what charge, exactly? Milling a man near ten years ago? With no proof, and no man to stand buff against him?"

"You could give evidence."

The Bull pushed out his lower lip. "I could say I had an inkling of what was about. But any black box worth a red cent will show I had no direct ken of the matter. And then there's the fact of who I am. And what I am."

"What?" Justy sneered. "You think the word of Bull Flanagan, community leader, might not carry much weight?"

The Bull smiled slightly. "It might if it was a community other than ours. No. I'd be more hindrance than help. That's if we could even get the slippery wee bastard in the dock in the first place. He's made a life out of sneaking about and hiding. I'd say he's long gone by now."

Justy's face was hot. "Well, I won't rest until I have him."

A chuckle. "Christ, but you've a fire in you, boy. I'm glad you're on my side and not on his."

"I'm not on your side."

He turned to Lars. The big sailor was sitting on the sidewalk, rubbing his wrists, an unhappy look on his face.

"Are you right, big fella?"

Lars stood up slowly. "I'm sorry, *a chara*. I walked right into it at Colley's house. I should have seen it coming."

"How so?"

"Ah, your girl Kerry was as twitchy and nervous as a first-year filly on race day. Wouldn't look me in the eye, wouldn't talk. She just pointed the way and then hid back in the bushes. I unlocked the back jigger easy enough, but as soon as I walked in, them two tonys stepped up out of nowhere, strapped like a squad of cavalry."

"Where's Kerry now?"

Lars looked apologetic. "Stroked if I know. She likely brushed the moment I went into the house. But that northern madge Campbell told me she's been part of this thing since the beginning. He even said she spotted those girls for your man Turner."

"Aye. Colley told me as much."

Lars shook his head, ruefully. "It'll be quite the merry chase, those two sleekit wee weasels running about after each other."

"Who?"

"Why, Turner and Kerry." His face fell. "Colley didn't tell you that part, then."

"Christ above, Lars! What are you talking about?"

"Turner. Colley told him to make her easy. Or that's what Campbell said."

Justy's heart was in his throat. "We have to find her."

The big sailor's hand was like a vice on his arm. "Slow down, now, Justy. Think for a minute. I know you have history with her, but she's done nothing but feed you gammon from the start. She sold you out. She sold both of us out. She can't be trusted."

"Fuck you, Lars." The anger was like a spike in his guts. He shook Lars' hand off his arm.

The big sailor drew himself up to his full height. "Fuck me, is it now?"

"Yes, Lars. Fuck you. I'd have thought you of all people could see through this. Kerry had no choice. You know what Colley did to her. What she feared he still could do. You heard her."

"I heard a story, right enough, *a chara.*" Lars' voice was soft. "But how do you know that wasn't a lie, just like all the other clankers she's dropped on you?"

It was like stepping out of a hot room into a cold wind. Justy's throat ached. The Bull was leaning on the door of his carriage, watching him.

He caught his breath. "Up on Cherry Street, Lars, when you went into the house. Did you see any sign of a child there?"

Lars shook his head. "I did not, Justy. I'm sorry."

His ears buzzed. There was a whining sound, as though someone had rung a tuning fork and held it beside his right ear. He felt someone throw an arm around his shoulders. It was like being wrapped in a ship's anchor line. Lars, he was sure. His best friend. He must apologize for the hard words he had used.

The arm pulled him towards a carriage. He saw men looking at him. Wide, expressionless faces under flat farmers' caps. His uncle's men. His uncle's carriage. Now he knew what people said when they talked about a puppet whose strings had been cut. Lars—it must be Lars—eased him up the steps and into the cab. He must apologize to his friend. The whining sound in his ears was louder now. A hand on his back pushed him forward until his head was between his knees and the blood thumped like a bass drum in his temples.

He closed his eyes and thought about Kerry. Skin the color of raw sugar, eyes like the sea. The girl he knew before had never lied, or stolen or betrayed anyone. But that girl was gone. The girl was a woman now, and she was broken, shattered like a piece of crystal.

But what had broken her? He let his mind sweep over the last few days, from the moment he had seen her lift a rich man's wallet to their last meeting in the church. All their conversations. Everything she had said.

He knew all about lies. He had spent enough time coaxing the truth from men, and he had learned that the most effective falsehoods were those that had a kernel of truth to them. The trick was finding out what was true and what was false.

He thought again about what she had said, and how she had said it. When she had looked him in the eyes, and when she had looked away. How her eyes had looked, and her face and her hands. She had learned how to double as a man. She was a good actress. But not a great one. He thought about the lies he knew about: about her knowing Colley—or not knowing him—about Campbell and Fraser; about her reasons for following him. He saw that she had rarely lied outright. Instead, she had been evasive and lied by omission. The more he thought about what she had told him, about meeting Colley, about the rape, about the child, the more he thought she was telling the truth. That she was trapped. That she had no choice. That, like it or not, she needed his help.

He rubbed his face and sat up straight. He was in the Bull's carriage, sitting on a hard bench. He saw two faces staring at him, lit by the dim glow from a street lantern and a weak moon. Lars and the Bull. His uncle and his friend, shoulder to shoulder on the bench opposite.

"He's alive, then," the Bull said.

Lars grinned, his big red beard bristling like a windblown hedgerow. "Looks that way. Something he ate, you reckon?"

"Something he had to swallow, for sure."

The Bull knocked twice on the wall behind him, and the carriage lurched forward. Lars wedged himself into the corner of the cab, folded his arms and closed his eyes.

"Where are we going?" Justy asked.

"We'll take Lars here down to his ship, and then get you home. I'll send ahead to have Corla make your bed up and warm something for you in the kitchen."

"No."

"No?"

"Thank you, but no. I'm going with Lars. We have to find Kerry."

Lars' eyes bounced open, as though he had been slapped awake. The Bull scoffed. "Jesus, boy. What do you want with that wee wasp now, after all she's done?"

Justy stared at his uncle. "Did you know it all?"

"I did not. I knew some of it. I knew she was thieving. I knew she was in and out of Colley's libben. But about a kinchin . . ." He shrugged.

"What about O'Toole? Does he ken what she's been about?"

"He does not. The man has enough on his plate."

"You don't want him distracted from doing your dirty work, is what."

The Bull looked amused. "You're right about that."

Justy shook his head. "I wish I knew what it was put her on that road."

The Bull was grinning now, the sickly light turning his teeth green.

"What?"

"What?" he mocked. "It was you, Justice. You put her on that road."

"Don't talk shite. Me?"

"You don't remember the way Kerry watched you when she was a tib? She worshiped you. Remember how you used to gurn on about changing your fate, finding a new life, escaping from the waterfront? About how just because you were Irish didn't mean you couldn't make it in the world? Well, I may not have listened to any of your bollocks, but she did. And when you upped and left, and she looked around, and saw where she was headed, she decided she wasn't having any of it. Marriage to some county Mayo shabbaroon, or cleaning rich coves' privies or making her money on her back? Not for her. She decided to do what the great Justy Flanagan done, and change her stars. And here we are."

There was a weight in Justy's stomach, a ball of leaded shot. He saw Kerry's thirteen-year-old eyes, wide and green under her fringe of dark hair, staring up at him as he talked and talked and talked.

"If I wanted to find Kerry now, where would she be, would you say?"

The Bull shook his head. "I'd steer clear, if I were you, lad."

"Aye, well, you're not me, are you."

The Bull made an exasperated sound and sat back heavily in his seat. The cab filled with the noise of the wheels rattling on the cobbles beneath them, and the creak and scrape and jangle of the carriage's wood and leather and brass. Lars was watching him, a question in his eyes. Justy shook his head, and his friend looked away.

It was a few moments before the Bull spoke. "What you said to Owens back there, about putting us right with the law. Is it possible?"

Justy shrugged. "Any lawyer could do it."

"Aye, but will you? You've made it plain what you think about the whole racket. I didn't say anything, but I can't see you kissing any arses to help raise money or find clients for a slave bawd."

Justy looked him in the eye.

"So why did you back me?"

"Because I wanted Colley. And Turner. And it was the only way of keeping you from getting milled." He smiled. "Plus, it gives me a way of poking that black bastard Owens in the eye."

"How's that?"

The Bull's grin widened. "Owens isn't a fool. He knows you're going to be about as useful to him as a paper hat in a house fire. He won't trust you to do anything you've said, except keep your mouth shut and stay out of the way. If you don't keep that part of the deal, you're dead, and there's nothing I can do about it."

"Fair enough. But if he knows I'm not going to do anything to help him, why give me what I want?"

"Because he doesn't need Colley as much as he needs me. He can hire people in the South if he has to, and he has Gracie to look after the Wall Street end. And he's sharp enough to twig that he can pay a lawyer to do what you said to do. But there's only one man can get his cargo off the New York wharves and up to Bedlow Street."

"Ho!" the driver called, and Justy looked out of the window of the cab. They were passing Dover Street. The carriage jolted as several of the Bull's men jumped off.

"So how big is your cut?" Justy asked.

303

"Twenty percent. Same as the rest."

"You, Owens, Colley, Turner and Gracie."

A smirk. "You haven't lost your head for figures, then."

Justy ignored the jibe. "What I can't figure is why you're taking the risk. I've never known you to take a percentage of anything. Whether it's whores or contraband or services rendered, it's always been payment up front with you. What makes this different?"

The wooden bench of the carriage creaked as the Bull shifted his weight. "How is it you think you know so much about my affairs?"

"Christ, Uncle. I lived in your house for five years, remember. You're not exactly the most subtle of creatures. All I did was keep my eyes and ears open. And ask a question here and there."

The Bull's mouth twitched. "That's what I get for keeping an Irish crew, I suppose. I never thought you had a mind to pay much attention when you were coming up."

"What else did I have to do, except study?"

A grunt of acknowledgment. "Then it won't have escaped your notice that there's not much chink in this business. I may own a fair whack of the properties on the East River front, but I employ a good portion of them that live there, too. Those men have to be paid. Their folk have to be looked after. And the buildings they all live and work in have to be maintained. That all adds up to plenty of plate."

"I can't say I've ever seen much in the way of maintenance."

A shrug. "It's a fine line. If I pour too much money into those properties, I'll never get it back. If I up the rents too much, folk will just up sticks and go to Canvas Town. Then nobody'll get paid, and I don't have a nice cushion of cash to tide me over until times get better, not like them puff guts up on Wall Street."

The wheels of the carriage screeched as they turned a corner, heading downhill now. Justy steadied himself on the bench with his hands. "So that's what this is about? Your retirement?"

The Bull scowled. "Don't mock me, boy. I've been trying my whole life to find a way to pull money out of the waterfront, and I'm telling you, it can't be done. Any investment I may make is too damned shallow to yield more than a pinch. Taverns, brothels, boardinghouses, they barely make any chink, so there's precious little skim, and they go out of business quicker than a rat up a beggar's blanket."

"But why a slave brothel, for Christ's sake? Why not shipping, or property or . . . anything else?" He could hear the pleading tone in his own voice. The Bull heard it, too, and he laughed.

"Why don't I go down Wall Street, you mean? Why don't I tiptoe into the Tontine fucking Coffee House and whiddle them dimber coves in their lace cuffs that the Bull's in the market for the right investment?" He laughed again, a harsh, grating sound, like an ass braying.

"Well, why not?"

The Bull sat forward suddenly, thrusting his face at Justy. "Are you fucking blind, son? Do you not see? I'm a teaguelander, a six and tips, a jumped-up, Fenian boglander Paddy bastard. Like you. Like your poor, stupid, cod-headed clunch of a father."

His face was dark. He sat back, breathing heavily. "No one's going to go into business with me. Or any other Irishman. Why do you think Francie was such a goddamned failure?"

Justy's chest was tight. "That's not true. What about Jarlath Cantillon? He had the run of the Tontine."

"Aye, but only as their serf. They only let the spineless, carrot-headed madge in the place because he told them his father was a Scotchman and he was raised an Ulster Protestant. The lying tosspot." He pulled a handkerchief from his pocket

305

and mopped his face. "I've been trying for years to get into something with a hint of a prospect, but these nativist bastards won't let me. Just like they wouldn't let your old man. The pigs are happy to pay the Irish to work, but they won't touch our fucking money. It's like it's diseased."

"But Colley was desperate."

"Yes, he was. He wanted to do the usual deal, cash for services, but he couldn't raise enough chink, and I saw I had a chance." He waved a hand dismissively. "Would I rather have been in something respectable? Sure I would, but a whore doesn't get to choose who parts her knees."

"You won't get respectable this way."

The carriage jolted over a pothole, and the Bull brayed his donkey laugh. "I don't want to be respectable, lad. I couldn't give a doxy's muff-wipe what the quality think of me. It's not their good opinions I'm after; it's their money."

"You look comfortable enough."

"Looks can be a lie." The Bull slid a self-conscious hand over his wide belly. "I remember your father saying to me once, 'It's one thing to make a few coins quick on the street, but if you want to fill a chest with gelt, the only place to do it is on that crooked lane that runs from Trinity Church to the water.' It's taken me twenty years to see he was right. And to see where he went about it all wrong. The dumb bastard went down there looking for partners, and no one would give him the time of day. But if he'd come with cash in hand, well, that would have been different. Money's got its own language, see? No one gives a cracked arse where it comes from; they just scoop it up and spend it. The problem is making it in the first place. And I will make it. I'll make a fucking barrel of it, and when I kick down the door of their fucking coffee house and pour the ducats in a heap on the floor, those Wall Street porkers'll shove their snouts right in. They'll call me Mr. fucking Flanagan, and say 'thank you, sir.'"

He sat back on the hard bench. "I suppose I'll have to wait for a while now, mind."

His face was deep in shadow. Justy could hear the slight wheeze in his breath over the sound of the carriage wheels on the road. The Bull was a huge man, mean, violent and dangerous, but he seemed pathetic now, like a rat trying to claw its way out of a hole it had wriggled into and grown too fat to climb out of again. But he was right about the way the New York elites saw the Irish. Like lice, streaming over the ocean, good for hard labor and whoring, and not much else. And what the Bull said about Justy's father made sense. He had barely grubbed out a living on the margins of Wall Street, denied a seat at the table by men who smiled at him with one side of their mouth and spat out insults with the other. "Brisket beater." "Red-letter man." "Craw thumper." "Catholic."

"What do you mean, you'll have to wait?" Justy asked.

His uncle shrugged. "I don't know if it'll even happen now. Things were already looking shaky before tonight. It took Jack a long time to get things going below the Line, and this Wall Street money-raising malarkey looks like a dog's breakfast to me. Never mind Cantillon. It's a miracle none of the investors have twigged us yet."

"People are too greedy to see what's plain in front of them."

"Most of the time, aye. But this anti-slavery carry-on is something else. Everywhere I look coves are reading pamphlets and handbills and newspaper editorials about it. I caught Duffy with a tract last week. Duffy, for Christ's sake! He said he got it from some cove making a speech on a fucking street corner. So I'd say you're dead on about Manumission getting stronger. The tide's been turning for a while. Jack reckoned the abolition bill passing was an opportunity, but now I think we're in danger of attracting the wrong kind of attention."

"I thought you didn't give a damn for how people see you."

"Nor do I. But I am bothered by how they see my businesses. And the whoring business in particular. The Quaker ladies of this city would love to shut down every nugging shop in the city, but their menfolk won't have it. You've never seen anyone boycotting a brothel, have you? Too many gents like their evening pastimes. But slavery's another matter. If word got out that we were involved in both the bawdy business and slaving, of any kind, those ladies would have a spree. We'd have a crowd of crows on the sidewalk up there, all singing lustily from the hymnbook. And that would be the end of that."

A queasy light from the streetlamps strobed through the windows of the cab, lighting the Bull's face one moment and casting it into shadow the next. They were going downhill again, slowly enough that the horse's hooves were louder on the stones than the carriage's wheels. Justy wondered what time it was.

The carriage pulled to a halt. The Bull opened the door, and the fresh smell of seawater and kelp filled the cab. Justy went to stand up, but the Bull stopped him, a hand on his thigh.

"I warn you, Justice. Lew Owens is in this thing up to his neck, now that he's bought Jack out. If you blow it all up, Lew has every right to come after you." He paused and looked Justy hard in the eye. "So I'm asking, will you stick to your end of the deal? To keep your mouth shut and not do anything to queer the lay?"

Justy waited for a moment before answering. "People are going to find out what you're up to, soon enough. You won't be able to stop word spreading, and were I you, I'd get as far from it as possible. Starting now. It won't matter whether you're legal or not. The city will do everything it can to shut you down." He held up his hands. "But I won't light the fuse, I promise. Like I told Owens, I'll not say a word more about this to anyone. Not to the law, not to your investors and not to your clients, not that

I know who they are anyway. From now on, I'll keep my nose out of Bedlow Street. You have my word."

The Bull gave him a long, calculating look. Then he patted his thigh. "Right you are, then. I'll see you around."

THIRTY-SIX

Justy and Lars climbed out into the street. They had drawn up beside an alley that ran down between two ancient warehouses. There was a strong smell of tobacco leaf, and between the two buildings Justy could see the water and the moonlight rippling and twisting on it, like silver filigree.

The wheels of the Bull's carriage screeched on the granite as it made a turn, men hanging on tight to the cab, their faces shadowed by their caps.

Lars took a long sniff, then spat into the gutter. "So that's the Bull. He's a scary big bastard, isn't he?"

"He might say the same of you."

"I'm like a pat of warm butter next to him. He reminds me of a skipper I knew once. He drowned a man for lighting a fire belowdecks in a storm. Hung him on a long rope from the bowsprit by his ankles. Dragged him for a league before he pulled him out."

"That sounds like the Bull, right enough. What did you make of that yarn of his?"

"Didn't strike me as a yarn, so much."

"You believed him?"

"Why not? He's right about the way most folks see the Irish in this town. Muscle and madge for hire. He wants to be seen as more than that, but an Irishman's got precious few options when it comes to making money. Your old man found that out, too, I'd say."

"You can't compare the two, Lars."

"No? They may have taken different roads, but they both wanted the same thing. To get the hell out."

"And they both had to sell their souls to do it." The words were out of his mouth before he had even formed them in his mind.

Lars' voice was soft. "Your da sounds like he was a brave one. It takes balls to beard the lion in his den. I wish I'd met the man."

"I wish you had, too."

They walked down the narrow alleyway between the tobacco sheds, their boots crunching on loose stones.

"I'm sorry about what I said before, Lars."

"You mean telling me to go bob meself? Don't fadge. Besides, you already apologized."

"I did?"

"About twenty times, when I was trying to stuff you into the cab there. You were slurring away like a rare old swill-tub. Quite like old times."

"Well, I'm sorry anyway." Justy glanced at his friend. "You think I'm spooney for trying to help Kerry, don't you?"

Lars shrugged. "I think you have plenty of history. And I think you feel guilty, too. Which is pure danna, by the way. How can you be blamed for choices that she made on her own, with you a thousand miles away? Your uncle's talking a load of cock."

"You don't think I influenced her?"

Lars shrugged. "I wasn't there, so I can't say. Maybe she did swallow all your trumpery when she was a tib, but she's a grown woman now. She has the hack of one who knows her own mind. And one who wouldn't take kindly to the idea that she could be steered one way or the other by anyone but herself."

"But I think she was steered, Lars; I think Colley got a hook in her early and she's been wriggling on the end of his line ever since."

"You believe her, then?"

"I do. I believe Colley raped her, and conned her and kept her."

"And the kinchin?"

"What else could force her to do what she did? Betray her oldest friend? What would it take for you to do that to me?"

Lars said nothing.

"She tried to warn me about Turner," Justy went on. "She told me to stop following her, and then tried to give me the slip. To stop him from coming at me. She didn't want to do any of this, Lars. I'm sure of it."

On the other side of the dock, the *Netherleigh* rose up against the dark sky, pale masts and black rigging, like a thicket of birch trees in winter. Justy stopped. "I'm going to try and find her, Lars. She needs my help. Turner will hunt her down. It's what he does."

"What about her cousin? Surely he'll take care of her."

"Even if Owens could give a dog's plug for her, and even if she trusts him enough to stay with him, she can't hole up in his libben forever. Turner will find a hidey-hole close by, and he'll settle into it, and he'll wait, as long as he needs. After that, he'll be in the wind. But right now, he doesn't know where she is, not for sure. Which means he's at large, looking for her, and that gives me a chance to catch him, before he goes to ground."

Lars took a deep breath. "And you want my help, I suppose."

"Only if you want to give it."

"I think you're cracked."

"Perhaps I am."

"But I owe you one. For dragging me out of that feckin' marsh."

"I keep telling you, Lars, you saved my hide enough times before. You don't owe me for that."

"For Gorey then." Lars' face was grim in the silvery light. "For helping me put those evil bastards to the sword for what they did to my ma."

They were quiet for a moment, remembering how redcoat blood had run like a river down the narrow Wexford lane, between a low cliff and a thick wood. How the flies had feasted and the Defenders had stood among the bodies, breathing hard through their mouths, their noses clogged with gunsmoke and the smell of the dead.

"We never got Hunter Gowan," Justy said.

Lars' beard bristled. "Perhaps if I light enough candles, God will allow our paths to cross one day."

"I'd like to be there to see it."

Lars chuckled. "All right then, I'm with you. Let's catch this rat. Where do we start?"

Justy nodded to the *Netherleigh*. "In your armory, of course."

Lars made a rumbling sound, deep in his throat. "You sneaking hog grubber. You had this all planned, did you? And what if I'd told you to go box yourself?"

"Then I'd have left you to climb into your scratcher and dream about the adventures we might have had." Justy grinned. "Now come on, big man. We've work to do."

They stepped quickly towards the ship, the heels of their boots loud on the granite blocks of the hard.

And then Lars stopped.

There was no breeze and the dock was silent, apart from the gentle slosh and suck of the water between the *Netherleigh*'s hull and the quay. And there was no sign of the duty watchman, either on the dock or on the ship. Lars frowned. "Someone's getting a slap."

Justy looked up to the top of the gangway. A thin layer of cloud had screened the moon, so that the light in the sky was hazy. He felt his skin prickle. Lars started up the gangplank. It creaked and groaned, rubbing against the gunwale of the ship as he climbed. When he reached the top, he squatted in the gangway and looked around.

He waved Justy up and pointed into the shadow cast by the side of the ship. A sailor lay there, his feet bare, his knees pulled up to his chest. He might have been asleep. But Justy could tell from the slack look to his limbs that he was dead.

The sailor's skin was pale and waxy. There was no hair on his cheeks, and when Justy lifted his chin, gently, he recognized Sandy's high forehead and ragged fringe. He pushed the boy's head back and saw a thin line across his neck. It looked blue in the moonlight.

He took the knife from his boot. The blade snapped open. *Turner,* he mouthed.

Lars made the sign of a pistol with his hand and raised an eyebrow. Justy ran a hand down the sailor's body and turned him. He shook his head. Lars winced.

The *Netherleigh* was a three-masted schooner. The captain's cabin and galley were housed in a small, square structure between the foremast and the bows of the ship. Another, similar structure towards the stern contained the chart room, a small storeroom and a top cabin used by the duty mates and the watch crew.

Justy and Lars pulled off their boots and walked silently to the center mast. Nothing moved. Lars bent to check the cargo doors were locked; then they split up, Justy moving forward and Lars aft.

The galley was empty. The windows to the captain's cabin were curtained. Justy put his ear to the cabin door and listened. There was no sound.

The hinges of all the doors on the *Netherleigh* were greased with pork fat, and the cabin door swung open silently. There was a high bunk against the back wall, with a built-in desk underneath. There was a man slumped in a chair at the desk, but the earthy smell of a voided bowel told Justy he was dead. He stepped into the cabin and pushed the dead man's shoulder, turning him so that the moonlight fell on his face.

Justy had only met the *Netherleigh*'s captain once, the day he boarded the ship. He remembered a tall man, with a neat beard and an amused look in his eye. Now those eyes were glazed and empty. Justy lifted the captain's chin and saw the thin line across his neck.

There was a map on the table, weighed down by a parallel ruler and a pair of dividers. The moonlight gleamed on the long brass points. Justy slipped the instrument into his pocket.

He stood in the cabin, listening, feeling the pulse in the cuts in his head, listening for anything other than the creak of the ship's timbers and the light slap of water on wood. There was nothing. He slipped out onto the deck and around the stern of the ship, in a long, slow, silent loop. Nothing moved.

He knew instinctively that something was wrong. Lars should have shown himself by now. Which meant Turner had taken him prisoner. Not killed him, because a pistol shot would have made too much noise and Lars would have fought like a wild man if Turner had tried the garrote. And there had been no noise. Which meant Lars was alive.

Justy squatted on the deck, facing the chart room door, his back against the aft mast. He knew the ship's routines, knew there were always three watchmen on board. One was dead. The other two would have been asleep in the top cabin, on the other side of the chart room, making them easy targets for Turner. He had to assume they were either dead or subdued. Either way, they would be no help to him.

He watched the chart room door. It was one of three places Turner could be, and the most likely: the storeroom was too small, the top cabin too cramped, especially if Turner had to share it with three bodies. He could sense Turner waiting for him. He thought of the layout of the room. It was the same size as the captain's cabin, but instead of a deep bunk, a shallow cupboard was fixed to the far wall. The door opened outwards. He guessed Turner would be sitting in the corner on the right side of the room to cover both the door and Lars, who would be wedged into the corner opposite. He pictured Turner, sitting on the floor, his back to the corner, pistol arm steadied on his knee, ready to fire.

He walked over and squatted to the right of the door, his back to the wall. He used the butt of his knife to tap twice, softly, on the door.

There was no answer.

"Turner? I know you're in there."

Silence.

He twisted his arm behind him and used the tip of his knife to lift the latch of the door. It opened outwards, swinging silently on greased hinges. He turned, and stepped back carefully, his head ducked forward, as he tried to get a look inside the room and not present too much of a target.

The moon was over his left shoulder. It sent just enough light into the chart room for him to see all the way into the corner. It was empty. In which case, Turner would be on one side of the entrance, pressed to the outer wall, his pistol pointed right where Justy's head would be.

But which side?

He took a deep breath and hurled himself through the doorway, his knife in front of him, angling to the right. There was no one there, and he instinctively dropped to the floor, rolling left, cringing in anticipation of the explosion and the pain of the ball in his back. But nothing came.

He bounced to his feet. The room was empty, except for a body crumpled in the far corner. There was enough light to see Lars' unruly beard and shaven head, and without thinking Justy went down on his knee to see if his friend was dead.

And then he heard the sound of something dropping lightly to the deck behind him.

"Drop the chive," Turner ordered, the Yorkshire accent thick in his voice, as though he had just stepped off the boat from England. "Stand up slowly."

Justy didn't move. He watched Lars, looking for a movement, his chest rising and falling, any sign that he was alive.

"Your friend's luckier than you," Turner said. "He went down hard when I hit him, but he'll be right in an hour or so. You won't be so crow."

Justy squeezed his knife tight in his hand. He could spin around and lunge, but if Turner was more than a long step away he'd be finished. And Turner wasn't the type to let a man get close to him a second time.

He dropped the knife. He stood up slowly.

"Hands clasped behind your head. And turn around. Easy now."

Justy did as he was told. Turner held the watchman's pistol, leveled at Justy's chest. He stood two long paces away, another sign that he knew what he was about. He was barefoot.

"Where were you?" Justy asked.

"On the roof. You both fell for it. Sloppy."

Justy cursed himself silently. Turner took a step back. He jerked his head. "Out. And don't even think about going for your chive."

The screen of cloud had dissipated, and the moon hung, fat and bright, in the sky. The scrubbed deck shone like a beach of white sand. Justy glanced at the pistol, at Turner's dark, birdlike eyes. "Get on with it, then."

"Oh, I'll not shoot you. I'd rather not make the noise." Turner grinned. "But I won't think twice if you push me."

"What then?"

"You'll see. Get round the back. To the storeroom."

It was a small cabinet, sectioned off at the end of the top cabin. Inside was all the equipment the crew might need in an emergency. Bailing buckets, gaffs, marlinspikes and coils of rope, stacked on shelves.

"Take that half-inch hawser out," Turner ordered. "Then come back here and tie it on to the rail." He jerked his head towards a section of the rail on the seaward side of the ship. "No one'll see us there."

Justy pulled the rope off the shelf. He felt cold inside, and his arms and legs were heavy as though cuffed with lead weights. The rail of the ship seemed a mile away.

Turner matched his steps, the pistol aimed at his chest. "Don't even think about jumping, Flanagan. If you step up on that rail without my say-so, I'll plug you. And then I'll go back and take care of your *marra*. But if you do like you're told, he'll live to see the sunrise."

Turner grinned. "When they wake up in the morning, they'll find you over the side, struck by the hempen fever. And they'll find this on you." He took something out of his pocket and dangled it in the air. It was a moment before Justy realized it was the garrote.

"You'll not get away with this."

"Oh, I won't?" Turner looked surprised. "Who was the last one to see Drummond alive? And Cantillon? And here's you on board a ship with two others milled the same way, and with the murder weapon in your pocket."

"Lars will tell the truth."

"Who's going to pay mind to him? He's your best pal; everyone knows that by now. Jake Hays'll listen to me first. It might take him a while to believe me, what with all the poison you've dripped in his ear, but it's always the physical evidence that speaks loudest for good old Jake. And then there's the clincher."

"What's that?"

"Why, that you committed self-murder out of remorse." Turner grinned. "Just like your poor dear daddy."

Justy stared. He felt as though his chest were being crushed.

Turner waggled the pistol. "There's that look again. Still want to cut my parts off, do you?" He spat on the deck. "Make a loop at the end of that rope. Then measure six feet and tie it off. And be sure to make it a solid knot."

Justy gritted his teeth. He tied a running knot, watching out of the corner of his eye. Turner kept two paces away, his pistol aimed steady. Close enough to be certain of his accuracy, but too far away for a rush. Justy considered using the rope as a flail, to knock the pistol out of Turner's hands, but what if he missed? If he took a bullet, he and Lars would both die.

He measured six feet from the knot and secured the rope to the rail. The rope was new, so it was coarse and stiff in his hands. It smelled like old hay.

"Put a stopper on it. I don't want it coming undone when you put your weight on it." Turner's eyes gleamed. "Now put the loop around your neck. Knot behind the left ear, like a proper topping cove would do. That's right." He threw the garrote onto the deck. "Pick that up. Put it in your pocket."

The wire was about three feet long, made of a dozen or more thin strands, twisted together and tied into two loops, wide enough to fit a hand through. The loops were wrapped with leather that was stained with blood and sweat.

"You're wondering if that was the instrument did for your daddy, aren't you?" Turner said. "I'd like to say it was, because that would make this even more sweet, but I doubt it. Jack's not really the sentimental type, and given he told me to get rid of his wire for him, I'd say he's not fool enough to keep an obvious murder weapon on his person for longer than he has to."

"Jack Colley?" It was suddenly hard to breathe. "Jack Colley killed my father?"

"Well, of course he did. Who did you think it was? Me? I'm a blade cock, not a wireman."

"You killed two men with a garrote tonight."

"Aye, well, you filched my knife, didn't you? Jack's wire was the only thing I had to hand. And it's not as though I don't know how to use a wire. They're just bloody awkward. There's no mess, I'll give you that, but it takes the bastards forever to die."

The sweat was cold on Justy's face. Turner laughed. "Look at the gurn on you. White as a virgin's belly. Colley fooled you, then."

"He said it was you. He said you killed them all. Drummond and Cantillon, too."

"Oh aye? Well, I couldn't have, could I? I was across the river in New Jersey when Drummond copped it. And I was stopping a fight at Beekman's Tavern when Cantillon was done. If you'd been half the fox you think you are, you'd have found that out before."

Justy said nothing. Turner was right. He hadn't questioned his own assumption that Turner had been the killer, and he had swallowed Colley's lie whole.

Turner waggled the pistol. "Enough talking, now. Pick that thing up and put it in your pocket."

Justy bent slowly. The coarse rope chafed his neck, and the knot bumped against his ear as he leaned forward to pick up the garrote. He slid the wire into his pocket. He felt a bump of excitement as his fingers touched something smooth. The dividers that he had taken off the captain's table. He squeezed the points together and slid the instrument up his sleeve.

The pistol jerked up again. "Onto the rail now. Face me."

Justy used a shroud to climb up. He tried not to look down, but he was acutely aware of the drop beneath him, thirty feet down to the dark, moonlight-striped surface of the sea. The points of the dividers dug into his palm. He turned and stood on the rail, his feet shoulder width apart, his right arm pressing on the shroud.

It was suddenly cooler. He looked over the roof of the chart room at the sleeping city. The air was quite clear, and he felt the slightest breeze at his back, bringing him the fresh smell of the sea. The streetlights had long gone out on Broad Street, but it cut a wide silver swath in the moonlight, down through the darkened buildings to the docks.

Nothing moved.

And then something.

A lithe figure appeared at the gangway, paused for a moment and then darted silently across the deck behind the chart room.

Justy felt a rush of warmth through him. It was never easy to see color in the moonlight, but he was certain the figure was a woman, and that the hat she wore was green.

He looked down at Turner, in his ripped coat, his hair pulled back from his battered face, tight against his scalp. The pistol seemed to point directly between Justy's eyes. It was an awkward angle for the Yorkshireman, holding a heavy pistol high in the air. Justy wondered how long he could keep his aim.

Turner licked his lips. "It's been a long time since I enjoyed topping a man this much."

"And you said I was the evil one. Looks like you're the one with the horn now."

Turner smirked. "You've only got a moment left, Flanagan. Don't you want to say something? One of your papish prayers, maybe?"

"Aye. Maybe."

He kept his eyes on Turner as Kerry came, slow and quiet, around the far side of the chart room. She carried a long gaff, with a wicked curved hook.

"Hurry up, Paddy," Turner snapped. "I haven't got all night."

Justy felt the wind on his back again. There was a long, creaking sound as the breeze hit the masts, and the *Netherleigh* rolled on its keel. The movement made Kerry stumble slightly, and the haft of her gaff thumped on the wooden deck.

Turner spun around, and Justy launched himself off the rail, the dividers sliding into his hand. He landed on Turner's back and stabbed hard at his right kidney. Turner gasped, his knees folding under him and the pistol skittering away across the deck. He groped hopelessly after it for a second, then rolled away, fast as an eel onto his back, lashing out with his fists at Justy's face. Justy ignored the blows and forced himself close, stabbing wildly. Turner hissed in pain as the spike caught him in the side, but instead of weakening, he grabbed for the rope around Justy's neck and pulled hard.

The rope went tight, and Justy took a deep breath and stabbed again, going for Turner's face now, his eyes. He felt the points of the dividers go deep, and Turner screeched. Blood splashed Justy's hand. He stabbed again, and felt one of the points of the dividers break off. Turner was screaming in pain now, but still hauling hard on the rope with both hands, dragging it tight over his shoulder and across his chest.

Justy could feel his windpipe being crushed. Panic snapped at him as he fought for breath. He jerked his head forward, trying to force the knot loose, but it was like a vice around his neck. Turner hauled on the rope again, bracing Justy's head against his own as he tightened the noose.

Justy felt something soft in his mouth. Turner's ear. He bit down hard, and Turner bucked under him, jerking on the rope, and Justy tasted warm blood and felt the rage boil through him.

His fists clenched, and the brass pivot of the dividers dug into his palm.

His mind cleared. The hawser was like an iron fetter on his throat, and his head felt as though it might burst, but he was laughing inside. His teeth were still sunk deep into Turner's flesh, and he jerked his head back and was rewarded with a grunt of pain. He lifted the dividers and braced the cool metal on his cheek. Then he tightened his grip, braced himself and rammed the unbroken point home, deep into Turner's ear.

The rope came loose. Justy rolled away, scrabbling at the coarse fibers, his vision graying around the edges as he tried to loosen the knot. It seemed to take forever, and then the hellish pressure on his throat was gone, and he was sucking air, over and over, staring up at the moon as the world closed in around him and dragged him under.

THIRTY-SEVEN

It was like being pulled out of a deep well. Out of the darkness into the light, soaked and shivering. He lay on his back, gasping like a landed fish, his neck burning.

Kerry stood over him, a dripping bucket in her hands. "Are you alive, then?"

He stared at her, anger and relief fighting inside him. He tried to speak, but his throat was closed. He made a strangled noise.

She dropped the bucket. "Well, if you can squawk, you can walk. Get up now. We've work to do."

He took her hand and she hauled him to his feet. There was a rain barrel lashed to the outside wall of the chart room, and he pulled the lid off and pushed his face into the cool water. He took a mouthful and swallowed hard. There was a tearing sensation, then a shock of pain, like a hundred needles being pushed into his throat. He gagged and spat.

He felt Kerry's hand on his back.

He dipped his head again, ignoring the pain as the cool water ran down the back of his throat. He coughed, spat and drank again until the pain was a dull ache. Kerry squeezed his shoulder. He stood up and pushed her away.

"You lied to me, Kerry." His voice was a wheeze, barely more than a whisper. "You helped Turner kill those girls. You led Lars into a trap. You nearly got me killed."

Her face was hard. "I had to. I didn't want to lie to you. I didn't want to do any of those things. But Colley made me. I told you."

"You told me a lot of things."

"You don't believe me?"

"I didn't say that." Justy touched his throat gingerly.

"Damn you to hell if you don't, Justy. You have no idea." Her eyes were suddenly bright. "I told you Daniel was with a nurse-maid. When all this started, Colley took me to see him. He was in his crib, sleeping. Colley pulled up his nightgown. He had a knife. He put the tip on Daniel's belly and said if I didn't do like he said, he'd gut him, then feed him to the pigs. Alive."

She held Justy's gaze. "I've seen what Colley's done. I know what he can do. He wouldn't think twice. So I did what I was told."

It was a moment before Justy spoke. "Where is Daniel now?"

"At my cousin's. Colley knew the Bull would turn over the houses on Bedlow and Cherry, so he brought the child to Lew's house for safekeeping." A hint of a smile. "He didn't reckon on you making that deal and cutting him out."

"How do you know about that?"

Her smile widened. "I was outside, in the garden. Under the window. I heard the whole thing, you crafty Turk."

"Owens said he hadn't seen you."

"Nor did he. I knew Colley would send one of his dogs after me, and I knew that Lew's place would be the first place they'd look. So I went in hugger-mugger, making sure no one tipped me."

"You saw Daniel?"

"I had to climb up the side of the bloody house to do it, but aye, I saw him. He's safe."

The wind gusted gently, and the boat heeled over. Justy stepped back to steady himself, then jumped as he felt something sticky under his foot. Turner was sprawled on his back, his eyes wide open, two inches of brass sticking out of his ear and a halo of black blood around his head. Justy staggered back against the barrel, frantically scraping his bare foot on the deck. It left a dark smear on the wood.

He felt panic snap at him, then Kerry's hands on his shoulders. Her face close to his. He was shaking. She hugged him tight. The coarse material of her hat bristled against his cheek. "You had no choice."

He pushed her away. He felt a terrible pressure inside him, words boiling up into his throat. But he could not speak. He spun around and plunged his head into the barrel. His head burned, as though it might boil the water. He closed his eyes, trying to push the thoughts away. But he could not. It wasn't the panic and fear that frightened him. Not the terrible clarity of the idea that he had to kill Turner or be killed. It was another sensation entirely. The breathless glee as he drove his weapon home. The raging triumph as the life came out of his enemy. He had enjoyed it.

He crouched beside the barrel, water running over his shoulders, gasping for breath for the second time that night. His throat burned, as though he had swallowed a bucket of flaming pitch, but he welcomed the pain.

Kerry watched him. "Come on, now," she said, eventually. "We need to be away from here."

He stood up slowly, wiping his face. Christ, but he was tired. "What are you even doing here, Kerry? Did you come after Turner?"

"I came after you. I wanted to explain. I followed the Bull's cab, but when I got here, I knew there was something off. I watched you go up, and when I saw the two of you take your boots off, I knew Turner had set a trap."

Justy thought about how long it had taken him to check the ship. First the galley and the captain's cabin. Then the chart room. After Turner had surprised him, it had taken several minutes more to go to the storeroom, collect the rope and begin tying it off.

"It took you long enough to come and help."

She said nothing.

He nodded. "You waited, didn't you? Until he showed himself. You didn't want to help us. You wanted to kill him."

"Aye, and why not?" She spat on the deck. "We were only supposed to find those girls and bring them back. Not kill them. But he gutted them, and cut their faces like they were dirt. I wanted to jam that spike into his guts and twist it until he squealed like the pig he was."

The moonlight had turned her face into a waxen mask. Her eyes were shadowed, but Justy could feel the hate and anger burning there.

"It wasn't just Colley, was it?" He kept his voice soft. "Turner too?"

"Jack liked to share me around. Turner. A sweaty pig called Barnes. A few others." Her tone was flat.

Justy felt as though he were standing apart from himself. His mouth was dry. He swallowed, but it was like forcing a handful of sand down his gullet. "I'm sorry."

She nodded. "So now you know the whole thing. Are you with me?"

"To do what?"

"To finish this. To kill Black Jack Colley."

THIRTY-EIGHT

They left Lars snoring in the cabin and were halfway down the gangway when Justy stopped.

"What are you doing?" Kerry whispered.

He pulled the garrote from his pocket. "That bastard had it when he came on board. He'll have it on him when they carry him off."

He ran up onto the deck and tucked the wire into Turner's coat. He went to pick up the watchman's pistol, but the hammer had broken when it hit the deck, and he left it where it lay.

Kerry was waiting for him on the dock, leaning on the wall in the shadow of the bailiff's office. She gave Justy a long look.

"What?" he asked.

"What about your deal with Colley?"

He looked her in the eye. "What about it?"

She smiled slightly. "He keeps valuables in all his kips, just in case. He'll visit them all, if he has time."

"How many places does he have?"

"Four. Bedlow Street, Cherry Street. A house in Greenwich and the warehouse at Hallam's Wharf. I don't know which ones he'll go to first."

"And we can't tear around the city after him. We can't count on him stopping to rest, either. We have to intercept him."

"Sure. But where?"

Justy swallowed, wincing at the tightness in his throat. The skin on his neck was tender, but when he touched it there was no blood. He tugged the silk band of his cravat up to cover the chafed skin. He thought of Cantillon, the way the lawyer clutched at his neck when he introduced him to Colley. "How about the Tontine? Do you think he kept anything there?"

Kerry nodded. "I hadn't thought of that, but aye, more than likely. He was always there. He kept papers and things there. So why not money, too?"

It was a short walk, made even faster by the lateness of the hour. There was no traffic to dodge, and no people to bother with. The streets were dark, the lanterns having long gone out, and the Tontine looked empty.

The door was locked. Justy tried to use the tip of his knife in the padlock, but the blade just brightened the brass around the keyhole.

Kerry pushed him out of the way.

She reached behind her head and pulled out the long hairpin that held her hat in place. She slipped the point into the keyhole and pushed on the steel until she had bent the pin into a thirty-degree angle. Her eyes narrowed as she played the point of the pin back and forth in the lock.

There was a sharp click. The lock fell open. She pushed the door wide and winked at Justy.

The Tontine was still. The huge chandelier in the lobby had been lowered, so that the servants could clean it, and Kerry and Justy had to walk in a long, wide circle around it. The doors to the Club Room opened smoothly. Moonlight streamed through the windows and cast long shadows from the armchairs and tables. The place smelled of damp ash and old leather. Kerry stood by a window, bending her hairpin back into shape, while Justy went to the long cabinet against the wall where Colley kept his sherry. It was full of bottles and stacks of paper. Justy knelt and pulled the papers onto the floor and began leafing through them.

Kerry hissed at him. She cupped her ear. He heard a carriage in the street. It stopped below the window. There was the hollow sound of boot heels on cobblestones, walking around the side of the building, and then silence.

He beckoned Kerry to the middle of the room. "He has a key to the back. We'll stay here and see where he goes."

"And then what?"

"We'll see. It may not even be him."

They stood either side of the doorway, listening to the muffled sounds of men moving through the building.

"Put it on the table, Mr. Fraser." Colley's voice carried through the dark from the dining room. Campbell wouldn't be far behind. Justy hoped they had left the carriage driver outside.

Two against three, at least two of whom would likely be armed. Not the best odds, but not the worst he'd ever faced. He still had the advantage of surprise. He closed his eyes and thought about the layout of the Tontine. He took the knife out of his boot. And then he walked quietly across to Kerry and told her what to do.

The moon had fallen far enough in the sky that its light now shone directly through the high windows in the Tontine's dining room. The long, polished table shimmered like a mirror, except where two black strongboxes marred its surface at the far end. Colley stood over one, separating its contents into two piles. Fraser stood behind him, watching, his pistols shoved into his belt.

It was a moment before Fraser noticed Justy in the doorway. He dragged out a pistol, but before he could level it Colley pushed it down.

"Mr. Flanagan. What a surprise. Come to see me off?"

"Hardly, Jack."

"No, I didn't think so. I can only assume you've come to . . . bring me to Justice."

"Very funny. But you won't be leaving New York tonight."

"What about our deal?"

"You lied to me, Jack. And that means there is no deal. Not anymore."

Colley closed the lid of the box. "I see. And what did I lie about, exactly?"

"About my father. About Drummond. About Cantillon. Turner told me everything."

"Did he? And how is the good Marshal?"

"Good and dead."

Colley smiled slightly. "You really are a very impressive young man, Justice. I do wish we had been able to find a way to work together."

"Do you deny it?"

"Deny what? Killing your father? Of course not. He deserved it. He was a pompous, self-righteous drone. We offered him the opportunity to become wealthy beyond his dreams, and then he turned on us. I gave dispensing with him no more thought than I would a capon, before I wrung its scrawny neck."

Justy had to squeeze his fists tight to stop himself from trembling.

Colley watched him for a moment. "I wonder, Justice. If you have come to kill me, where are your weapons?"

"I didn't say I was going to kill you. I mean you to hang, like the gutless, murdering pimp that you are."

"Of course you do." Colley's face snapped shut. "Well, you should have brought more than that pathetic knife of yours. Mr. Fraser? Shoot him."

Fraser was quick. His arm swung up and there was a loud crack. The doorjamb disintegrated. But Justy was already gone.

331

He ran to the doorway to the Club Room and stood in the moonlight, listening to Fraser's boots, hammering on the floorboards. He waited until Fraser saw him, and then he stepped back into the dark.

Fraser followed, running across the expanse of the lobby. There was a strange moaning sound. He felt a breath of wind on his face. He stopped. He screamed.

Justy had drawn all the curtains in the Club Room except one, which he had torn down and cut into strips. He had fashioned a makeshift rope, then taken it to the lobby. The chandelier hung from the ceiling, its hawser attached to an iron hook on the wall opposite the dining room. He and Kerry worked quietly, aware that Colley was in the dining room, only a hundred feet away. Justy had pushed the massive wheel of oak to one side, and Kerry had secured it to the hook with the velvet rope. The chandelier became a pendulum, halted in mid-swing. The only snag was, both the rope that suspended it and the strip of velvet that held it to the side were now tied around the same iron hook in the wall.

"It's dark, so be careful. If you cut the wrong one, you'll bring that thing down on your head and Fraser'll be free to plug me any way he pleases," Justy whispered.

"I wish you'd stop treating me like some totty-headed moll."

He grinned. He handed her the knife. "I'm not. I'm trusting you with my life."

The chandelier was made of solid oak and banded with strips of iron. It weighed more than a ton. When Kerry cut the strip of velvet, releasing the huge wooden wheel, it swung through the still air, faster than a man could run, making the slight moaning sound that made Fraser stop. When he saw what was bearing down on him, he barely had the time to open his mouth before the edge of the chandelier caught him square in the face. His scream was abruptly cut off as his head was torn from his shoulders.

The impact did nothing to slow the chandelier. It carried on and struck the far wall with a splintering sound, like a tree being felled. Kerry dropped to her knees and crawled towards Fraser's body as the wheel swung back over her head. She grabbed the pistols and squirmed across the parquet floor to the Club Room.

It was pitch-black inside, the only light coming through the door that led to the lobby. Justy took his knife from Kerry and pushed her towards the window. He sniffed the pistols to see which one Fraser had already fired, then gave her the loaded gun. "Get behind the curtains. There's only two of them now, but they'll both be armed. They won't want to come into the room, but I'll try and draw them in. When I say, throw the curtain open and shoot whoever you see."

He went to the center of the room and knelt behind one of the big leather chairs.

He felt, rather than heard, them. There was a slight thickening of the darkness around the doorway. He ducked his head down. He was confident the overstuffed chair would stop a ball, even at close range, but his guts were still churning.

"I'd tell you to run, Jack, but you won't get far!" he shouted. "Not now that the Bull knows what you did."

"That's if you had the time to tell him." Colley's voice floated across the room. "If I was bent on exacting revenge, I'm not sure I would make a detour to Dover Street first. I think I would come direct to the rendezvous."

Justy closed his eyes and cursed himself for a goddamned hotheaded clunch. If Colley killed him, there would be nothing to stop him from getting out of the city. And even if Colley didn't kill him, if he ran now, he would likely still make it out. It would be impossible for Justy to get to the Bull first.

He felt the thud of his pulse in his crushed throat and his cut hand. He imagined himself sitting at a green baize table opposite Colley, cards facedown in front of them. "Perhaps you're right, Jack. Perhaps I did come direct. Perhaps not. But if I did, don't you think I'd have sent word with one of his water rats first?"

Silence. He imagined Colley weighing his options. He could kill Justy or run, but if word had already made it to Dover Street the Bull would catch him and give him a long, slow, painful death. And was Justy such a fool, to make such an elementary mistake? The odds were long, and the stakes were high. Which left Colley with just one option: to capture Justy and exchange him for his life.

There was a shuffling sound in front of him. Justy crawled backwards and to the right. He hid behind another chair.

"That was a nasty trick you played on Mr. Fraser," Colley said. Justy could tell he was still beside the door.

"A face like that, I did him a favor."

Again, the shuffling sound, off to his left this time.

Justy took a deep breath. "Now!"

Moonlight flooded the room. Campbell was crouched beside one of the chairs, his pistol in his hand. He spun towards the source of the light, firing at the shape in the window. Kerry fired at the same time, and Campbell's head snapped back. He crumpled to the ground. Kerry was gone.

The room stank of gunpowder. Justy glanced around the chair, but Colley was no longer by the door. He crabbed left. He needed to get to Kerry.

He crawled to Campbell's body. The ball from Kerry's pistol had entered above the right eye and blasted out the back of his head. There was no second pistol in his belt. Justy kept moving left, listening for Colley.

Kerry screamed.

Justy risked a look over the chair he was hiding behind. Colley was standing by the window, his pistol resting on his shoulder, pointed at the ceiling. He looked relaxed, like a man out for a walk in the country.

He shifted his weight, and Kerry screamed again.

Justy stood up. Kerry was lying on the floor by the window. Her coat was dark, but it was darker still around her shoulder, where Colley's boot rested, pinning her to the floor.

Colley grinned. "It's a bad one, Justice. The shoulder. You've seen wounds like this, haven't you? All those blood vessels coming together in one place. A long, slow bleed. And then there's the nerve endings. So many. So much pain."

He pushed down again with his foot. Kerry's scream seemed to go on for minutes, before ending in a tearing, retching sound.

"Enough!" Justy shouted. "What do you want?"

"The same arrangement as before. Safe passage out of the city. A day's grace."

"The Bull will never let you go. Not when he finds out what you did."

It was as though all the air had been sucked out of the room. Justy felt the blood thump in his temples.

Colley smiled.

"So he doesn't know yet. You haven't told him. You were so caught up in your own vengeful thoughts that you failed to send word. That changes things, doesn't it?"

Slowly, he straightened his arm and brought his pistol to bear. Justy watched it come, his heart like a trip-hammer as the barrel leveled at his chest, yawning like a round grave.

"Any last words?" Colley asked.

Justy said nothing.

Colley shrugged and pulled the trigger. There was a loud click.

Justy grinned.

"Half-cock, you cunt."

The blade of his knife snapped into place and he hurled himself at Colley, his left hand going for Colley's eyes, the blade in his right aiming for his neck. Colley staggered backwards, flailing with the pistol. He was lucky. The pistol hit Justy's hand and the knife spun away across the room. Justy ignored the pain in his fingers and kept coming, ploughing into Colley, grabbing his coat and hammering his head forward.

His forehead smashed hard into Colley's nose. Colley screamed as the cartilage gave way, and blood spurted over his face and into his mouth. He spat in Justy's face, smashed the butt of his pistol into his temple and drove his knee upwards into Justy's groin. He clawed at Justy's eyes and snapped at his ear with his teeth. It was like grappling with a cornered wolf. Colley was more than twenty years older, but he had muscles like a ship's hawsers and he used everything he had to fight.

Justy felt a spike of fear. He threw an elbow at Colley's head and rolled away, reaching for his knife, but Colley was on him instantly, his knee in Justy's stomach, pinning him to the floor as they both scrambled to get their hands on the weapon.

Justy's fingers felt metal. The blade of the knife. His hand closed on it, and then he screamed as Colley pulled the knife away, the blade slicing deep into Justy's palm. He writhed, one hand trying to push Colley off him while the other held the knife away, but Colley squirmed on top of him, belly to belly, and held him down. He pressed himself as close as a lover, jamming his knees into Justy's thighs, pinning him to the floor. Then he rocked back on his knees and brought the knife to his chest with both hands. Justy went with him, trying to sit up, using one hand to punch at Colley's face and then wrapping both hands around the knife, trying to push it away.

Colley pushed forward again, the blade pointed down. Justy's back hit the floor. His arms were locked. He dug his fingernails into the backs of Colley's hands, trying to push him left, then right, but everything was slick with blood and sweat, and Colley's weight was like a wall above him.

The blade was smeared with blood. Colley's face was a bleeding, sweaty mask. He was panting like a dog. And then he chuckled. He leaned harder, and Justy felt his elbows buckle.

Colley grunted. His eyes bulged and he slid sideways, dropping the knife, one arm reaching behind him. Justy pushed him away, grabbed the knife with his left hand and struck hard. He felt the blade go deep, and then he rolled away, dragging himself to his feet, the breath like fire in his throat.

Colley was on his knees, his forehead pressed to the floor, one hand clutching at the knife wound in his side, the other reaching behind him, groping for something. Justy stepped closer and saw a glittering inch of silver hairpin sticking out of his back.

Kerry was slumped in one of the Club Room chairs. Her face was gray, and her right sleeve was soaked with blood. He undid her coat, then stripped off his cravat, folding it into a wad that he pressed against the wound in her shoulder before buttoning the coat tight.

"Is he dead?" Her voice was slurred.

It was an effort for him to speak. "Not yet. But soon."

He leaned over Colley, took hold of the end of the long silver hairpin and pulled it out. Colley moaned and fell onto his side.

Kerry's lips moved. He leaned close. Her eyes were dull, and her skin was clammy. He knew he had to get her to a surgeon, and quickly.

"You should finish the job," she whispered.

He looked at Colley, lying on his side, his head lolling on the soft blue carpet. Blood trickled steadily out of his mouth and he was breathing in short hiccups, without exhaling. Justy knew the signs. Between them, he and Kerry had cut an artery and punctured a lung. Colley was drowning and suffocating, all at the same time.

He wiped his knife on Colley's coat, folded it and tucked it into his boot.

"Let him bleed."

THIRTY-NINE

Monday

The rain came down in sheets out of a bruised sky. There was no wind, and the deluge was constant. It drenched the slack canvas of the *Netherleigh*'s sails, turned the spars into gutters and the masts into downpipes. It sluiced over the deck like a river in spate.

Justy stood, shivering at the stern of the ship. His hair was drenched. The wound on his scalp was still healing, and it was too painful to wear a hat. He wiped his face with his bandaged right hand and watched over the open water as a longboat pulled closer to a sleek two-masted clipper with a white hull and decks made of varnished pine. On a sunny day, with a full array of sail, the clipper would look glorious. But now its rigging hung wet and slack, and it wallowed in the gray, oily roll of the ebbing tide.

Both ships were anchored in Sandy Hook Bay, where ships heading for New York made the turn northwest into the channel between Staten Island and Brooklyn. The skipper of a fast three-masted schooner had told Lars about the white-hulled clipper with a human cargo that had left Savannah on the same day but was slowed by its smaller rig and delayed further by the bad weather.

The longboat pulled close to the clipper, and a figure in a red coat climbed up a fixed ladder, followed by five big men in black greatcoats.

There was a low growl of thunder, far away in the east, and a small gust of wind eased the *Netherleigh* round on its anchor. Keeping the clipper in view, Justy walked along the rail until he reached one of the stays that held up the rear mast. It was a moment before he realized he was standing right where Turner had held him at gunpoint, two days before.

He looked down at the deck. The oak had been scrubbed clean. He touched his neck. It was still raw and bruised, and his throat still hurt when he swallowed.

He had carried Kerry to the surgeon who lived next door to Sarah Boswell. He had waited until the man had dug the ball out of Kerry's shoulder, bandaged her and put her to bed. Then he went to the law.

Marshal Jacob Hays had remained silent as Justy had told his story. He had appeared unmoved by the carnage in the Tontine Coffee House: Campbell with a small hole in the front of his head and a crater of gore in the back, Fraser with no head at all. And Black Jack Colley, facedown, pale and lifeless, in a lake of his own blood. Hays had said nothing when they found the *Netherleigh* as Justy had left it, Sandy dead by the gangway, the captain murdered in his cabin and Lars still unconscious in the chart room. Only when Justy had shown him Turner, lying on his back, staring at the sky, with a garrote in his pocket and two inches of brass sticking out of his ear, did Hays finally speak.

"I can see why Turner would come after Miss O'Toole. She was an eyewitness to his depravity. But why you? All you had was your suspicions."

"Because he knew I wouldn't stop. He knew I would keep coming after him, until I put him in a box, either one in front of a judge or one under the ground."

"You know this how?"

And Justy had smiled despite himself. "Because he and I were much alike."

"Not too much, I hope." Hays had smoothed the lapels of his red coat and looked around the deck of the *Netherleigh*. "He set you a pretty trap here. How did he know you'd come back?"

Justy had been asking himself the same question. He thought he knew. "We were both scouts, trained to think in a certain way. The man who taught me my craft in Ireland fought over here, too, in the Revolutionary War. He was at Valley Forge, so it's possible he knew Turner. Perhaps even fought alongside him. He was the one who told me the best place for an ambush is where the enemy feels safest. And what safer place than your best mate's ship?"

The rain began to soften. Another belch of thunder rolled in across the ocean from the east, but there was no flicker of lightning or break in the cloud to indicate which way the storm was moving. The sky was a smear of grays, indistinct from the sea. The horizon was a blur.

Water trickled down the back of Justy's neck. He saw movement on the deck of the clipper. One by one, the men in long coats climbed back down into the longboat, and then there was a dull smear of red as the last man descended the ladder.

The boat slid back across the water towards the *Netherleigh*, faster now with the tide, and it was only a few minutes before Justy heard the boarding bell rung by one of the oarsmen.

Hays was first onto the *Netherleigh*'s deck. His red coat was soaked, and the collar of his shirt had turned pink with the dye. Rainwater dripped out of the three funnels made by his tricorn hat. He turned and watched as the clipper weighed anchor.

"Well?" Justy asked.

Hays pushed his hat back and looked up at Justy. He was a powerfully built man, with broad shoulders, but now he looked shrunken. His face sagged, and his shaggy eyebrows appeared to be forcing his eyes closed. He wiped a hand over his forehead. "I hoped I would never see the like."

Justy felt his mouth go dry. He had never seen inside a slave ship, but he had heard what conditions were like. Men and women were packed together in the holds like sardines, bound with ankle fetters and linked with chains. Choked by the stench of vomit and urine and feces. No light, no air. No mercy.

"It's like a kind of hell, I'm told."

Hays gave a mirthless laugh. "Hell is right. But not the kind you're thinking of." He looked at the clipper as it moved slowly past them, carried by the tide. "I've never been on such a luxurious craft. The cabins are small, but beautifully appointed. Silk sheets, blankets of the softest wool. Calfskin. Brass. Mahogany. . . ." His voice trailed off.

Justy frowned. "What then?"

Hays turned back. His eyes were dark, and whether it was the rain or tears that were smeared on his cheeks Justy couldn't tell. "They were children, Justice. Little girls. Some no more than six or seven years old."

Justy felt a spike of ice in his guts, and the chill spread through him. A rare and precious commodity, Colley had said. There was bile in his throat, and though he was chilled to the bone, he felt the rage bubble like lava inside him.

"How many?"

"Fifty." Hays' voice was grim. "They have no idea what's in store for them. They've never seen anything like that kind of luxury. They've come from farms and plantations and mills. They're dressed up like little ladies, in colored dresses, with their faces painted. The whole way up they've been getting lessons on deportment and manners. Every one of them curtseyed before they spoke to me. Lowered eyes, soft voices . . ." His own voice trembled, and he wiped his face again. He was crying freely now, his head tilted back into the rain. His men stood back beside the chart house, the rain dripping off their leather helmets, their faces like stone.

Hays took a deep breath. "The captain seemed a decent man, believe it or not. Courteous. Reasonable. The kind of chap I might take a glass with, if I didn't know the nature of his business. And he knows his business, well enough. He pointed out that I have no jurisdiction, and that his . . . cargo had already been auctioned and paid for, so he was merely acting as a passenger vessel, and not breaking any law."

"What did you say?"

"I told him that was a matter for the court to decide. That I would impound his ship on arrival in New York, and confiscate his cargo on suspicion of the intent to sell these children in contravention of the Act." He gave a sour smile. "That he and his employers might indeed prevail in the courts, but I would arrange things to ensure that it would be at least a year before a judge heard the case, by which time the city would be in an uproar."

"And that convinced him?"

"We shall see."

Hays turned to watch as the clipper moved out of the shelter of the spit of Sandy Hook. The ship shuddered slightly as its bows slid into the chop, and its wet sails billowed. Men busied themselves aboard, hauling on ropes and tightening the sails, and the clipper seemed to float for a moment above the water before turning into the wind, towards the east, out to sea and away from New York.

Justy put a hand lightly on Hays' shoulder. "You did well today, Marshal."

Hays' jaw was tight as he watched the clipper pick up speed. "I wish I could have done more. No doubt the villain will just jig up to Providence or down to Norfolk, where this corruption is still tolerated."

The fo'c'sle bell clanged, and the sailor on watch in the bows of the ship called out. Justy and Hays turned to see Lars hurrying out of the captain's cabin.

"All hands!" he roared, and the deck was suddenly a hive of activity, as the crew poured out of the belly of the ship into the rain and began preparing the *Netherleigh* for sail.

Lars walked back to the stern of the ship, his hands behind his back. He wore a new blue coat with brass buttons and black frogging. A wide tricorn, trimmed with gold, was perched on the back of his head.

Justy bowed ostentatiously. "Good afternoon, Captain. May I compliment you on your hat."

"Shag off, ya madge," Lars said, his beard bristling like an angry red hedgehog. He spun on his heel to watch the slave clipper slice through the growing chop of the open sea. "She's a beauty, eh? I hope she sails well in heavy weather."

The sky over the ocean was turning from gray to black. Justy could see what looked like wisps of smoke turning in the cloud. "You heard what they found on board?"

Lars kept his eyes on the clipper. "I heard."

He whistled to his new first mate, a stocky man whose face was dark with tattoos. They conferred, and a few minutes later the anchor was hauled up and stowed, the sails were set and the *Netherleigh* turned north, towards Fort Hamilton and the channel to New York Harbor.

Lars led Justy and Hays to his post in the fo'c'sle. The *Netherleigh*'s sails filled with the freshening wind, and the ship jolted forward as it picked up speed. Hays held tight to the rail and wiped his face with a handkerchief.

"What is the duration of your commission, Captain?" he asked.

"Until I get back to Liverpool. I'm hoping they'll confirm the appointment there, but they might just make me first mate again."

Hays nodded. "I wish you every good fortune."

"Thanks, Marshal."

"It is I should thank you. For allowing the city to commission your ship on this mission." He lowered his voice. "I shall have to write a report, but I can leave the name of the vessel blank, if you would wish."

Lars shook his head. "The owners of the *Netherleigh* are firm Quakers, sir. They don't hold with slavery. They'll be happy to hear they could help."

"In that case you'll permit me to write a letter, thanking them and commending you."

Lars looked pleased. "Thank you, sir."

Hays took off his hat, smoothed his hair and lifted his face into the breeze. He looked suddenly younger. He shot Justy a look. "And what about you, Mr. Flanagan? Will you return to England with Captain Hokkanssen?"

"I don't think so. I've caused him enough trouble."

"What will it be, then? Back to Wall Street?"

Justy shrugged. "Perhaps. I haven't decided."

Hays looked at the bulk of Fort Hamilton in the distance. "I believe that we are the best guides of ourselves. That we do best when we are not tied up in a knot of rules. But I also believe that men are weak. That they too often fall prey to their basest, most predatory instincts." He rapped the rail with his knuckles. "Rules and laws, then, are necessary. To protect the weak, the naive. The young."

He turned to watch the slave clipper struggling east, into the wind. "But laws are useless on their own. We need men and women to enforce them."

He looked meaningfully at Justy.

Justy gave a dry laugh. "You're asking me to join you? Perhaps you've forgotten I killed a Mayor's Marshal. Stabbed him in the ear, not twenty feet from where you're standing."

Hays smiled. "I'm well aware of the irony. But the fact that you found Turner out, exposed him and disposed of him, all without help, convinces me that you're exactly the kind of man I need. This city is growing at an incredible rate, as you know. We have too many people, and not enough space for them to live, or work for them to do. Every day brings more people and more trouble, and I need help keeping it all in check."

"I'm not sure I'm built to be a crusher."

Hays waved the comment away. "I have plenty of stout men who are quick with a club. What I need are steady men who are quick with their brains. I plan to reform the Watch, to turn it into a real police force, properly paid and administered, with a remit not merely to protect the populace, but to seek out those who commit crimes, and bring them to justice. To do that I need educated men, thinkers, people who know this city, who call it home, who can help me keep it safe for all who live in it." He rapped the rail again. "Whatever their creed or their color might happen to be."

Justy glanced at Lars, who raised an eyebrow but said nothing.

"What about my relationship to the Bull? The Mayor won't like that."

Hays gave a slight smile. "It might be useful to have a man on my staff who has an eye on the underworld. Besides, your actions in today's matter have shown me which side of the moral divide you favor. The Mayor is strong for Manumission. He will not take much convincing once he hears about today."

Justy shook his head. "You must keep my name out of this, Marshal. If my uncle or Owens or anyone else finds out I was involved, the next time you'll see me someone will be dragging me out of the East River on the end of a gaff."

Hays frowned. "Of course. Not a word, then." He paused. "Will you think on it?"

Justy nodded. "I shall. I'll come to see you at the Hall tomorrow."

Hays nodded, satisfied. He rapped on the rail a final time and went to attend to his men, buttoning his coat around him. The red cloth was so soaked with rain it looked almost purple, and its tails flapped around his thighs as he strode aft.

Lars watched him go. "So you're to be a copper, are you?"

"Well, it's about as daft a notion as you being a skipper."

"Fair enough." Lars chuckled. "I have to thank you for something, by the way."

"Oh yes?"

Lars looked awkward. "Introducing me to Sarah."

Justy laughed. "Sarah Boswell? Well, well, you old dog. I thought I caught a gleam in your eyes there. What about your girl Lise?"

"Sulks too much. Sarah's more . . . worldly."

"I bet she is. Well, I'm happy for you."

"Thanks."

Lars leaned his back on the rail and looked south, where the clipper was now a distant blob of white against the gray. "So, what will you do if the Bull finds out you told Hays about all of this?"

"Told him what? I said to the Bull I'd say nothing more about all of this to anyone. And I didn't. Hays already knew about the scheme. I'd already told him about it. It was you gave him the rest, not me. You got the word about what ship they were using, and you told Hays. I was in the room, right enough, but I didn't say a word, if you recall."

"You think Owens'll swallow that?"

"I don't give a damn." He jerked his chin at the clipper, as it was swallowed by the mist. "All I know is I couldn't live with that on my conscience."

"Me neither." Lars' beard bristled.

347

Justy smiled. "There's that look."

"What look?"

"The one that says some poor bastard is going to get a hammering."

Lars said nothing.

"Forget it, *a chara*. By the time you've dropped us and turned about, you'll be a day behind him. And you don't even know which way he's going."

"Do I not? That storm's coming up hard from the south. He won't want to battle through it, so I'd say he'll run with the wind. Where might he land north of here?"

"Providence is the obvious place. They wouldn't let him into New London or Boston. He could try for Portsmouth, but it's a long haul, and there's no trade to speak of there."

"Providence, then. Perhaps I'll make a stop on my way up to Boston. Pay a wee visit to some stout fellows I know there."

"Mind how you go."

"Oh, I'll be careful all right." Lars pulled the brim of his hat lower over his eyes. "But should I have need of a lawyer . . ."

"Then be sure to send word." Justy smiled. "I might even give you a discount."

FORTY

Thursday

The silent bodyguard with the scarred face pushed the door to Owens' living room open and stepped aside.

The bizarrely furnished room looked smaller in the daylight. New York was blanketed by low cloud, and the hard white light made the gaudy furniture look washed out and cheap.

Justy stood by the mantelpiece and looked into the grate. A servant had swept it clean and piled kindling, ready to be lit. The pile shifted slightly, and a beetle crawled out and along one of the sticks.

Justy turned at the sound of the door opening. Owens stood in the doorway, dressed in a spotless white shirt, sleeves rolled up above the elbows, like a working man.

"You've got some sand, coming here." The soft, Welsh accent.

Justy said nothing, and Owens walked across to the fireplace. "You kill two of my business partners, and now you expect to walk in and out of my house as you please?"

"I'd have thought I did you a favor. Now you, the Bull and Harry Gracie can split your filthy profits without ever worrying about anyone else coming back for a handout."

Owens looked into the grate. He stepped forward quickly, crushing something under his foot, then gave a flat smile that didn't reach his eyes.

"What about you, then? Up at Federal Hall, I heard."

"That's right."

"I don't suppose you had anything to do with that cossack Hays turning away my cargo a few weeks back. Or the story in *The Gazette* the next day."

Or the deluge of editorials in all the newspapers that had followed. A week of large-print headlines, trumpeting outrage at the notion of children being trafficked into sexual slavery.

"No one got any information from me."

Owens' face twisted, as though he had tasted something sour. "No. It was that bloody skipper. I'm told the week before he left Savannah he went out and got nazie every night, and blabbed my business all over the port."

"So what happened to . . . the cargo?"

"Back to Savannah, of course."

So the schooner had gone south through the storm after all. He wondered how long Lars had searched before he gave up the hunt. And then he thought about the children. What had happened to them?

Owens leaned on the mantelpiece. "You were right, by the way."

"About what?"

"About the quality. After the newspapers got started, I had Gracie ask around. Seems coves are come over a bit crank about the idea of having a slave-doxy all to themselves. It's going out of fashion, see?"

"I won't say I'm not relieved to hear it."

"Makes things easier in some ways. Takes care of our trouble with the law. And it means I don't have to go grubbing about for talent in the Carolinas, or wherever."

Justy couldn't stop himself from sneering. "Just another New York nugging house, then. A pity your ambitions have been brought so low."

"Bedlow Street ain't a brothel, boy. It's a club, for a particular type of gent. The kind of place that a swell can go without fear of having his pocket picked or his plug tail poisoned. Discreet. Exclusive. Expensive."

"Not as expensive as it would have been, though, surely. You can't expect to make anywhere close to the kind of money you had planned."

Owens grinned. "You'd be surprised. See, Jack was right about one thing. The quality's got some mighty odd tastes. Exotic. Not the kind of thing your waterfront mott can help with. Takes a special kind of titter to meet the needs of such folk, and a high price to secure her services. Or his. Lucky for us, we don't have to travel to find the talent. It's right here in town."

"What do you mean?"

"You've seen the ships coming in. Hundreds of new arrivals every day, plenty of them young motts, desperate to make their way. They need to be schooled, of course, and that takes time, but I made a few quid off the trade down in Savannah, and that'll tide us over."

A few quid. So the children had been sold, and God only knew where they were now. Waiting at a table in some wealthy man's townhome, perhaps, or sent back to a plantation.

Better than what had been in store for them here.

"What about your Wall Street scheme?"

The sour look twisted Owens' face again. "The sooner we're out of that trumpery, the better, I say. With Colley gone, those Wall Street porkers won't stop asking questions about the nature of the venture. Gracie's holding them off for now, but we're going to have to start giving people their money back before long."

"Can you afford to?"

"Not yet. But soon. Bedlow Street's already making plenty of chink, and when it's all squared away, it'll be a gold mine. You'll

351

have to come and see it all for yourself." He smiled. "And bring your fellow officers of the law."

"Don't you ever get tired of pimping, Lew?" Kerry's voice was weak but still barbed with scorn. She walked slowly into the room and eased herself into an armchair upholstered in mustard-yellow velvet. She wore a pair of dark riding breeches and a man's white shirt, the right sleeve hanging loose. Her hair was pulled back sharply from her face.

"Shouldn't you be in bed?" Justy asked.

"Not if I don't want to go mad with boredom."

"Bed doesn't have to be boring, girl," Owens said.

Kerry glared. "Fuck off, Lew."

"Right you are then, that's me told." He smirked at Justy. "I meant what I said, now. Standing offer for you and your boys."

"Fuck off, Lew," Justy said.

For a moment, Owens was very still. And then he threw his head back and boomed with laughter. He grabbed Justy by the shoulder. "That's very good, boyo. Very good."

Owens jammed his thumb into the soft flesh of the shoulder socket, digging for the nerve. His teeth flashed in his face. His eyes were hard.

"Lew!"

He ignored her. "You like to walk the line, don't you, boyo? Gives you a rise, don't it?"

Justy said nothing. He kept his eyes steady and his jaw clamped tight.

"Lew!" Kerry snapped again.

Owens let go. "You're a brave man with her and your uncle in your corner, aren't you, Justice Flanagan? How would you be on your own, I wonder?"

Justy resisted the urge to rub his shoulder. "You should hope it never comes to that."

Owens gave him a long look. "I'll be watching you, boyo."

"And I you."

Owens nodded. He turned and walked out of the room, brushing his fingers gently against Kerry's hair as he went.

"Not much of one for making friends, are you?" she asked when Owens was gone.

"He may be your cousin, but that doesn't make him any less of an evil bastard."

"Only to those that cross him."

"And those he wants to use."

A high-pitched squeal came from the room above them. Kerry winced.

"Is that Daniel?" Justy asked.

"That sound he makes. It's like a goddamned spike in your ear." She grinned. "So to speak."

The child screeched again, but she ignored the sound. "Thanks for coming to see me."

He sat on a dainty, spindle-legged chair. "Thanks for asking."

"I wanted to say I'm sorry. About everything."

"I understand. Lars will, too, when I write and tell him about the wee man upstairs."

She gave him a hard look. "So you didn't believe me."

"Most of me did. But a part of me wasn't sure." He shrugged. "You sold us out, Kerry. You even led Turner on to me."

"I tried to warn you off."

"You did, but you must have known I'd come after you still. And that he'd be watching."

She turned her face away and looked out of the window. There was a man in the garden, dressed in a brown smock and a wide hat. He shuffled along, bending every few steps to pick fallen apples and put them in a basket. The red apples looked like flowers in the grass.

"But I wanted to thank you anyway," Justy said. "For Turner. And for Colley. If you hadn't been there, and done what you did, one of them would have put me in my eternity box, for sure."

Her eyes were like chips of green stone. "I wish I'd had the bastards to myself. I wouldn't have made it so easy for them."

"They're in the ground now. No way they can hurt you. And that's all that matters."

She looked into the garden, watching the gardener's brown back dipping and rising rhythmically as he picked the apples. "So what happens now?"

He shrugged. "You heard I took a position at Federal Hall?"

"Aye. Lew told me. You're to be a copper."

"That's right. Jacob Hays wants to create a kind of new police force for New York. He wants me to be a part of it. But that's not what you're asking about."

"No."

Somewhere inside the house, farther away now, the child began to cry. Kerry's eyes flickered. "Back in the church, when I asked if we'd get married, you said, 'Why not?' Did you mean it?"

Justy nodded. "I did then."

"And now?"

"And now I don't know."

Her eyes hardened. "Too good for me, are you? Too good to marry a Negro half-caste with a gangster for a father, a pimp for a cousin and a bastard for a bairn."

"You know that's not it."

"What then?'

He shrugged. "I thought I knew you, Kerry. I thought I knew who you were. What you were. But I was wrong. After all this, I realized I don't know you at all."

Her fingernails scratched on the yellow velvet arm of the chair. "So what am I to be, then? A nursemaid? Locked up in this place?"

Justy shook his head. "You don't need a husband to make

354

you someone, Kerry. You've already proved that. You can be anything you want. You made yourself into a man, for heaven's sake. And one of the smoothest pickpockets in the city."

She made a face. "Aye, well, I think my tooling days are over."

"Didn't you want to be a teacher, once?"

"A teacher?" She laughed. "There's a geg for you. I don't even know my letters, remember?"

"You can still learn. I'll help you."

"I don't need your charity."

The dainty chair squeaked as he stood up. "It's not charity. And it's not that I owe you, though I do. You're my friend, Kerry. You're my family."

"Oh right. I'm like a sister to you, then."

He grinned. "Hardly. Not the way I've thought about you sometimes."

Her mouth softened. "You really think I could learn to read and write?"

"I don't see why not. You learned how to fool the whole city when you were out thieving."

"Almost everyone." She had a faraway look in her eyes.

He knelt beside her and took her hand. "He's dead, Kerry. He's gone. It's just you now."

"No, it's not." She pushed his hand away. "I've the wean to worry about, too."

"All the more reason to make something of yourself."

A door opened somewhere, and the sound of crying came down the hall. Kerry sighed. "Help me up."

Justy put his arm around her. She stood up, gritting her teeth. "How is it?" he asked.

"Hurts like the Devil's peg, if you must know."

She walked away slowly, then turned in the doorway. "Bring one of them books the next time you come, then. We'll see what we can do."

"I will."

She smiled and left, and he stood for a moment, feeling the vibrations in his hands and his chest, and the smile on his own lips. And then he took a deep breath, walked out of the gaudy pimp's parlor, through the door and into the day.

AUTHOR'S NOTE

The Devil's Half Mile was supposed to be a history book. The idea was to tell the story of America's first financial crisis, the Panic of 1792, and its aftermath, which culminated in the establishment of securities trading rules and the creation of the New York Stock & Exchange Board in 1817.

Fascinating stuff.

Too fascinating, perhaps. I disappeared down a research hole early on, trying to get a sense of what Aaron Burr, Alexander Hamilton, and other Wall Street players of the time were really like. Despite numerous historical tomes and an award-winning musical, we still know very little about these people, what motivated them, and how they really behaved: it was all history and not enough story. And I really, really wanted to tell a story.

I also needed to get words down on the page. So, as a kind of side project—just to keep my hand in, you understand—I decided to write a murder into the narrative. That proved to be a lot more fun than combing through collections of correspondence, and after a time the scale tilted. Six months later, I had two-thirds of a novel written and the history project was consigned to a dusty folder deep in the bowels of my hard drive. And I was having a lot more fun.

As absorbing as it was to learn about how Wall Street changed in the wake of the Panic, discovering how New York changed in the same period was even more so. The city was little more than a large town in 1799, when Justy Flanagan stepped off the *Netherleigh*. What eventually became the Five Points was still a freshwater lake, and the tiny village of Greenwich was surrounded by open fields. But the city would double in size over the next twenty years, straining its capacity, its tolerance, and its way of life.

I was also struck by New York's complicated relationship with the slave trade. It was perhaps the most important port in the country, and slavery was an important part of the national economy. But the tide of opinion was turning hard against human trafficking, and a bill for the gradual abolition of slavery was passed by New York State early in 1799. Bad news for the port, perhaps, but good news for the city, which had the largest concentration of free Negroes in the country and was already quite tense enough, as blacks fought with newly arrived immigrants for work.

I would not have been able to learn about any of this were it not for the collections of maps, letters, and other documents kept by various libraries. The New York Public Library, the Los Angeles Public Library, and the libraries of several universities, including Yale, Columbia, and Boston, were particularly helpful, not least because they have done such an excellent job of making so much of their materials available online.

Unfortunately, a lot of these materials contradict one another. Paintings of the period have a tavern on one corner of Wall Street and Water Street, while a letter from one merchant to another has it diagonally opposite. One map, dated 1798, shows New York built all the way up to what is now Canal Street. Another, dated 1803, shows only dotted lines above Chambers Street. These contradictions made it difficult to recreate an exact picture of New York. I found myself making changes, then changing them back and then back again. Eventually I decided to go firm on just one version, resigned to the fact that any rendition of a city two centuries distant will inevitably be flawed.

The Devil's Half Mile is a work of fiction, and I hope that my countrymen will not be too dismayed by how the story portrays our forebears. Ireland is a country with a deep and wide cultural and intellectual heritage, and I have found that the people of its diaspora are great representatives of our homeland. Unfortunately, in the late eighteenth century, the deck was well stacked against us. Irish Catholics were oppressed and discriminated against by the British in Ireland. They were shut out of higher education until late in the century, and it was difficult for them even to get started in a trade. Most of the population were farmworkers and manual laborers, if they could find work at all, and many of these people made the dangerous trip across the Atlantic out of desperation.

Unfortunately, when they arrived in New York, they found things were not much different from the way they had been in Dublin. The English may have lost the Revolutionary War, but many still lived in New York, and their view of the Catholic Irish was the prevailing one: subhuman, stupid, useful only for the most menial work. It would take more than twenty years and the sheer force of numbers to give the Catholic Irish any kind of power in New York. Until then, they were mostly confined to the bottom of the economic barrel: to service, hard labor, and crime.

I doubt any of them would have named their son Justice. The Irish tended to name their children after the saints, and names like Justice, Hope, and Charity smack of Protestantism. But I imagined that an Irishman keen to advance his son in New York society might have chosen the name Justice, in the hope of fitting the boy in. If such a man did well enough to send his son to college, it would probably not have been in America, however: those few universities that existed were staunchly

Protestant and did not generally welcome Papists. Trinity College in Dublin was an option: it was opened to a handful of Catholics in the late eighteenth century; but I liked the sound of the brand-new Royal College of St. Patrick, which was founded in Maynooth in 1795.

I have taken liberties with Justy's college curriculum. I doubt a jurisprudence course at Maynooth included a concentration—or even a class—in criminal law, but if Justy had wanted to spend some time with a police force as part of his studies Paris would have been the place to go. France established its first police force in 1667, and Paris had been patrolled by a force of inspectors since 1709. The city's waterfront commissariat provided the model for England's first experiments in policing on the wharves of the Thames in 1798.

That Irish students took part in the Irish Rebellion of 1798 is not in doubt. It was a short-lived but brutal affair that took place from May to September of that year. Lars' home of Gorey in Wexford suffered badly. The town was used as a garrison for loyalist militia forces, and the people of Gorey had to endure some of the most appalling atrocities of the conflict, including murder, rape, and torture on a large scale, until the militia evacuated following the United Irish victory at Oulart Hill on May 27. The pitchcap was one of the most common methods of torture, although I should note it was used by both sides. The militia commander Hunter Gowan existed. He was born in Gorey, served as a magistrate, and led a yeomanry corps in the area called The Black Mob. He was infamous for summarily murdering Catholics suspected of rebel sympathies, and for using a human finger to stir his cocktails. These kinds of outrages united the Catholic population and inspired groups of rebels to rise up all over the country to fight British forces and the loyalist militia. Much of the action took place in county Kildare, close to Maynooth. Justy would have felt the shock waves that swept across the country in the aftermath of the Curragh massacre, when 350 men and boys surrendered to the English, only to be subsequently gunned down in an open field, just twenty-five miles from Justy's college. It is not a stretch to imagine a young, idealistic lawyer joining the Defenders to fight. It is perhaps harder to believe that such a man would be able to survive the particular horrors of guerrilla warfare and return to school to complete his studies, but that, I would answer, speaks to Justy's resilience and his spirit.

Justy, Kerry, John Colley, and the Bull are all fictional, but several of the characters in this novel did exist. Alexander Hamilton appears briefly, and I have described him as he appears in a portrait dating from that time, not long after he stepped down from the position of Secretary of the Treasury.

Jacob Hays was made a Mayor's Marshal in 1798. He had a reputation as a hard charger who led from the front and did not spare the rod. "Old Hays" became so feared and respected that his very appearance was enough to break up an unruly gathering. He had little in the way of men or resources to work with, but his tireless work laid the ground for the creation of New York's police force in 1845. Whether he wore an ostentatious scarlet coat I do not know, but he struck me as the kind of man who might.

William Duer was a onetime congressman turned speculator, who did indeed die at home, on release from debtors' prison. I have not invented his friendship with all sorts of eminent people, including Alexander Hamilton, who wrote to him often but refused to bail him out. I have not invented Duer's pivotal role in the Panic of 1792: he indulged in the kind of behavior that would give the New York Attorney General a slam dunk in an insider trading and stock manipulation case today. My story of Duer's involvement in a trafficking ring and a Ponzi scheme, however, is entirely fictional.

It is interesting to compare the Panic of 1792 and the Financial Crisis of 2008. Like his successor Hank Paulson, Alexander Hamilton feared the Panic would bring the country down, but while the 2008 Crisis triggered a torrent of new rules in the Dodd-Frank Act, the 1792 Panic ushered in very little in the way of change. Like most Americans, who felt they had thrown off the shackles of government interference along with the tyranny of the Crown, Wall Street men thought they should be able to regulate themselves. The result was that there were few, if any, rules when it came to securities trading and the entire system was based on the twin pillars of trust and *caveat emptor*. Consequently, the markets lurched from one crisis to another, trust was eroded to a nub, and cynicism reigned. Even the New York Stock Exchange was conceived as a power grab from the auctioneers who dominated the system at the time.

Many people might look back at those days wistfully: it's certainly easy enough to find Wall Street players happy to argue that banks and investment houses can regulate themselves and government should just get out of the way. Unfortunately, experience has proved that a poorly regulated system is too easily abused and that cynical bankers and traders—whether frock coated and bewigged in 1792 or clad in business casual today—are quite willing to abuse it.

Paddy Hirsch
Los Angeles, June 2017

ACKNOWLEDGMENTS

This book would not have been written had I not been lucky enough to get a place on the inaugural Crime Writing Residency at the Banff Centre in Alberta, Canada. I found my community at Banff: Louise Welsh and Michael Robotham gave me the tools and the confidence I needed to overhaul and finish my manuscript, while Don MacDonald, Kim Murray, Sandy Conrad, Hope Thompson, Marie Fontaine, and Tony Berry, were—and continue to be—a constant source of support.

I owe a particular debt to Don, Kim, and Sandy for taking the time to slog through my first draft, identifying everything from plot holes to spelling errors, and offering excellent advice. It's one thing for fellow writers to read one's attempts; it's quite another for friends to do it, which is why I am so grateful to Kirsten Love DiPatri, who read my second draft at lightning speed and gave some very useful notes, just when I needed them.

Michael Price and Monica Holloway, two of the most gener-ous people under the sun, inspired me, fed me, liquored me up, and made me laugh. Monica introduced me to Lisa Gallagher, a wonderful person and an outstanding agent who somehow always manages to make me feel that I'm her most impor-tant client. Doug Krizner, Brendan Francis Newnam, John Buckley, David Willis, Millie Jefferson, David McGuffin, Fiona Ng, Rodney Yap, Kalika Yap, Damian and Esther Chew, Mark

Locklin, Ian Sears, Richard diPatri, Lindsay Hollister, Justin Richmond, Steve Chiotakis, and Tess Vigeland all cheered me on when I needed it; Sarah Gilbert and Jon Gordon kept me gainfully employed; and Charlie Hauck's words of advice kept me putting words on the page—even if I only managed to write for five minutes on any given day.

I'm immensely grateful to all of the team at Tor/Forge in the U.S. and Corvus, Atlantic Books in the U.K. My editors, Diana Gill and Sara O'Keeffe, really transformed the manuscript. I know firsthand how tough the editing process can be, which makes me doubly grateful for their insights and hard work, as well as for Diana's finesse and diplomacy.

Finally, my thanks to Eileen. For keeping my head straight and my spine stiff. And for bringing me along to San Jose.

GLOSSARY

a chara my friend, buddy, pal (Irish)

a mhac my friend (Irish)

bairn a child
balderdash diluted liquor
barking iron a pistol
bawd a pimp
bawdy house a brothel
beak a judge
beard splitter a pimp
beaters a pair of boots
beour a woman (Irish)
bimble stroll
black box a lawyer
black joke a woman's private parts
blackthorn a stick made from blackthorn, popular with the Irish
blade cock a man who specializes in knife work
bob masturbate
bobtail a prostitute
boglander an Irishman
Bojeley Beaujolais wine
bollocks testicles; also rubbish
bounce nerve; courage
bouncer a ruffian
box the Jesuit masturbate
breeks breeches
bumper a large glass, filled to the brim

calibogus spruce beer

cant street slang
charley a big man; an oaf
cheese it be quiet
chink money
chive a knife
clunch a fool
coat buzzer pickpocket
cock a man
colt bowler a young man
cossack a policeman
cove a man
cracked mad
crackers buttocks
crow fortunate
crusher a policeman
cull a man

danna excrement
death hunter an undertaker
dimber pretty; handsome
doxy a prostitute
drumbelo a fool
dub o' the hick a bump on the head
ducats money
duds clothing

eagle ten-dollar coin
earth bath a grave
eternity box coffin

fadge a farthing; also, to care
fart catcher a valet
farting crackers breeches
Fenian a Catholic Irishman

filch to steal
finger smith woman who performs abortions
fizzog a face
flash fancy; elaborate; also slang
flicker a medium size glass
fork (verb) to pickpocket

gammon rubbish
gelt money
glad (verb) to saunter
glimms eyes
goose to fool
grapple raw liquor
grunter a pig
gull (noun) a gullible person
gull (verb) to play a confidence trick; to fool
gundiguts a roly-poly fellow
gurn (verb) to complain; to drone on (Northern English)
gurn (noun) a face; an expression (Northern English)

hack appearance
half seas-over tipsy
heavers a woman's breasts
hector a ruffian
hessian coarse cloth; sacking
Hispaniola the island of Haiti and the Dominican Republic
hose stockings
huff (noun) a blowhard
hugger-mugger stealth
hush to kill

jarvie a coachman
jigger a lock
judy a prostitute

kinchin a child
kip (noun) a house; a sleep
knap to steal

knuckler a thief; a pickpocket

lambskin man a judge (because of his long wig)
laycock a woman's private parts
libben a house; a home
lift (verb) to steal
lobster a redcoat; a King's soldier
long-shanks long-legged
lutefisk fermented herring

mab a woman; a wench
mackerel a wallet
mackerel-back skinny
madge a woman's private parts
marra friend; mate (Northern English)
matelot sailor
mauld drunk
member mug a chamber pot
mill to kill
moll a woman; a mistress
mort a woman
mott a woman's private parts; a prostitute
muff-wipe a sanitary towel

nazie drunk
nug to copulate
nugging shop a brothel

peg a penis
pettifogger a lawyer
phiz a face
pike to run away
pink (verb) to stab; to pierce
pipe a penis
plug; plug tail a penis
poker a sword
poundies an Irish potato-based dish
prancer a horse

prig a thief
privy a lavatory
puff guts fat
pug cider cider made with
    ingredients other than
    apples

queer the lay disrupt the plan
quid money; dollars; pounds

rag carrier a cavalry standard
    bearer; an ensign
rantum scantum sexual
    intercourse
rum strange; odd

sand courage
sapscull an idiot
scaly miserly
scamp (verb) to run away
screwsman a lock-breaker
shab off run away; escape;
    desert
sharper cheat
shoot the cat to vomit
shoulder clapper a policeman
simkin a fool
six and tips a cheap cocktail of
    whiskey and beer, favored by
    the Irish; also an Irishman
snakesman a small burglar who
    sneaks through windows
spooney foolish
stampers footwear
stand buff to give evidence
stingo strong drink; rotgut
strapped armed
strommel hair

suck the monkey binge drink
swede a head
swill-tub a drunkard
swive sexual intercourse
swizzle a cocktail of beer, rum
    and sugar

tackle clothes; belongings
tarrywags testicles
Teaguelander an Irishman
the gunner's daughter a
    cannon
thieftaker bounty hunter
tib a young girl
tile a hat
tilt fight
tip (verb) to inform; to notice
titter a young woman
toasting iron a sword
tony an albatross; a big man; a
    thug
tooler a pickpocket
top (verb) to kill
topping cove a swell; a gentle-
    man
tosspot a garbage can; insult
trumpery rubbish; hot air
tup to copulate
turk a bad man; a thug
twig to spot; to discover

wean a child
whiddle to talk; to tell
wireman a man who kills with
    a garrote, by preference
wit to understand

yarum warm milk